Daddys howse

Lake

Daddy

Me!

by Tyler Montgumry, age 4½

ABOUT THE AUTHOR

Emily Dalton has loved romance since she first read *Pride and Prejudice* and *Jane Eyre*. When it occurred to her that it might be fun to write her own romances, she began with several Regencies and historicals. Now she concentrates on contemporary romances for Harlequin American Romance, and this year won *Romantic Times Magazine*'s Reviewers' Choice Award for Best Harlequin American Romance of 1997, *Wake Me with a Kiss*.

With three boys at home, none of whom are quite grown up yet—including her husband!—she enjoys juggling her career with homemaking and motherhood. Besides writing, Emily loves to travel, read other people's books, take long walks and eat chocolate truffles.

Books by Emily Dalton

HARLEQUIN AMERICAN ROMANCE

Instant Daddy

EMILY DALTON

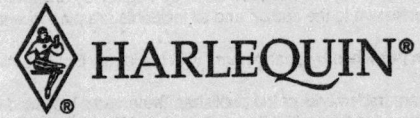

HARLEQUIN®

TORONTO • NEW YORK • LONDON
AMSTERDAM • PARIS • SYDNEY • HAMBURG
STOCKHOLM • ATHENS • TOKYO • MILAN • MADRID
PRAGUE • WARSAW • BUDAPEST • AUCKLAND

To my sisters in Alaska, Cyndi Romberg
and Cheri Woods
I'll always have wonderful memories and a grateful heart
for the years we lived together as a family.
Love you,
Danice

ISBN 0-373-16783-0

INSTANT DADDY

Chapter One

"Here, Cass. Check this out. Maybe you'll find your dream man in Alaska."

Cassie automatically caught the magazine Susan tossed from halfway across the bookstore. She glanced at the periodical, its glossy cover showing a grinning hunk of guy in a red flannel shirt and tight jeans against backdrop of majestic mountain peaks. When she read the title, *Single Men of Alaska*, she immediately set it aside on a nearby table and returned to her job of unpacking magazines and arranging them on shelves.

"The store opens in twenty minutes, Susan. I don't have time—*we* don't have time to goof around. There are still three boxes full of women's magazines to set out for display."

"All work and no play makes Cass a dull girl," Susan retorted. "Aren't you even tempted to check out all the cute guys advertising for companionship from the icy back of beyond?"

Cassie turned and threw her friend a rueful grin. "If they have to advertise, I can't imagine that they're any great catch."

Susan shook her head vigorously, the chestnut brown curls bouncing against her cheeks. "That's where you're wrong, Cass. These guys advertise for the simple reason that there's about five times as many men in Alaska as women." She moved to the table where Cassie had put down the magazine on a stack of *Cosmo*'s. She picked it up and flipped through a few pages, then shoved the open magazine to within two inches of Cassie's face. "Do these guys look like losers to you?"

Cassie gave an exasperated laugh, took the magazine and sat down on the edge of the table. "All right. If it will get you off my back and back to work, I'll look. But only for a minute. Besides, aren't you forgetting that I've got a boyfriend?"

Susan crossed her arms over her chest and snorted. "I suppose you mean Brad?"

"Who else? We've been dating for two years, haven't we?"

"That's exactly my point. Dating but not *mating*. You two haven't even slept together."

Cassie felt herself blushing. "Susan, you know I don't believe in rushing things. I'd like to be sure of my feelings for Brad before we get intimate."

"I understand why you feel that way, Cass. I mean, after what happened to you..." Susan's words trailed off.

Cassie said nothing. Susan, and just about all her other friends, thought that what had happened to her five years ago was the worst thing that could happen to any young woman. Cassie didn't agree, but there was no point in arguing.

After a tactful pause, Susan continued persistently. "But I still don't see how you can date a guy for two years and abstain from sex the whole time unless something's just not clicking between you. Face the facts, ma'am. You're *never* going to be sure about Brad. In all fairness you should either make a commitment to the poor guy or give him his walking papers and let him get on with his life. Sometimes I think you just use your relationship with Brad as an excuse not to get involved with anyone you might *really* fall in love with.''

Susan's lecture was interrupted by the phone's ringing. She gave Cassie one last admonishing glance and went to answer it.

Cassie hung her head and thumbed idly through the magazine. Though she'd muttered under her breath a time or two, Susan had never before spoken so forcefully on the subject of Cassie's ambiguous relationship with Brad. She herself had never considered the possibility that she was using him, and she'd certainly never consciously done so. She cared about Brad, *only*...

Susan was right about one thing. The guy deserved to know where he stood. She really should make a decision one way or the other about Brad. But every time he tried to get close, every time marriage crept into the conversation, she got cold feet.

There was certainly nothing wrong with Brad Callahan. In fact, he was a great guy. He was good-looking, kind and loving, and wasn't too shabby as a cowboy-cum-businessman, either. After all, he'd taken a small, struggling cattle ranch he'd inherited from his uncle three years ago and turned it into a thriving concern.

Brad's ranch was five miles outside of town, just down the road from Cassie's home, the much larger spread owned and operated by her father, Jasper Montgomery. As neighbors do in the mostly rural Big Sky country of Montana, Brad and Jasper spoke over the fence while straddling their horses and eventually became good friends as the older cowboy shared his years of ranching experience with the novice. Now Brad was more like a son than a neighbor to Jasper, and nothing would make both of them happier than for Cassie to formalize the connection by saying "I do."

Jasper's wholehearted endorsement wasn't the only one. Tyler adored Brad. However, Cassie felt her barely four-year-old son was too young to be clearheaded in his judgment, particularly about a man who carried Jolly Rancher candies in his pocket and wasn't ashamed to use them as bribes.

Cassie felt her heart swell with love at the thought of the most important "man" in her life. Tyler might be a mistake in the eyes of most of the residents of the tiny town of Nye, Montana, where she was born and raised and now ran a combination bookstore-coffee bar called The Buzz, but Cassie could never regret the night of passion that had brought Tyler into the world nine months later.

No, even if Tyler hadn't been the result of that night of indiscretion, Cassie couldn't bring herself to regret the most incredibly romantic experience of her life....

She'd been barely twenty. She and three of her girlfriends had gone to the annual Fourth of July fair sponsored by the local cattle ranchers and town merchants. Nye had retained a lot of rough-and-tumble ambiance from the first rush of miners who came in droves when ore was first discovered in the surrounding mountainsides in the last century, and summer brought a fair number of tourists to enjoy that ambiance.

They'd gaze up at the angular, painted timber buildings that still stood along Main Street, buildings that used to be mostly saloons, but which now housed antique shops, candy stores and restaurants, including Cassie's bookstore.

So, when Cassie and her friends were strolling along the grassy fairway, eating pink cotton candy, they weren't surprised to see a lot of strange faces in the crowd. But when a certain face turned in their direction and a handsome young man disengaged himself from the surrounding people, walked deliberately up to them and began a conversation, they were awestruck. Nye had rarely seen the likes of this guy. With his chiseled face and devastating smile, his dark hair and sky-blue eyes, he was movie-star gorgeous.

He told them he was just passing through town at the end of a short course of summer college classes. He was staying at Cavana House, the bed-and-breakfast run by Mr. and Mrs. Tuddenham, and he'd been excited to find out there was a fair in town. Would they tell him which of the animal exhibitions were the best, and which concessions stand had the spiciest hot dogs? As he chatted about the town, the fair and the mild July weather, he oozed charm from every refined pore.

Jamie, the bravest and most flirtatious of their

group, invited him to tag along with them for the evening. He'd happily agreed. But as the evening wore on, Cassie found herself, rather than the forward Jamie, more and more the object of his interest. Cassie, bookish and shy, only pretty in a quiet sort of way with her straight blond hair, gray eyes and pale complexion, was more surprised by his interest in her than anyone else.

They rode together on the Ferris wheel. He knocked down bottles and won her a large stuffed Wile E. Coyote. They ate hot dogs and caramel apples, then nearly got sick on the merry-go-round. At the end of the ride when he lifted her off the aquablue horse with the gilded harness, dizzy and laughing, she felt a strong stirring of sexual desire the likes of which she'd never experienced before.

Later, while the other girls went home in Jamie's car, the handsome stranger walked Cassie to hers. She ended up giving him a ride to the bed-and-breakfast...then sneaking in with him and staying all night.

Nothing like this had ever happened to Cassie before. Up until that night, she'd been a virgin and with no great temptation to be anything else. But this stranger, this man who only wanted to be known by his fraternity nickname, "Bogie"—which he said had come about because of his rapt involvement in a Humphrey Bogart marathon on cable one year despite looming final exams—had swept her off her feet and into his bed by the sheer power of his considerable charisma.

In the wee hours of the morning, he walked her to her car, kissed her lingeringly through the open window, and made arrangements to meet her the following day for a picnic.

Giddy with excitement, Cassie prepared a basket of food and drove to the park where they were to tryst. After waiting an hour for him to show up, she went to the Cavana House to see what was keeping him. Mr. Tuddenham explained that "Mr. Bogart," which was the name he'd actually registered under, had received a long-distance call that morning and left in a great hurry.

Cassie was disappointed, but life went on and she would have tucked away her romantic memory of that night for the occasional indulgence of lazy afternoon daydreaming, if a month's worth of throwing up and a pregnancy test hadn't changed everything...changed her life forever.

"Cassie? Cassie, where are you, girl? By that grim look on your face, you must not like whoever you're reading about."

Susan snatched the magazine and stared at the page Cassie had randomly opened to.

"Oh my *gaw*... If you don't think *he's* cute, there's something definitely wrong with you, Cass. And what a neat name. Adam Baranof. Must be Russian. Didn't a bunch of them Tolstoy types settle in Alaska eons ago? Geez, he's even a marine biologist. Brainy *and* brawny. What more could you want?"

Cassie glanced down at the page Susan was waving under her nose. "I'm just not interested, Su—"

Cassie's heart stopped beating, then came to life again with a hard thump she felt clear to her toes.

"Cass? Cass, what's wrong? You look just like

my mom did when she got food poisoning after eating Aunt Ida's home-canned succotash. Are you gonna be sick?''

With trembling fingers, Cassie took the magazine out of Susan's hands and stared disbelievingly at the picture of a dark-haired man with sky-blue eyes. A man who was movie-star gorgeous.

''It's...it's *him*.''

''What do you mean *him?* Don't tell me you know this guy?''

Cassie nodded slowly. ''Oh, I know him all right.''

''As in the *biblical* sense you know him? But I thought the only guy you'd ever slept with was Tyler's—''

Susan fell silent. Cassie glanced up and saw her friend's mouth hanging open like a hungry baby bird's.

''Yes, it's Tyler's father, Susan,'' Cassie confirmed in a raspy voice. ''I thought I'd never be able to tell my son who his father is. But now I know.''

''Are...are you sure?''

''I could never forget that face.''

''I can see why.''

Now they both lapsed into stunned silence, staring at the picture of Adam Baranof.

Adam Baranof. Cassie thought the romantic name suited him...or at least suited the memory she had of him and of his suave charm. The ad seemed fitting, too. He wasn't advertising for a wife or a long-term relationship like some of the other men in the magazine. He was advertising for a *friend.* Someone to share a few good times with, a few laughs, a few walks on the beach. To the right woman he was willing to send a first-class airplane ticket for a weekend rendezvous in Alaska. Seldovia, Alaska, to be precise...wherever that was.

Cassie shook her head. After five years and several early and futile attempts to track down Tyler's father, she found it hard to believe that his identity could be revealed to her in this weird, accidental way.

"So now that you know, what are you going to do, Cass?"

Susan's softly spoken question was a good one.

"I...I don't know," Cassie answered. "I always thought he should know about Tyler. I didn't want or need financial support or anything, but it just seemed right to tell a man he'd become a father. But it's been so long since he was here. He might not remember me. He might not even *want* to know...you know?"

"Well, I think he *should* know," Susan stated, growing indignant as the shock wore off. "He obviously wasn't very careful that night or you wouldn't have gotten pregnant. And then he left town willy-nilly the next morning, leaving you to go through the whole ordeal alone."

"It wasn't an ordeal, Susan," Cassie reminded her in a firm tone. "I loved every minute I was pregnant with Tyler, and that little boy is the center of my universe."

"I know all that, Cass," Susan hastily assured her. "That's not what I meant. It's just that men shouldn't go around getting women pregnant, then taking no responsibility for it."

"He didn't know I was pregnant."

"Well, he sure as heck knew you could be, didn't he? It's one of the things that can happen when two people...you know...tango!"

"Neither of us thought about the possible consequences, Susan. Neither of us was careful. It was as much my doing as his." Cassie felt her cheeks glowing with warmth. "We were just sort of... *carried away* by our passions."

Susan grabbed Cassie by the shoulders and gazed intently into her face. "You still have the hots for this guy, don't you?"

Cassie shrugged, embarrassed and confused. "Of course not."

"But I'll bet you'll never forget that night *or* that man," Susan persisted.

"It *was* a pretty magical night. And he *was*—" Cassie shook her head, sighed and smiled "—pretty incredible."

"And pretty unforgettable. If that night was as great as you say, I'm sure he feels the same way about you."

"I doubt it," Cassie answered bluntly. "He didn't make any effort to contact me, did he? I apparently didn't make quite the same impression on him as he did on me."

"There's only one way to find out for sure," Susan suggested with a coyly raised brow.

Cassie stared suspiciously at her friend. "To find out *what* for sure?"

"If you made an impression on him. Answer his ad, Cassie. Send him a picture. You'll find out fast enough if he remembers you."

Trying to ignore the way her heart fluttered with excitement, Cassie paced the floor. "If I *were* to get in contact with Adam, my object wouldn't be to try to rekindle something between us. It would be to tell him about Tyler. That's all."

"But I thought you weren't sure if you *should* tell him about Tyler?"

"You're right. I'm *not* sure!"

Susan nodded sagely. "Well, I agree, you're right to be cautious. I mean, how much do you really know about this guy except that he's great in the sack?"

Cassie stopped pacing and whirled around to face her friend. "Susan! I know more than *that!*"

Now Susan raised both brows. "Oh, you do? *What* exactly? He left town without even telling you his real name. Did you know he was a scientist?"

Cassie frowned and shook her head. "No, but—"

"No buts. You really don't know this guy from Adam." Susan stopped abruptly and laughed at her own unintentional joke. "Seriously, Cass, what if he's really not a very nice man? What if he doesn't like kids? What if he *does* like them and wants Tyler to spend six months out of the year in Alaska?"

Now Cassie's heart fluttered with apprehension. "Are you trying to scare me, Susan?"

"No. All I'm saying is that you ought to get to know this guy before you tell him about Tyler."

"How am I supposed to do that?"

Susan sighed and raised both hands in the air.

"Answer the ad, Cass. Just answer the ad. It's that simple."

DRIVING HOME for lunch, as she passed through a flat stretch of grassland where range cows stood in the warm June sun and a loping coyote chased a field mouse across the road, Cassie thought about Susan's arguments for answering Adam's ad. Susan had made it sound simple, but it wasn't. It was complicated, and what complicated it the most was the person who mattered most in her life. Tyler.

Would he hold it against her someday if she decided not to contact his father when she had the chance? People moved around. If she didn't write to Adam now, he could disappear from their lives as quickly as he'd accidentally reappeared.

But contacting him could also possibly cause an upheaval in their lives they'd never recover from. What if he wanted to be part of Tyler's life? What if he wanted to be part of *her* life again?

Cassie pushed that idea out of her mind before the Cinderella scenario could take over and she started envisioning herself and Tyler snugly ensconced in some palatial log cabin in Alaska with a Russian prince.

Being part of a family, having more children with a man with whom you were at least on a first-name basis, was a dream she cherished. But such a dream seemed far more likely to come true with a stable man like Brad, who lived next door, than with a marine biologist advertizing for a "friend" in some remote town called Seldovia in faraway Alaska.

Cassie crossed the bridge over the fast-flowing Stillwater River and drove more quickly than usual through the open gate under the Lone Mountain Ranch sign that was suspended high above the dirt road from a rustic pine framework. Dust flew in the wake of her Subaru Outback, but she was eager to see Tyler and anxious to talk to her father about her incredible discovery.

She skidded to a stop in front of the fieldstone-and-log ranch house she called home, with the familiar forested mountains behind it and outbuildings of every size and variety scattered on the grounds around it. Tucking the *Single Men of Alaska* magazine under her arm, she stepped out of the car and trained her eyes on the front door.

She wasn't disappointed. The door flew open and Tyler flew out, his granddad following in long, lazy strides, making no attempt to keep up.

"Ty! How's my little cowboy?"

"Me and Granddad caught two trouts!" Tyler announced as his mother scooped him into her arms for a quick kiss and hug. "And Sylvie's cookin' 'em fer lunch!"

"That sounds delicious," Cassie said with enthusiasm, although with her stomach in such a nervous state she wasn't sure if she'd be able to eat a single bite. She smiled down at Tyler, marveling again— after seeing the photo of Adam—at how much he looked like his father. He had the same dark hair and blue eyes. And that dimple in his chin would undoubtedly grow into a cleft just like Adam's.

"Your foot was pressed to the metal comin' down the drive, hon," her father observed in his usual laconic drawl. "Did ya think ya saw smoke comin' from the house, or are ya just hungry?"

Cassie looked at her father, at his tall, rangy figure in jeans and a Levi's shirt, at the sun-weathered face and drooping gray mustache that made him look a little older than his fifty-seven years. Today there was a twinkle in his pale blue eyes, but they had blazed with anger five years ago when he'd found out some passer-through had impregnated his daughter, then flown the coop.

Time had worked its magic and he'd long ago come to terms with the way Tyler had become part of their lives. Now he was just grateful for his grandson, for the sheer pleasure and vitality he brought to their little family which had seemed so diminished after the death of Cassie's mother six years before.

Jasper spent a good part of his day with the boy, sharing the ups and downs of child-rearing with Cassie and their sixtyish nanny-housekeeper, Sylvie. The influence of a cattle-rancher grandfather was evident; Ty was only four but he already rode a horse and knew how to rope a steer. He wore his boots to bed—they had to be removed after he was asleep—and he didn't leave the house without his Stetson, grooved just so at the crown and curved at the brim just like Granddad's.

"No smoke. Just anxious to get home," Cassie replied with a smile as she held Tyler's hand and walked alongside her father to the door. Then, she added in a lowered voice, as Tyler hurried ahead to the kitchen toward the smell of fresh trout sizzling in the skillet, "Actually, there is something I need to talk to you about, Dad. Something important."

Her father's eyes narrowed and he looked at her keenly. "All right, hon. We'll talk after lunch when Sylvie puts Ty down for his nap. That all right?"

Cassie nodded and released a shaky sigh. "That would be perfect."

STANDING IN her father's study, which was paneled in warm, honeyed tones of knotty pine, with a huge trout hung over the mantel and copies of Remington sketches framed on the walls, Cassie watched Jasper Montgomery's face as he took his first look at Tyler's father. He wasn't smiling.

"So this is the scoundrel," he muttered.

"Dad, I thought you'd gotten over wanting to wring his neck!" Cassie exclaimed.

"I thought so, too. Guess I was wrong."

"As I've told you before, I was a consenting adult. In fact, I was more than willing."

Her father grimaced, then sighed. "Yes, I know. But spare me the details, will ya, Cass?" He tossed the magazine onto his desk, folded his long arms over his broad chest, and peered at her from under sternly lowered brows. "So now I suppose you've got some fool notion of writin' to this fella?"

Cassie averted her gaze and nervously trailed a finger along the smooth edge of her father's massive walnut desk. "You don't think I should?"

"I don't think it's going to matter what I think," her father said with a sniff. "You've probably made up your mind already and, just like your ma, you'll do what you want no matter what I think."

Cassie looked up, suddenly realizing that her father was right. She *had* made up her mind and no amount of talking would change it.

"Dad, I have to contact him. It's only fair."

"Fair to who? I was all for findin' this fella when

you were pregnant, and even when Tyler was just a baby. But it's different now, Cass. Ty's four years old. He's used to us...and we're used to him.'' Jasper's scowl deepened and his arms tightened against his chest. For the second time in her life, Cassie detected fear in her tough ol' daddy's eyes. The first time was when her mother was diagnosed with cancer.

Cassie moved to stand next to her father and laid a gentle hand on his arm. ''You don't think I'm going to allow Adam to take Ty away from here, do you?''

''As a father he'll have rights. He might want joint custody.''

''But there's a much greater chance he won't want anything to do with Tyler,'' Cassie reasoned. She turned away and resumed the idle occupation of tracing invisible designs on her father's desk. ''Besides,'' she began carefully, ''if I write to him and he writes back, and *if* I actually go up there, I might find out he's a jerk. And if that's the case, I'm not even going to tell him about Tyler. I mean, after all, I really didn't get to know him before. We had such a short time together and we weren't exactly exchanging anecdotes about our lives, our families, our aspirations. He might not be the kind of man we want in Tyler's life at all.''

Jasper was silent for such a long time, Cassie was almost afraid to turn and look at him. Because of his strong love for Tyler, Jasper might be reluctant to admit that Adam Baranof had a right to know he was a father, but in the end he'd opt for doing the honorable thing. Would Jasper agree with her that holding off until she knew Adam better was the honorable thing to do?

She turned slowly and faced her father. He was still frowning, but that uncharacteristic frightened look was gone from his eyes. "I don't know if it's the right thing to do or not, Cass. But I don't care. If Ty's gonna have a father in his life, we'd better make damned sure he's a good one. You go ahead and answer that ad and see what happens. Go to Alaska if you want to and keep your secret as long as you need to. You've raised that boy for four years and you've got more rights than this Baranof fella by a long shot. Take it a step at a time, that's what I recommend."

Cassie smiled her relief. "I appreciate your support, Dad."

He patted her on the shoulder and headed for the door. "You've always got it, sweetheart. You know that. Now you'd better get busy and write that letter. If it has to be done, there's no point in putting it off. Use my desk and stationery, if you like."

"Thanks, Dad. I will." Cassie moved to the back of the desk and sat down in her father's cushy leather chair, scooted in and picked up a pen. Then, just before her father was through the door, she called, "Oh, Dad?"

He popped his head in. "Yeah?"

"Do me a favor. Don't tell Brad anything about this till things are more settled, okay?"

He frowned, hesitating. "Okay," he said at last. "But you can do me a favor, too."

"What's that?"

"Be careful this time, will ya?"

Cassie knew her father was referring to more than birth control. What happened with Adam could affect all their lives forever. She hoped her smile conveyed more confidence than she felt as she replied, "Don't worry, Dad. This time I'll look before I leap."

Chapter Two

Wearing his white terry bathrobe and a pair of Nike running shoes, Adam jogged out to the mailbox a half mile down the remote road that led to his cabin, dug out the many envelopes crammed inside and jogged back to the warm house. He dumped the mail on the kitchen table and started sorting it. As had been the case ever since the last issue of *Single Men of Alaska* came out, the stack of letters from women replying to the ad was as high as his orange juice carton. And this was every day. He couldn't wait until he figured out a way to get back at his brother for sending in that stupid ad without his permission.

"I just want you to find a girl and be as happy as I am, bro," his brother had said with that disarming, innocent look of his.

Adam tried to ignore his growing irritation as the stack grew ever higher. He hoped that somewhere at the bottom of this mess he'd find what he was really waiting for—a letter from the National Science Foundation in Washington D.C. telling him that his research grant had been awarded. He was kept busy enough working on the consulting committee for the new aquarium going up in Seward, but he wanted more than anything to continue his research on marine mammal behaviorism and was hoping to start it before summer's end.

When the last envelope turned out to be pink and covered with heart-shaped stickers and lipstick kisses, he had a pretty good idea that it wasn't from a scientist.

Adam swallowed his disappointment, took a sip of coffee from a steaming mug and picked up his letter opener. He'd grudgingly promised his brother to at least read all the letters, even if he had no intention of replying to them. It wasn't that some of the women weren't attractive or didn't sound interesting; it was just that he felt no burning desire to get involved in a relationship right now.

But that was exactly why he'd worded the ad the way he had, his brother had said. Although Alex could vouch for happily-ever-after love as being the best kind ever and worth looking for, none of the women answering the ad would expect more from Adam than friendship.

Adam begged to differ. He opened up the pink envelope first and a photo fell out that was obviously done by one of those boudoir photography studios. The woman was heavily made up, her hair teased to an impossible height, and a pink feather boa encircled her bare shoulders. And talk about cleavage… Her name was Sugar. Sure.

He forced himself to wade through Sugar's flowery scribbles. She wanted candlelight dinners, walks in the rain, single roses on her pillow and…a good stock portfolio. How much did he make as a marine biologist, anyway? Was he interested in moving from Alaska to somewhere more lively…like Vegas?

That one went directly into the trash and was followed by many others. Adam was no longer shocked when he received nude photos or blatant sexual overtures. But he likewise was no longer even remotely interested when the women seemed normal, literate and nice.

By the time he'd made it to the bottom of the pile, his vision was glazed. There was one more letter to wade through, however and, after all, he'd promised. The envelope was a plain white one, which was a welcome sight after so many fuchsias and lavenders. Adam glanced at the return address. This one was from Montana, and the writing was crisp and neat without all those swirls and curlicues it seemed some of the women thought were necessary to convey a proper feeling of romance.

He opened the letter and a photo fell out. He picked it up, glanced at it without much interest, then glanced at it again. It was a young woman, tall, slender, blond, standing by a copper-colored horse. In the background were mountains covered with fir trees and a blue, blue sky. The woman was wearing jeans and a yellow gingham shirt tucked into her belt.

He set down the picture, then picked it up again. There was something about her face…Something so natural and refreshing in the way she'd posed so casually, the wind blowing her straight, shoulder-length hair in a swirl around her head. She was very attractive. Very appealing.

He picked up the letter and read it. Her name was Cassandra Montgomery. Most folks called her Cassie, she wrote. He thought it was a nice name that suited her girl-next-door appearance. She owned a bookstore and coffee bar in a little town called Nye.

Adam tried to remember if he'd stopped in Nye during a trip through Montana a few years ago, but he couldn't recall whether he had or not. There had been so many quaint little towns—especially in the west—he'd lost count of them by the time he'd seen most of the lower forty-nine.

Adam stared at the picture again and tried to imagine her voice. Then he did something he never thought he'd do in a million years. He found some stationery, picked up his pen and wrote back to her.

CASSIE STOOD at the mailbox and held the envelope with trembling fingers. There was no mistaking it. The return address read "Seldovia, Alaska." It was from *him*. Adam. Tyler's father. The only man she'd ever slept with.

"He remembers me," she whispered under her breath as she walked slowly toward the house. Since her father and Sylvie had taken Tyler into town for a matinee, she had the place to herself, and for this she was deeply thankful. She didn't want anyone to see her in this weird state of mixed excitement and dread.

She went to her father's study, which stayed cool even during the hottest summer days, sat down behind his desk and picked up his letter opener. She slit the envelope and removed a neatly folded single sheet of stationery.

She read the short, friendly letter, then read it again. And again. Then she set down the letter and stared at the wall opposite the desk.

"He doesn't remember me," she whispered dismally. But how was it possible that he didn't remember her? And why had he written to her, otherwise? According to his letter, hers was the only letter he'd replied to! Was he lying? But surely she wasn't special enough to pique this man's interest over all other respondents vying for his attention without some remembered history between them. What was going on?

Cassie got up and paced the floor. In the letter he invited her to come to a wedding, his brother's wedding, which was to take place two weeks from Sunday. He said he would send a round-trip, first-class airplane ticket. She could come out on a Thursday, spend the weekend and they'd get to know each other a little bit. At the same time she'd be providing him with a date for the wedding and a safeguard against his Great-Aunt Zelda who would try to set him up with every spare female at the reception afterward.

Cassie appreciated the casual charm and sense of humor evident in his letter writing, but... But why didn't he remember her? Had that evening, which had meant so much to her, meant so little to him?

Two hours later, her father, Sylvie and Tyler came home. Tyler, half asleep, went immediately down for a nap, and Jasper took Cassie by the arm and guided her ahead of him into the study. He closed the door and turned to face her.

"He wrote to you, didn't he?"

"How did you know?"

"You haven't been this pale since you fell off your horse last year and broke your ankle."

Cassie nodded, smiled wanly. "You can read me like a book."

"You're disappointed."

"He didn't remember me. Or if he does, he isn't saying so."

"Why wouldn't he say so?"

"Well, I never let on that *I* remembered *him*."

Jasper shook his head. "Maybe he's just playing a game he thinks you started. Maybe you should have told him exactly who you are."

"I'm glad I didn't."

"Why?"

"Because, Dad, he doesn't remember me!" Cassie exclaimed, then immediately regretted raising her voice. "Sorry. I'm just not sure what to do now."

"If I were you, I'd still go. If you don't resolve this one way or the other, you'll never stop fretting."

Cassie thought about it, but not for long. "You're right, Dad. I'll write back and tell him to send the ticket. But I want you and Tyler to go with me."

Jasper's eyes widened to the size of silver dollars. "I thought you weren't going to tell him about Tyler until you got to know him a bit? And then only if he impressed you as a good man."

"I still feel that way. I just want you to come with me as far as Anchorage. Adam won't have any idea I didn't come alone. You and Tyler could take in the sights—go fishing for some of that legendary salmon up there—while I find out what I can about this guy. He lives on the Kenai Peninsula, about two hundred miles south of Anchorage. If I tell him about Tyler and he wants to meet him, you guys'll be right there within a half day's road travel. If I don't tell him, or he doesn't want to meet Tyler, well, no big deal. You've said many times that you'd like to visit Alaska. Think of it as a vacation.''

At Jasper's continued doubtful expression, Cassie added cajolingly, ''Besides, Dad, I could use the moral support. Knowing my two favorite guys in the whole world are nearby will really help.''

Although he still looked troubled, Jasper relented and managed a weak smile as he wrapped his arm around Cassie's shoulder. ''Hon, if that's the way you want to do it, I suppose I'll go along with the plan as long it doesn't look like it's about to blow up in your face.''

Cassie nodded gratefully, then added with a furrowed brow, ''What will we tell Brad?''

''That we're taking a vacation. It's partially the truth, but I suppose that means it's partially a lie, too. I hate this, Cassie. Why don't we just tell Brad what's going on?''

''Because I don't think I could deal with Brad's emotions on top of everything else. He's bound to feel threatened.''

Jasper nodded thoughtfully. ''I suppose there's no use worryin' him.''

Cassie agreed wholeheartedly.

BRAD INSISTED on driving them to the airport in Billings, which meant Cassie couldn't relieve any of

her tension by talking to her dad about the situation.
Instead they were forced to put on a cheerful front
as if they were really just going to Alaska for a short
vacation.

"My sister and her husband went on a cruise to
Alaska a couple of years ago," Brad commented
conversationally as they sped along the interstate.
"She couldn't quit talking about it for weeks after.
She said Prince William Sound was the most beau-
tiful place she'd ever seen."

Cassie turned to look at Brad, at his strong tanned
hands on the steering wheel, at his clean, honest
profile below a thatch of blond hair, the sun-
wrinkles around his blue eyes. She was almost sure
he suspected something was going on that he wasn't
included in, but he was being polite and patient as
usual. Sometimes Cassie wished he'd be just a little
demanding and difficult. Maybe if he had been,
they'd be married by now and she'd have one thing
less to worry about on this trip.

Cassie glanced into the back seat where her father
and Tyler were reading a book together. Her gaze
locked with her father's for a moment and she knew
they were sharing the same concerns.

"Will you see Prince William Sound?" Brad
asked her, turning his head to look at her.

"I'm not sure," Cassie answered with a smile.
"Our itinerary isn't exactly worked out yet."

Brad nodded, looked at her doubtfully for a minute, then turned his gaze back to the road without
saying another word.

Yep, thought Cassie. *He knows something's up.*

AFTER SEEMING to almost skim the peaks of the Chugach Mountains east of the city, the plane descended quickly to land at Anchorage International Airport at five o'clock Thursday afternoon. For a minute, Cassie thought they were going to land in Cook Inlet itself, but soon realized that the gray water adjacent to the regular landing strips of the airport was Lake Hood, which the pilot had mentioned over the intercom as being the busiest seaplane base in the world. It was fascinating to look down on hundreds of small, colorful planes docked in the water.

Since Adam had arranged to meet her at the gate, Cassie said goodbye to her father and Tyler in the airplane, then waited for them to get off and far enough away before she disembarked. Tyler was happy to go with his granddad, and he was assured that his mommy would see him in a couple of days. He was reminded of when she went away every once in awhile to booksellers' conventions. He knew she'd always come back and, in the meantime, he and his granddad could go fishing. He was enthralled with the possibility of catching a fish bigger than he was.

As Cassie walked through the covered ramp, clutching her purse and the two carry-ons which held everything she'd brought for the trip, she hoped the long flight hadn't made her look like death warmed over. You couldn't tell anything by those tiny mirrors they had in the in-flight rest rooms, but she had made sure her hair was neatly combed, her bangs smooth and her lipstick fresh.

As for her clothes, the only reasonable choice for

surviving a long flight with a small boy was to wear jeans and a casual wrinkle-proof knit top—navy blue, so stains wouldn't show as much. And, as she knew it got cool in the evenings in Alaska even in summer, she'd tied a blue-and-white-patterned sweater around her shoulders to wear later.

The last one off the plane, she emerged from the ramp and stopped cold, looking around cautiously. She suddenly realized that she was absolutely petrified. But it was too late to turn tail and run because there he was. *Adam.* He was headed straight for her, as big as life, all smiles and twice as handsome as she remembered. He wore jeans and a crew-neck sweater that was the exact shade of sky-blue as his eyes.

Memories of that night came flooding back.

The feel of his lips, the taste of him.

His strong arms as he held her close...

Cassie's heart was beating so hard and fast she had a sudden unreasonable fear that Adam might actually be able to see its frantic rhythm under the thin fabric of her blouse.

"Hey, I was beginning to think you'd chickened out," he teased, standing in front of her with his hands propped casually on his lean hips.

He sounded exactly the way she remembered. "I...I almost did," Cassie admitted, smiling shyly.

He stared at her for a few seconds, his gaze studying her features with an intensity that made Cassie hope he was remembering, too.

"Your voice..." he began.

"Yes?" Cassie prompted eagerly.

He smiled again. "It's just like I imagined it

would be. That's what really made me write to you, Cassie. After seeing your picture, I had to find out how your voice sounded.''

Cassie hid her profound disappointment and glibly replied, ''So if I sounded like Olive Oyl you'd have put me on the next plane back to Montana, I suppose?''

He laughed and reached out to take her luggage. In the process, their hands brushed and a thrill went up Cassie's arm like a shock of electricity. Startled, she didn't dare look at him and instead stared at the floor. She couldn't believe the attraction could be so immediate—and stronger than ever!

''We only have a short way to walk,'' he said, his voice calm, his manner collected as he took her elbow and guided her toward the open terminal. The light touch of his fingers against her skin gave her goose bumps.

''Are you cold?'' he asked suddenly.

Cassie gave herself a stern mental lecture. She had to pull herself together. She was ashamed to be so easily attracted to this man. Especially since he didn't seem to be affected by her in the same way.

She forced a smile. ''Maybe a little. The plane was hot and it's really open in here.''

''Alaska is famous for its wide-open spaces. I think you're going to like your visit. This is incredible country. But then Montana's pretty incredible, too.''

Cassie searched his face. ''Have you been there?''

''Yes. But it was several years ago and I have to admit I don't remember a lot about it. You'll have to refresh my memory. Now, why don't we stop for a minute so you can put on your sweater?''

While Adam solicitously helped her on with her sweater, Cassie fumed. *Oh, I'd like to refresh your memory, all right. How about with a cricket mallet to the head?*

''There, is that better?''

Cassie nodded and smiled, outwardly all sweetness and light, inwardly getting more frustrated by the minute. How could he have forgotten her so completely? Surely, though, once they'd talked for four hours during the trip to Seldovia, he'd start to remember. And, if he didn't, it would serve him right if she just surprised him with the news suddenly—kind of like a splash of cold water to the face. *Something* was needed to wake this guy up!

But Cassie soon found out that it wasn't going to take four hours to get to their destination. Adam walked her through the terminal to a shuttle, which quickly transported them to Lake Hood.

''We're going in a floatplane?'' she squeaked as she peered through the shuttle window.

Adam chuckled, then climbed out and turned to face her. ''It's a fast way to get around and a great way to get your first glimpse of the land, Cassie. Are you nervous?''

''Are you the pilot?''

''Yes. But don't worry. I've been flying since I was sixteen. Trust me?''

He held out his hand and she looked at it for a minute, traitorous memories recalling the feel of his caresses, then placed her hand in his. ''Sure, I trust you," she said flippantly, although she'd never been in a plane smaller than a jet in her life.

"You'll love it," he assured her.

And she did, right from the minute she climbed aboard the compact blue-and-white plane and took off in an exhilarating spray of water.

"It's a de Havilland DHC2 Beaver, but I call her *Tashya.*"

Thinking of "Bogie," Cassie turned to him. "You like nicknames?"

"If they apply. I named this little beauty after my grandmother, Natashya Nikolski Baranof. Small and beautiful, almost delicate-looking, but strong and reliable and full of spunk."

Cassie liked the "reliable" part, because it seemed as though they were barely airborne when Anchorage abruptly ended and a vast wilderness began! There were mountains, meadows, rivers and lakes. Oh, so many lakes! Despite her tumbled emotions, she couldn't help but be delightfully distracted by the incredible scenery she was flying over.

"What's that? It looks like a field of snow."

"It's arctic cotton. And that meadow over there at the base of the mountain is full of red fireweed and purple lupine."

"Beautiful. And what about that mass of brown. I think it's moving!"

"It's a herd of caribou. I doubt you'll ever see as many animals anywhere as you'll see here in Alaska. Look, there's a flock of migrating cranes."

Cassie looked and looked and asked a million questions—even forgetting in the excitement of the moment that she was peeved at the pilot. But, really, hitting a man with the news that he was a father as the result of a one-night stand he didn't even remember while he piloted a plane over the rugged terrain of Alaska did not seem the wisest move, anyway. There'd be a right time for telling him later, and meanwhile she could try to get to know something more about the man who'd fathered her son.

Adam proved to be a font of information, a definite lover of the land. "Have you always lived in Alaska?" she asked him.

"Yes. In fact, my roots go back to the eighteenth century. My Russian ancestors settled on Kodiak Island and now they're all over the state."

"What about your immediate family?"

"My immediate family is settled mostly around Cook Inlet in small towns like Homer and Seldovia. In fact, my father runs a charter boat business out of Homer. You know, tours for fishing, hunting and sight-seeing. My mother used to work in Dad's business, but she stays at home now and thoroughly enjoys that."

"What about your brother?"

Adam smiled at her as if surprised and flattered by her curiosity. "My brother is a marine geologist, rather than a biologist like me. He works for the oil companies by helping them locate sites on the seafloor to drill for petroleum and natural gas. He's a lot more practical than I am."

Cassie couldn't resist it. "Is that why he's getting married and you're not?"

Adam chuckled and eyed her warily. "I've never considered marriage a practical goal. I just figured two people met and fell in love, realized they wanted to stay together forever, then got married as the next natural step.''

Cassie couldn't argue with that. In fact, he hadn't said anything that she could argue with. He seemed intelligent, polite, friendly and a perfect gentleman. So far, there had been absolutely nothing in his conversation or manners that could remotely justify not telling him about Tyler…except for the fact that he didn't seem to have the vaguest memory of having slept with the mother of his son! But maybe, although it was a crushing blow to her pride, Cassie shouldn't hold his faulty memory against him. After all, what did that have to do with Tyler?

They were following the shoreline of Cook Inlet now, on the east side of Kenai Peninsula where the mountains gave way to dense forests that rolled down to narrow beaches. In the space of about an hour, during which they continued to chat about a wide variety of things—excluding one-night stands and unplanned pregnancies—they touched down in the deep-blue waters of Kachemac Bay, an arm of the inlet. They taxied to a wooden dock, pulling abreast a tied-up motorboat. From the dock, rustic-looking stairs climbed the thickly forested hillside and disappeared into the shrubbery.

''This looks like a beautiful place,'' Cassie said as she peered through the front window of the plane. ''But sort of remote.''

''That's the way I like it,'' Adam said, as he turned dials and flicked switches on the control board. When he was finished, he gave her a devilish smile. ''It's even more remote than you think, Cassie. The only way to get out of Seldovia is by ferry or plane, so even if you decide this blind date is a bummer, you're at my mercy till you can figure out the ferry schedule or learn to fly. Although, sometimes my brother Alex drops by. He lives in Seldovia proper, near the ferry dock. You could always plead your case to him.''

Cassie laughed nervously at his teasing, not so much worried about being at *his* mercy as she was at being at the mercy of her own traitorous attraction to this Alaskan hunk.

''Homer—you know, where my folks live—is on the other side of the bay,'' Adam told her when they stood on the dock and Cassie stared in awe in a different direction across the inlet at huge, snow-capped peaks that rose from sea level, and at what seemed like a river of blue ice.

''That's Grewingk Glacier,'' Adam informed her without waiting for the question that hovered on Cassie's lips. ''I'm glad it's clear today, so you can see it. Pretty amazing, huh?''

Cassie could only nod. She was trying to withstand the double whammy of being thrilled simultaneously by the man at her side and the breathtaking scenery that surrounded her.

''Let's get you up to the house,'' he said, after allowing her a couple more minutes of awed staring. ''We'll have plenty of time to sightsee, and there's a lot I want to show you. Come on, Cass.''

Cassie preceded Adam up the stairs toward a large wood-frame cabin set on rock pilings. As she ascended, she saw and heard birds and insects and small animals grubbing through the undergrowth. The place pulsed with life.

At the top of the stairs where the land leveled off, Cassie saw a green Jeep Cherokee parked on a gravel driveway next to the cabin. They went inside the cabin, which, if not palatial was definitely substantial in size, quite open and airy, and with all the modern amenities.

After a quick tour of the house—which, as one might expect in a bachelor pad, was rather sparsely furnished and decorated—Adam surprised her by taking her outside again and walking her to another, much smaller cabin just a few yards away. It was connected to the main house by a wooden walkway that bypassed a large, screened-in hot tub nestled among spruce and birch trees.

"I guess you could call this the guest house for want of a better term," he said when she looked to him for an explanation. "It was kind of a bonus when I bought the place. I don't use it much, but my parents sometimes send family and out-of-town guests over here when they run out of room at their place. Since we don't know each other that well yet, I thought you'd be more comfortable out here."

Cassie nodded mutely and followed him inside. Remembering how quickly they had gotten chummy at their first meeting, she had been prepared to ask for her own separate bedroom. But he was actually putting her in a separate *house!* Either he'd become more reserved over the past five years, or she just didn't turn him on anymore. Confused, Cassie wasn't sure which explanation she preferred.

Adam showed her through the cozy cabin, then moved to the door, saying, "Feel free to use the hot tub. It's a great way to loosen up after a long flight.

Dinner'll be ready at eight-thirty." He grinned. "I'm a pretty good cook, so I hope you're hungry."

"Oh, I am," Cassie lied. She didn't think she could swallow a bite. There was too much left unsaid, too much tension. She was dying to blurt out the truth, to tell him that he had a son that looked exactly like him, right down to the cleft in his chin. And to demand to know why the hell he didn't have the slightest memory of having slept with the mother of their adorable child!

Adam smiled again, oblivious to her frustration. "Good. Don't bother knocking when you come up to the main house. Just walk in. See you later."

"Yeah. See you later," she echoed.

As soon as Adam shut the door behind him, Cassie sank onto the bed, physically and emotionally exhausted. She realized there was no way she was going to be able to keep up this charade much longer. And maybe there was no reason to.

Maybe Adam had slept around a lot five years ago and that's why he didn't remember her, but appearances seemed to indicate that he no longer practiced that same life-style. Otherwise, wouldn't he have at least put her under the same roof so it would be easier to get her into his bed?

Cassie sighed and made a resolution. She was done with this waiting game. At dinner—maybe even *before* dinner—she was going to tell him everything.

ADAM FOUND himself whistling as he prepared trout almandine, a spinach salad and crusty rolls, then set the table with the good dishes his mother had given him as a housewarming gift three years ago which he had never used. He even picked some yellow arctic poppies from the yard and plopped them in a vase he found collecting dust in the back of his cupboard, then lit a couple of fat emergency candles he kept around in case the electric generator broke down and arranged them near the flowers. Maybe they weren't elegant tapers, but their flickering flames still set a sort of mood.

Adam couldn't believe he was so intrigued by this woman, so immediately attracted to her, so eager to make a good impression. It wasn't in his nature to be impetuous, but he already knew without a doubt that he wanted to get to know as much as he could about Cassandra Montgomery.

He leaned against the counter as the fish sizzled in the pan and thought about her. She was lovely and natural. Despite her many questions, there was a reticence about her, a sort of "mystery." But this was a welcome change from all the women who came on like gangbusters on the first date.

He was actually thinking of calling his brother to thank him for putting that stupid ad in the magazine! But there was no time. Cassie would walk through that door any minute and he had no intention of being on the phone. Tomorrow things would start getting hectic, beginning with a morning trip into Kenai for a final fitting of his tux. Saturday was the rehearsal, Sunday was the wedding, and Monday she was scheduled to fly home. Suddenly four days just seemed like far too little time to get to know this lovely woman. But maybe, if things went well, he could convince her to stay longer.

"Knock, knock?"

He turned and saw her standing just inside the door. He liked what he saw. She had changed into a pair of beige linen slacks and a long-sleeved, silky-looking white blouse. Her hair fell in a shiny blunt cut to her shoulders and her bangs were brushed to the side. She wore a minimum of makeup and pale freckles dotted her small, straight nose. She managed to look natural and elegant at the same time.

"Come in, Cassie." He walked up to her and impetuously took her hands, gazing into her gray eyes until she blushed and turned away. "You look great."

She pulled her hands away and walked past him into the room, stopped at the table, then turned to face him. "This is nice." She made a sweeping gesture of the neatly set table. "You must do a lot of entertaining."

"Hardly," he said with a rueful smile. "I cleaned the place just for you, and this is the first time those dishes have seen the light of day. I usually eat off paper plates."

She looked at him doubtfully as if she didn't believe him. "I'm sure you don't serve wonderful dishes like trout almandine—that *is* what I'm smelling, isn't it?—on disposable dinnerware to your guests."

Adam walked back to the stove to tend to dinner and spoke to her over the counter that separated the kitchen from the dining area. "No, I don't. I don't because I hardly ever have guests. In fact, I've been so wrapped up in my work lately, the last time I had a date was—" he paused and mentally ticked off the time ''—two months ago, to be precise. And I didn't bring her here because I couldn't be bothered to clean up the place. Bachelors will be bachelors, you know. We're very predictable.''

She nodded, her smooth brow furrowing slightly. ''Oh, I wouldn't say that. At least *you're* not.''

Adam didn't know what to reply, but it appeared that he wasn't expected to. Cassie immediately turned away and began to slowly pace the living room floor, apparently deep in thought.

Now Adam frowned. It didn't seem to him to be a good sign for your date to be in a contemplative funk not five minutes into the evening. He turned off the stove and walked around the counter to stand by the table with his arms crossed over his chest, watching her.

When she appeared not to even notice his presence, he finally asked, ''Is something the matter, Cassie? You seem very preoccupied.''

She turned abruptly, a strange sort of urgent expression in her eyes. ''Something *is* the matter, Adam.''

He took two steps forward. She took two steps back and began to wring her hands. ''What is it?'' he demanded, starting to worry. All sorts of possibilities were going through his head. Hell, he hoped she wasn't going to tell him she was married!

''There's something I have to tell you.''

He sighed. Such a beginning did not sound promising. ''Go ahead.''

Her head bobbed nervously. She gave a wan smile and wrung her hands a little more. ''It's about when you were in Montana before—''

"Yes?" he prompted.

"You and I..." She paused again, blushing.

Now he was really confused. "You and I what?"

"You and I—"

But Cassie had no chance to finish her confession, or revelation or whatever it was she was trying to say, because just then the door swung open and a man breezed in.

"Hey, bro," Adam began, then caught sight of Cassie just as she caught sight of his brother. Her eyes widened and her lips parted on a startled gasp. That's when Adam realized he hadn't told Cassie that he and his brother were—

"Twins," Cassie said in a shaky voice. "Oh, my God. You're *twins*."

Chapter Three

Cassie grabbed the back of one of the dining room chairs for support. She felt faint. Her insides were topsy-turvy. She couldn't believe she was looking at two men who were absolutely identical in appearance, from handsome head to toe, both of whom—no, *either* of whom—could be the father of her child! But since Adam didn't seem to remember her, maybe it was his brother who was actually Tyler's father. There was only one way to find out.

"Cassie, you don't look too well," she heard Adam say as he laid a hand on her shoulder and peered worriedly into her face. "Maybe you should sit down."

"I don't want to sit down. I want to ask your brother a question."

Looking perplexed, Adam gazed back and forth between his brother and Cassie. Alex had no expression on his face whatsoever. He simply stared, as if in a trance. "You want to ask Alex a question? But you two don't even know each other." He paused, then his brows lowered. He turned back to his brother. "Or do you?"

"That's a good question. *Do* we know each other, Alex?" Cassie quickly echoed, hating the note of desperation that had crept into her voice. But now that she'd started, she couldn't stop. She wanted an end to this uncertainty. "Are you the man I met five years ago at the Fourth of July fair in Nye, Montana, whom I then spent the night with at the Tuddenhams' bed-and-breakfast?"

Cassie heard Adam gasp, but her gaze was fixed on Alex, willing him to speak, to react in some way. When he continued to appear stunned and confused, she turned back to Adam, tears beginning to sting the back of her eyelids. "Or is it you, Adam, and you just don't remember me?"

Now both men appeared stupefied. "Don't just stand there like a couple of idiots!" Cassie exclaimed, beyond exasperation. "One of you *must* remember me, because one of you happens to be the father of my four-year-old son! He looks exactly like you—exactly like *both* of you! Right down to that damned cleft in your chins!"

In almost perfect unison, Adam and Alex both fumbled for chairs and sat down.

"I'm not telling you this because I want money from you," Cassie hurriedly explained. "I don't want child support for Tyler. We're perfectly fine the way we are. He's got plenty of male influence in his life, too, and doesn't necessarily need a father. I just thought you should know about him, that's all. And, someday when he asks, I want to be able to tell my son who his father is. That's why I answered Adam's ad. That's why I came up here. I saw the face of Tyler's father in that magazine, staring back at me after five years, and it was the only way I knew him. Now what I want is a name. Is it Adam or is it Alex?''

Adam and Alex seemed to be in states of shock because neither of them said anything. It was either that or...

Cassie dropped her head into her hands. "Oh, my God. *Neither* of you remembers me, do you? Adam, where's your bathroom? I think I'm going to be sick.''

This announcement finally stirred Adam to action. He hurried to his feet, caught her arm and guided her to a bathroom that seemed miles away by the time Cassie got there. She sagged down onto the edge of the tub and gratefully received the washcloth Adam quickly dampened and handed to her.

"Are you really going to be sick?" he inquired gently.

"I don't know," Cassie answered dully. "But if I do get sick, I don't want you here to see it. With my luck, you'd remember the sight of me puking my guts out even if you can't remember making love to me all night long."

"Cassie, I—"

"Go away. Shut the door and go away. I need some time."

Cassie waited until he left, then she turned on the tap, redampened the washcloth with steamy-hot water, bent her head and gratefully pressed the washcloth to the back of her neck. She kept the tap running to drown out the sound just in case she started crying.

All the tension, all the doubt of the past couple

of weeks had come to a head…and *still* nothing was resolved! Damn it, she almost wanted to cry—maybe it would make her feel better—but a stubborn part of her refused to. She'd have her little time out, then she'd march out there again for another dose of necessary humiliation. By sorting out travel agendas of five years ago, surely they'd be able to figure out which of the forgetful Baranof twins was Tyler's father.

WHEN ADAM RETURNED to the dining room, Alex was still seated in the chair, looking dazed. Adam crossed his arms and stood over him, his knees locked, his legs slightly spread in an almost military stance. He stared down at his brother until Alex raised his head to meet his stern gaze.

"Is she going to be all right?"

"That depends. *Do* you remember her, Alex?"

Alex sighed. "Of course I do." Wearily, he ran a hand through his hair. "I recognized her immediately. It was such a shock, for a minute or two I couldn't even breathe." Then in a quieter, softer tone, he continued, "It would be impossible to forget that night."

Alex felt a sharp stab of jealousy which he tried to squelch. This was a serious matter that needed to be discussed calmly and rationally, without emotional distractions.

"Was it just one night?"

"Yes. We had a date for lunch the next day, but I left town before she came by."

Adam fought the urge to whack his brother upside the head. "That was a crummy thing to do."

"I didn't mean to do it. I got a call from Mom. It was when Dad got that concussion and he was in critical care. We all rushed to his bedside, remember?"

Adam nodded, then asked gruffly, "Didn't you two even exchange names?"

"She told me her name, but I only told her my frat nickname."

Adam grimaced. "Bogie?"

"Yeah."

"And she was satisfied with that?"

Alex shrugged tiredly. "I guess so. Hell, I was just having fun, Adam. I even registered under Mr. Bogart. I did that all the time, back then. I was going to tell her my real name the next day." He looked earnestly at Adam. "I know I've done a lot of stupid, irresponsible things in my life, bro, but I certainly never intended to get Cassie in trouble then abandon her."

Adam's anger subsided…a little. Anyway, he had an inkling that his anger was partially based on the fact that his brother had found Cassie first…and had left with her such a permanent reminder of himself.

"What are you going to do about the child?"

"The child." Alex shuddered. "I can't believe this. How can this be happening little more than forty-eight hours before my wedding? When Kelly finds out I have an illegitimate son, she'll… she'll—" He shook his head woefully. "Hell, I don't have a clue what she'll do, but it'll definitely put a damper on what's supposed to be the most wonderful day of her life. As for her parents…I've

got a pretty good idea how *they'll* react to the news.''

Adam knew exactly what Alex meant. Alex's intended in-laws were quite a bit older than their own parents and had had Kelly, the youngest of their seven children, late in life. They were old-fashioned and very protective. When they'd found out that Kelly had been living with Alex since their engagement three months before, Mrs. Armstrong had cried and Mr. Armstrong was so angry he almost refused to fly out from their home in Florida for the wedding. Kelly mollified him by moving into her own apartment until she and Alex were actually married.

Adam had met Mr. and Mrs. Armstrong at a family dinner the day before and, while Mr. Armstrong was polite and pleasant, he clearly adored his daughter and did not seem to be the sort of man who could easily overlook the sudden appearance of a woman from Alex's past claiming a child as the result of a one-night stand.

Mr. Armstrong strongly disapproved of alcoholic beverages, too, not just for himself but for the whole world, and was opposed to serving it at the wedding reception. Kelly gave in to him on this, just as she had on her living arrangements, and champagne was omitted from the menu.

Adam felt that people had a right to make their own choices about whether or not to drink alcoholic beverages, and felt it was rather selfish of Mr. Armstrong to try to force his own personal code of behavior not just on his adult daughter but on everyone else. Unfortunately, if Mr. Armstrong was that opinionated about champagne consumption, he would probably have even stronger opinions about one-night stands and accidental babies. Adam was beginning to feel some reluctant sympathy for Alex.

"I don't suppose there's any chance Cassie's lying," Adam suggested tentatively. The two brothers locked gazes and simultaneously shook heads. "No, I didn't think so, either," Adam muttered. He hardly knew her, but he instinctively realized Cassie was probably too honest for her own good. Besides, all she had to do was produce a picture of Tyler, and if he looked as much like Alex as she said, who could dispute that kind of evidence?

"She was a virgin," Alex suddenly revealed.

Adam clenched his jaw. That was more information than he wanted. "I repeat, Alex, what are you going to do about the child?"

With much effort, Alex pulled himself to his feet and began to trudge about the room, his hands stuffed in the back pockets of his jeans. "Hell, I don't know! What am I supposed to do?"

"By Cassie's account, nothing. She doesn't seem to care whether you're part of the child's life or not. She says she doesn't want money, or your influence as a parent. I think she just wanted to end the embarrassment of not knowing the name of her child's father." Adam paused, then asked, "Don't you have *any* interest in the boy, Alex?"

"Not really," Alex admitted a little sheepishly. "Right now all I can think about is Kelly and the life we've got planned, and how all that's in jeopardy now! You know how long I've waited for a woman like Kelly, Adam. I can't stand the thought that I might lose her."

Alex moved to the window and looked out over the heavily wooded hill behind the cabin. Adam watched the glum profile of his younger brother—by exactly three minutes—and his sympathy grew. It was true, Alex had waited a long time for a woman like Kelly.

Well, perhaps *waiting* wasn't the right word to describe Alex's activities before he met Kelly. Charm incarnate, Alex had always attracted more women than he knew what to do with. As a scientist and a scholar, he was exemplary. As a date or a lover, he was irresponsible and fickle. That is, until steady, levelheaded, strong-minded—except when up against her parents—lovely Kelly Armstrong came along. Paradoxically, being head-over-heels in love with her had grounded him for the first time in his life.

They were both geologists, both career-minded, and had jobs lined up in Florida, where they planned to move after the honeymoon. Kelly was just what Alex needed, and her presence had considerably lessened Adam's struggles with his younger twin, as well. Lord knew he'd helped his brother get through the hassles of countless soured relationships over the years, and it was a relief to see Alex finally happy and committed. It would be a terrible shame to have it all blow up in his face because of something that happened five years ago.

"Adam?"

"Hmm?" Adam roused himself from thought and was surprised to find his brother looking at him with something like hope on his face.

"I think I've got a solution to this problem.

Something that will satisfy Cassie and save my marriage, too.'' He spoke in a whisper now, darting a look toward the hallway from which Cassie might emerge at any moment.

Adam frowned suspiciously. ''What are you talking about, Alex?''

Alex moved closer, his tone urgent and excited. ''Just tell Cassie that *you're* Tyler's father! That it was *you* who slept with her five years ago!''

Adam instinctively recoiled from such an idea. ''What? You're crazy, Alex! Number one, it wouldn't be fair to lie about something as important as a child's paternity. Number two, she wouldn't believe me. I haven't shown a single sign of having recognized her since she arrived.''

Alex grabbed Adam's shoulder in a clench so tight it hurt. ''Number one, you're the kid's uncle, aren't you? You look just like his real father, don't you? You're a Baranof. How much closer to the real thing could she get? And, number two, just tell her that you were drunk that night, or...or something. That *now* you remember her. That she'd seemed familiar all along, but it took the jolt of her news to jog your memory.''

''I would never have forgotten sleeping with Cassie, drunk or sober,'' Adam stately grimly. ''*You* didn't forget.''

''No, but she doesn't know that. She went into the bathroom not knowing which of us was the father, thinking that whoever it was had forgotten the whole...er...incident. Hell, she'll be relieved to find out it's you and not me! She'd probably be the last person to want to mess up anyone's wedding.''

Adam shook his head. "There has to be another solution. What if Cassie agreed to keep quiet about Tyler's paternity till after the honeymoon? You could break it to your fiancée then without her father around to fan the fire. Or tell Kelly now, just keep it from her parents. She'd probably understand."

"Would she? I don't know. She's caved in to her parents more than once. She moved out on me when her father voiced his disapproval of our living arrangements, remember? And why should *I* take the risk?"

Alex cocked a brow. "Because *you're* the father?"

"But *you* don't have a fiancée to worry about! Besides, I'll bet Cassie would be hurt if we tried to hush up the whole thing. It would be best for everyone if you just claimed paternity. Cassie'll go home happy and I'll go on my honeymoon happy."

Adam wanted to ask, *but what about me?* There was nothing about this situation making *him* happy. Cassie may have only answered Adam's ad because she thought he was Alex, but he had written to her because of an immediate and unexpectedly powerful attraction to her. Meeting her in person had only intensified that attraction. It seemed grossly unfair that she was suddenly off-limits to him because of a complicated history with his brother. His brother...who probably wished he'd never set eyes on Cassie in his life.

And she was definitely off-limits. Without honesty between them, to try to initiate an intimate relationship would be brutally unfair. Considering his attraction to her, if he went along with Alex's idea and she stuck around for the wedding as planned, the next three days could be a living hell.

But maybe he deserved a little bit of hell for such a great big lie...if he agreed to tell it.

And what about Cassie and what *she* deserved? Did she deserve the truth, which would almost certainly put many lives in upheaval? Or did she deserve a lie that would probably—excluding himself—smooth the way for them all?

Tyler wouldn't suffer. He was far away in Montana and would never have to meet either him or Alex. Tyler's life would go blissfully on and when the day came when he asked his mother about his real father, he'd find out it was a man in Alaska named Baranof. Did the first name matter?

Why *not* take the path of least resistance? Adam rationalized. Alex's self-interest notwithstanding, maybe he was right. Maybe it was the best course to take, after all.

"I'm back."

Adam's head jerked up to find Cassie standing just inside the room. He expected to see her eyes pink from crying, but they weren't. She was very pale, but she stood straight and tall, with her chin up. *Stoic.* He wished he could take her into his arms to caress and comfort her until the color crept back into her cheeks and that grim look about her soft mouth disappeared.

"Are you okay?"

She nodded, tried to smile. "Yes, I'm much better now. It was just a shock, you know, seeing you both together like that. I had no idea..." She gave an uncertain chuckle. "It shot my theory all to heck about who Tyler's father absolutely had to be. Now there are two possibilities.'' She looked from Adam to Alex, who was standing with his back to the room, facing the window again, then back to Adam. ''Has...has either of you remembered...anything?''

Alex looked over his shoulder at Adam, his eyes pleading, urging. Cassie's expression was wrenchingly hopeful. Adam had never felt more torn in his life. While his conscience screamed foul, his emotions were nevertheless winning the battle.

Finally, with a sigh of surrender, he said, ''Yes, Cassie. I remember. I remember that night with you.''

Adam was immediately rewarded for his lie. Cassie's eyes lost their bleakness, her shoulders their rigidity, her mouth its grim pucker. And, in the background, Alex's head dropped in an almost prayerful pose of profound relief.

''Then...then you're Tyler's father,'' Cassie said, as if needing to reassure herself by stating the obvious.

Adam's gaze darted to Alex, then away. It was hard to look at his brother and lie about the father thing. ''Yes. Yes, I guess I am.''

Cassie nodded slowly. ''Then I guess we have some things to talk about.''

''That's my cue to leave,'' Alex spoke up, turning and walking briskly past them to the door. With his hand on the knob, he glanced back at them, a smile plastered on his face, but Adam detected behind the politeness the look of a hunted man who had just escaped a death trap. ''You guys do have a lot to talk about. I'll see you tomorrow in Kenai for the tux fitting. Cassie, you can meet Kelly then. You'll love her.''

Cassie nodded absently, her eyes still fixed on Adam.

Alex paused, then added nervously, ''Right, Adam?''

Adam looked at his brother, his expression carefully neutral. He already had a sinking feeling in his stomach that what he'd just done was terribly wrong. But the die was cast. ''Right, Alex. See you tomorrow.''

ALEX WAS GONE and Cassie was alone with Adam. Now that the truth was out, she felt horribly self-conscious. She had been prepared to feel awkward at this point, but the surprising arrival of Adam's twin had almost turned the drama of the situation into *melo*drama.

''I feel like I'm living in a soap opera,'' Cassie confessed, hoping to lighten the mood.

''All the key elements are present,'' Adam agreed with a grim, rueful smile. ''Amnesia, babies out of the blue, evil twin.''

''*Evil* twin?'' Cassie teased gamely. ''Which one?''

Adam looked away and shrugged. ''Are you hungry, Cassie? Dinner's still edible.''

''I don't think I can eat a bite till we've cleared some things up,'' she admitted.

He nodded and pulled out a chair for her. ''Okay. Sit down. We'll talk, then eat.''

She sat down, scooted her chair near the table, then rested her clasped hands in front of her. Adam sat opposite her, but he leaned back, his arms crossed high over his chest. Cassie thought the pose rather standoffish and defensive and it prompted her first question.

"You're not at all happy about this news, are you?"

His lips twitched. "I would have thought the first thing you'd want to know is why I didn't remember you right away."

"That *is* a good question. Another good question is, why do you remember me now?"

Adam's blue eyes narrowed slightly as his gaze trailed over her features. She felt warmth creep up her neck. "Your face immediately caught my attention, Cassie. Your face out of hundreds of faces on hundreds of photos."

"I suppose that *does* mean you remembered me, whether you knew it or not, because otherwise you would never have written to me out of all those respondents to your ad. It would just be too weird. Too coincidental…or fated."

He blinked, smiled tightly. "Right. Too coincidental, too fated."

"Then, when I blurted out the bare facts, I can see you finally putting two and two together. But, honestly, I can't understand you forgetting so *completely* until then."

"The details are fuzzy, Cassie, because…because I was drunk that night."

Cassie stared. The confession seemed to have been wrenched out of him. "You're kidding. You certainly didn't act drunk. You were very… well…*coordinated*." If he was so skillful and romantic when he was drunk, what was he like sober? She didn't dare think about it.

"You'd be surprised how drunk a man can be and still...er...perform normally," he informed her with another grim smile.

She may never have been with another man, but Cassie knew Adam had to be above average in the lovemaking department. She just knew it.

She noticed a muscle ticking in his jaw. Had she made him angry?

"You don't seem to care for this line of questioning," she suggested.

"I feel stupid about remembering so little." He uncrossed his arms, crossed a long leg ankle to knee and absently tapped the sole of his shoe with a forefinger. His movements and mannerisms were still graceful, still fascinating to watch. "Aren't you insulted?"

Cassie recalled her wandering thoughts. "Yes, I suppose I am...a little. Especially since I remember so *much*."

Adam grunted. There was a beat of uncomfortable silence, then he said, "I know one detail that's rather significant."

"What is it?"

"It was your first time."

Cassie blushed again and stared at her clasped hands. After such an unpromising beginning, he was certainly remembering more than she expected him to.

"I suppose you remember that because I was a klutz that night. Because I didn't know what I was doing till...till you showed me. But it all seemed so natural, and I got the impression that you enjoyed yourself as much…as much as I did.''

When he didn't immediately answer, Cassie braved a glance at him. The muscle in his jaw was ticking more frantically than ever. ''I've put you on the spot, haven't I? I'm sorry. I don't know why I even brought up any of this. Anyway, how can you reassure me about something you barely remember?''

Adam stared at Cassie's flushed, embarrassed face. He'd never felt so frustrated in his life. While he wanted more than anything to reassure her about that night, he'd be treading through uncharted territory to do so. He could only guess how things had gone that night, only suppose they'd gone well. By her and Alex's reactions to every mention of it, perhaps *extremely* well. Besides, if Cassie had enjoyed herself so much, it stood to reason that Alex couldn't have helped but enjoy himself, too. *Damn* him.

Adam gazed into her clear-as-crystal eyes just before Cassie ducked her head shyly and looked down. He decided that there probably wasn't a man on earth who could resist such a woman's charms. Least of all his three-minutes-younger brother. And since he'd already told Cassie an enormous lie to ease the way to happiness for that brother, he shouldn't feel the least compunction about telling smaller lies that would make her happy, too.

''You weren't a klutz, Cassie.''

Up flew her downcast eyes. ''I wasn't?''

''Far from it. As you said yourself, it…it was all very natural. Very lovely. I enjoyed myself very much and I was sorry I couldn't meet you for lunch the next day. I got a phone call, you see. My father had a fall and my mother called to—''

''Ah.'' Her eyes lit up, her lips curved in a tentative smile. ''So it *was* an emergency. You didn't stand me up?''

He smiled back and answered honestly. ''A man would be a damned fool to break a date with you for any reason short of a major emergency.'' Impulsively he reached across the table and took her hands. ''I'm sorry that I... What I mean is, I'm just sorry you had to go through so much alone, with the baby and all.''

She squeezed his hands and her smile broadened, its sweetness sending an unwilling surge of emotion through him. ''There's nothing to feel sorry about when it comes to Tyler. I loved him from the moment he was conceived. I loved being pregnant and I've loved being his mother.''

Adam nodded doubtfully. ''Yes, but there must have been difficulties—''

''Oh, there were,'' she answered with a wry chuckle. ''Not the least of which was my father, who wanted to tar and feather you.''

Adam released her hands and sat back. ''That's understandable,'' he murmured.

''But he doesn't want to do that anymore, because he's as crazy about Tyler as I am.''

Adam couldn't help but be impressed by Cassie's obvious love for her son. Just talking about Tyler made her glow like a...well, like a Madonna. It was reassuring to know that his little nephew was being raised by such a loving and committed mother, and a doting grandfather, too. But it only made Cassie more appealing to him, *damn* it. He sat there silently, stewing over the whole situation.

"This brings me back to my original question," Cassie said, interrupting his unpleasant thoughts. "You're not happy about this, are you? Does this mean you don't want to have anything to do with Tyler?"

How did Adam answer such a question? If Tyler were *his* son, he'd sure as hell want to see the little guy. At least he *thought* that's how he'd feel... Oh, hell, he didn't know! Until Cassie showed up, having kids had been the last thing on his mind.

"You look very undecided," Cassie suggested. Before Adam could answer, she slipped a hand inside her blouse and pulled out a small snapshot. She handed it to him and he automatically took it. It was still warm from nesting against her breast and it smelled like talcum powder. But these sensations were secondary to the visceral reaction of looking at a pint-size replica of himself.

"My God," he rasped. "He looks just like—" He stopped himself. Tyler looked just like his father. His father, *Alex*. Not Adam. *Alex*.

"Handsome, isn't he?" Cassie said, her voice humming with motherly pride. "And you're right, he looks just like you, right down to the cleft in his chin."

Adam could only nod stupidly.

Then she asked, shyly, "Would you like to meet him?"

Adam swallowed hard. Of course he'd like to meet him, but that was something that could never happen. Alex had no intention of being part of his son's life, and since he, Adam, was pretending to be the boy's father, that meant he mustn't show any interest in Tyler, either.

But when he looked over the snapshot and into Cassie's hopeful eyes, Adam found he couldn't be as straightforward as he ought to be. "Well, Montana's not exactly next door. Maybe if the little guy were closer—"

Cassie's eyes shone like stars. "He *is* closer. He's in Anchorage with my father, staying at the Voyager Hotel. If you'd like to, we could fly up there tomorrow and you could meet him."

Chapter Four

Unless Adam specifically expressed an interest in meeting his son, Cassie had not intended to tell him that Tyler was in Anchorage with her father. But from the way his eyes lit up when she showed him Tyler's picture, she could have sworn he was instantly smitten. Thus the spontaneous suggestion that father and son meet. Now she wasn't so sure about Adam's reaction to the picture. Suddenly he looked more alarmed than intrigued.

"We don't have to tell him you're his daddy," Cassie quickly assured him. "And if you decide you don't want to be part of his life, I'm sure he won't remember meeting you."

Adam placed the picture on the table between them and sat back in his chair, a troubled expression on his face. "Do you want me— Do you really want Tyler's father to be part of his life, Cass? And what exactly does that mean, anyway?"

Cassie sat back, too. Her emotions were in turmoil. She wasn't sure what she wanted. And she wasn't sure why she seemed actually to be *encouraging* Adam to be part of Tyler's life. If her father were there, he'd be kicking her backside for sure. After all, Tyler was as happy as possible the way things were. She still didn't know Adam that well. What if he turned out to be a complication that Tyler could have done much better without?

"Never mind," Cassie said quickly. "It was a stupid idea."

"It wasn't a stupid idea. It's just that—"

"It should have been *your* idea," Cassie interjected, her gaze nervously flitting here, there, everywhere but at Adam. "I wasn't going to tell you Tyler was in Anchorage unless you said you wanted to meet him. But I didn't give you the chance and now you're feeling pressured and—"

Cassie was silenced when Adam gently grasped her shoulders and forced her to look at him. His expression was concerned, sympathetic. "It wasn't a stupid idea, Cass," he said succinctly. "Nothing you've thought or said or done is stupid. You're his mother. Your motives are pure and unselfish. You're only thinking of your son, which is more than I can say for the rest of us."

Cassie was torn between the pleasure of feeling his hands on her shoulders and having his face so close, and confusion at his choice of words. "The rest of us? What do you mean?"

Adam sighed, released her, sat back again. "I mean *me*. Just me. *I'm* being selfish. I'm protecting myself."

"In what way?"

"I *would* like to meet Tyler. I'm just not sure it's such a good idea."

She nodded, trying to understand. "Because

you've already decided that you don't want to be part of his life?"

"Because it would be impossible to be part of his life."

Cassie still didn't understand Adam's reasoning— in fact, he seemed almost to be hiding something— but his intentions were clear. Adam didn't plan to be part of Tyler's life.

Well, her father would be happy. As for herself, she knew she ought to be relieved, but she was actually disappointed. Maybe it was because she couldn't conceive of being a parent to a remarkable, adorable child like Tyler and not rejoicing in the fact. Even if he wasn't such a remarkable, adorable child, wasn't it normal and natural to be drawn to your own flesh and blood?

In a way, Adam's almost frightened reaction to news of Tyler's close proximity lessened her good opinion of him. Yes, as he'd said himself, it showed him to be a bit selfish. After all, if he met Tyler he might start caring for him. And caring for someone, whether it was a woman or a child, meant a certain amount of commitment. And commitment meant time and responsibilities and emotional risk. And, though she had already tried to reassure him about that, perhaps he thought it also meant *money*.

"I don't think I like what you're thinking."

Startled, Cassie looked up and into Adam's eyes.

"You think it's the money, don't you? Actually I would be more than thrilled to contribute to Tyler's upbringing and education, but I don't think you'd approve of that unless I was also part of his life.

And that's the rub. I *can't* be part of his life, Cassie."

Cassie waited, but no further explanation was offered. So, hiding her hurt, she shrugged and said, "Okay. If that's the way you want it."

"It's the way it has to be," he said, rather stubbornly, she thought. And she still didn't understand. Was there something she didn't know about the situation?

Adam knew she didn't understand, but how could he explain? He supposed he should just say he didn't want to meet Tyler because he didn't like kids, even when they were his. She could write him off as an unfeeling bastard and leave it at that. But he *did* want to meet Tyler and he wasn't an unfeeling bastard—just a lying bastard—and he was fighting the urge to tell her they'd fly up to Anchorage right after the tux fitting tomorrow.

"I'll reheat dinner," he said, forcing a cheerful tone as he stood up and moved to the counter. "You must be starved by now."

"To tell you the truth," she began, standing up, too, and turning to face him, "I'm not hungry. I wasn't hungry earlier, either. Too nervous. Now I'm just—"

"Disappointed," Adam finished for her. He could see it in her eyes. She was disappointed and, he feared, about to announce that there was no point in staying in Alaska now that she'd broken the news about Tyler. Undoubtedly it would be best if she flew back to Montana as soon as possible, but even though it would create a special kind of hell for him if she didn't, he was startled to realize how much he'd depended on her staying for the next three days.

"It's not as if I were dying to show off my new puppy or something," Cassie tried to explain. "Although I *am* tremendously proud of him. But Tyler's your *son!* From what I can see, Adam, you seem to be a pretty nice man. If I thought you were a jerk, I wouldn't even have told you about Tyler. But while I don't think you're a jerk, I *do* think you're behaving a bit like a…well, a.…"

"Coward?" he offered ruefully.

Tactfully, she did not agree, but might as well have when she continued by asking, "What are you afraid of? Or do I already know?"

She partially knew. He *was* afraid. Afraid of falling for the kid and the mother, too. Trouble was, it was more complicated than that. He had no *right* to fall for the kid or the mother. *Especially* the mother. He wasn't the man she thought he was…in oh-so-many ways! If he really were Tyler's father, he wouldn't hesitate to make plans for a trip to Anchorage. But he wasn't Tyler's father. He wasn't anybody's father. He was a phony.

Adam stared at Cassie's bleak expression, aching inside. He couldn't stand the idea of her leaving, disappointed and disgusted by him. And so he couldn't resist giving in to what they both wanted. Damn it, he'd take her to Anchorage! He'd fly up there to meet Tyler and the formidable grandfather who had once mentally tarred and feathered him. Or, rather, he'd mentally tarred and feathered Adam's twin, the original culprit. Now, in Adam's opinion, both Baranof men deserved punishment.

Although Tyler wasn't his son, he *was* his nephew, Adam continued to reason, setting aside culpability for the moment. What was the harm of getting to know and even getting to like one's own nephew? It was the mother he'd have to watch himself around. For now, however, all he cared about was making her happy again, wiping that sad look off her face.

"If I told you that we could fly up to Anchorage right after the tux fitting tomorrow morning, do you think you might get your appetite back?"

Instantly the bleakness in her eyes disappeared, but just as quickly a cautiousness crept in to tamp down the joy. "Are you sure? Or have I just forced you into doing what I want?" Her lips quirked. "Dad says I've got a way of doing that. Just like Mom."

"You've got a way about you, that's for sure," Adam acknowledged in the same rueful tone. Boy, did she ever. He had an unsettling notion that, if exposed too long to her wiles, he'd do just about anything she asked.

"No, Cassie, I actually do want to meet Tyler. However, I think, just as you suggested, it would be best if we didn't tell him I'm his father."

Cassie nodded. "Agreed. We'll just get together, the three of us, and see what happens. No expectations, no promises."

"Don't you mean the four of us?" Adam reminded her. "By the way, does your father still want to tar and feather me? He might like the result of our one-night stand, but he might still feel antipathy toward the perpetrator of the crime." It occurred to

Adam that he wouldn't mind Mr. Montgomery's ire if he'd actually had the pleasure of making love to Cassie all night long. In fact, if that were the case he wouldn't mind a lot of things.

Cassie smiled and sat down, picked up Tyler's picture and tucked it back inside her blouse. *Lucky picture.* "Like I said, Dad's settled down since I first told him I was pregnant. That was five years ago, Adam. He's not the sort of man to hold a grudge. The only way you'd get him riled up now is if he caught you doing something *new* he considered detrimental to his precious daughter."

Something new, like lying to her about who was the real father of her child?

"I think I'm hungry again," Cassie said happily. "That fish smells delicious."

Adam was glad Cassie's appetite had returned, but his had completely disappeared.

Cassie noticed that Adam didn't eat much, but then he had received quite a shock that evening. And as for conversation, she carried it while Adam pushed food around on his plate and nodded distractedly only when a response of some kind was absolutely necessary.

Finally Cassie took pity on him, stood up and dropped her napkin on the table. He gazed at her, blinking like a man just emerging from a trance. "It's getting late."

He stood, too, instantly apologetic. "I'm sorry, Cassie. I've been lousy company. Stay and have some coffee. I promise to perk up." He grinned. "No pun intended."

"Adam, I think the kindest thing I could do for

you is leave you alone so you can digest the fact that you've become a father overnight.''

''Isn't that usually the way it happens?'' he teased gamely.

''It's usually not such a big surprise, and the child never arrives wearing toddler-size cowboy boots. Good night, Adam. Thanks for dinner. I'm just sorry you couldn't enjoy it, too.''

''My appetite will be back by morning,'' he assured her, as he walked her to the door.

When he placed his hand lightly on the small of her back, ready to follow her outside, shivers ran up and down Cassie's spine. She turned, disconcerted to find his face, his lips, just inches away, and said rather breathlessly, ''You don't have to escort me to my cabin, Adam. I know my way.''

''A gentleman always takes his date to her door at the end of the evening,'' Adam insisted.

''Is this still a date?'' Cassie asked, finding it hard to think while they stood so close to each other.

''I remember it starting out that way, but I feel like light-years have passed since you walked through my door at eight-thirty.''

''Is that a polite way of saying I've aged you?''

He chuckled. ''Just let me walk you to your cabin, Cass, if for no other reason than to protect you from the occasional bull moose, bear, or some other wild beast that might be roaming around at this hour. Remember, you're in Alaska now. You have to be a little more careful about certain things.''

Cassie nodded and allowed Adam to guide her through the door, his hand still lightly pressed against her lower back. She was from Montana and not as frightened of wild beasts as Adam might think. She was much more frightened of accidentally revealing that he still did crazy things to her blood pressure and pulse. Afraid that if he bent his head to lightly kiss her on the cheek, she'd throw her arms around his neck and press her lips against his.

The night air was cool and damp and smelled of pine; and the sky, despite the fact that it was past ten o'clock at night, was the pale purple of early dusk. They accomplished the walk to the cabin in tense silence and when they reached the door, Cassie hesitated, unable to make herself turn to face him.

"Cassie?"

"Hmm?"

"Don't worry. I don't expect you to invite me in."

She turned slowly, then looked up. He smiled down at her.

"This is awkward as hell, isn't it?" he said.

"Yes. Yes, it is."

He put his hands on her shoulders, his fingers kneading her tense muscles. It felt wonderful. *Too* wonderful. "Like I said, don't worry. I'm not going to put the moves on you just because we have some history together. I know we can't pick up where we left off, and I wouldn't want to."

She winced and blushed. *"Oh."*

"No! That's not what I meant," he hurriedly explained. "Believe me, I find you very attractive...er...*still*. But things are different now."

Cassie nodded mutely. She wasn't sure she understood how he perceived the situation to be different, but she was wholeheartedly in agreement that, because of Tyler, they needed to go slowly and carefully in the romance department. Things could get even more awkward if they got involved and it didn't work out.

Of course there was always the other side of the coin...fairy-tale ending with she and Tyler and Adam becoming one big happy family. But Cassie wouldn't allow herself to entertain such an idea. While Adam might be attracted to her, he was obviously ambivalent about their son, and possibly opposed to any kind of commitment.

"You understand, don't you?"

"Do I really need to?" Cassie countered. "All that's important is that we both understand the need to avoid...well...*what happened before,* even if we both have different motivations."

Adam frowned. "It sounds like you've decided that my motivations are less than admirable."

She shrugged. "No. Since you haven't told me your motivations, I can't judge one way or the other. Maybe if you *explained*—"

His hands slid off her shoulders and fell to his sides. "I can't."

She lifted her chin. "Fine. Keep it to yourself, but I'm going to tell you my motivation, whether you want to hear it or not. I just don't want anyone getting hurt."

He reached up and gently cupped her jaw, his thumb moving in feathery circles against her skin. "Neither do I, Cass," he whispered, looking earnestly into her eyes. "Neither do I."

He turned and walked away, not looking back. Cassie chewed her bottom lip, watching with narrowed eyes until he disappeared behind some low-hanging tree branches.

What wasn't Adam telling her? What *were* his motivations? Were they purely selfish, or was he thinking of her and Tyler, too?

Who *was* he protecting, anyway?

"ALEX?"

"Oh, hi, bro." There was a pause on the other end of the line, then the whispered question, "Is something the matter?"

Adam settled in his reclining chair with the portable phone, throwing his leg over the well-padded arm. "Hell, yes, something's the matter. I didn't like this from the start and now things are worse. Cassie's brought her fath—"

"Let me call you back," Adam interrupted. "*Kelly*'s here."

Adam couldn't miss the underlying anxiety in Alex's voice. He sighed. "No, don't bother. I'm going to bed."

After another strained pause, his brother said, pointedly and in a deliberately cheerful tone, "I've told Kelly about Cassie and Tyler."

Adam sat up. "You *what*?"

"You heard me," he continued, obviously playing to an audience of one…Kelly. "With Cassie here for the wedding, it would have come out sooner or later."

"Who said you could decide that sooner was better than later?" Adam demanded to know. "Or did you spread the word early on because you figured it would make it harder for me to change my mind?"

"Cassie would have been hurt if it had been handled any other way," Alex continued. "I thought
we both understood that."

Adam scowled across the room and through the
window that gave back a beautiful view of wooded
mountainside. Alex was right. What made him think
he could take part in this deception without also lying to Kelly and every other member of the family?
By claiming Tyler as his, he'd only thought at that
moment of protecting Alex and making things easier
for Cassie. He hadn't considered the domino effect
put in motion by that first lie.

"Adam? You still there?"

"You're right," Adam conceded grimly. "Everyone should be told about *my* involvement with Cassie and *my* son. I'll tell Dad tomorrow at the tux
fitting."

"Dad won't be there tomorrow."

"He won't?"

"No. He went in today to get fitted because he's
got too many charters booked for tomorrow. That's
why I called him an hour ago and told both him and
Mom about Cassie and...and the kid."

"Don't call him 'the kid.' His name is Tyler."

"Whatever. I mean...okay."

"Weren't Mom and Dad a little surprised that the
news that I'd fathered a child hadn't come from
me?" Adam inquired dryly.

"I told them you were with Cassie, working
things out."

"I suppose they're chomping at the bit to see their
first grandchild?"

"They know that you...well...that you *may* not want to be part of his life."

"So you told them that, too? I'm sure Mom was impressed with my parental instincts."

"She didn't understand at first, but when I explained how you feel—"

"You mean how *you* feel."

"—I think they understood."

"Explain it to *me,* then, Alex," Adam muttered, "because I sure as hell don't understand not wanting to be part of your own child's life."

"What? I didn't hear you. Kelly was saying something."

"It wasn't important."

"Anyway, Kelly says she's anxious to meet Cassie and that it's too bad she didn't bring Tyler with her."

"Well...not to Seldovia."

"What do you mean...not to Seldovia?"

"Tyler's in Anchorage with his grandfather. I'm going up there tomorrow to meet him."

There was another pause, much longer this time. "You're kidding."

"No, I'm not."

In a furtive whisper, "Hell, Adam, I had no idea something like this would happen! Hold on, I'm going into the other room."

Adam waited while Alex made up some excuse to leave the room. He listened to muffled voices and fuzzy static for a couple of minutes, then Alex finally got back on the line.

"Why didn't you just tell her no?"

"Because it seemed really important to her for

me…for *Tyler's father*…to at least see his son before making any decisions about future involvement.''

"It sounds more and more like she wants you…*me*…to actually be a father to this kid."

"His name is *Tyler*."

"What're you doing to make her so pro fatherhood, bro? Turning on the charm?"

"Hardly. I barely spoke to her at dinner. I was shell-shocked, I guess. I think she just sees me as a decent guy and wants to be fair."

"Well, apparently you're doing *something* to encourage her, so cut it out."

"Maybe I should just haul off and smack her one, Alex," Adam drawled sarcastically. "That's sure to make her see me in a different light."

"Damn it, Adam, I don't know! I'm *so* sorry about all this. I really am. I know this must be tough on you. You know how grateful I am, don't you? This just wasn't something I could hit Kelly with two days before our wedding."

"How do you know for sure? Kelly's a big girl. Maybe you're underestimating her. Maybe she'll understand. And maybe she won't care a rat's rear what her parents have to say about it."

Alex released a long sigh. "Adam, she told me she was glad I wasn't Tyler's father. She said it would have ruined everything."

Adam was silenced. But only for a minute.

"It seemed like the right thing to do at the time, Alex, but now I don't know. I hate lying to Cassie."

"It's not hurting her or anyone else," Alex argued. "Far more people would be hurt if I admitted to being Tyler's father...Cassie included. It'll be over soon, bro. She'll go home to Montana on Monday and we can forget any of this ever happened.''

Easy for you to say, Adam thought to himself.

''I like her,'' he said, finally.

''I'm sorry about that, too,'' Alex answered, and Adam could hear the sincere regret in his brother's voice. ''Tough luck, both of us taking a fancy to the same face. If there was any other solution...''

''What if I like Tyler just as much?''

''Like I said, someday we can forget any of this ever happened,'' Alex repeated, sounding just as tired and disheartened as Adam. ''Go to bed, bro. Get some sleep. Tomorrow's another day.''

''Right, Scarlett,'' Adam grumbled.

CASSIE YAWNED and stretched in the four-poster, listening to the singing of birds and humming of insects outside. Despite the tension of the night before, Cassie was surprised to feel both rested and cheerful. Though she didn't understand Adam's attitude toward Tyler and was frustrated because he wouldn't confide his feelings to her, she couldn't squelch an unexpected excitement at the prospect of introducing him to their son that day.

Cassie hadn't realized until then how much she'd missed sharing her parental pride and love for Tyler with the man who'd helped create him. Surely once the two of them met, Adam would lose his ambivalence toward their child and they'd all become friends...if nothing more.

She enjoyed a hot shower, then made a cup of Irish breakfast tea in the tiny kitchen and drank it while she dressed. Not sure what to wear to a tux-fitting, followed by a father-meets-son-for-the-first-time outing, she put on a short denim jumper embroidered on the bib, with a pink T-shirt underneath. It was casual, but it was still a dress. She applied a minimum amount of makeup and pulled her hair into a loose ponytail, tied with a pink scarf.

Since the guest house didn't have a phone, she walked up to the main cabin at eight-thirty and knocked on the door. She would have to call her father and Tyler at the hotel early, before they left on some fishing expedition, and arrange a time and location to meet.

After waiting a couple of minutes, Cassie raised her fist to knock again, but changed her mind. Adam might still be in bed. She didn't have a clue how late he normally slept and they hadn't made any plans the night before about when to start the day.

She was about to turn away and come back in half an hour when the door suddenly opened. Well, she hadn't got him out of bed.... It was worse. She'd got him out of the shower.

Chapter Five

"Hi, Cass. Sorry about this." Adam ran both hands through his wet hair and smiled sheepishly. "I couldn't relax last night and I ended up oversleeping."

Cassie tried not to stare at his chest, at the taut, glistening skin that showed through the gap of his white terry robe. She tried to keep her eyes trained to above the neck, but that didn't help her sky-rocketing blood pressure much. Freshly shaven and glowing from the shower, his chiseled cheekbones stood out magnificently. And his eyes glinted like jewels below the arch of his brows and the slicked-back Valentinolike hair.

"I...I just thought I'd better call the hotel before my dad and Tyler take off for the day," she stuttered.

He pushed open the screen door. "Good idea. Come in."

"I...I could come back later."

His lips quirked in a smile. "Why? Just get in here and make your call. Don't worry, I won't come out of the bedroom till I'm decent."

Cassie felt herself blushing as she sidled past him into the room. If not for their history together, he'd probably think her woefully naive and prudish. Or perhaps he thought so, anyway. Maybe he was only being polite last night when he told her she wasn't a klutz five years ago at the Tuddenham's bed-and-breakfast.

"Earth to Cassie."

Cassie nearly jumped. "What?"

"Did you hear me say the phone was right over there?"

He motioned toward a phone in the living room by a large, overstuffed reclining chair.

"Thanks," she mumbled, too embarrassed to look him in the eye. Unfortunately, that drew her gaze to his bare legs, descending from the bottom of his robe. Rivulets of water trailed sinuously down the well-muscled calves, which were lightly dusted with dark hair. She remembered how those legs had felt entwined with hers... Her brows furrowed. Only she didn't remember them being so well defined. Perhaps he'd been working out more in the past five years. Or running. Or—

"What's the matter, Cassie? Don't you have the phone number?"

Cassie looked up and into Adam's eyes. She wasn't sure, but she thought she detected an amused twinkle lurking there. Up came her chin. "Of course I have it. You don't think I'd put my child and my father in a hotel two hundred miles away and not know how to get in touch with them, do you?"

Adam grinned. "I didn't think so."

"What...what time should I tell Dad we can

meet? And where?'' Damn it, why did he have to be so gorgeous?

"We'll have to take the ferry to Homer, then drive to Kenai. Then we'll have to come back for the plane. We should be able to get up there by two o'clock, but since I can't be exact about the time, let's just tell your father ballpark two o'clock and meet him and Tyler at the hotel.''

"Okay.'' Cassie smiled wanly, clutched the phone against her chest and stared at him.

"I'll leave you now, so you can concentrate on what you're doing,'' he finally said, the twinkle in his eyes more apparent than ever.

Cassie was about to declare that he hadn't bothered her concentration in the least, but realized that it would make her look guilty as hell of just the opposite. Instead she turned her back on him and began to dial. She heard him pad away, then pressed the receiver button down and dialed again. Her first attempt at dialing would probably have connected her with some poor confused soul in China.

"Hello. Lone Mountain Ranch. I mean—''

"It's okay, Dad. It's me.''

"Cass. What's goin' on, honey?''

"Plenty, Dad. I told him about Tyler.''

There was a pause on the other end. "You made up your mind about him pretty fast.''

"He's a nice guy. He'd be a good father to Tyler…if he wanted to be.''

"He doesn't want to be?''

"I don't think he knows what he wants. The whole thing was a bit of a shock. We're coming up there today so he can meet Tyler.''

"You think meetin' Tyler will help him decide what he wants?"

"I don't know, Dad. I'm confused, too."

"Well, let's not get *you-know-who* mixed up in this until you're a little less confused, okay?"

"Of course, Dad." Cassie smiled. She could hear Tyler in the background, wondering aloud if that was Mommy on the phone. "I take it *you-know-who* wants to talk to me. Have you guys been having lots of fun?"

"We're having a great time. He's in the other room eatin' some pancakes I ordered up. I don't want to put 'im on the phone till we settle this."

"Don't worry, Dad. We're not going to tell Tyler who Adam is. We'll just introduce him as a friend, or an uncle. You know, like Uncle Brad. That way if Tyler never sees him again, no big deal."

"No big deal, eh? Humph! This whole thing is a lot bigger than I wish it were. Too bad you ever got hold of that magazine, Cassie."

"Now, Dad... Let me talk to Tyler."

Cassie talked to an animated Tyler for ten minutes, listening to all the details of his first evening in Anchorage. Despite the lateness of their arrival, they'd still managed to do some fishing at a lake located within the city limits, then fried up the fish in their hotel room, which they'd chosen specifically because it had a kitchen. There was nothing Jasper and his grandson liked better than fresh skillet-fried fish.

They'd even visited Potter Marsh, apparently a game refuge, seen lots of migratory birds, a couple of beavers and a moose!

"Honey, I'm so glad you're having a good time," she said, smiling into the phone and picturing Tyler's happy face.

"When are you comin' to the hotel, Mommy? Granddad says we can go out on a boat and do some fishin' and I think you'd like that a lot, Mommy!"

"I'm coming today, Tyler."

"Really?"

"And I'm bringing a friend."

"A friend? Like my friend Justin?"

"Well, no. He's more my age. Kind of like an uncle, I guess."

"Like Uncle Brad?"

"Yes, like that. He wants to meet you and spend some time with you, too."

"Oh."

"Don't worry. He's very nice."

"Does he like t' fish?"

"Yes. I think so. We had fish for dinner last night. Now put Granddad back on the phone, Ty. I've got to arrange a time to meet you guys."

After finalizing plans with her father, Cassie said goodbye to Tyler and hung up. She turned to find Adam standing in the entryway to the hall, one shoulder resting against the doorjamb, his arms crossed over his chest. He was frowning.

"What's the matter?" Cassie asked.

"Don't tell him I'm his uncle," he said tersely. "Just say I'm a friend, okay?"

"Sure," Cassie replied quickly. "I only meant it as a sort of honorary title, you know. That's what he calls Brad."

Cassie realized the minute the name came out that

it was a mistake to mention her boyfriend back home.

"Brad? Who's Brad?"

Or maybe it wasn't a mistake…

Adam straightened up and moved into the room. He was wearing tan slacks and a forest-green sweater, the sleeves pushed up to reveal sinewy forearms.

"Just a friend of mine," Cassie said offhandedly.

"How many uncles has Ty got, Cass?" he inquired gruffly.

Cassie laughed. "You sound jealous, Adam Baranof! After forgetting my existence for five years, I find that even more mystifying than your objection to being called 'uncle'!"

Adam stared at her for a couple of minutes, his brows still lowered in a frown. Then, suddenly, he shook off his scowling demeanor and smiled. "I guess it's okay if he calls me uncle."

"Kids like to categorize the adults in their lives," Cassie explained.

"Yeah. I understand. As for being jealous, you're right, I have no business. Of course you have a life of your own back in Montana. I guess I just assumed that because you answered the ad, you were free."

"I *am* free. But, as you know, that's not why I answered the ad. I was looking for Tyler's father."

Adam shrugged and shoved his hands in his pockets. "And you found him, so I guess that closes that subject." He cocked an elbow and glanced at his watch. "We'd better get a move on. The ferry for Homer leaves in twenty minutes."

Cassie wasn't sure what to make of Adam's attitude. Part of her was pleased by what appeared to be his jealousy, but another part of her was puzzled by his objection to being called "uncle." She'd like to think it was because he really wanted Tyler to call him "Daddy," but just wasn't ready to admit it yet. As she followed him to the car—irresistibly admiring the view of a tight rear and long legs—she smiled to herself and allowed a smidgen of hope to blossom.

Careful, Cassie, she told herself. *Don't start getting dewy-eyed about this guy. At least not with so little to go on.*

Fortunately it was another clear, beautiful day and Cassie was able to distract herself from the scenery inside the Jeep with the scenery outside the Jeep. Seldovia was charming. Most of the timber houses were on pilings and the town proper was highlighted by a picturesque boardwalk that, according to Adam, dated back to the 1930s. They stopped at the Two Sisters Bakery to pick up muffins and coffee to go, then headed for the ferry dock.

"How many people live here?" Cassie asked as she peered curiously around and nibbled on her muffin.

"Four hundred or so. Fishing, timber and tourism supports most of the residents. Then there's guys like me and Alex who just like it here. We're away a lot, though."

With a wave at the man standing inside the pay booth, Adam drove the Jeep onto the ferry.

"Away doing what?"

"We both do some teaching at Fairbanks University and at the university extensions scattered around the state. I get a few research grants and am frequently on-site for that, and Alex does a lot of contracted work for the petroleum companies. When he and Kelly move to Florida, though, they'll both work full-time for the same company. They'll still be required to travel a lot, though, mostly to the Middle East.''

"No more teaching?"

Adam parked, pressed the security brake, finished off the last of his muffin, then helped Cassie out of the Jeep. "Alex is too ambitious to teach. It doesn't make enough money. And he can't stand staying in one place for too long. He's looking forward to the traveling.''

"He's lucky he found a woman who shares his views and his talents. They seem very compatible.''

"They are.''

"What about children?"

Adam had taken her arm and was leading her to the railing that faced north toward Kachemac Bay, holding his coffee in his free hand. She felt his fingers spasm, momentarily tighten around her elbow, then gradually relax. "What do you mean?"

She tried to catch his eye, but his gaze remained fixed on the bay. He squinted into the sunshine and the cool breeze off the water, sipping his coffee.

"Are they planning to have kids? All that traveling might be hard to do with kids in the picture.''

"Alex and Kelly aren't interested in having a family right now. Not now, and maybe not ever. As I told you, they're both very career-oriented. Kids simply don't figure in.''

Cassie nodded. "Then I guess it was a good thing

you're Tyler's father and not Alex. Even if he chose not to have anything to do with Tyler, Kelly might have freaked out a little...you know?''

He turned, gazed at her briefly, then said, ''Yeah. I suppose that's possible.''

''Have you talked to Alex since last night? Did he tell anyone about...about me and Tyler?''

''Yes, I have talked to Alex. I hope you don't mind, but he did tell Kelly and our parents about you and Tyler.'' He watched her and waited.

Cassie raised her brows. ''*I* certainly don't mind, but I'm a little surprised. I didn't think you'd want your parents to know about us unless you'd decided to be part of Tyler's life.''

''I didn't give Alex permission to tell everyone, he just did,'' Adam admitted.

Cassie's stomach knotted up. ''In other words, you're sorry he told them.''

''No, that's not it, Cassie,'' Adam said with a sigh, looking earnestly into her eyes. ''It's just that—like you said—maybe I would have kept quiet at least until I'd decided what I wanted to do about Tyler.''

Cassie nodded. His reasoning was sound and sensible. He was behaving the way most men would in such a situation. Actually *better* than most men. She certainly couldn't blame him for that. And, if he was a little uptight this morning, she knew he was probably just nervous about meeting Tyler and her father.

As they approached Homer Spit, Kachemac Bay turned into a veritable hubbub of maritime activity. Fishing boats, sailboats, motorboats and ferries came and went. Overhead and on the shore seabirds of every description screamed and chattered. Adam pointed out a bald eagle sailing high above the spruce trees that lined the shore. When Cassie smiled in delight, he slipped his arm in hers and leaned close, suddenly seeming far from uptight.

"There's an eagle's nest near my house in Seldovia. I'll have to show it to you before you leave."

His breath against her ear thrilled Cassie, and her heart fluttered like a schoolgirl's. She wondered why Adam did that to her, and why Brad didn't. Especially since Brad was the one who stuck around and Adam was the one that got away. She wondered, did he always make a point of getting away?

Homer was bigger than Seldovia, but just as charming. The long narrow gravel bar that was the "spit" was lined with visitor shops, eateries, art galleries, commercial wharfs, docks for waterborne sight-seeing and fishing cruises, parking places, campsites and a port for the huge oceangoing ferry, the *Tustumena*.

"I'd show you my dad's boat, but he's already out on his first charter," Adam said. He drove slowly through the tiny town, pointing out sights of interest, then took the Sterling Highway to Kenai.

Minutes later, they were entering Harold's Tux Towne. Still dazzled by the bright sunshine and the way it glinted off the water that had seemed to greet them at every turn in the road, Cassie had to blink a few times before her eyes became adjusted to the artificial light inside the formal-wear shop.

When she could focus, the first sight to greet her

was Adam looking dashing in a black tuxedo. No, that couldn't be Adam, that had to be—

"Hi, Cassie. I want you to meet my fiancée, Kelly. Kelly, this is Cassie."

Cassie was shocked all over again at how exactly alike Adam and his twin were. It took her a minute to drag her gaze away from Alex to look at his fiancée.

Kelly was a tall woman, slim, auburn-haired and beautiful. Her expression was friendly but cautious, and Cassie couldn't help but feel that she might harbor a bit of suspicion about her. Possibly she was simply feeling protective toward her soon-to-be brother-in-law and was hoping Adam wasn't being taken in by a floozy. Of course, all of this was mere speculation. Or paranoia!

"Hi, Cassie." Kelly extended her slim hand and gave Cassie's a firm, feminine shake. "It's nice to meet you."

Cassie smiled wryly. "But a bit awkward, isn't it? I'm sure you don't have any idea what to say to me."

Kelly's chuckle sounded relieved. "I'm glad you said that. You're right. I wasn't sure what to say. I didn't know whether to bring up your little boy or not."

"Please do," Cassie said, her chin raising automatically. "I love talking about my son."

"Alex says you're going up to Anchorage today so Adam can meet him." Her gaze shifted to Adam, who was standing behind Cassie and had so far said nothing. "That should be…er…fun."

Cassie waited for Adam to say something. How

he spoke of Tyler around his friends and family could make or break her good opinion of him. She'd be very upset if he acted embarrassed or ashamed.

Adam rested a hand on Cassie's shoulder. "I'm looking forward to meeting Tyler," he said. "Judging by his picture and the twinkle in his mother's eyes every time she talks about him, he's quite a kid. I'm glad she brought him to Alaska with her."

Adam spoke with a firmness and conviction that delighted Cassie and filled her heart with gratitude. She turned and smiled up at Adam, hoping to convey how very admirably he'd risen to the occasion.

When Cassie turned and smiled at him, Adam was nearly knocked over by an onslaught of emotions. She was glowing, her eyes shining, her lips trembling ever so slightly at the corners. His heart swelled with tenderness and he wanted to take her in his arms and hold her close. But he couldn't. He had no right. She was only feeling gratitude toward him for behaving like *Alex* should have been behaving. As it was, both brothers were first-class jerks, only Cassie didn't know that. Sweet Cassie was too damned trusting for her own good.

"When are you going up?" Alex asked, breaking the odd mix of tension in the room. Adam looked at his brother, seeing the barely contained anxiety behind his bland expression. He probably couldn't wait to get rid of them, but didn't dare show it.

Again Adam felt an unwilling surge of sympathy for his brother. He gave Alex a brotherly punch in the arm, something they frequently resorted to as a show of affection that wouldn't embarrass them at the same time. "We're leaving right after I try on that monkey suit you expect me to wear at the wedding. If I'd known being best man was going to be so uncomfortable, I might have bailed out.''

"That's a bunch of baloney, bro," Alex said. "You'd never bail out on me."

Adam didn't answer, didn't meet his brother's searching gaze.

"Did you bring Tyler's picture with you, Cassie?" Kelly suddenly inquired. "I'd love to see what he looks like."

Cassie's face lit up even brighter than before. "Of course I brought a picture. I take one with me everywhere." This time, instead of pulling it out of her blouse, Cassie took the picture out of her purse. She handed it to Kelly and Alex peered at it over his fiancée's shoulder.

"Oh, my gosh, he looks just like you, Adam," Kelly exclaimed. "Right down to the Baranof cleft in his chin. Doesn't he look like your brother, Alex? Isn't he adorable?"

Adam watched the play of emotions on his brother's face. Surprise, confusion, fear. "Yeah. He's the spitting image of his father all right." His gaze flicked up to meet Adam's. Like most twins, they were very tuned to each other's thoughts and feelings. But, for once in his life, Adam didn't have a clue what was going on in his brother's head. Was it possible that a bit of fatherly feeling and paternal pride had surfaced?

While Adam watched and tried to analyze Alex's reaction to seeing his son for the first time, Harold, the diminutive, balding owner of the shop, bustled up to him with a tuxedo shrouded in a plastic bag draped over his arm. He led Adam away to the dressing room, all the while lamenting over the Baranof twins' broad shoulders and what they might do to the seams of his tuxedo jackets.

Alex followed them into the dressing room, but with Harold hovering and assisting and dictating, there was no opportunity for the brothers to speak privately.

Finally trussed up in his tux, Adam emerged from the dressing room to stand before the triple mirrors alongside Alex. In the mirror's reflection he saw Kelly and Cassie talking animatedly at the other side of the store where they'd left them.

"I wonder what they're talking about?" Alex said nervously.

Adam waited until Harold moved away to greet another customer, then answered, "Probably about something that has nothing to do with you or me. Don't panic."

Alex sighed. "My nerves were bad enough just getting ready for the wedding. Now *this*."

Adam tugged on the cuffs of his shirtsleeves and looked at Alex's eyes in the mirror. "Lying is very stressful, but it doesn't have to be this way. It's not too late to come clean."

"Are you crazy? Coming clean is the last thing I want to do."

"Even after seeing Tyler's picture?"

Alex grimaced. "What do you mean by that?"

"Didn't you feel anything when you looked at the picture?"

"Oh, I felt *something*. I was shocked that he really does look just like me. Is that what you mean?"

Adam knew that if he had to explain to Alex what a father might feel when looking at the spitting image of himself, there was really no point in going into it. You either felt something or you didn't. He was rather amazed, though, that *he'd* felt something and Alex hadn't.

"Wow. God was in a good mood when he made you two," Kelly said as she and Cassie approached. "Two more gorgeous men I've never set eyes on before."

Alex did some playful preening for his fiancée and kissed her cheek, but Adam quickly changed the subject. "What were you ladies talking about?" He looked at Cassie, but she didn't answer. She just kept gazing back and forth between him and Alex, her expression thoughtful.

Kelly just ignored the question, still in a mood to tease and flatter. "Yep. Since you came as a matched pair, it's a good thing you're easy on the eyes. You know, sometimes when you two are dressed alike, I can hardly tell you apart."

Cassie looked interested. "You mean there are times you actually *can* tell them apart? How?"

"Well, there's a slight difference in their builds for one thing. Adam's a runner, so his calves are more developed, but that doesn't help when he's wearing long pants. Another way to tell is by their hands and the way they use them. For example, if you tied Alex's hands behind his back, he wouldn't be able to talk." Kelly got a coy look on her face and ran her hand over Alex's chest. "Then there's the difference between their—"

Alex gave Adam a warning look in the mirror.

"Kelly, don't give away all our secrets," Adam said with a forced chuckle. "And, speaking of secrets, are you or are you not going to tell us what you two were talking about while I was being manhandled in the dressing room?"

Kelly grinned. "Girl talk."

"That sounds ominous," Alex said with a nervous chuckle.

"Oh, it's nothing *bad*, Alex. It's something I think the whole family will appreciate."

"Don't keep us in suspense, Kelly," Adam prompted.

"You tell him, Cassie," Kelly invited.

Adam looked at Cassie, who appeared to be teeter-tottering between feelings of excitement and doubt. "I hope you'll think this is okay, Adam."

A feeling of dread he knew Alex shared swelled in Adam's chest. He smiled encouragingly. "Just spit it out, Cass."

She wrung her hands and tried to smile back. "Well...Kelly's been nice enough to invite Tyler and my father to the wedding, too. She wants us to bring them back with us when we fly to Anchorage. Is...is that okay with you, Adam?"

Chapter Six

Out of the corner of his eye Adam saw Alex stiffen. He could feel his brother's anxiety on a visceral level and, combined with his own, that was a pretty miserable sensation. Things were getting way out of hand.

"I've asked too much," Cassie suggested. Her voice was calm, she was half-smiling, but Adam could see the blossoming hurt in her eyes.

"No, Cass. Not at all," Adam immediately assured her, feeling like a bone in a tug-of-war between starving dogs, about to be torn in two. He knew Alex didn't want to see Tyler, much less have the little guy, his mother and his grandfather attending the wedding! What a nightmare!

On the other hand, Cassie would be devastated if Adam refused to bring them down for the wedding. It would clearly imply that he saw his son as an unwanted intrusion into his life, his family. It would make Cassie think he was ashamed of Tyler. Ashamed of his and Cassie's night together.

And that simply wasn't true. *If* he'd slept with Cassie five years ago, *if* he really was Tyler's father, he wouldn't hesitate to bring them down from Anchorage to meet the entire Baranof clan. And since he was doing Alex a favor by standing in for him as both ex-lover and father, he decided that *he'd* make the decision without worrying overly much about how uncomfortable it would make his twin brother. In fact, maybe it would be good for Alex to feel a little uncomfortable…

"I think it's a great idea, Cass," Adam told her, then watched as her face lit up. He loved the way every feeling, sad or happy, was reflected in those beautiful gray eyes of hers. He thought he heard a small gasp coming from Alex's direction, but he refused to look at his twin, finding it much more enjoyable to gaze at an honest face over one racked with guilt and fear. He refused to look at his own reflection for the same reason.

"You're sure?" she murmured.

Kelly chuckled and leaned close to Cassie to whisper in her ear, "Don't give him a chance to change his mind!"

"I won't change my mind," Adam stated. "It's a done deal, Cassie."

She smiled her pleasure.

"Isn't this great, Alex?" Kelly chirped, slipping her arm in his and leaning against his side. "Most of my brothers and sisters and their families are flying in from Florida, your huge family is ferrying and flying in from all parts of Alaska, and, to cap it all, there'll be surprise guests from Montana! Heck, we'll have the whole fam-damily at the wedding!" She laughed. "That is, unless *you've* got an adorable little son stashed away somewhere I don't know about. But in that situation I think I might feel just a *teensy* bit less inclined to extend an invitation. Not to mention, Dad would have a cow!''

The others chuckled halfheartedly at Kelly's attempted joke, but no one looked particularly amused. Adam knew why he and Alex weren't busting a gut, and he was pretty sure he knew why Cassie wasn't laughing, either. As any mother would be, she was sensitive to any suggestion that Tyler was somehow unacceptable because of the circumstances of his birth. Sure, it was okay with Kelly as long as *Adam* was Ty's father. But if it was *Alex*...

Adam decided that it was time to leave. Ignoring his brother's pale, shell-shocked appearance, he summoned Harold, hurried along the final fussings over his tuxedo, quickly changed into his street clothes and ushered Cassie to the Jeep.

Kelly waved from the door as they sped away toward Sterling Highway.

''She's really nice,'' Cassie said, waving back and looking over her shoulder through the window until they'd turned a corner.

''You still think so despite that bit about feeling less inclined to invite a child that belonged to Alex?'' Adam inquired dryly. ''That wasn't very tactful of her.''

Cassie settled in her seat and turned toward him with a thoughtful expression. ''No, it wasn't tactful. But she wasn't intentionally trying to hurt or offend me.''

''No, I'm sure it wasn't intentional,'' Adam conceded.

''I certainly didn't expect her to invite my father

and Tyler to the wedding,'' Cassie continued thoughtfully. Her face brightened. "It's going to be great to have Ty with me for the weekend. I miss him even when we're only separated for a day." Her smile broadened, became coy. "You'll find out what I mean, Adam. You're going to love him."

Adam nodded, swallowed, smiled weakly. That's what he was afraid of.

She cocked her head to the side, watching his reaction with interest. "Does this mean you've changed your mind about not wanting to be part of Tyler's life?"

Adam sighed and looked at the road. "I'm not sure what this means, Cass. We'll just have to wait and see."

WE'LL JUST have to wait and see. Those words kept swirling through Cassie's mind during the entire trip to Anchorage, teasing her, tempting her to hope that Adam wasn't going to vanish from their lives like he had before. She didn't try to analyze her feelings, to separate her desire for Tyler to know and benefit from a father's influence and her own very grown-up desires of the heart. As Adam had said, she'd just wait and see what developed. She was a mature adult and she could handle it if, while being a father to their son, Adam only wanted to be friends with her. At least she was pretty sure she could.

Sometimes she thought of Brad and felt guilty. Not guilty because her heart was being unfaithful to him—he'd never really captured her heart, nor had she given it—but guilty because she couldn't feel about him after three years the way it would be so easy to feel about Adam in four minutes.

"What are you thinking about, Cassie?" Adam inquired as they began their descent onto Lake Hood.

Cassie automatically answered, "Brad."

Adam raised a brow and gave a half smile. "I see."

No, you don't, Cassie thought. But she didn't dare explain everything she'd been thinking and why, or he'd definitely run for the hills!

They reached the Voyager Hotel that afternoon by one-thirty and headed straight to the room where Tyler and her dad were staying. With a mother's pride and confidence, she knew Adam wouldn't be able to help falling in love with Tyler. Most people liked her dad, too...once they got past his prickly facade. She just hoped her Montana men took to Adam as quickly as she had.

"This is it," Cassie said as they reached room 230 and paused outside the door.

"Yep," Adam answered laconically.

"You're nervous," Cassie stated, suddenly noticing how strained he appeared. She'd been so caught up in her own excitement and happy hopes, she hadn't noticed Adam's deteriorating composure until just then. Oh, most people wouldn't think he was nervous at all. He wasn't fidgeting or shifting or pacing. He was standing perfectly still. But there was a tiny furrow between his eyes she'd never noticed before and a barely perceptible muscle ticking in his jaw. That muscle had been ticking the night before, just after he'd found out he was a father.

Adam smiled, but Cassie could tell it was done with an effort. "Sure, I'm nervous," he said finally. "I'd be some kind of a hard case if I weren't."

"You've got a point," Cassie agreed with a sympathetic nod, then turned and rapped lightly on the door. "But try not to worry too much. I have a feeling all three of you guys are going to hit it off."

Adam wasn't so sure about the "all three" part of Cassie's prediction, but he nodded and smiled anyway. A second later the door creaked open about four inches and, toward the very top of it, a large nose and a long gray handlebar mustache poked out. "That you, Cass?" a gruff voice asked in a whisper.

Cassie chuckled. "Yes, Dad," she whispered back. "You were expecting maybe the mob?"

The door opened a few more inches. Pale eyes in a leathered face rested on Cassie, warming to an azure blue as he smiled down at her. Those same eyes, as they turned on Adam, became as cool and steely as gunmetal.

"I don't have to ask who you are," he announced in a slightly sarcastic drawl. "The boy couldn't look more like you if he'd been cloned."

"So I hear," Adam replied, careful not to allow his gaze to shift away from the older man's piercing scrutiny. He extended a hand. "I'm happy to meet you."

Jasper Montgomery stared down at Adam's hand for a protracted couple of seconds, then he extended his own hand and the two men shook. *Score one for me,* thought Adam. *I didn't back down and he didn't refuse to shake.*

"Why are we standing in the hall, Dad?" Cassie

asked, her voice tinged with amusement. "And why are we all whispering?"

"The boy's asleep," Jasper announced, opening the door and standing to the side. "The sunlight and the excitement got him confused last night and he didn't doze off till the wee hours. 'Fraid it's all caught up with him this afternoon. He's been down for a couple of hours, though, so I expect it wouldn't hurt to wake 'im up now."

Adam followed Cassie into the hotel room, down a hallway past the bathroom to an open suite containing bedroom and kitchenette. There in the middle of the room in the middle of a king-size bed lay a pint-size boy. He was flat on his back, sprawled like a starfish, his arms and legs flung away from his body. On second thought, with his cowboy boots still on and his hat on the nearby pillow, Adam decided he looked more like a star of an old-time western than a starfish, staked out by the black-hatted villains in the middle of the desert to die of sunstroke and ant bites.

But more than that, Tyler looked like Alex. And he looked like *him*. And, strangely enough, he was sleeping in Adam's favorite childhood sleeping position! Uncontained and comfortable, Adam had paid no attention to his brother in the same double bed, leaving Alex to sleep clinging to his own narrow portion of the mattress on the very edge.

"My God," Adam whispered under his breath. Cassie was standing beside the bed, gazing down at Tyler, but Adam had stopped a few feet away, stunned and immobile.

"Hadn't you seen a picture of 'im?" Jasper

asked. He stood on the other side of the bed, opposite Cassie. He peered narrowly at Adam from under bushy brows.

"Yes. Yes, and I could see the resemblance then. But seeing him in person…" Adam's voice trailed off. He couldn't help himself; he added, "And he sleeps just like I used to sleep, hogging the whole bed."

"Yep, he's a helluva bed partner," Jasper agreed with a proud sniff. "Always was."

"You really slept like this, too, Adam?" Cassie asked, her eyes wide with delighted interest. "Gosh, I wonder how many ways you two are alike?"

This brought Adam up short. Yes, how many ways were Tyler and his *uncle* alike? It stood to reason that some of Adam's traits had found their way into Tyler's personality. But it also stood to reason that he'd have more traits in common with Alex.

"Come closer, Adam," Cassie urged, waving him over. "He won't bite. At least not while he's asleep."

Tentatively, Adam obeyed. He walked slowly to Cassie's side of the bed and joined her in the decidedly mommy-and-daddylike activity of watching a child sleep. Who else would find such a way of passing time anything but extremely boring?

But Adam wasn't bored. God help him, he was enthralled. The child, who was no doubt a ball of fire while awake, looked like an angelic choirboy in sleep. Long, thick lashes lay against round, flushed cheeks. His lips were tilted, almost smiling, above a stubborn chin with a deep dimple that would someday be the Baranof cleft.

"He's dreamin' of fishin'," Jasper theorized. "Or flyin'. I used to dream of flyin' all the time when I was a kid."

"Well, let's wake him up and let him experience the real thing," Cassie said, bending over the bed to carefully trail her fingers through the thick, dark hair that fell over Tyler's forehead.

"What d'ya mean?" Jasper immediately demanded to know.

Cassie looked up at her father, smiling. "Adam's flying us down to Seldovia. We're all three going to stay at his house and attend his brother's wedding."

Quick as a trigger finger, Jasper turned those steely eyes in Adam's direction, full of suspicion. "We are? How come?"

"My brother's fiancée extended the invitation just this morning," Adam explained, feeling a bit sheepish. Jasper had every reason to be suspicious, to wonder what was in the works.

"They all know about Tyler...about you and Cass?"

"They will by the end of the weekend," Adam answered. "So far, only my brother, his fiancée and my parents know."

Jasper cocked a brow. "Your parents, eh? Well, what do they think about the sudden appearance of a grandchild?"

"Frankly, sir, I don't know. I haven't talked to them yet. It was my twin brother who—"

Now both brows flew up. "Your brother's a *twin*?" His keen eyes flitted to Cassie, then back to

Adam. "Then how the hell does Cassie know which of the two of you is Tyler's real father?"

Adam's stomach felt like a dishrag being twisted in the hands of a hefty housewife. His heart was drumming in his ears and he felt as close to fainting as the day when he was ten years old and he'd buried a fishhook an inch deep in his thumb.

Cassie's easy laugh partially revived him. "Dad, how can you ask such a question?" she said with a mildly scolding look. "I know Adam's the father because he told me so."

Jasper grunted. "Yeah, but when you got his reply in the mail, he didn't remember you."

"Not at first. But he remembers everything now."

"That true, son?" Jasper looked at him until Adam felt as if the old man could see right through to the troubled soul inside. It was obvious this Montana rancher was as canny as a coyote. He didn't miss much, that's for sure.

Adam was close to spilling everything. He wanted to. He wanted to in the worst way. But he'd promised his brother to protect his wedding day and if he intended to renege on that promise Alex should be the first to know what his intentions were. Such being the case, the first thing Adam would do when he got back to Seldovia was corner Alex and talk sense to him, hopefully talk him into coming clean. Together they could confess and throw themselves on the mercy of the women. Cass and Kelly could then decide what the lying Baranof twins deserved.

"Dad, I'm sure Adam doesn't appreciate being grilled," Cassie said, looking worriedly at Adam, then back to her father. She blushed. "Believe me,

I know he remembers that night because…because he mentioned something very particular and personal about me that he couldn't possibly have guessed."

Jasper grunted again, spun on his boot heels and stalked to the kitchen mumbling something about "more than he needed to know."

Adam sighed with relief. He was saved for now, but the reckoning was coming. He wanted it to come. He was hating this deceit more and more. Cassie was just too trusting. She was apparently so honest herself she was incapable of being suspicious of others' dishonesty.

"Adam?"

Adam had been gazing down at Tyler, fighting that recurring idea that everything would be just fine if only he really were the boy's father. He looked up at Cassie. "Thanks for coming to my rescue."

"Listen, don't worry about Dad. He'll come around. He's just very protective of me and Tyler." She smiled. "Maybe when we get to Seldovia you can show all three of us that eagle's nest."

"If you can wake up Tyler," Adam teased. "The kid sleeps like a rock." Just like he used to. A brass band could be marching through the room and it wouldn't wake him.

But when Cassie leaned down and whispered in Tyler's ear, "Wake up, sleepyhead," he blinked open his eyes and sat up, as alert as if cymbals had crashed over his head. Tyler was just like him in that respect, too. Once awakened, Adam was instantly alert.

"Mommy? Mommy, you're back!"

Adam watched as Tyler threw his arms around Cassie's neck. Mother and child obviously had a great relationship. He'd known that all along, of course, but now he was seeing it in the flesh.

Cassie sat down on the bed and drew Tyler next to her, hip to hip. She looked up at Adam, and Tyler followed her gaze. Soft gray eyes and bright blue ones were staring up at him, their ingenuous and trusting expressions almost identical. It was damned unsettling. "Honey, I want you to meet my friend, Adam. You know the one I told you about over the phone?"

Tyler rubbed one eye with a fist and nodded. "Hello, Uncle Adam."

"No, Tyler," Cassie said quickly, "just call him—"

"I told you it was okay, Cass. Remember? *Uncle* Adam's fine," Adam stated. "Pleased to meet you, Tyler." Cassie looked uncertain at first, but Adam's smile and shrug reassured her that he really had changed his mind and was okay with the honorary title. Even if his true relationship was thrown in his face every time Tyler said his name, Adam figured it was no more than he deserved. He just hoped that Jasper—who was watching them from the kitchen with a grim expression on his weathered face, his lanky frame propped against the counter—wouldn't notice that every time Tyler used the avuncular term, Adam had to fight the inclination to cringe.

"Do you like t' fish?" Tyler immediately wanted to know.

"Love to. Do you like salmon?"

"I like trout th' best, but salmon's good 'nd it's bigger, too."

"I know a great place where you can catch salmon that's twice your size, Tyler."

His eyes lit up. "Really? When can we go?"

Cassie laughed. "As soon as you and your granddad are packed."

"Cass, can I have a word with you…er…*over here?*" Jasper called from the kitchen area. He was speaking to Cassie, of course, but he was looking at Adam with the expression of a man about to round up a posse.

"If you two want to talk in private, I can wait downstairs in the lobby," Adam offered, already headed for the door.

"No." Cassie stepped in front of him, putting her hands on his chest. The contact seemed to startle them both at first and for a couple of seconds they simply stood there, staring into each other's eyes.

Adam glanced at Jasper. He was looking more and more in the mood for a lynching. "I don't mind, Cass. Really."

Cassie glanced at Jasper, too, removed her hands and nervously clasped them behind her. "It would be more efficient time-wise for Dad and I to talk while I walk him down to the lobby to pay the hotel bill and check out. You wouldn't mind staying with Tyler for a few minutes, would you? He's always hungry when he gets up from a nap. Maybe you could fix him something to eat. I'm sure Dad's got something in the cupboard for snack attacks."

While Adam hesitated, wondering how to reply, Tyler slipped off the bed and moved to stand by his mother. "I am hungry," he admitted. "Granddad bought some peanut butter 'nd jelly at the store." He pointed at Adam. "Can he make sand'iches?"

"I'd be surprised if he couldn't," Cassie answered, her hand resting on the back of Tyler's head. "He's a very good cook. He makes fish almost as delicious as Granddad's."

Adam tried to look humble as Tyler gazed up at him with a new respect. He realized Cassie's endorsement might be good for *him,* but Jasper might not appreciate competition in the sacred fish-cooking category.

"Okay," Tyler said. "Let's go, Uncle Adam." And with that he headed for the kitchen, smiling up at his grandfather as he passed, seemingly completely unaware of the tension in the room. Jasper smiled back and tousled his grandson's hair. It was only during that brief expression of affection for his grandson that the scowl left Jasper's face for even a nanosecond.

"I guess I'll be making sandwiches while you guys check out," Adam announced, meeting Jasper's fierce gaze unblinkingly as he followed Tyler into the kitchen. He realized that the best way to handle Jasper was probably by not showing fear. And he really wasn't intimidated by the stern old man, anyway. He understood and empathized with his feelings and suspicions completely. What Adam was really feeling to the point of misery was guilt.

"See you in a few minutes, Tyler, Adam. Come on, Dad," Cassie called from the door. "The sooner we get you guys checked out, the sooner Tyler can get his first floatplane ride."

Tyler stopped in the middle of licking peanut butter off his thumb. "Flying? We're going *flying?*" he squeaked.

Cassie grinned. "Yep."

"In another plane?"

"I hear it's the only way to go," Cassie answered solemnly, her eyes sparkling. "But I'll let Uncle Adam tell you all about his plane. Bye, hon."

When the door finally closed behind Cassie and her father, Adam looked down and found a peanut-butter-smeared face gazing up at him expectantly. "Well, Uncle Adam? Are ya goin' t' tell me about your plane or not?"

"WHAT WAS that all about?" Jasper nearly shouted as soon as they'd walked ten feet down the hall in the direction of the elevators.

Cassie slipped her hand around her father's elbow and smiled determinedly. "What was what all about, Dad?"

Exasperated, Jasper stopped in his tracks and flung an arm in the direction of room 230. "*That!* What was *that* all about? Are you crazy leaving Tyler with a total stranger?"

Cassie crossed her arms over her chest and faced him. "Adam's no stranger. Adam is his father."

"Well, that may be true, but—"

"What do you mean *may* be true? I told you he knows something about me that's quite personal and—"

Jasper lifted both hands, palms forward. "Never mind. I don't want to know. What I *do* want to know is why you're acting so featherbrained and teachin' Tyler all kinds of wrong lessons?''

Cassie angled a brow. ''Featherbrained?''

''As a peahen. Why else would you leave your son alone with a man he just met?''

''Is that what you mean by teaching wrong lessons?''

''He'll be going to school soon, Cass. Do you want him to think he can hobnob with just anybody off the street?''

''That's not going to happen, Dad, and you know it. Tyler knows I approve of him staying with Adam and that's the only reason he's comfortable doing it. He realizes that I trust Adam.''

''And why *is* that? Why do you trust him? We've been in Alaska less than twenty-four hours and this fella's apparently won you over already. Hell, doesn't this cozy scenario seem just a little too familiar to ya, Cass?''

Cassie felt her face heating up. She waited until a couple passed them in the hall, then said in a lowered voice, ''Dad, you aren't implying that I—that Adam and I—''

''Not implyin'. Askin'. Have ya done the mattress dance with 'im, Cass?''

Cassie laughed, embarrassed, indignant and amused at the same time. ''Where on earth did you pick up that phrase? I think you've been watching too many talk shows, Dad.''

''Bah! You're being evasive.''

Cassie sighed. ''Come on, let's walk while we talk.'' She took his arm and they proceeded again toward the elevators.

"Are you going to answer my question or not?" he persisted.

"Yes, Dad, I—"

She could feel him stiffen. "You mean you actually *did*—"

"Listen to me. Yes, I *am* going to answer your question."

"Oh."

"And *no,* I haven't slept with Adam. I told you things would be different this time and…and they are. Actually, in many ways *he* seems different this time."

They reached the elevator bank and her father pushed the Down button. He gazed at her thoughtfully. "But you are attracted to him, aren't you? I can see it, Cass, so don't even try to deny it."

Cassie returned her father's gaze directly. "Yes, I'm attracted to him, but I'm trying very hard not to let it influence the way I handle his and Tyler's relationship. I'm trying to be objective."

Jasper snorted. "Hell, honey, I don't think you *can* be objective."

She poked him in the chest. "Apparently neither can you. And while I think that partially has to do with your protective feelings toward me and Tyler, I also think you're thinking of Brad."

Jasper's brows lowered. Soberly, he asked, "What about Brad?"

Cassie shook her head, just as sober. "Dad, you know I care about Brad—"

"But?"

"I know you love him like a son, and Tyler adores him."

"But?"

"But after three years you'd think I'd have married the guy by now. Bottom line, we just weren't meant to be. When we get back to Montana I'm going to have to tell him how I feel so he can get on with his life."

Cassie felt like a villain. Her father's face showed how terribly disappointed he was. "You've never talked this way before. You've never let on that there was no hope at all of you and Brad getting together."

She shrugged helplessly. "I guess it took this trip to make me see the truth."

He shook his head. "That scares the hell out of me."

"Why?"

"For the same reason it scares you, I expect. It's Adam. In just a day, you like *him* better than Brad."

Cassie nodded. Earlier that day, she'd been thinking the same thing.

"Where's this goin', Cass?"

She gave a helpless chuckle. "I wish I knew." She hesitated, then continued, "Dad, you know I respect and appreciate your opinions—"

"I should hope so."

"—but if you're not objective about Adam your opinion isn't worth much, is it?"

He grimaced. "No, I guess not."

"Besides, he *is* Tyler's father. Isn't that reason enough to give the guy a chance?"

The elevator pinged and the doors opened.

"I guess so," he agreed grudgingly as they stepped into the elevator. He gave her a quick kiss on the cheek and faced forward. "But being objective doesn't mean I'm not allowed to watch 'im like a hawk."

Cassie also turned to face the closing doors. "I know, Dad," she said ruefully. "I know."

Chapter Seven

During the twenty minutes Cassie and Jasper left him alone with Tyler, Adam got to know a lot about his nephew. He learned that he made a pretty mean peanut butter and jelly "sand'ich" all by himself, but didn't like eating alone. Adam hated the gooey consistency of peanut butter, but he gagged down half a sandwich anyway just to be sociable.

He learned that Tyler refused to eat jam with seeds in it because the seeds stuck between his teeth. He said it felt kind of like having sand in his mouth like when he fell off his horse, Buster, last year. No, he didn't break anything, just got a "gritty mouthful" as Granddad said. He didn't cry, either. He wasn't a crybaby, he informed Adam proudly, not even when he got shots at the doctor's.

Next to fishing, his favorite thing to do was listen to stories about animals, especially big ones like elephants and dinosaurs and whales. His four favorite people were Mommy, Granddad, Sylvie and Uncle Brad.

Someday Mommy and Uncle Brad were going to get married and he was going to have little brothers.

No sisters, just brothers. No, Mommy never said so, but he just had a feelin' that someday Uncle Brad was going to end up being his daddy. He'd never had a dad before, you know. By the way, did Uncle Adam have any Jolly Ranchers in his pocket?

By now Adam was beginning to realize that although Cassie had claimed to be free of romantic entanglements back home, this Brad fella had to be a pretty big part of their lives. He was certainly important to Tyler. And while he also realized that once Cassie found out he'd lied about being Tyler's father there was little to no chance of having a relationship with her. He was so jealous of Brad his jaw ached from clenching it at the thought of her kissing some Montana cowboy who probably looked like Kevin Costner in *Silverado*... you know, romantically heroic. Or like Michael Landon as Little Joe on *Bonanza*, all roguish charm. Or like Gary Cooper in *High Noon*, the strong, silent type.

As Cassie and Jasper walked in, Tyler was inexpertly wiping down the table with a damp paper towel while Adam packed in a sack the small amount of groceries Jasper had stored in the cupboard. Still thinking of Cassie and Kevin Costner, or some other cowboy of the same studly ilk, Adam looked up with a frown on his face. He quickly realized that Cassie had mistaken his gloomy expression as a distaste for baby-sitting.

Her cheerful smile wavering, her gray eyes searching his, she inquired, "Did you two manage okay without us?"

"Sure, Mommy," Tyler answered for them. "We

ate sand'iches and now we're cleanin' up. Can we go now?''

"As soon as we're packed, bud," Jasper told him. "Come on over here and help me unload this drawer."

Tyler did as he was told and Adam and Cassie were left in the relative privacy of the kitchen.

"We had a great time and Tyler's a great kid," Adam immediately told her.

She didn't look convinced. "Then why were you frowning when we came in?"

"I was thinking about Kevin Costner," he replied dryly.

Her eyes narrowed, her lips tilted. "Say again?"

"Look, don't ask. Just believe me when I say I wasn't frowning because of Tyler. He behaved perfectly and we had a couple of great 'sand'iches.'"

Finally she smiled. "Okay, I believe you." She looked like she wanted to say more, to ask questions and find out what he was thinking and feeling, but she didn't. For this he was grateful.

"Did your father give you much trouble?" he asked in a low voice. He eyed Jasper across the room, tossing clothes in suitcases and keeping up a nonstop conversation with an excited Tyler. "He looks a little less bloodthirsty now."

"Don't worry about Dad. He'll warm up to you. It just takes him a while to trust people."

You could take some lessons from him, Cassie, Adam thought, but since it wasn't time for a confession, he kept this opinion to himself.

Soon Jasper and Ty were packed and ready to go. In just a few minutes they were taking off from Lake

Hood with Tyler in the front passenger seat, and Cassie and her father in the rear. Tyler's excitement was palpable, his eyes enormous, his cheeks rosy with color. If he was a little frightened during the takeoff he didn't show it and once in the air he couldn't quit asking questions.

Cassie was sitting behind Adam and she leaned forward to whisper wryly, "Like mother like son."

Adam smiled and nodded. Yep, they were alike all right, equally intelligent and inquisitive, equally engaging. Thank God, though, Tyler proved he wasn't too perfect. Toward the end of the flight, he started getting irritable and bored, then announced that he had to go to the bathroom...*now.*

"Honey, why didn't you go before we left the hotel?" Cassie asked in a beleaguered voice.

"No one tol' me to."

"Some things you shouldn't have to be told, Tyler," his grandfather stated unequivocally. "I'm sure you can wait till we land."

"When will we land?" Tyler wanted to know, his voice grown slightly whiny.

"In about five minutes," Adam said. "We'll land in the water right by my house, Tyler, and all you'll have to do is run up the stairs to the bathroom. Think you can make it?"

Tyler considered, then mumbled, "Yeah, I think so. I'll tell ya if I can't."

"I'd appreciate that," Adam murmured. He caught Cassie's chagrined expression in the overhead mirror and he smiled at her. She was so eager that Ty make a good impression, but she shouldn't be worrying. If Tyler didn't whine or get bored or have to go to the bathroom at the most inconvenient moment, he wouldn't be normal. His normalcy certainly took nothing away from Adam's appreciation of his nephew. Actually it just made him more real and lovable. He wondered if Alex would see it the same way...

As soon as they docked in Seldovia, Cassie accompanied Tyler up the stairs at a brisk trot to the nearest bathroom while Jasper and Adam followed more slowly with the suitcases.

"I've always wanted to see Alaska," Jasper commented as he took in the view. "It doesn't disappoint."

"There's no place like it," Adam agreed, then added politely, "but Montana's nice, too."

"It's home," Jasper said, then turned his gaze on Adam. "For all of us."

Adam suspected a double meaning. Perhaps Jasper was cautioning him about trying to take Tyler away from the only home he'd ever known. Since he had no right to do so even if he wanted to, Adam quickly reassured him. "You have nothing to worry about, Mr. Montgomery."

"I don't?" Jasper had stopped on the stairs and was looking Adam straight in the eye. "Would you care to elaborate on that?"

Adam smiled wanly. "No. Just please believe me when I say I don't want Cassie or Tyler hurt any more than you do."

Jasper stared at Adam for a minute, then sniffed and looked away. "Don't know why, but I think I actually *do* believe you," he said grudgingly.

"Doesn't mean I won't be watchin' you like a hawk, though."

Adam chuckled and started up the stairs again. "Can't say I blame you, sir."

"Adam?"

Adam turned. "Yes?"

"Don't call me sir. Makes me feel like an old fart. Jasper's the name. Use it."

Adam suppressed a smile and nodded soberly, liking Cassie's father more by the minute. At the top of the stairs, Adam directed Jasper to the main cabin and down the hall to one of the two extra bedrooms, passing Cassie and Tyler in the kitchen getting drinks of water. He set down the suitcase he was carrying and said, "Furnishings are kind of spare, but this is the best mattress of the two available."

"All I need is a place to lay my head." Jasper looked around consideringly. "You say you've got two empty beds? How many bedrooms have you got in this house, anyway?"

"Three."

Jasper was immediately on the alert. "Where's Cassie sleepin', then?"

Adam pointed toward the window. "See that little cabin down the hill a ways? Cassie has it all to herself."

Jasper's eyes narrowed. "You put her there right from the start, not just when you heard I was comin'?"

"I'm very happy to say that yes, I put her there right from the start," Adam answered with rueful amusement in his voice. "Very happy, indeed."

This drew a reluctant grin from Jasper. "I'll bet you are."

Adam nodded, the two of them understanding each other perfectly. "So where will Tyler stay, with you or Cassie? Or would he like his own room?"

"He's got his own room back home, but while he's here I expect he'll want to stay with me or his mom. We'll let him choose, but I'll put his clothes in this chest of drawers with mine." He turned toward the door where Cassie and Tyler had just appeared. "That okay with you, hon?"

Cassie shrugged, smiled. "Fine with me. Tyler can sleep where he wants. It's up to him." Cassie looked down at Tyler. "Where do you want to sleep, Ty? Here in the big house with Granddad, or with me in the little house down the hill?"

"I'll sleep with the guys," Tyler answered importantly, strutting into the room and sitting down on the edge of the bed. "Say, when are we goin' to see that eagle's nest you tol' us about, Uncle Adam?"

"As soon as you guys get unpacked and settled in, we'll do some sight-seeing, get a good look at the eagle's nest, then take the ferry over to Halibut Cove for some dinner."

"What about fishin'?"

"We can do that tomorrow morning before the wedding rehearsal. Sound okay?"

Tyler wrinkled his nose. "Who's gettin' married? Do we hafta go to the weddin'?"

"I'll let your mother explain about the wedding," Adam said, exchanging an amused smile with Cassie. "I have to get something in my car."

Adam left and went straight to his car, picked up his cell phone and called his brother's home number. For what he had to say to Alex he needed privacy. The phone rang five times, then went to Alex's answering machine.

"Damn," Adam grumbled. He wanted to talk to Alex and make his position known immediately. He wanted to tell Cassie the truth. The sooner the better. The fact that they'd soon be on honest terms with each other was the only thing that gave him the courage to keep up the charade.

After the beep on Alex's answering machine sounded, Adam said, "Alex, we have to talk. To-night." He hung up without going into further detail just in case Kelly was around to hear the recorded message. No point in tipping their hand before Alex had time to prepare his fiancée for the startling news.

Adam pressed the Off button on his phone and turned just in time to see Cassie walking slowly down the wooden walkway to her cabin. She didn't glance his way but seemed preoccupied with her own thoughts…apparently happy ones, judging by her serene expression.

Adam shook his head sadly. Too bad he was going to have to burst her bubble soon. But until that dreaded moment, he was going to make sure she and Tyler and Jasper had a wonderful afternoon and evening. For Adam their time together would be bittersweet, because after his and Alex's confession it was highly unlikely that Cassie would ever want to speak to him again.

WITH THE THREE most important men in her life as company, Cassie had never spent a more wonderful afternoon and evening. Adam drove them all over the place. They saw mountains and hanging glaciers and streams and lakes. They got out and took short hikes into the forest and saw moose and caribou and even a black bear. The highlight of the trip, though, was the eagle's nest.

They'd parked in a meadowlike clearing that was covered with glorious purple lupine, the area surrounded by old conifer and cottonwood trees. They stood, four abreast, by the Jeep. Adam handed Cassie and Jasper each a pair of binoculars, then turned to Tyler.

"Here's your pair, kiddo. Are they too heavy for you?"

"No, o' course not," Tyler answered stoutly.

"Good. Now come here and let me hoist you up on my shoulders. Take your hat off first." Adam grabbed Tyler under the arms and lifted him over his head easily. "I'll tell you where to look, okay?"

"Will there be baby eagles in the nest?" Tyler asked as he settled himself on Adam's shoulders.

Adam held Tyler loosely by his ankles. "There should be. Usually the nests are built in April, the eggs are hatched, then by the end of July most of the eaglets are ready to fly. See where I'm pointing?"

"Yeah?"

"Look through the binoculars at that tree, the really tall one in the middle of the three that are clumped close together. Do you know which one I mean?"

"Think so."

"Good. About a third of the way down you'll see the nest. It's pretty big, so—"

"I see it! I see it!" Tyler bounced on Adam's shoulders, accidentally bumping Adam's head with the binoculars.

Adam winced, but didn't mention the unintentional assault. Cassie pressed her fingers against her mouth to stifle a giggle.

"Do you see the eaglets?"

"Yeah! They look funny. All fuzzy and feathery."

Adam chuckled. "Yep, they look pretty funny when they're little. It'll take awhile before they get sleek and beautiful like their mom and dad."

Suddenly they heard an eagle's cry in the sky above them and an adult eagle fluttered gracefully down to perch on the edge of the nest.

"I'll be damned," Jasper muttered. "Ain't that a pretty sight?"

"Yes. The prettiest sight I've ever seen." But Cassie wasn't talking about the mother eagle and her young. She held the binoculars away from her eyes and was gazing at Adam and Tyler, both of their faces rapt and smiling. Her heart ached and a lump of emotion filled her throat. She wished she knew if Tyler and his father would be enjoying more excursions together in the future, but Adam still wasn't giving her any clues.

From the Homer harbor they took a ferry to Halibut Cove, which Adam said was an artists' colony, with about a dozen blocks of wooden walkways that connected galleries, eateries and private homes. They ate at the Saltry where they sat at a window that overlooked the boat dock and the cove. Everyone had seafood, Adam and Cassie enjoying some exotically prepared halibut, Jasper and Tyler sticking with pan-fried fillets of salmon.

Tyler was nodding by the time they headed home, sated with good food, fresh air and breathtaking scenery. Even Cassie, despite the growing yearning she felt for a fairy-tale ending of this incredible trip to Alaska and the almost nonexistent chance of such a thing ever happening, felt contented to the core. She was living in the moment, savoring the day for all it was worth. Who knew when she'd ever be this happy again?

Back in Seldovia, Cassie helped Tyler into his pajamas and into bed, where he fell asleep immediately.

"I'm hittin' the hay, too," Jasper announced as he stifled a yawn. "But I'll walk you down to your cabin first."

"No need, Dad," Cassie assured him.

Jasper peered at her concernedly, obviously struggling to keep his eyes open. "You *are* goin' straight down to the cabin, aren't you?"

"Yes. It's ten-thirty and we're supposed to get up at the crack of dawn to go fishing, aren't we? Dawn comes pretty early up here in the summer, so I think it's best I get some sleep."

Jasper looked past her to the door. "Where's Adam?"

Cassie shook her head, grinned ruefully. "Dad, I told you not to worry. Adam's already said goodnight. He took the car and went into Seldovia to see Alex about something. He said he'd be late."

Jasper nodded. "Good. Then I'll say good-night, too, sweetheart. Sleep tight."

"I will, Dad." She kissed him on the cheek, then stooped to kiss Tyler, too.

"Close the door in case Adam's not so quiet when he comes in," Jasper told her.

She obeyed and was soon on her way down to her own private little retreat. It was still light outside and she looked toward the gravel drive by the house half hoping that Adam's Jeep would pull up while she was watching. She'd been disappointed when he'd announced that he was going to Alex's. She had hoped they could spend a little one-on-one time together at the end of the evening. She was anxious to know how he was thinking, feeling. About Tyler, of course. But also about *them*.

While Jasper was around, there was no possibility of physical contact of any kind, but Cassie had felt the sexual tension between them all day long. Even now, even when Adam was nowhere in sight, she positively *ached* for him. But now it wasn't just physical desire she felt. She wasn't being swept off her feet by a handsome, charming stranger who hadn't even told her his real name before making passionate love to her. This time she was getting to know him, seeing him in his natural surroundings, watching him with their son. If they made love now, it would be different. It would mean something more...

As Cassie prepared for bed, she tried to force visions of their lovemaking out of her mind. By the time she'd showered, brushed her teeth and slipped into her nightie, she realized that she wasn't going to get any sleep at all that night. She was too keyed up. She needed to relax somehow. Then, suddenly, she remembered the hot tub.

ADAM KNEW it was probably fruitless, but he drove past Alex's house one more time. Sure enough, there was no car in the drive, no light on in the house. It wasn't possible his brother was spending the night with Kelly in Kenai because her parents were staying at her apartment, but they could be out on a late date together and he just hadn't received Adam's phone messages yet.

Adam sighed and headed home. At least by now Cassie, her father and Tyler would be in bed and asleep. He wouldn't have to be around Cassie until tomorrow, wouldn't have to fight his ever-growing desire to kiss her, hold her, make love to her. After she learned the truth, she'd probably hightail it back to Montana as fast as she could. Then there'd be no more temptation, no chance of doing something so morally bankrupt as making love to a woman he'd blatantly lied to about something as sacred as the paternity of her child.

Adam was careful to be very quiet when he entered the house. He noticed that Jasper's door was closed and heard loud snoring coming from behind it. He wondered how Tyler managed to sleep through such a ruckus, but then remembered that kids could sleep through just about anything, bless 'em. And troubles didn't keep them up at night, either. They were either too innocent to realize they should be worried, or were too optimistic to think that troubles might actually outlast the night and reappear the following morning.

Adam wished he had a small portion of such innocence and optimism. Enough, at least, to get him through what might be the longest night of his life. That Cassie was sleeping just a few yards away nearly drove him crazy.

He showered, brushed his teeth, pulled on his pajamas, then hit the sack with the latest techno-thriller guaranteed to keep you enthralled until the last chapter. Fat chance. After ten minutes, he threw the book on the lonely-looking pillow next to him, tossed off the covers and tore off his pajamas. Stepping into his swim trunks, he grabbed a towel and headed for the hot tub.

Just feet from the screened-in patio that housed the sunken hot tub, Adam stopped short. In the gloaming of approaching midnight, he could see that the tub was already occupied. It could only be one person, of course—*Cassie.*

Adam's heart began to thump wildly. His breathing accelerated. His skin tingled and anticipated. This was the best and the worst coincidence possible.

If he was smart he'd turn around and head back to the house pronto. But he wasn't feeling smart. He wasn't feeling much of anything beyond a yearning to see, to hear, to *touch* the woman who had been dominating his thoughts since her letter arrived two weeks ago. And every hour in her presence since then had intensified his desire for her.

Slowly Adam moved closer and closer to where the hot tub bubbled away invitingly. But far more inviting than the warm, pulsating water was the idea of sharing it with Cassie. Standing in the shadows of a low-hanging tree branch, he stopped and stared, at war with himself. He knew he shouldn't be spying on her, but he couldn't help himself.

Cassie was up to her collarbone in water, her arms stretched out on either side, the back of her head resting against the molded side of the tub. A smile played on her lips, her eyes were closed. He feasted on the sight of her, the curve of her long throat, that pulsing dip at the base of it, the gentle slope of shoulders, the suggestion just below the frothy waterline of small, firm breasts.

That's when he realized she was naked. That's when he knew he'd better leave. He was no Peeping Tom. He turned to go.

"Adam? Adam, is that you?"

Adam turned back, but looked everywhere except directly at Cassie. At a *naked* Cassie. "Yeah, Cass. It's me. But I'm headed back to the house. I didn't know the tub was occupied."

She chuckled. "It's a big tub, Adam. Why don't you join me?"

He flitted an alarmed look at her—at those big eyes, that glistening skin—then away again. He swallowed hard. "I don't think that would be a good idea."

"Why not? This would be a great time and place for us to talk. We haven't had a private moment all day."

He felt the heat creep up his neck and pool in other more sensitive areas of his body. "Talking's okay. It's the privacy part that worries me, Cass. Maybe if you had some clothes on—"

This time she laughed out loud. "Adam! I do have clothes on. My bathing suit straps have just slipped off my shoulders, that's all. See?"

Nervously he allowed his gaze to shift, then rest on Cassie. She had pulled herself out of the water until she was exposed from the waist up. Sure enough she was wearing a bathing suit, a peach-colored bikini that had appeared flesh-colored under the water. The straps were up again, but the minimal covering of her slim, sexy body accomplished by the bikini wasn't enough to tamp down Adam's growing ardor. On the contrary...

"Look, if you're afraid we'll...we'll get involved, I promise to stay on my side of the tub. I promise not to try to seduce you." She slipped back into the water and smiled coyly. "I promise," she repeated.

That's when Adam started to feel like an idiot. Obviously Cassie wanted some company. *His* company. Obviously, they were both adults and they both knew the unfeasibility of getting involved with each other right now. So, surely with both of them attempting to keep cool heads, despite the hot and steamy environment, surely they'd succeed in doing so. It wasn't as if he were some out-of-control hormone-riddled teenager.

"Sure, why not?" he said at last, with more bravura than he felt. He opened the screen door and advanced to the edge of the tub. Staring down at her and seeing her without the blur of the wire meshing between them was startling. She was so beautiful.

Her skin so creamy pink and white, so shiny with moisture.

Perhaps he'd made a mistake…

"For heaven's sake, Adam, get in," Cassie coaxed. "These waters are not shark-infested."

Adam chuckled nervously. Sharks he could maybe handle. A wet and sexy Cassie was something else.

Adam dropped his towel and stepped into the tub. Going down, he couldn't help but feel that, figuratively as well as literally, he'd soon be up to his neck in hot water.

Chapter Eight

Cassie watched as Adam slowly slid into the water. It was the body she remembered, only better somehow. The calves so sinewy and well-developed, the taut thighs, the narrow hips, the flat stomach, the smooth, hairless chest…

Cassie's brows furrowed. Hairless? She distinctly remembered that Adam had had a light dusting of black, curly hair on his chest five years ago. Her fingers had delighted in the silky feel of it. Was it possible that, during the passage of time, a man could go bald on his chest? Not likely!

Then she realized that he could be waxing it. Lots of men did, although she would never have pegged Adam as the type of guy who would feel the need to tamper with nature. She was curious to know the reasoning behind the cosmetic change, but how did you ask such a question? Maybe it had something to do with being a marine biologist and all that scuba diving he did. In her opinion, either way was fine. Hairy or hairless, he had a fine chest.

Adam leaned back in a corner seat of the hot tub,

the water nearly to the top of his shoulders. He closed his eyes and released a long sigh.

"Feel good?" she inquired with a shaky smile.

"Yep."

"It was a pretty tense day for both of us," she continued, eager to talk if for no other reason than to take her mind off what she really wanted to do. She had another good reason to talk, though. She really did want to know what Adam was thinking and feeling about the most important thing they had in common, their *son.* "It's not surprising we both thought of using the tub."

"Uh-huh."

"I couldn't sleep a wink. I kept thinking about…about—"

Adam opened his eyes. "About who? I mean, about what?"

"You were right the first time. I was thinking about you and—"

"Me?"

"You and Tyler."

He closed his eyes again. "Oh."

She waited, but he offered nothing further on the subject. Growing irritated, she demanded, "Adam, are you going to talk to me about Ty or not?"

"Or not," he answered without opening his eyes. "I'm here to relax, Cassie. I can't relax and talk about serious, life-altering issues."

"Okay, but when *will* you talk to me about Tyler?"

"Tomorrow."

"Really, Adam?"

"Absolutely. After tomorrow, you'll know everything you need to know."

Well, that seemed to settle that. "Then what shall we talk about *now?*" she asked rather anxiously.

"Do we have to talk?"

"I *want* to talk. I mean, if we don't talk…"

Adam opened his eyes a crack, their deep blue a striking contrast to the sooty black of his eyelashes. "Cassie, we've been talking all day. Don't feel the need to entertain me. I think we're beyond that. I know you're conversable."

"That's not why I want to talk."

"Then why?"

"Because it gives me something to do, something to think about besides…besides…" Deciding she'd better shut up, she licked her lips nervously.

Adam's eyes flew open. He sat up, cocked his head to the side, gave his bottom lip a cursory chewing. "Cassandra Montgomery, you *promised.*"

Thrilled and frightened by the abruptly sensual tone of his voice, she sat up straighter. "What? What did I promise?"

"You promised not to try to seduce me."

"I'm…I'm *not.* Look, I'm clear over here." She fluttered her hands over the water, indicating her side of the tub.

"You don't have to *do* something to be seductive," he informed her ruefully. "In your case—at least as far as it applies to *me*—all you have to do is be you."

"Oh." Cassie was pretty sure she'd been complimented, but the details were fuzzy. "I still don't know what I'm doing that's so—" she made a comical Greta Garbo face and stretched the word out in a throaty contralto "—*seductive.*"

He grinned. "For one thing, you're being too damned honest for your own good...as usual. You just now practically told me that *you're* thinking about the same thing *I'm* thinking."

Was it possible to blush when you were already up to your chin in hot, bubbling water? "I did?"

"*Cassie...*"

"Yes, I guess I did," she confessed.

He nodded knowingly, then his gaze shifted to her lips and stayed there. His grin disappeared. "You're wondering how it would feel if I kissed you."

"But...but I *do* know."

"No, you don't," he stated firmly. "Believe me, Cass, my kissing you now would be totally different than the kisses you remember from that night in Nye, Montana."

After considering her answer for a few nervous seconds, she admitted, "I've been thinking so, too."

"But—things being the way they are—you and I both know it might be best if neither of us found out for sure."

She didn't like the suddenly depressed tone of his voice. "Things being the way they are? You mean unsettled?"

"Yes. Unsettled. Precarious. Dangerous."

"I see," she said soberly. But she didn't see. He still said things that made her think he knew something she didn't. Something that he was afraid to share. Could there be another woman, a *significant* other woman, that he didn't want to tell her about?

He leaned back and sighed again, as if soul-weary, peering at her from under those thick, sexy lashes. "That's why it's really stupid that we're in this hot tub together. We're just tempting fate."

"But I *did* keep my promise, Adam," she reminded him. "I *did* try not to seduce you."

His smile was lazy and rueful. "Thank you for at least trying."

"You're welcome." She paused, bit the inside of her lip. "I have just one last question."

"Yes?"

"Did I succeed in not seducing you...or not?"

That was it. That was the clincher. Adam couldn't stand it anymore. He had to kiss the lips that uttered such inflammatory words with such utter ingenuousness. Whether her innocence was an act or not, he didn't care. The effect was the same.

She watched wide-eyed as he crossed the churning water between them in two floating strides, grasped her shoulders and pulled her against him. A feeling of serenity, of profound relief in the final surrender of will to fate swelled through him like a soothing tidal wave. Her skin felt so soft, so warm and welcoming under his hands. He'd wanted to touch her like this for so long! Then the serenity turned to exhilaration and urgency.

"That was one question too many, Cassie," he explained. "But since you asked, here's your answer." He cupped her face and lowered his head until his lips touched hers. He had meant to be gentle, to bank the fiery desire he felt and keep the kiss as restrained as possible. Foolish man. Stupid idea. The minute his lips connected with Cassie's, he was lost.

And it didn't help that she seemed as eager as he, as curious, as lost…

As the kiss deepened, he pulled her close, relishing the feel of her slim curves against him, exulting in the sweet, heady taste of her. His hands slid over her shoulders, her back, into the dip of her waist. Hesitantly at first, then bolder, Cassie touched him, too, her seeking fingers caressing his back, then moving sensuously upward to sink deeply into his hair.

Desire was drowning out the screams of his conscience. Emotion was overcoming his reason. Nothing, no one had ever felt so right.

Cassie was in heaven. Nothing, no one had ever felt so right. Not even her memories of five years ago could compete with the way she was feeling now, today, in Adam's arms and enjoying his kisses as if for the first time.

It *was* different this time. It was better. She had thought it might be better, but not like *this*. There was an emotional intensity behind the kisses and caresses that took her completely by surprise. They seemed connected on a spiritual as well as a physical plane. Oh, but the physical was good, too. So very, *very* good.

Deep in another kiss, their tongues exploring, seeking, tasting, Cassie brought her hands forward to his waist, then up and over the smooth expanse of his chest. Beneath her sensitized fingertips she could feel every nuance of muscle. She pulled back from his kiss just long enough to murmur against his mouth, "I like your chest smooth like this. At first I wondered why—"

Cassie abruptly broke off when she felt him stiffen. She leaned back and peered into his face. The sun was finally setting and his features were partially hidden in shadows. He didn't look at her but past her, into the quickly darkening forest that surrounded them. "Have I offended you? I wasn't going to mention that I'd noticed the difference, but I just sort of got carried away. I *do* like it."

"Well, I suppose I'm glad you like it," Adam said in a strangely strangled voice. "But why do you feel compelled to compare everything *now* to *then?* Hell, Cassie, I feel like I'm competing with myself! That night in Nye is ancient history. *Ancient history!*"

He released her and turned away, leaving Cassie startled and devastated by his apparent anger.

"Adam, I'm so sorry," she whispered, staring helplessly at his back. "I...I had no idea you felt this way."

Abruptly the stiffness went out of his back and his head fell forward in a defeated pose. "It's not your fault, Cass. It's mine. I should never have allowed this to happen." He turned to throw a weak and wistful smile over his shoulder. "I'm the one who should apologize."

Suddenly cold and shaken to the core, Cassie crossed her arms over her chest. "Instead of apologizing to each other, why don't we dry off and go inside so we can talk?"

"No, Cass," he said tiredly. "No talking until tomorrow. That's when everything that needs to be said will be said. I'm going to bed now and I suggest you do the same. It'll be dark in a matter of minutes.''

Before Cassie could say another word, Adam stepped out of the hot tub. Water streamed down his body, accentuating the musculature of his well-honed physique. Gazing at him Cassie couldn't even remember her name, much less find the words to urge him to stay and have a heart-to-heart. He bent to pick up his towel, gave his torso and legs a few cursory swipes, then opened the screen door and headed up the wooden walkway to the house without ever looking back.

Back in her cabin, Cassie tried in vain to understand what exactly had happened in the hot tub between her and Adam. She felt shocked, betrayed, bereft. One minute they were kissing, the emotion and electricity between them equal forces driving them to the inevitable act of lovemaking. Then, suddenly, after her mention of his smooth chest, he had turned away from her as if she'd forcefully applied her knee to his groin!

She didn't believe he could possibly be so vain that mentioning the chest waxing—or rather alluding to it—was taken as an insult. But he was certainly upset about something related to comparing him *now* with him *then*. But why? She knew she'd never sleep if she didn't demand an immediate explanation.

Quickly throwing on jeans, a T-shirt and a pair of slippers, she tied her hair back in a ponytail, then took a flashlight and headed to the house. She knew he was still up. She could see a light on in one of the back bedrooms and in the kitchen.

The back door was ajar, so she pushed open the screen door and quietly went in. She didn't want to wake up her father or Tyler. She tiptoed into the dimly lit kitchen and saw Adam standing in front of the open refrigerator, his back to her. He was fully dressed in jeans and a blue flannel shirt. She supposed he was anticipating a sleepless night, too.

Filled with yearning, filled with the need to fix things between them, she laid the flashlight on the counter, walked soundlessly up to Adam, slipped her arms around his waist and pressed her cheek against his back.

"Adam, I just couldn't leave things the way they were."

Adam jumped when she touched him, then turned around and gazed down at her with an astonished expression. "Don't look so surprised," she whispered, her hands resting flat against his chest. "I had to know why you shut down on me like that. Something's bothering you and I want you to tell me what it is."

"But—"

She touched her fingers to his lips. "I know you said you didn't want to talk tonight, but I can't wait. We can talk about Tyler tomorrow, but, please, let's talk about us *tonight*."

"But I'm not—"

Cassie silenced him with a kiss. When he didn't immediately respond, she just tried harder. She twined her arms around his neck and gave it everything she had. In fact, she was so busy trying to make *him* respond, it took her a while to notice that *she* wasn't feeling much of anything, either.

"What the hell is going on here?"

Cassie froze at the sound of Adam's angry voice. Her eyes flew open as she stared up and into the apologetic and amused expression of a man she had no business kissing. With abrupt and sickening clarity she realized that she'd mistaken Alex for Adam and was liplocking the wrong twin!

ADAM HAD TO force himself to remain calm. Alex had arrived just moments before and Adam had gone to his bedroom to put on some clothes so that he and his brother could take a walk and have a long talk. But coming into the room and seeing Cassie kissing Alex was like a bad dream come true. Because he knew they'd kissed and more before, the image had intruded from time to time, but he never thought he'd actually see them together in the flesh.

"Adam! I thought...I thought he was *you*," Cassie stammered, then practically jumped away from Alex when she realized she still had her arms around his neck.

"I can believe that," Adam said evenly, "but who did Alex think *you* were? You and Kelly could hardly pass for twins."

"Hey, bro, don't get the wrong idea here," Alex cautioned in a cajoling voice, his hands raised in the classic pose of innocence. "Cass took me completely by surprise."

Adam crossed his arms. "Yes, I noticed you were stunned speechless," he said dryly. "You couldn't even pull yourself together long enough to say the three little words that would have cleared things up immediately."

"Three little words?" Alex repeated with a puzzled frown.

"You know... 'I'm not Adam.'"

Cassie moved toward Adam, her hands clasped, her face devoid of color. "Adam, I can vouch for the fact that Alex was stunned. He just stood there while *I* kissed *him*."

Adam raised a brow. "So are you saying that if he hadn't been stunned, he *would* have kissed you back?"

"You know that's not what I'm saying," Cassie exclaimed in an incredulous tone. "Adam, I don't understand why you're acting like this. You have no reason to suspect Alex of wanting to behave improperly with me. And you certainly have no reason to think that *I* would want to put the moves on *him*. He and I have no history together and, besides, he's engaged to be married! Not only that, but he's my son's uncle!"

Adam had no reply to this. Cassie's reasoning was based on more falsehoods than truths, but she didn't know that. He had immediately accepted that Cassie had made a mistake, that she had mistook his brother for him, but what about Alex? Had he allowed the kiss—perhaps even welcomed it—because of a lingering curiosity about Cassie and the potent memory of her kisses? Was there still a spark between them?

Now Alex approached him and spoke in a low voice. "Listen, bro, I can tell you're thinking way too hard about what just happened here. Plain and simple, this was a mistake. In case you need reminding, let me tell you again that I'm getting married in less than forty-eight hours to a woman I'm crazy about. I wouldn't do anything to jeopardize that. Adam, you *know* I wouldn't.''

Adam stared into his brother's eyes and knew he was telling the truth. His gaze shifted to Cassie. She looked confused and hurt and angry. He didn't blame her a bit. He'd been behaving like a jackass. His own frustration had spilled over into a ridiculous display of suspicion and jealousy.

Adam released a long sigh. ''I'm sorry, Alex, Cassie. I obviously jumped to the wrong conclusion.''

Relief showed immediately on Alex's face. ''Don't worry about it, bro,'' he said, punching Adam on the arm.

''What about you, Cass?'' Adam inquired with a chagrined half smile. ''You still look upset.''

Although her hands had relaxed and her color was back, her brows were fixed in a frown. ''I don't want to be upset with you. I just want to *understand* you. That's why I came up here looking for you, Adam. I want you to explain why you got so upset when I mentioned—'' she darted a look at Alex, then blushed adorably ''—*you know*...the chest thing.''

Adam quickly moved to her side, cupped her elbow and turned her gently toward the door. ''By some miracle, I think your father and Tyler may still be asleep. But if we talk all night in this room, they're sure to wake up eventually.'' As they passed the counter, Alex picked up the flashlight Cassie had brought with her from the cabin.

Cassie watched what he was doing and set her chin at a stubborn angle. ''How long would it take for a simple explanation, Adam? Besides, aren't you and Alex planning to talk?''

"Yes, but not here." Adam smiled, hoping she'd let it go, but Cassie wasn't about to be placated so easily.

"Can't you and I talk first? I don't think Alex would mind."

"It's late, Cassie. Alex wants to get home so he can be rested for the rehearsal tomorrow. And don't forget, we've got a fishing date with Tyler bright and early. I was just getting ready to leave with Alex when you arrived and sort of…stirred things up."

By now, although she was obviously reluctant, he'd managed to maneuver her out the door and they were headed down the walkway toward her cabin.

"Geez, Adam, getting you to talk is like getting Tyler to eat beets," Cassie said at last. "I have questions—"

"I promise you, Cass, tomorrow I'll answer all your questions. We'll have a long talk and clear everything up."

"Everything?" She sounded unconvinced.

"Everything," he assured her.

At the door of the guest house, she turned and peered up at him. In the moonlight he caught a glimmer of a grudging smile. "I suppose I should be flattered that you were jealous when you saw me with Alex. But, really, Adam, I didn't feel anything when I kissed him. He may *look* like you, but he's not you. He could *never* be you."

She stood on tiptoes and kissed his cheek, then disappeared inside, leaving Adam to ponder the irony of her words. After a few seconds, he shook his head and walked quickly back to the house. Alex was waiting for him and he wasn't going to miss this opportunity to get his twin brother alone for a little mano a mano talk.

Alex was standing on the porch, the door to the house closed behind him. "So she picked up on the chest thing. She's got a good memory, I'll say that for her."

"I suspect it's because she's not been with many men."

Alex shrugged. "Maybe. Here, I brought your jacket. Where to, bro?"

Adam took the jacket and slipped into it while Alex held the flashlight. "Let's just walk down the road a bit."

Alex hopped down from the high porch, stuffed his hands in his jean pockets and led the way. "When I got your message, I figured you needed to unburden yourself again. With such an admiration for absolute truth, you'd make a lousy lawyer. Did the kid get to you or something?"

Adam fell into step beside his brother, the bobbing flashlight illuminating the narrow dirt road in front of them. "Hell yes, he got to me. He's an incredible little boy." He took a quick glance at his brother, but could only make out a dim profile limned by moonlight. "I don't suppose you'd want to spend a little time with him and find out for yourself?"

"Not likely," Alex drawled. "Why would you even suggest it...unless you're getting cold feet again and want to bail out on me?" Alex stopped and turned to stare at Adam. Adam didn't have to see his brother's eyes clearly to know the expression in them was anxious and accusing.

"I'm sorry, Alex, but that's exactly what I want to do," Adam answered firmly. "I can't keep lying to Cassie. It's wrong and it isn't fair."

"It isn't fair to whom?" Alex demanded to know. "Cassie? I don't think so, because it seems to me *she's* perfectly happy with the way things are."

"Too happy," Adam said gruffly. "She'd like me to be involved with Tyler, be a father to him."

"Well, why not?"

"Alex, haven't you got a conscience at all?"

Alex ignored him, adding, "By the looks of things, I think Cassie would like you to be something to *her,* too, Adam."

"I wish it were possible—"

"It *is* possible!" Alex exclaimed, exasperated. "Don't be so damned stubborn and self-righteous! You and I are the only two people in the world who know you're not Tyler's real father. I'm sure as hell not going to tell anyone anything different. Why should you?"

Adam closed his eyes on a weary sigh. "Because it's not the truth," he growled between his teeth.

"Truth can be highly overrated," Alex scoffed. "Sometimes, for certain people in certain situations, fiction over fact can make for a much happier existence. Besides, how much closer to being Tyler's real father could you be? You and I share an almost identical DNA makeup—amounts of chest hair excepting—so if you'd actually fathered Tyler he'd probably be no different than he is now!"

"You have this rationalization thing down to a

science, Alex,'' Adam muttered in grim amazement, edging past his brother to continue their walk.

"Can you blame me, Adam? I'm fighting for my life.''

"You're exaggerating.''

"Kelly *is* my life. If I lose her—''

"I don't think you'll lose her.''

"Can you be sure of that?''

Adam paused, then admitted, "No.''

"Well, there's one thing we can both be sure of,'' Alex said. "Whether you tell Cassie the truth or not, you're going to lose *her*.''

The harsh, measured words hit Adam like stones to the heart. Alex was right. He was going to lose Cassie whether he told the truth or not.

"Face the facts, Adam,'' Alex continued mercilessly. "You're so guilt-ridden about lying to her, you'd never let yourself get fully involved with Cassie. You could be a father to Tyler, a husband to her—if that's what both of you wanted—but you won't let that happen. You won't allow the three of you to be happy, because you're too damned honest and upright!''

"If I were really honest and upright, Alex, I wouldn't be in this damn mess in the first place.''

"Regardless of when your overzealous conscience kicked in, bro, it's too late for you and Cassie. If you tell her the truth now, she'll be devastated. She'll never forgive you.''

"In other words, little brother, you're saying I'm damned if I do and I'm damned if I don't,'' he commented bitterly. "So what's the definitive point?''

"The point is, since things don't look too good

either way for you, why not save *my* skin? Why not let me and Kelly be happy? Even if you opt to stay out of their lives, Cassie and Ty would ultimately be happier believing you were his father. If you hit her with the truth now, she'll have a bitter taste in her mouth for the rest of her life about Tyler's side of the family. It seems to me that—just to ease your own conscience—you're willing to put the rest of us through hell!''

Adam listened with growing frustration and anger. His brother certainly had a way with words. *He* certainly wouldn't have had any trouble taking up the practice of law. Alex was making him feel as though he were the most selfish person on earth.

Adam knew it wasn't true. He knew he only wanted to do what was right, but he couldn't completely dismiss Alex's argument that by doing what was conventionally ''right'' he'd be messing up his one-and-only brother's rosy future and breaking the hearts of Cassie and a lot of other people, too.

Adam wasn't sure he believed that fiction was better than fact in any situation, but sometimes the truth hurt so badly it was hard for people to pick up the pieces and go on. Was he, somewhere deep inside, hoping that if Cassie knew the truth she'd be able to handle it, to pick up the pieces and eventually forgive him so they could have a life together? After telling such a huge and sustained lie about something so personal and important, it would probably take a miracle for her to forgive him...but a miracle seemed to be the only hope Adam had.

If he was hoping for a miracle, did that make him selfish? Or just crazy?

"Adam, what are you going to do?"

Without consciously deciding to, Adam and Alex had turned around and had walked to within a few feet of the house. Alex just stood there, his rigid stance a mix of defiance, deference and desperation, waiting for Adam to say something.

As the seconds passed, then the minutes, Adam's anger and frustration built on itself until he was ready to explode. How could he put his brother, Kelly and Kelly's whole family through the misery Alex was so sure would result from Adam's truth-telling? How could he *not*?

"I know you, Adam. If you had decided to tell her the truth, we wouldn't still be standing out here," Alex finally said. Then, sweetly he added, "How can I ever thank you?"

"Don't bother," Adam growled.

The air between them was fraught with tension and resentment. Alex shifted from foot to foot, gave an uneasy chuckle, then suggested, "Look, if it will make you feel any better, why don't you just haul off and hit me?"

The offer was made in jest. But Adam wasn't in a jesting mood. He pulled back his fist and sent it flying.

Chapter Nine

Cassie lay awake in bed thinking about what had happened between her and Adam that night. She also thought about the different things that had happened during the day—things said, looks given—all of which left her no choice but to conclude that Adam was keeping something from her. And Alex knew what it was.

This secret between them was undoubtedly why Alex had paid a midnight visit to Adam on a night when he would have been better off going to bed early so he could be chipper for rehearsal day activities. It had to be something important, something that was really bugging Adam...and maybe Alex, too.

Cassie wasn't stupid. A little naive and trusting, yes. Inexperienced with the opposite sex, definitely yes. But stupid, no. That's why she had to consider the possibility that her father might have been on to something when he'd wondered how the hell she knew which of the Baranof twins was Tyler's father.

She'd answered him quickly and with confidence. It had never entered her mind not to believe that

Adam was telling the truth about being the man she'd made love with five years ago, the man who had fathered her child. To lie about something like that would be cruel and unforgivable. She felt she knew Adam well enough to know he was incapable of being so duplicitous.

Besides, he'd known that she was a virgin when Tyler was conceived. The only way he'd know such a thing is if he'd actually been there, or if, during the five measly minutes she'd spent in the bathroom after announcing who she was, Alex had filled his brother in on all the intimate details of that night in Nye. What a horrible idea!

Cassie sat up and pounded her pillow, then tried to find a cool, comfortable spot on it. She was getting a headache even considering the possibility of such deceit. She refused to believe it was possible for Adam to have made up his mind in five minutes to tell such a huge lie, then act on it for the past two days without breaking into a cold sweat every time he looked at her, her father, or—in particular—her son.

And how had he picked her letter out of hundreds of others if he didn't remember her from somewhere? She'd said it herself and Adam had agreed, it would have been too coincidental, too predestined, for him to have chosen her without some memory prodding him.

Cassie turned on her side and curled up, hugging the covers in tight fists against her chest. She liked Adam. She liked him a lot. And she knew he liked her, too. She was determined not to jump to conclusions. She would put these horrible ideas out of her head for now. She'd give him the benefit of the doubt, give him a chance to explain himself.

One thing in particular she hoped he could explain was the chest hair discrepancy, because now she remembered how Kelly had stroked Alex's chest at Harold's Tux Towne while enumerating the differences between Alex and Adam. There was no denying the fact that her lover of five years ago had had chest hair. Adam didn't. Did Alex? She supposed she could ask Kelly about it, but how did one bring up such a subject?

Cassie squeezed her eyes shut and willed unconsciousness to take over, to rescue her from thoughts that threatened to ruin every hope of happiness she'd entertained in the past two days...but sleep didn't come for a very long time.

Cassie was awakened that morning at the relatively late hour of eight o'clock by Tyler shouting, "Mommy, get up! We've made ya some eggs and you'd better eat 'em so we can get fishin'."

Cassie sat up, pushed her hair out of her eyes and tried to focus. Tyler was leaning on the end of the bed and her father was standing just inside the door.

"We were going to leave you alone till you woke up on your own," he informed her, peering at her appraisingly from under his bushy brows. "But by the looks of things, you'd probably have slept till noon. Have trouble dozin' off last night, did ya?"

"Yes, I guess the sunshine or something has my internal clock all messed up."

"You should've set the alarm," her father told her.

Setting the alarm had never occurred to Cassie.

She'd had serious doubts about ever getting to sleep at all, much less having trouble waking up.

"Don't worry, guys," Cassie said, flipping off her covers and throwing her feet over the side of the bed. "I'll be ready to go in a flash. Keep the eggs hot, I'll be up to the house in ten minutes or less, I promise."

Tyler left with his grandfather, all smiles, and Cassie was as good as her word. She took a quick shower, pulled on the same jeans and pink T-shirt she'd had on the night before when she'd inadvertently kissed the wrong twin, brushed her hair into a ponytail and applied just a dab of lipstick and mascara. She was sure she wouldn't wow Adam with her glamour, but somehow she didn't think salmon fishing and glamour went together, anyway.

Her stomach was in knots as she walked up to the house and she was wondering how she was ever going to eat and keep down a plate of eggs. And now that her mind was filled with suspicion, how was she going to act natural around Adam? She had decided that she would wait until he decided the time was right to talk. She wasn't going to push things. And maybe she was in no hurry to hear the truth, the whole truth and nothing but the truth...

Adam had a hard time meeting Cassie's eyes as she came through the back door, then had trouble looking away. She smiled at him as if nothing had gone down the night before, as if they hadn't kissed and quarreled and promised to clear things up today. It made him hope that maybe she wouldn't push him to talk.

After last night's debacle with his brother, Adam

wasn't sure how to handle things anymore. He still wanted to tell Cassie the truth, but he wanted Alex's full cooperation. And he was determined not to lose his cool again—with Cassie, as he had in the hot tub, or with Alex, as he had during their talk.

After the fact, he'd felt terrible about giving Alex a shiner, especially since he'd still be wearing it for the wedding. And, although Alex had been surprised that Adam had actually taken him up on his suggestion to belt him one, Alex had pulled himself up off the ground without a whimper or a complaint. He'd simply smiled ruefully and hoped his brother felt better.

Trouble was, nothing short of the truth was going to make Adam feel better. He'd thought about all of Alex's arguments last night in favor of keeping mum. In the clear light of day, they didn't wash. Alex thought he was protecting his happiness with Kelly by lying—he even thought he was protecting Cassie and Tyler's happiness—but the truth always came out eventually. And when that happened, no one would be happy.

"Good morning, Cass," Adam said warmly. "I hope you like scrambled." She looked wonderful, so fresh and girl-next-door.

"Scrambled is great," she answered, sitting down at the table.

"Hurry, Mommy," Tyler said, his hands linked around her elbow as he bounced on his heels. "Eat fast, okay?"

"Tyler, leave your mother to eat in peace," Jasper ordered from the living room where he was thumbing through a fishing equipment catalogue. "Have you got your tackle ready, bud?"

Tyler took off, leaving Cassie and Adam alone in the kitchen. Even this marginal privacy felt awkward after last night. And despite her cheerful front, Adam could tell Cassie was tense. She wasn't eating.

"At least drink your orange juice," he suggested.

She looked up, embarrassed. "I'm just not hungry, I guess."

He smiled. "I understand completely."

Cassie nodded, but said nothing. He was a bit puzzled by her restraint, but was too grateful for it to ask questions. She drank her orange juice and they left for Beluga Point in Kenai. Adam had picked that spot for fishing because in addition to salmon he hoped they'd see some white beluga whales for Tyler.

The weather had been excellent since Cassie's arrival on Thursday, but Adam could see clouds gathering over Grewingk Glacier as they found a good spot to throw out their lines. Tyler proved to be an excellent fisherman and his eyes lit up like stars when he got his first nibble. Adam helped him reel in the salmon and laughed out loud at the expression on Tyler's face when he first caught sight of the enormous fish.

"Wow! Look, Mommy. Look, Granddad. He's a *giant!*"

Adam grinned and lifted the ever-present cowboy hat off Tyler's head to ruffle his hair, meeting Cassie's eyes over the crown. "There's some even bigger ones out there, Ty. But we'll catch only enough for dinner and a couple for the freezer, okay?''

"Spoken like a true marine biologist," Cassie commented approvingly.

Jasper limited his catch to just one so Tyler could fish for more than his share, while Cassie watched and cheered them on.

"I thought you'd fish, too," Adam said. "I brought you a rod."

"I love to fish, especially with Ty and Dad, but this experience is so special for Tyler I'd rather just be an observer. His expressions are so fun to watch."

"I know what you mean," Adam agreed. "I can't wait till he sees a whale."

When Tyler did see a whale, his enthusiasm was exhilarating, so much so that Adam realized he must have grown rather blasé over the years to the wonderful creatures he saw on nearly a daily basis and even had the privilege to study. Maybe it was true that you had to see the world through a child's eyes to really appreciate it. And maybe you had to actually spend time with children to appreciate *them*.

Since he and Alex were the only children in his immediate family, there were no nieces or nephews to bounce on their knees or throw in the air until they squealed. They only saw their smaller cousins at large family gatherings, so their experience with children was quite limited. But Adam had found it surprisingly easy to relate to Tyler, to enjoy his company. Maybe if Alex had the same opportunity to spend time with Tyler, he'd decide that chancing Kelly's displeasure was worth the risk to be a father.

This idea stuck with Adam and he made up his mind to make sure, before Cassie and Tyler went back to Montana, that his brother knew what he was giving up by not acknowledging Tyler as his.

By eleven o'clock it had started to sprinkle, then to rain in earnest. They packed up, had lunch at a diner in Kenai, then headed back to Seldovia to get ready for the rehearsal, which was to take place at three o'clock. Tyler immediately went down for a nap in Jasper's room and Cassie retired to her own little cabin without once showing signs of being impatient for their talk. In fact, she seemed as eager as Adam not to be alone with him.

Adam puzzled over this for some time, but Jasper was in a talkative mood and Adam exerted himself to play host until time to get ready for the rehearsal.

ADAM HAD assured her that the rehearsal was informal, followed by dinner at a family-style restaurant in Soldotna, but Cassie took the event quite seriously. She and Tyler would be meeting Adam's family for the first time. She wanted to make a good impression. She still hadn't been given information to the contrary, so she was stubbornly holding on to the belief that Adam was Tyler's father. Especially after watching the two together that morning, Cassie was convinced that Adam couldn't possibly be lying.

Cassie put on a pale yellow, fitted pantsuit, gold hoop earrings and a matching bracelet. She wore her hair down and applied her makeup carefully. She dressed Tyler in a nice pair of khaki pants and a blue pullover shirt that brought out his beautiful blue

Baranof eyes. Her father wore gray slacks, a white Western-style shirt and a black string tie. With his handlebar mustache, he looked like one of the Statler Brothers.

Ironically, Adam's clothing choices were almost identical to what Tyler was wearing! Khaki pants and a blue pullover brought out Adam's beautiful blue Baranof eyes, too. Seeing him and Ty together took Cassie's breath away. Again she told herself he couldn't possibly have lied about being Ty's father, especially since he was going to be introducing them to his family. He wouldn't lie to his whole family, would he?

It had been raining off and on all afternoon, the showers interspersed with brilliant sunshine. Tyler had counted three rainbows so far. The bright blue sky was filled with streaks of fast-moving clouds when they left for the church, which Adam told her was in the old, original town of Ninilchik, a few miles north of Homer on the beach.

Cassie had seen a few Russian Orthodox churches with their charming architecture and onion domes since her arrival, but she was completely unprepared for the picturesque view that greeted her as they came over the hilltop and down into the tiny village at the mouth of the Ninilchik River.

The church was built of white timber with a steep green roof. Although it was quite small, it had five onion domes topped with crosses. To one side was a graveyard filled with more pristine-white crosses, many of the burial sites enclosed within white picket fences about two feet high.

"This is so charming!" Cassie exclaimed. "I can

certainly see why Alex and Kelly decided to have the ceremony here.''

''At sunset, the view as you look across Cook Inlet can be breathtaking,'' Adam told her.

''Who all's going to be here, son?'' Jasper asked from the back seat.

''The church is quite small, so just the wedding party...which is big enough as it is with Kelly's four sisters as bridesmaids. Their spouses and kids and other immediate family members of the wedding party will meet us at the restaurant for the rehearsal dinner later. You won't meet the whole batch of Baranofs and Armstrongs till tomorrow.'' Adam added wryly, ''That'll be a mob scene.''

''Will there be *some* kids today, Uncle Adam?'' Tyler wanted to know, his voice a bit plaintive.

Adam smiled at Tyler in the rearview mirror. ''There'll be two. Kelly's niece and nephew are flower girl and ring bearer. I think they're just about your age, Tyler.''

Tyler nodded. ''Good.''

Adam parked in front of the building just as another four-wheel-drive pulled into the lot. ''It looks like Mom and Dad are here,'' he announced.

Now the flutterings in Cassie's stomach magnified, felt more like hummingbirds than butterflies. What would they say? What would *she* say? What would they think of her and Ty? Would they blame her for bringing Tyler to Alaska? For being careless enough to get pregnant in the first place?

By the time everyone was out of the cars and lined up on the walkway in front of the church for introductions, Cassie had worked herself into a panic. She was surprised and comforted when Adam slipped his fingers over hers and held her hand tightly. She looked up into his face and realized he was as nervous as she was.

"Mom, Dad, this is Cassandra, her son, Tyler, and her father, Jasper Montgomery. Jasper, Cassie, Ty...my parents, Peter and Monica Baranof."

Adam's father was tall and dark with striking wings of gray over his temples. His mother was tall, too, and—surprisingly—a blonde. They were handsome people both, and Cassie could see where Adam and Alex got their good looks. Neither parent looked much over forty, although they'd have to be even if they'd had the twins at an early age.

"It's nice to meet you," Peter said politely, his brow slightly furrowed, his gaze tense and uneasy as he briefly scanned Cassie and Jasper, then settled with keen interest on Tyler.

"Same here," Jasper returned as he reached out to shake Peter's hand.

The two fathers shook hands, then Tyler extended his hand to Mr. Baranof, too. Adam's father looked surprised but rather pleased and bent to shake Tyler's hand. Neither Cassie nor Monica had spoken yet. Cassie was still drumming up her courage, and Monica was too busy staring at Tyler.

"My goodness, it's uncanny how much he looks like—"

"Er...Mom, did I mention that Ty caught some king salmon this morning?" Adam quickly interrupted. Apparently Alex had told their parents everything but the *tiny* little detail that Tyler didn't know Adam was his father. "Show her how big they were, Tyler."

"*This* big," Tyler said, his eyes wide with remembered awe, his arms stretched as far as they would go. "Uncle Adam helped me reel 'im in."

Monica and Peter stared at Tyler as if entranced. Then, finally, Monica broke away long enough to flit a puzzled and disapproving glance at her son. "*Uncle* Adam helped you?"

"Yeah. We caught four of 'em. Two for dinner and two for the freezer."

Tyler's words were followed by silence. Cassie still hadn't said anything and Adam's parents seemed tongue-tied and incapable of doing anything but staring at their grandson. Tyler was beginning to fidget, so Jasper made a move.

"I think I'll walk Tyler around the grounds," he told them. "I expect you four need a little time to…er…clear the air. Come on, son."

After Jasper walked away with Tyler toward the quaint and beautiful graveyard, Peter and Monica's gaze shifted to Adam. "Why does he call you uncle?" Peter immediately demanded to know.

"It was my idea, Mr. Baranof," Cassie said. "I didn't want Tyler to know Adam was his father until…until certain things were worked out."

Monica and Peter turned their attention to her. As if seeming to finally recognize how uncomfortable Cassie was, Monica smiled and touched her arm. "Please call us by our first names, Cassie. This must be hard for you, dear, and we haven't made it any easier, have we? We haven't exchanged a single civil word! You'll have to forgive us for behaving so strangely. It was such a shock when Alex told us. I mean, to find out you have a grandson who is four years old that you had no idea existed... Then, just when we thought we were getting used to the idea, seeing him in person threw us both for a loop." She turned to Peter. "Isn't that right, dear?"

Peter nodded, but looked sternly at Adam. "What I don't understand is why you haven't called and spoken to us directly, Adam. Why did we have to hear everything from Alex?"

"I found out about this the same night you did," Adam answered, his tone a bit defensive. "I've needed time to think."

"Well, if he's still calling you Uncle Adam, it sounds to me like you haven't been thinking nearly enough...or *clearly* enough. Alex told us you were having doubts about what to do. I gather you still haven't decided whether or not to be a father to the boy?" Peter glanced down at Cassie and Adam's locked hands. "What *is* going on, Adam?"

Cassie was feeling more and more uncomfortable. She had thought Adam would have called his parents by now, would have talked the situation over with them, explained that Tyler was unaware of the familial connection between them. That he hadn't done so made Adam appear less committed and more confused and conflicted than ever. But she certainly didn't want Adam in their lives if he had to be coerced and shamed by his parents to do it.

Hurt and discouraged, Cassie said, "Maybe I should leave you and your parents alone to talk, Adam." She pulled her hand free and turned to go.

"Cassie, I'll go with you," Monica said hurriedly. "Why don't you and I get to know one another a little better before the rest of the wedding party arrives?"

Adam watched Cassie and his mother walk away, his heart heavy. He hadn't handled this very well. He should have called his parents before today and made sure they understood what was going on, saved Cassie this confrontation. But how could he do that when, from hour to hour, *he* wasn't even sure what was going on? Alex had put him in a damnable position... No. *He* had put himself in a damnable position. And Cassie, too.

"Well, Adam, *are* you going to tell me what's going on?" his father repeated.

Adam was tempted to tell him exactly what was going on. Oh, was he ever tempted! His dad had always been a tremendous support to him, a great confidant in times of trouble. But, no, Adam still wanted Alex's willing cooperation in this coming-clean business. He felt the only way Alex would really learn from this situation was to come to the conclusion himself that truth was more important than any tenuous happiness based on lies. Alex had to be the one to recognize his responsibility in this situation and fess up, or he'd blame Adam for squealing on him for the rest of their lives.

Adam lifted his hands in a helpless gesture. "Dad, things are still up in the air. I *can't* tell you yet what will happen. And, please, although I'm sure the news will be whispered from ear to ear and everyone will know anyway—thanks to Alex—I'd rather the fact that I'm Tyler's father isn't *publicly* discussed. Tyler mustn't know. It's for his own protection."

Adam's father didn't try to hide his displeasure. "Adam, I'm disappointed in you. If I were father to that child, I'd claim him immediately and be as much a part of his life as possible. Obviously, Cassie would welcome your involvement…and not, I think, just for the boy's sake. Do you really think you're being fair to her, leading her on this way?"

Adam rubbed his forehead. "Dad, I *care* about Cassie. I care about both of them!"

"Then why doesn't Tyler know who you really are? And why aren't you publicly acknowledging him as your son? As much as he resembles you, even if Alex and the others who know are discreet, everyone will guess the truth, anyway. Aunt Zelda in particular can spot Baranof blood from a block away. She won't be here today, but you'll have to face her tomorrow for sure. *And* all the others. As for Cassie…"

He looked over to where Cassie and Monica were standing several yards away, looking out over the tiny cemetery where Jasper and Tyler were carefully wending their way around the neatly fenced graves. Both smiling, they were deep in conversation. "She seems very sweet, Adam. Too sweet to trifle with."

Adam clenched his jaw. He never imagined it would be so hard to lie to his father, to endure his disappointment and censure. "I told you, Dad, I need time," he repeated wearily.

His father shook his head. "This isn't like you, Adam. I think there's more to this than you're saying. But let me leave this word of wisdom with you, son. Family is more important than anything else. If you really do care about Cassie and Tyler—and if it's the kind of caring that families are built on—don't take too long to figure out what to do.''

Adam nodded, a constriction in his throat making it impossible to speak. His father didn't know the whole story, but even if he did he'd still be disappointed in him. Maybe more so. But he'd said words that rang true, words that fueled Adam's own sense of urgency. *If you really do care, don't take too long to figure out what to do.*

His father squeezed his shoulder and walked away as Kelly's car pulled up with her four sisters inside. He saw two other cars coming down the hill, neither of which were Alex's. He wondered how his brother would explain his black eye.

The way Adam was feeling at that moment, he would have gladly blackened Alex's other eye so he'd have a matched set! He wished more than anything that he could announce to the members of his family attending this rehearsal that he really was Tyler's father. Then repeat the announcement tomorrow at the wedding reception in front of the entire Baranof clan. Hell, he wished he could shout it from the summit of the highest peak of the Chigmit Mountains!

But it wouldn't be true. And it wouldn't be fair to Cassie and Tyler. Tyler must never be told such a lie because when the truth came out—which it inevitably would—Cassie would have to try to explain to her son that it wasn't Adam but Alex who was his father. Talk about confusing a kid. Talk about childhood trauma!

No, it seemed Adam's only recourse was to work

on his brother to come clean of his own free will. But how?

AFTER LISTENING to Adam's defensive exchange with his father, Cassie had been close to tears. But Monica Baranof had changed all that. With a warmth and graciousness Cassie couldn't help but respond to, Monica made her feel right at home.

First she asked Cassie questions about her life in Montana, her job, her pastimes. Then, as Jasper and Tyler rejoined them, she encouraged Tyler to tell her all about his Alaskan adventure. By the way her eyes lit up as he enthused about fishing, whales and the eagle's nest, it was obvious she was as thoroughly smitten by her grandson as Cassie had hoped she'd be. It didn't hurt, of course, that he was the spitting image of her own beloved boys. Tyler responded to her, too, but how could he not when she looked at him with such love in her eyes?

The possibility that Monica might not be part of Tyler's life when this trip was over was a thought that couldn't help but dampen Cassie's happiness, but she hadn't given up hope on Adam finally realizing how important Tyler was to him...and, dare she hope, how important *she* was, too?

Monica took Jasper by the arm as she walked them around the outside of the church, pointing out the historically significant details of the building. She explained that they couldn't go inside because the priest—John, a family friend—hadn't arrived yet to open the doors. And once they were inside, reverence for the religious sanctity of the small building would preclude social chattering. John would guide them through the wedding rehearsal and then they'd leave to do more socializing at the restaurant.

Cassie appreciated Monica's attention to her father. She was sure he was feeling threatened by the sudden introduction of more grandparents in Tyler's life, but was too fair-minded and caring to show it.

She glanced over at Adam right after his father walked away to welcome Kelly and four other women. Their eyes met. Adam's gaze conveyed a sort of sad apology. She supposed he was sorry he hadn't been able to make up his mind yet, hadn't better prepared her and his parents for this meeting. Her heart ached, but she didn't go to him. *He* would have to come to *her*. She wasn't going to even inadvertently put pressure on him, especially here among his family and friends.

Things started getting boisterous as the rest of the wedding party seemed to arrive all at once. Cassie watched from a distance as two young men jumped out of a Jeep with mud-encrusted tires. They had a little boy with them. A gray-haired couple arrived in a rented sedan with a little girl bouncing in her seat belt between them. They smiled but seemed reserved and a little disapproving of the festive exuberance of the young people.

"Those are Kelly's parents," Monica explained.

"But they're so much older than you and Peter!" Cassie exclaimed without thinking.

Monica smiled. "They aren't that much older, but they did have children at a later age than most couples. See all those bridesmaids and the two ushers?"

"Yes?"

"All Kelly's sisters and brothers. Kelly's the youngest."

"Oh." Cassie was amazed. She had no idea Kelly's family was so large. And the children seemed so different from the parents, so talkative and full of life.

"Come with me and I'll introduce you to them, then to the others."

Tyler, always a sociable child, immediately asked his mother's permission to make friends with the girl and boy. She said, "Okay, hon. But don't go out of the churchyard and stay away from any mud. And when the rehearsal begins, you must come inside, sit quietly and be respectful." Only half listening, Tyler nodded eagerly and was off to make friends.

Cassie noticed with pleasure that Adam joined their group en route to meet the Armstrongs. He gave her an encouraging smile. She smiled back, glad he would be there to support her while the introductions were performed.

Halfway there, however, another four-wheel-drive pulled into the parking lot. There were two men inside, Alex and another usher, she supposed. Suddenly she stopped in her tracks and stared. Alex stepped out of the vehicle, smiling sheepishly...and sporting a big black eye!

Chapter Ten

As he moved to the center of the group, Alex's appearance caused a general uproar. There were exclamations, questions and jokes about his eye.

"What a shiner!"

"Trying to match your eye to your tux, Alex?"

"How'd that happen? Run into someone's fist?"

"Kelly's, I bet. You two smoothin' out last minute wrinkles in the prenup?"

Alex laughed and shrugged while Kelly hung on to his arm. "Kelly knows better than to hit me where it shows," he joked, after which Kelly punched him playfully on the shoulder. "The truth is—" his gaze traveled across the few feet that separated him from Adam "—my brother hit me."

Cassie was stunned. Everyone was stunned, including, apparently, Adam. He stood as stiff as a board, meeting his brother's bold gaze with a guarded question in his. Or was that a *hopeful* expression? Cassie couldn't really tell.

"What's going on?" Jasper whispered in her ear.

"I don't know," Cassie whispered back. "I...I

never thought Adam would actually hit Alex over what happened.''

"What do you mean...over what happened?" Jasper asked suspiciously.

"Shhh, Dad."

Adam finally spoke up. "Alex is right. I did hit him in the eye last night."

Both sets of parents exchanged glances. "But why, Adam?" his mother wanted to know.

"Why don't you tell her, Alex?" Adam suggested.

Alex continued to stare at Adam with a sort of belligerent half smile on his lips. Cassie was horrified. It seemed like her innocent mistake last night was about to be broadcast to the world! But why would Adam encourage his brother to embarrass her like this?

Suddenly Alex broke eye contact with Adam, looked around at the tense, expectant group and laughed. "Boy, I sure had you guys going, didn't I? It was an accident! Adam and I were horsing around last night, doing a little fake boxing by moonlight, when his fist accidentally connected with my eye. Take my advice, never box in the dark. We had a good laugh over it, but neither of us thought it would turn this ugly. Did we, Adam?"

"No, I never thought it would turn this ugly," Adam answered in measured tones.

The black eye explained, everyone laughed and continued to socialize. Well, not *everyone*. Cassie was still feeling a little shaken by what she had feared would be an extremely embarrassing way to be introduced to the group, not to mention her certainty that Kelly might get a little upset if she found out about the accidental kiss.

The Armstrongs stared at Alex and looked as if someone had forced them to eat worms, and Adam and Jasper stood on either side of Cassie, silent as tombs.

Suddenly Monica took her arm and Jasper's arm and steered them toward the Armstrongs. "Come on, you two," she whispered. "Kelly's parents can't take their eyes off Alex's black eye. Let's divert them!"

Cassie looked over her shoulder and was relieved to see Adam following them. Monica introduced her and Jasper to the Armstrongs and they did manage to divert the scowling couple from unpleasant thoughts connected with the black eye...possibly thoughts having to do with how they were going to answer the impertinent questions that would be asked when they showed off their daughter's wedding pictures! But now those disapproving gazes were fixed on Cassie.

"Nice to meet you," Cassie said in a determinedly friendly tone.

"Same here," Jasper added, as he reached out to shake Mr. Armstrong's hand.

"Nice to meet you, too," they answered in unison, but Cassie could immediately tell that the Armstrongs had heard all about her and Tyler and didn't approve. Their manner was outwardly polite, but she'd seen that appraising look before. Her assessment was unfortunately confirmed when Mrs. Armstrong asked, "Oh, so you decided that it would be best not to bring the little boy?"

Cassie bristled. Did Mrs. Armstrong mean what she thought she meant? That Tyler was an embarrassment? She probably thought it would be best if all three of the Montgomerys stayed at home!

"I take Tyler everywhere I go, Mrs. Armstrong," she quietly assured her, smiling faintly. She looked around the churchyard, saw Tyler and pointed. "That's him right over there. He's the one who looks *just like Adam.*" She probably shouldn't have, but Cassie couldn't help rubbing it in a little!

But Cassie regretted rubbing it in when Mrs. Armstrong blushed and looked flustered. She probably hadn't meant to be offensive. Cassie didn't want to offend anyone, either, much less Kelly's parents, but when it came to Tyler she never made excuses. A terrible tension hung over their little group.

"Come on, Cassie, Jasper," Monica said, her smile forced. "I have several more people to introduce you to."

"Let me introduce them, Mom," Adam offered.

Monica nodded gratefully, looking as embarrassed by Mrs. Armstrong's comment as if she'd made it herself. Adam took Cassie's elbow and guided her into the center of the group. Jasper followed. Adam smoothly introduced them both, then announced proudly, "And I'm sure you know who that little guy over there is...the one who looks just like me?"

Now it was Cassie's turn to be flustered...but in a *good* way! A *very* good way! Adam had seemed passively supportive before, but now he was taking control and actually behaving as though he were proud of Tyler and wanted the whole world to know!

"I see John's coming," Adam said, lifting his chin in the direction of another car coming down the hill. He turned to Alex. "Before he arrives and gets the rehearsal underway, would you and Kelly like to meet Tyler?"

Cassie thought Alex hesitated, but then he casually answered, "Sure. Why not? It's about time I met the nephew I've been hearing so much about."

"I'd love to meet him, too," Kelly assured them. "It looks like he's already made friends with my other niece and nephew."

Now Cassie was sure Adam was coming around to this fatherhood thing! He certainly seemed determined to introduce Tyler to his Uncle Alex. She threw Jasper an encouraged smile as she walked away with Adam, Alex and Kelly. She was disappointed when he did not return the smile, but instead looked rather grim.

When they reached Tyler, he was demonstrating the best way to throw a lasso. "If I hadda rope, it'd be a lot easier," he was explaining to the little boy and girl sitting cross-legged on a dry patch of sidewalk and watching him raptly.

"Ty?"

Tyler turned and looked up at Cassie. "Yeah, Mom? Is it time for the dumb ol' weddin' rehearsal already?"

Cassie smiled apologetically at Kelly. "Just about."

"But we were havin' fun!"

"Watch how you talk about the wedding, sweetheart. We've brought the bride and the groom over to meet you.''

"Oh," Tyler said quietly. Chagrined, he looked up shyly at Alex and Kelly. Adam was standing right next to Alex and it abruptly occurred to Cassie that Tyler had never seen them together before or even knew that Adam had a twin.

His eyes widened with interest. "I can tell you're brothers," he stated. "I can tell 'cause you look a lot alike."

Cassie laughed. "They're not just brothers, Ty. They're twins. They look *exactly* alike."

Tyler cocked his head to the side. "No, Mommy. Not ec'zactly alike. One of 'em's got a black eye."

Everyone laughed. "You're right, but Alex hasn't always got a black eye, Tyler. When his eye looks normal, there's really no way to tell them apart."

"*I* can tell them apart," Tyler insisted. "Even without the black eye."

Cassie knew Tyler wasn't just bragging and she was impressed by her son's perception. She looked at Adam and Alex and still saw absolutely nothing physical about them that was different enough to be able to tell them apart. But there definitely was a difference in their expressions as they looked down at Tyler.

It was strange, but Alex seemed anxious and impatient. Perhaps because he knew the priest had arrived, he was eager to get on with the rehearsal. Or maybe he just wasn't used to children and didn't know what was expected of him.

Adam, on the other hand, had a gleam in his eye that clearly revealed an affection for Tyler. To Cassie it was just further proof that Adam was Ty's father, not Alex.

"You're right, Ty. This is my brother, Alex," Adam said, leaning down and resting his hands on his bent knees so he could be eye-level with Tyler. "He's the lucky guy getting married to that pretty lady over there." He hooked a thumb over his shoulder. "Her name is Kelly. Why don't you shake hands?"

Adam watched while Tyler reached up and Alex reached down. He knew he was forcing this meeting, this contact between them. But, if left to his own devices, Alex would probably have avoided Tyler completely.

"Pleased t' meet cha," Tyler said, shaking hands in a very manly way.

"Pleased to meet you," Alex answered rather faintly.

"Oh, Alex, isn't he adorable?" Kelly cooed.

Tyler frowned at the sissified adjective being applied to him and snatched a glance over his shoulder at his little friends to make sure they weren't laughing. Adam couldn't believe Kelly was talking about Tyler as if he weren't even there.

"Those eyes, that *chin!* Alex, it's just like your—"

"So, I hear you went fishing today, Tyler," Alex interrupted as he gave Kelly a gentle elbow in the ribs.

"Yeah. Me and Uncle Adam caught some really big salmon." His head cocked to the side, his brows drawn together in concentration. "Say, if he's my uncle, are you my uncle, too?"

Adam watched Alex's reaction. He wondered if he would be able to tell Tyler to his face that he was his *uncle*. At least Adam had had the advantage of actually being his uncle. There was an instant of painful confusion in Alex's expression, but then he quickly answered, "Sure, Tyler. Call me uncle. I like the sound of that."

Adam was disappointed. Alex seemed to have put up an impenetrable barrier, making certain that Tyler would have no effect on him at all. He was single-minded in his goal to get married without making any earth-shattering—or *engagement-endangering*—confessions.

Alex turned to Kelly with a smile. "I think it's time we got this show on the road, don't you, hon? I see John's opened the doors to the church and our parents are waiting for us."

"Kelly, why don't you and Cassie and the kids go on in?" Adam said pleasantly. "I need to speak with Alex for just a minute."

Kelly chuckled. "Okay. But try to control yourself, Adam. Don't blacken his other eye, too!"

Cassie left, but threw a questioning look over her shoulder as she urged Tyler ahead with a hand resting on his neck. As soon as the women were out of earshot, Adam turned his back to the church, crossed his arms, and faced Alex. "What was that little show you put on when you first got here?" he inquired grimly.

"What show?" Alex muttered.

"You know exactly what I mean."

Alex shrugged. "Oh, you mean telling them that

you'd hit me? I suppose you thought I'd tell them I'd walked into a tree or some dumb thing.''

"I certainly never expected you to tell the truth, but I wish—''

"You wish I hadn't scared you like that? Well, Adam, you're so keen on telling the truth all the time and I just thought I'd give you an idea—just the *tiniest* taste, of course—of what it would be like to tell Kelly, Cassie and our families the truth about who Tyler's real father is.''

"Alex, I wasn't going to say I wish you hadn't scared me. I was hoping like hell you'd spill your guts, tell it all! I was praying you'd finally realized that there was no other choice but to tell the truth. I was so disappointed when you backed down and resorted to that stupid boxing story.''

Alex sneered. "I don't believe you.''

"Believe me. No matter how much trouble it causes initially, you know you have to tell Kelly, and I have to tell Cassie, exactly what we've done. We have to tell the truth. You *know* it, Alex.''

Alex shook his head. "No, I don't know it. And what about you and *your* little tricks? What's the idea of dragging us over here to meet Tyler? Meeting him doesn't make any difference in the way I feel. He's a nice kid, but so what? You're wasting your time and your breath, bro. Give it up.'' He looked over Adam's shoulder at the church. "Now, if you don't mind, it's not polite to leave a bride waiting at the altar.''

As Alex walked past, Adam caught his arm and growled, "Fine, little brother, but think about what you'll be saying tomorrow when you take your vows for real. Think about what it means to be the person Kelly will promise to love and honor for the rest of her life, and what it means to love and honor her back. Think about it, Alex.''

CASSIE HAD NEVER before attended a marriage ceremony in a Russian Orthodox church, or anything like it. While this was simply a rehearsal, she was still deeply moved. The priest explained each of the steps in the ceremony, its meaning and importance, then actually walked them through some of it.

The couple exchanged rings right at the beginning, then held hands throughout the rest of the service. The theme that stood out most to Cassie was the idea that as husband and wife they'd share everything, joys as well as sorrows. That they would bear one another's burdens.

Watching Alex's and Kelly's profiles from her seat on the far left in the front, she thought Kelly glowed. Alex, on the other hand, seemed wooden and preoccupied. Not *pleasantly* preoccupied, either. She caught Adam's eye once during the rehearsal and his smile was bleak. This was supposed to be a joyous event, but the brothers Baranof didn't look very happy.

When Adam had sent them ahead into the church so he could have a private moment with Alex, she couldn't help but wonder if they were exchanging angry words over last night's accidental kiss. And how about Alex's black eye? Was that really an accident, too?

Cassie knew she couldn't ignore the tension between the brothers anymore and blind herself to clues that pointed in a direction she couldn't bear thinking about. She had to find out what was going on between Adam and Alex and if it had anything to do with a summer's night five years ago in Nye, Montana. She had to ask Adam questions and demand answers. She had to know the truth, no matter how much it might hurt.

She sighed and it must have been louder than she thought. Her dad's arm crept around her shoulder and she looked up into sympathetic eyes. "Don't worry, Cass," he whispered, almost as if he'd read her mind. "We're gonna sort this out...*real soon*."

SOMEHOW CASSIE made it through the rehearsal dinner. Tyler had fun with the children and Cassie enjoyed meeting more of Adam's family, all of whom treated her with friendly, congenial attention, but underneath it all, she felt a stomach-churning tension. There was never a private opportunity to speak to Adam alone, so she had no choice but to wait until they got home before unburdening her heart and mind of so many emotions and questions.

Adam and Alex kept a healthy distance between them the whole time. And when toasts were made to the happy couple, Adam's was conspicuously absent. When finally asked why the best man wasn't proposing a toast, Adam answered, "I'm saving mine for tomorrow."

It poured rain on the way home. Everyone in the Jeep was quiet and Tyler fell asleep en route, not even stirring during the ferry ride. He was happily exhausted from hours of playing with Kelly's nieces and nephews. Cassie tucked him in bed as soon as they got home, then eagerly went back to the living room to find Adam and demand to know what was going on between him and Alex and what it had to do with her. But when she got there, she found only her father waiting for her.

"Dad, where's Adam?"

"He's down at your cabin, waiting for you."

Cassie bit her lip. "So, he knows I want to talk?"

"Looks that way."

Cassie started toward the door, but Jasper stopped her with a light touch on the shoulder. "Cass?"

Cassie turned. "Yes, Dad?"

"Before you go, I just want you to know that while I've kept my mouth shut for a spell now, I've been keepin' my eyes and my mind open. If you're still confused after talking to Adam, you talk to me. I have some pretty good ideas about what's going on here, but I think it's best Adam tells you first." Cassie nodded. Her father sounded so serious and certain. That wasn't a good sign. Suppose it was true that Adam wasn't Ty's father? Suppose—

"Get goin', Cass. The sooner the better," her father advised.

Cassie nodded again, her stomach a labyrinth of knots. She stepped out onto the porch and closed the door behind her. The rain drummed on the roof like thunder. There were two umbrellas leaning against the outside wall of the house, but, on an impulse, she ignored them and ran down the path to the cabin without any protection from the downpour.

The shock of cold rain against her skin felt wonderful! It cleared her mind, sharpened her determination to face whatever possible unpleasantness lay before her. But she still hadn't given up hope that there was a logical explanation for the animosity between Adam and Alex, for the conflicting messages she got from Adam about his feelings for her and Tyler, and for the "chest thing."

She reached the cabin, went in and stood dripping on the hardwood floor by the door. Adam was standing in the kitchen, but turned when he heard her enter. His eyes narrowed with consternation.

"Cassie, what were you thinking coming down here without protecting yourself from the rain?" He hurried to the bathroom and came out with a towel. "That rain is damned cold. You'll get sick!" He held the towel out to her.

Cassie said nothing, did nothing, just stood with her arms crossed over her chest like a naughty, humbled child. She was starting to feel the chill, but Adam's concern seemed so real, so wonderful! If she got sick, maybe it would be worth it just to have seen Adam a little frightened, to have enjoyed him being a bit of a fussbudget for her sake. He stood over her, scowling like a thundercloud, and she couldn't help but smile up at him.

She watched him melt, relent, then finally smile back at her. "You're an idiot," he said tenderly, then started to blot the rain off her face with the towel, his ministrations as gentle as a lover's.

Cassie hadn't had seduction on her mind when she left the big house, but now she did. How could this man be so gentle and caring and be the remorseless liar he'd have to be if her and her father's suspicions were true? How could she feel this way about him if he wasn't the wonderful man he seemed to be?

Maybe if he held her… Maybe feeling warm and safe in his arms was the cure for all her doubts and fears. Maybe if he made love to her again, as he had in Nye, she'd recognize her lover from all those years ago. Maybe…

ADAM WAS ENCHANTED. He had asked Jasper to send Cassie down to the cabin so they could talk. But looking down at her now, at the glistening rain on her soft skin, the wet shine on her coyly curved lips, the shivering pose, the loving and hopeful expression in her eyes, all he wanted to do was take care of her. Protect her. Warm her up…one way or the other.

He knew which way he'd *like* to warm her up…but he also knew which way he *should* warm her up. Steeling himself against her sweet allure, he ordered, "Get in the bathroom right away, Cass. Rub yourself down with a towel, dry your hair and change into something warm. I'll have a hot cup of tea waiting for you when you get out."

Cassie seemed simply amused by his sternness, and she didn't budge an inch. He knew she must be freezing because he could see the goose bumps on her arms.

Exasperated, he asked, "Cassie, what's wrong with you? Do you want to get sick?"

She rolled a shoulder. "Will you take care of me if I do?"

Adam swallowed. He had certainly not expected this blatant flirtatiousness from Cassie, especially now when they had important things to discuss. But he liked it…*a lot*…and it was wreaking havoc with his good intentions. He had asked her to meet him here so he could apologize for the tactlessness and narrow-minded behavior of the Armstrongs. So he could explain why he'd been so wishy-washy about everything. So he could tell her the *truth*. He couldn't wait for Alex forever. He didn't even seem to know his brother anymore.

"Cassie, I asked you here so we could talk. We can't talk till you've warmed up. Why are you being so difficult?"

She rolled that sexy shoulder again. Hell, where had she learned to do that? "I'll change if you'll help me undress. My fingers are numb with cold. I don't think I can manage the buttons."

Adam raised a dubious brow. "They are? Let me see." He reached out and took her hands in his. She was right! Her fingers were like ice cubes! If she was already this cold, there was no time to lose.

"I don't know why you're doing this, Cass, but it's not going to work," he informed her. She looked up at him, demure and unrepentant. She was adorable with wet, straggling hair in her eyes, a come-hither pout to her lower lip.

"We're *not* going to make love, because we have to talk, do you hear?" he continued to bluster like a frustrated schoolteacher. She said nothing, but her teeth were starting to chatter and that was the last straw. He bent and swooped her into his arms. She gave a little surprised squeal, then twined her arms around his neck. "I'll help you undress, but that's all. That's *all*, Cass!"

Adam carried her into the bathroom, feeling her slim body shivering against him. He realized only a hot bath was going to warm her up. He set his jaw with grim determination. Somehow he was going to get through this without making love to her.

Adam set her feet on the bathroom floor, reached down to remove her shoes and thin cotton socks while she braced her hands on his shoulders to keep steady. He straightened up, then barked like a drill sergeant, "All right. Take off your clothes."

"I…I t-told y-you, Adam, my f-fingers are t-too cold."

He believed her. She was shaking all over. Quickly he unbuttoned the top of her pantsuit, embarrassed to observe his own warm fingers almost as shaky as hers. He peeled off the wet top and tried not to notice the pretty lace bra she was wearing, especially since the rain had soaked through and rendered it virtually transparent. Rosy, erect nipples showed through the delicate netting.

"Turn around," he ordered, his voice gruff and almost angry.

"D-don't be such a b-bear," she complained, wrinkling her nose at him before turning around. "I d-didn't d-do this on p-purpose."

"That's the damnedest thing about you, Cassie," Adam said ruefully. "You don't plan to be sexy as hell. It just happens naturally."

"Th-thank you, I th-think," she stuttered.

"Don't thank me, just try to stand still."

He unsnapped her bra, slipped the flimsy straps over her creamy shoulders, then the insubstantial scrap of lace fell to the bathroom floor. She started to turn around. He held her still with firm hands on her upper arms. "No. Stay facing that direction, if you don't mind."

She turned her head and smiled back at him. "W-what if I d-didn't plan the seduction, b-but now I w-want it, n-need it, m-more than anything?"

"What you need and ought to want more than anything, young lady, is a hot bath," Adam informed her, trying to ignore the way her words had fanned the hot flame of desire already burning in every molecule of his body. "Now let's...er...get those pants off."

There was a zipper on the side of Cassie's slacks. He unzipped it, then hooked his thumbs in the waistband. As the wet slacks slid over her shapely hips, a pair of white bikini panties was revealed. Swallowing hard, he shut his eyes until the slacks were on the floor, then she leaned on his shoulder with one hand and pulled them over her feet.

"You can leave your panties on. Now stand to the side while I turn on the water." Adam continued to avert his eyes from the beautiful, shivering, almost naked woman who stood not twelve inches away from him as he turned the water on full bore and adjusted its temperature.

Maybe this was part of the payback he deserved for lying to her, he mused as sweat collected on his upper lip. Having her so close, so willing, and so unattainable... Well, he deserved to suffer. But if he'd had a choice, he would have rather had hot bamboo shoots shoved under his fingernails than *this*.

"It's just right now, so step in. Be careful. Don't slip."

"W-what about b-bubbles?"

Adam laughed and looked up at her, inadvertently glimpsing lovely pale globes and pink, puckered nipples behind her loosely crossed arms. He looked away, but not before the rest of her slim curves had made an impression on his already hysterical hormones.

"Just get in, Cass."

He waited, but she didn't move, so he heaved a beleaguered sigh and stood up. "I'll look in the cupboard, but since I'm a bachelor, I can pretty well guarantee—"

Whoops. There it was, a big bottle of vanilla-bean-and-gardenia bubble bath. Now he remembered dimly a weekend with a pretty brunette from Sitka and her penchant for frequent soaks in scented suds.

"Y-you found s-some, d-didn't you?"

"Yes," he answered tersely. "And I'll only let you use it if you don't ask me where it came from. Now get in the tub, Cassie, before I throw you in!"

This time she obeyed. Not a little relieved to finally have his hypothermia patient in hot water— not to mention a foreseeable end to this session of torture he was enduring!—he waited until she was sitting down, then stood over the tub and stared at the wall as he poured the bubble bath somewhere, he hoped, near the running water.

"Hey! You're sp-splashing it all over the place!" Cassie exclaimed, laughing. "G-get closer, Adam. I d-don't bite!"

"That's what you said in the hot tub," he muttered, setting down the bottle of bubble bath on the vanity counter.

"I didn't b-bite you, did I?"

He wouldn't have minded it she had...

"C-come on down to my level, Adam. It's the only w-way you can swoosh w-warm w-water over my back. I'm still s-so c-cold!"

She did still sound cold. "Well, I'll swoosh your back with water, but then I'm leaving. But before I start swooshing, I want you to splash the water around and make lots of bubbles. It'll...er...provide a little camouflage for your...er...self." *And some much needed peace of mind for me!*

She chortled like a child, gleefully enjoying his agony. "All right, I'm splashing. There! Is that g-good enough?"

Adam took a cautious look. She was smiling up at him through a veritable bonanza of bubbles. The water was still pouring into the tub and Cassie was nearly up to her chin in big, round, shiny bubbles. Foamy white suds dotted her face, stuck to her hair and the end of her nose, and even floated in the air around her. She looked adorable...and more desirable than ever.

"Maybe I overdid the bubble bath," he said wryly.

"Well, it certainly covers me up. Isn't that what you wanted?"

"You don't sound cold anymore," he hedged. "Are you sure you still need your back swooshed?"

She immediately started chattering her teeth. "Faker," he accused, but he got down on his knees anyway, turned off the tap, picked up a big blue sponge and started squeezing hot water over her back.

"Oh, Adam, that feels sooo good," she crooned,

her eyes closed, her eyelashes fat and spiky against her pink cheeks. "Don't stop. Please don't stop!"

"You sound like one of those organic shampoo commercials," he teased weakly. *Or my favorite dream about you.*

"Just don't stop," she repeated in a husky voice.

Adam didn't want to stop, but pretty soon he'd have to. He quit squeezing the water over her back and started moving the sponge up and down her supple skin, admiring the curve of her backbone, the graceful dip of her slim waist.

It was plenty hot and steamy in the bathroom, but Adam knew his rising temperature had more to do with his occupation than his location. And if he didn't get out of there pretty soon—

Suddenly she opened her eyes and turned to look at him. Her face was only a couple of inches away. Her mouth kissably close.

"Come on, Adam. I know you want to kiss me. So why don't you already?"

He shook his head firmly. "No, Cass. We have to talk."

She stuck out her bubble-dappled chin. "If you don't kiss me, I'll have to take matters into my own hands."

He paused to wonder what she meant, to consider what to do, to say…an instant too long. She laughed and grabbed his shirtfront with surprisingly strong foam-covered fingers. There was a brief struggle, after which Adam found himself dragged over the rim of the rub and into the bubble bath with Cassie.

Chapter Eleven

"Cassie, *what're you doing?*"

Water lapped over the side of the tub and onto the floor as Adam struggled to sit up. There was obviously way too much water in the tub for two bodies. And way too much temptation...

She slid into a position behind him, wrapped her legs around his waist and her arms around his chest. "I should think it's perfectly obvious what I'm doing, Adam. I'm simply trying to warm myself up by borrowing a little of your body heat."

Well, he had plenty to share.

He tried to gently pry her arms from around his chest. The feel of her warm, firm breasts against his back, even through the thin material of his shirt, was too delectable for words. She was stealing his breath away. She was stealing his will to resist.

"That's a bunch of hooey," he argued halfheartedly. "You're as warm as toast by now."

"Oh, you have no idea," she murmured against his ear, then kissed and nuzzled his neck.

"Oh, I think I do," he answered in a rasp. "But this bath business is risky stuff. If you've ever bathed with a man before, you know it can lead to…to *more,* Cass, and I don't think we're…we're ready to—''

"You know, I've never taken a bath with another person. Certainly not someone of the opposite sex," she mused, her breath against his ear sending chills up and down his spine. "In fact, you're the only man I've ever slept with."

This confession stunned Adam. He knew she'd been a virgin when Alex slept with her, but she hadn't slept with another man since then? Obviously, this was not a woman who gave herself easily. It was a humbling thought. She'd struck him as being inexperienced, but he'd never have guessed just how inexperienced she really was! But for one with so little practice at the art of seduction, she definitely had a natural instinct.

"Adam? Have I surprised you?"

"You never fail to, Cassie."

Her hands roamed up and down his chest, then her fingers—no longer too cold to function, but working at their dexterous best—began to undo his shirt buttons.

"Cassie, before you get me too excited to think straight—"

"You mean you aren't there yet?" she whispered provocatively, her warm mouth working its way down his neck and across his shoulder as his shirt gaped open. Eventually she had all the buttons undone, his shirt off and tossed onto the flooded bathroom floor. Now her fingers massaged his bare chest.

Adam's eyes fluttered shut. His head fell back and

Cassie slid around him, kissing his neck the whole time, until she straddled his waist from the front. Her wet, bare breasts were pressed against his chest now, the hard nipples teasing him to the point of insanity. Soon he would have to touch her.

He opened his eyes and swallowed hard. "You're so beautiful...and so damned determined," he whispered, looking at her flushed face, her sultry, half-closed eyes.

"When something's right, I am," she said. "And tonight I'm determined that you and I are going to make love. Wanna bet against me, Baranof?"

"I'd be crazy to."

He was licked. He knew there was no turning back now. He wanted her so badly every part of him strained to be near her, every nerve tingled with the thrill of her proximity. With a sigh of surrender, a silent prayer that she'd forgive him when she knew the truth, he pulled her to him with a roughness born of desperate need and what felt like a lifetime of denial.

His mouth found hers, hard, eager, demanding. She kissed him back with the same intensity, their bodies arching into each other, their hands curious, seeking, pleasuring.

They parted for air and he ran his hands up her arms, then held her away from him, just so he could look at her, really look at *her* for the first time. Her breasts were so beautiful, so perfectly shaped and weighted to fit in a man's hand. He reached out and cupped them both, then found he'd been right. Cassie's breasts had been made for a man's hands...but not just any man's. *His* hands. A surge of almost painful possessiveness washed over him.

He bent his head and, in turn, took each rosy nipple in his mouth and suckled. She moaned and threaded her fingers in his hair, clutching him to her, arching against his mouth. Her response incited him to a higher and higher state of arousal, of yearning, of soul-deep need.

"We're getting out of this tub," he whispered hoarsely.

Her face crumpled. "No." The word came out a barely audible plea.

He smiled. "And onto the bed."

She smiled and nodded, her lips parted, her breath a thin whistle of air.

He stood up and nearly fell, the bottom of the tub was so slick with bubble bath. Holding on to the towel bar, he managed to step out and onto the floor where a rug floated in the flood waters.

"You should take off your slacks in here," Cassie advised, her eyes wide and full of wonder as she stared at him. "That way, you won't drip as much water through the rest of the house."

He nodded and stared back at her as she rose from the water, naked except for a transparent strip of panties. Oh, she was so beautiful....

HE WAS so beautiful.... Cassie just stood and watched as Adam unzipped his pants and pulled them down, then kicked them off along with his Jockey shorts. Fully aroused, he was the most beautiful specimen of male she'd ever seen. Well, he was the *only* specimen of male she'd ever seen, but she knew he had to be above average in oh-so-many ways.

"Now it's your turn," he said, meaning her panties should come off, too, she supposed. She willingly complied and they stared at each other for another minute or two before he finally reached out and helped her step over the tub. They walked carefully out of the bathroom, grabbing a couple of towels as they went, then rubbed each other down—in between kisses—before falling onto the bed.

By some unspoken mutual agreement they left the lights on. They wanted to see each other, to look into each other's eyes. They wanted to go slow…but they couldn't. Kisses and caresses moved quickly to the need for an ultimate joining.

With his forearms braced on either side of her, his body covering hers, he gazed down at her with a look in his sky-blue eyes that was both joyful and sad. "Cassie, I want you to know I've never wanted to hurt you. I hope you believe me. I hope we can work this—"

She reached up and pressed her fingers gently against his lips. "Just love me, Adam. Love me now and we'll talk later." She moved her hips impatiently under his, connecting with that most intimate part of him. He closed his eyes and a tremor went through him from head to toe. Cassie could see, feel, sense, that he was as deeply affected by her as she was by him. Her power over him was exhilarating, humbling. *Wonderful.* His power over her was welcome and real.

He entered her. They moved together with a passion and tenderness that Cassie had never experienced before. *Never* experienced before.... Not with this man, not with any man. And when they reached their climaxes, even as their bodies were racked with wave after wave of ecstasy, their souls seemed to meet, kiss and converge...for the first time.

That's when Cassie knew Adam had been lying to her all along.

He was not her lover of five years ago. Not Tyler's father. That singular honor belonged to the other Baranof twin...Alex.

From her new perspective, Cassie also realized for the first time that she and Alex had been physically attracted to each other and swept away by a fleeting infatuation, and nothing more. And she knew that now only because she had connected with Adam on a much deeper level. Unfortunately, Adam's lies had made their lovemaking a bittersweet travesty.

Stunned and deeply hurt, Cassie pulled away and turned her back to him when Adam tried to hold her.

"Cassie? Are you all right?"

"Just sleepy," she murmured, too confused and full of pain and anger at that moment to confront him with the truth. She needed to think and she couldn't do that with him holding her.

"Okay, so now I know you don't like to cuddle after lovemaking," he teased, then kissed her shoulder and scooted minimally away...not nearly far enough to allow her to capably sort through her myriad emotions.

As they lay in the afterglow of lovemaking, Cassie felt as though she'd turned to stone. Pretending to be falling asleep, she slowly, ever-so-gently, inched farther away from Adam. Away from the magic of his touch, his heat, she could think. She could decide how to get away before the wedding without causing too big a ruckus. It would kill her to stay.

The Baranof twins had lied long enough and hard enough to ensure her silence. She would accommodate them and leave tomorrow, never to return. Tyler didn't need a father and she certainly didn't need a charming liar in her life.

As the minutes ticked by, the silence of the room punctuated only by Adam's soft breathing, Cassie felt the full tragedy sweep over her. Silently she cried, wiping each tear carefully away with the edge of the sheet. He would never know how much he'd hurt her. How much she'd loved him.

NOW HE'D DONE IT. He'd done exactly what he'd promised himself he wouldn't do. He'd made love to Cassie before she knew the truth! But then maybe he'd done so because he knew once the truth was out there was a snowball's chance in hell of her giving him the time of day, much less her body and soul.

Yes, that was her soul he'd melded with during the most sublime moments of their mating. He loved this woman—yes, he *loved* her—and they seemed to be meant for each other. If only...

Adam shifted carefully in the bed and peered over Cassie's shoulder to look at her face. She didn't move. Her eyes were still closed. How he wished his mind was as untroubled, then maybe he'd be able to sleep, too.

Oh, if only he hadn't lied to her! If only he'd told her the truth long before tonight, instead of waiting for his brother, trying to teach him a lesson, to take some responsibility. If only Alex—

The door opened, someone came in.

Adam sat up in the bed. It was Alex.

"Who is it?" Cassie mumbled, turning to look toward the door, holding the covers to her throat. "*Alex?* What are you doing here?"

Alex simply stood by the door and stared. He looked numb and shaken.

Adam could tell something was wrong. *Terribly* wrong. But he couldn't even get out of bed and go to his brother because he had nothing on and nothing to put on.

"What's the matter, Alex?" he asked, dreading the answer.

"I told her," he said simply. "And I came here to tell you that it was okay to tell Cassie. But I see you already have." He attempted a smile, but it turned out strange and twisted. "I wish Kelly had been as understanding as Cassie. The wedding's off, Adam. It was just like I feared. She called the wedding off."

"Sit down, Alex," Adam said, stretching out a hand as if he could physically detain him that way. He pulled on the sheet until it was free, leaving Cassie the comforter for cover, then wrapped it around his waist. "I think I've got some extra clothes in the back of the closet."

Alex obediently dropped into a nearby chair, hung his head and stared at his hands. He was obviously devastated.

While Adam looked for something to put on, he snatched glimpses of Cassie out the corner of his eye. He found it very strange that after her initial "What are you doing here?" she hadn't asked another question. Hadn't said another word. It was as though she already knew. Already understood. He remembered how she'd pulled away after their lovemaking and got a sick feeling in his stomach.

Could she know? Did she understand exactly what was going on? Why Alex was there? And if she did...would she understand why he and Alex had chosen to lie and forgive him for it? That was the question that would gnaw at him until he got a chance to talk with her.

Adam took the musty-smelling clothes he found and put them on in the bathroom. When he came out again, Alex was still sitting silently and Cassie was propped against some pillows, watching him with a sad expression. He hoped that meant she'd have similar feelings of sympathy for *him*...jerk that he was! He knew he'd done something horrible and didn't deserve forgiveness. But forgiveness was exactly what he hoped and prayed for.

"I'm going to take Alex back to his place so we can talk."

Cassie looked down and nodded.

"I may have to stay with him for a while."

"I understand."

"And when I get back, I'll explain all of this to you."

She nodded again.

"Cassie?"

She looked up slowly, reluctantly. He couldn't tell

what she was thinking, feeling. She seemed remote, fenced off. It scared the hell out of him!

"I was going to tell you before..."

Dully, she said, "I guess you tried."

"Yes."

She looked down again.

"I'd better get Alex home. I'll be back as soon as I can, but go ahead and get some sleep. It may be morning before you see me again."

He didn't expect her to reply and she didn't. He moved to the chair where Alex was slumped and pulled him to his feet. As they were leaving, Cassie surprised him by calling out Alex's name instead of his.

They both turned.

"I'm sorry about Kelly," she said simply.

Alex nodded, tried to smile, then turned and stepped into the rain. Adam followed.

IT WAS a long night. Adam really hadn't expected Kelly to call off the wedding. He had expected anger and tears and maybe a postponement. But his faith had been so strong in the love Kelly and Alex had for each other, he believed they'd somehow work it out and the wedding would go on. He believed, and he still did, that truth between them—even when it was late in coming—was more important than ignorant bliss. But so far Kelly wasn't appreciating this distinction.

Adam understood her initial distrust and disillusionment. She would be wondering why Alex felt the need to lie in the first place. Was it really because he was afraid he'd lose her or alienate her parents? Or was it because he still had feelings for Cassie?

Adam tried to convince Alex that Kelly just needed time. Time to sort through her feelings, time to realize she loved him enough to forgive and trust him again. Alex needed to be patient.

But patience was a hard virtue to press on a man on the eve of his canceled wedding day. There was nothing to look forward to in the morning but humiliation and the disappointment of dozens of family members who had come to share the most important day of his life. They would blame him, and he deserved it.

Adam and Alex watched the sun come up at 4:35, sipping coffee in Alex's kitchen. They'd talked all night and had downed a pot of java between them just to keep them going for the difficult day ahead.

"Are you going to be okay?"

Alex smiled grimly. "Unfortunately, yes. It would be easier if I just gave up, quit eating and faded away to nothing. But I'm not going to give up on Kelly. Somehow I'll get through this nightmare and try again."

Adam smiled. "It's good to hear you talk this way. I hope it's not just the caffeine."

Alex chuckled. "Could be a little bit. Oh, I'll still have some tough times, Adam. But as long as you can talk me through the worst of it, I'll manage."

Adam stood up and thumped Alex on the shoulder with his open hand. "If I'm around, I'm yours."

Alex frowned and looked up at his brother. "Maybe I shouldn't have taken you away from Cassie last night…just when I did. You've still got to make things right with her.''

Adam nodded. ''Wish me luck. I'll need it.''

''I do wish you luck, Adam. I should never have dragged you into this in the first place.''

''I'm a big boy. You didn't twist my arm.''

''But when you wanted to end it sooner, I wouldn't let you. I was a real bastard.''

''Yes, you were. But you were scared. You weren't yourself.''

''Lord, I *hope* that wasn't me!''

''Gotta go,'' Adam said, peering through the window at the lightening day. ''Glad it's not raining.''

''Yeah, Mom and Dad can display my head on a stake in bright sunshine.''

''I'm sure they'll sharpen a stake for *my* head, too, Alex. See you later, dead or alive.''

Alex pushed himself to his feet with a weary sigh and followed Adam to the door. Adam opened it, and they both stared at the person standing on the other side.

''Hi, Alex,'' Kelly said, pale and pink-eyed but with a tremulous smile. ''Can I come in?''

ADAM DROVE home with renewed hope in his heart. Maybe there'd be a wedding after all! It was certainly a good sign that Kelly was there bright and early on Adam's doorstep and not carrying a gun!

It gave him hope for his own situation, too. He hadn't had a chance yet to explain himself to Cassie. He didn't even know how much she already knew, but he was certain she knew enough to be hurt and angry.

Cassie was really the one with the most to feel hurt about. The fact that the whole deceit had involved the most precious thing in her life—her son—would make it difficult for her to forgive. She was fiercely maternal. It was just one of the things that made her so lovable, so wonderful.

Adam's heart was in his throat as he pulled into his driveway. He wasn't sure if she'd be in the guest cabin or in the main house. It was still early, so he tried the cabin first.

He walked in, her name on his lips. But the bed was empty. And made.

Terror gripping him, he moved to the closet and threw it open. Just as he feared, Cassie's clothes were gone.

There was still a chance she was at the main house. After all, how could they have got out of there without assistance? The ferry didn't run between 1:00 a.m. and 5:00 a.m. and neither of them could fly. Of course, Kelly had somehow gotten over from Kenai. Where there was a will there was a way, he supposed. But it wasn't exactly an inspiring or comforting thought just at that moment.

He hurried into the house and...found his father sitting at the table. His heart sank to his toes.

"Dad."

"Adam."

"You flew them out?"

"As soon as the rain stopped around two-thirty."

Adam nodded, weariness and misery threatening to overcome him.

"Come and have some coffee, son. I expect I need to do for you what you just did for Alex."

Adam was grateful for his dad's support, but the one big difference between his hope for happiness and Alex's—a difference his father could never fix—was the absence of a woman at the door, asking…"Can I come in?"

AS THE PLANE approached the Billings airport, Cassie looked out over the familiar countryside with an aching but grateful heart. This was *home*. It wasn't as lush and majestic as the Kenai Peninsula, but it had its own brand of wide-open beauty, rugged mountains and endless skies. Here she hoped she'd find peace of mind again, settle into the life she knew and loved before this dreamlike detour to Alaska.

She turned to observe her father, just waking from a nap, and Tyler between them, still sleeping. The last twenty-four hours had been exhausting for all of them, especially Ty. He'd been awakened in the middle of the night for the trip to Anchorage, then they'd had to wait in the airport for hours for the next flight to San Francisco and another to Montana. That's what happened when three people who weren't scheduled to fly out until the next day decided to go standby. Her father called it the hurry-up-and-wait dilemma.

Now it was nearly eight o'clock, the long purple shadows of the evening creeping over the landscape. The sun went down here at nine o'clock at the latest in early summer, unlike Alaska, the land of the midnight sun, where everything incredibly beautiful was illuminated until the night was nearly over.

Incredibly beautiful. Like Adam's face as he'd

looked down at her in the midst of their lovemaking. The curve of his throat from that angle, the loving expression in his eyes. How could she have ever mistaken one brother for the other? In Adam's lovemaking there had been such a depth of tenderness and meaning. He and Alex were *so* different...

Yet, in one respect, too much alike. They had conspired together to dupe her into believing a lie that made things simpler, easier for them.

She'd meant it when she told Alex she was sorry about Kelly. Sorry that he'd lost Kelly because of *her*. She truly believed he loved his fiancée—and dreaded the influence of his formidable in-laws—and perhaps that's why he'd resorted to such a deceitful trick. But that didn't excuse it.

Cassie just wished she'd never set eyes on that magazine, never written to Adam, never gone to Alaska. If she hadn't, the wedding would have gone on as planned. Alex would have lived his life ignorant of the fact that he was father to the most wonderful little boy in the world. But Cassie knew that *she* had received the greater blessing in knowing and loving Tyler, in having him a part of her life forever.

As for Adam...

Cassie wasn't sure why she couldn't feel the same compassion for Adam, the same understanding. She supposed he was only trying to help his brother. But because of what had happened between them—not just the physical lovemaking, but the bonding with Tyler, the friendship that had so quickly blossomed into love—his lies seemed like the worst kind of betrayal.

He'd said he wanted to talk to her last night, before they'd made love, and maybe he was going to tell her the truth then. She didn't know. She'd never know. Would it have made any difference?

As the airplane wheels hit the runway, Cassie looked at the tinted windows of the terminal. Somewhere in there Brad was waiting for them. Faithful, bighearted Brad.

Brad would never lie to her.

Chapter Twelve

The wedding was on. Kelly and Alex still had some talking to do, but they were committed to working everything out between them because a most important and vital fact remained: they loved each other deeply.

So, they kept their overnight rift to themselves, confiding the particulars of it to only two people besides those directly involved. Other than Kelly, Alex, Adam, Cassie and Jasper, only Peter and Monica were privy to the fact that Tyler was Alex's biological son, not Adam's. And that's the way they planned to keep it...if Adam agreed.

As Alex and Adam dressed for the wedding, they had time to talk this over.

"So, *why* do you still want everyone to think I'm Ty's father?" Adam demanded to know, astonished at such an idea, particularly after everything they'd been through.

All dressed in his tuxedo except for his jacket, Alex was adjusting his bow tie in front of the small, square mirror over the dresser in their old bedroom in the folks' house in Homer. Two twin beds still rested at opposite sides of the room, pennants hung on the walls along with posters and pictures from their teenage years. Adam, fully dressed, sat on the bed that used to be his, fiddling with a cuff link.

Alex turned with a serious expression on his face. "Don't worry, bro, I'm not trying to weasel out of anything here. I never intended to be a father to Tyler. You know I'm not the fatherly type. Kelly and I may *never* have children. She thinks they're cute, but that's as far as it goes. And the people who *should* know I'm Tyler's biological parent have already been told. Kelly knows the truth and so do the folks. As for Kelly's parents," he added wryly, "we've decided that they're on a need-to-know-only basis. Those two have the unenlightened mentality of the Dark Ages."

Adam couldn't disagree about the Armstrongs, but he still had reservations. "But I wonder what Cassie would think about this? Would she think it was still an act of deceit just to make things easier for you?"

Alex raised his brows. "I don't know. But if you're worried about it, why don't you call her and ask her what she thinks? She'd probably be thrilled to know that Kelly and I worked things out."

"Oh, that was smooth, Alex," Adam drawled. "I suppose you think that would be a clever way to insinuate myself back into Cassie's life. I don't think she'd even talk to me. In fact, I don't think I'll ever see her again."

"Well, if that's how you feel, why are you worried about what Cassie thinks, anyway?"

"It's the principle of the thing," Adam insisted.

"We've handled that end of it, bro," Alex argued. "Like I said, the people who matter, the people who have a right to know the truth, have been told. As far as Tyler's future goes, it's no longer important who supplied him with the Baranof genes. That's been established. In an impulsive and irresponsible act of romantic lust, *I* did."

"Don't remind me," Adam muttered.

"Does that mean he should be chained to a father like *me* forever? Hell, I should hope not. Biology doesn't make a man a real father. Love does. And if I ain't mistakin', bro, you grew real fond of that kid while he was here."

"Well, sure, I *care* about Tyler, but I'm not—"

"But you could be. As far as I'm concerned, Adam, Tyler's yours."

Adam gave an incredulous bark of laughter. "With or without his mother's consent, I suppose?"

"You want him, don't you?"

Caught off guard, Adam blurted, "Sure, I do. I wished he was mine right from the beginning."

He immediately looked chagrined, but Alex smiled, satisfied to have so cleverly extracted the confession. He slipped into his tux jacket.

"Then what's the trouble?"

"Oh, some father I'd be a thousand miles away and with no access to the kid!" he exclaimed, standing up to pace the floor. "Cassie wouldn't let me within a hundred miles of him."

"Then it sounds to me like this—if you want to see your son, you'd better make up with his mother."

Adam sat down on the bed again, resting his elbows on his thighs and letting his hands dangle between his knees in a defeated pose. "She made her feelings pretty clear when she left without even giving me a chance to tell my side of the story…not that that would have helped much."

"Maybe she left because she loves you too much."

"Oh, sure. That makes a load of sense."

Alex turned back to the mirror and gave his bow tie a final tweak. "Think about it, bro. But if you haven't done anything to remedy this sad state of affairs by the time Kelly and I are back from Hawaii, I might have to take matters into my own hands."

Adam rose and stood behind his brother, their reflections identical except for Alex's black eye and Adam's scowl.

"I'll handle this *my* way, little brother."

"Which means, I suppose, not at all," Alex said with a sniff.

"Alex…"

Alex smiled. "Let's not quarrel on my wedding day, bro. It's a miracle it's taking place at all. Be happy for me."

Adam's scowl faded away and was replaced with a reluctant grin. "I *am* happy for you, Alex. Now shouldn't we be going?" He patted his coat pockets and the scowl reappeared. "Damn, I think I've lost the rings!"

"Adam…"

Now the grin was back. "Fooled ya."

A WEEK AFTER Cassie was home, she was rocking in the porch swing on a hot Saturday afternoon, drinking lemonade and waiting for Brad. It was the first day she'd taken off since returning to Nye and she was feeling extremely lazy. No, make that lethargic. No…make that *depressed.* No point in lying to herself.

She heard the screen door open behind her and looked up at her father. "Ty asleep?"

"Yep."

"Good." She took another sip and pushed off with one dangling foot for another languorous swing.

"He wanted to stay up and see his Uncle Brad, but I told 'im you and Brad had some private talkin' to do."

Cassie smiled faintly, her half-closed eyes watching the dusty road beyond the fence. "How did that go over?"

"Not too bad, actually. He figures you and Brad are fixin' to set the weddin' date."

Cassie was startled out of her listlessness. She gazed up at her father. "Where did he get that idea?"

"Don't know. But I reckon we need to sit him down one day soon and give him the lowdown with no frills attached."

Cassie turned to watch the road again. "You mean tell him that I'm not going to marry Brad…ever?"

Cassie waited nervously through the long pause that followed. Finally her father muttered gruffly, "Cassandra Montgomery, don't tell me you've changed your mind about Brad…*again!*"

Cassie hitched up one shoulder and ever so

slightly shoved out her bottom lip. "Well, I don't know. It's just that I've been thinking lately—"

"Cassandra, look at me."

When her father used that tone of voice, Cassie obeyed. Jasper looked as grim as an undertaker. "Er...yeah, Dad?"

"If you're thinkin' what I think you're thinkin', you got another think coming."

"What's *that* supposed to mean?"

"You don't love Brad. You told me so yourself. And I know for certain that you're in love with someone else."

Cassie turned away, blinking back tears that came on suddenly at the slightest, most distant allusion to *that man in Alaska*. The nights were the worst, though. The quiet darkness offered no interruptions for her traitorous thoughts of missed kisses and looks and wonderful times spent together. "I've learned that love is highly overrated. I much prefer a man I can depend on, a man who will tell me the truth, *always*."

"Hell, Cassie, no one tells the truth all the time."

"But the size of the lies makes a big difference."

"Even good men make mistakes."

Cassie turned her head sharply to glare at her father. "I suppose you're going to tell me that you think Adam Baranof is a good man?"

Jasper nodded. "Damn right I am. You asked me to give him a chance and I did. I found out real fast that I liked the boy."

"He's no boy and...and he knew better."

"I think that's what he was planning to tell you last Saturday night when you were hell-bent on hightailing it out of there faster than a jackrabbit in heat."

"Tell me what? That he knew better?"

Jasper nodded again. "Yep. That boy suffered over it. Tellin' lies didn't sit well with 'im. I could see that, easy."

"Then he shouldn't have agreed to cover for his brother in the first place."

"Yep. I'm sure he knew that about three minutes after the fact."

Cassie gave an exasperated hiss. "Dad, why are you sticking up for him? It's *over!*"

Jasper snorted. "Is it?" Then before Cassie could launch another flurry of arguments, he continued, "But, as far as Brad's concerned, it doesn't really matter what's goin' on with you and Adam. You don't love Brad and it'd be damned selfish of you to keep danglin' that carrot in front of his nose, Cassie. Cut 'im loose, hon. Cut 'im loose. It's the humane thing to do."

After regaling her with his horse analogies, Jasper left Cassie to stew. But it didn't take her long to admit that, no matter how it had been put into words, her father was right. When Brad came, she'd have to cut 'im loose.

She wasn't sure why she had even been considering dangling that carrot a second longer. She knew she wasn't in love with Brad and never would be, and simply feeling secure with him because he was trustworthy and devoted wasn't enough of a reason—for *either* of them—to hang on to a going-nowhere relationship.

In the past week Cassie had avoided talking to

Brad by working late at the store almost every day, then coming home to spend a couple of hours with Tyler before going to bed exhausted. The exhaustion hadn't helped her sleep or block out the constant thoughts of Adam, but the nonstop busyness had at least helped her cope during the daylight hours. Susan watched her slave away at the store and clicked her tongue, but no amount of sympathy or advice from her faithful friend slowed Cassie down.

She just couldn't sort out all the confusing thoughts and feelings! How could she be so in love and so hurt at the same time? How could she want him every minute, yet wish he didn't exist?

Five minutes later, Brad's truck passed through the front gate and pulled to a stop in front of the house. Cassie watched him swing his long legs out of the cab and saunter up the sidewalk to the porch. She shook her head with rueful wonder. He had a damned sexy saunter, but it didn't get to her in the least. What was the matter with her! Most women would give their eyeteeth for a suitor with a sexy saunter like Brad's!

Lean and tan and leggy in snug jeans, his fresh-washed blond hair glinting in the sun, he was a fine figure of a man. Why she was able to appreciate this fact and still be completely unmoved was a mystery to Cassie. Brad needed and deserved a woman who couldn't wait to peel off those jeans and get down to business.

"Hi." He smiled and sat down in the swing beside her, smelling faintly of aftershave. Brad was subtle, right down to the nice way he smelled.

"Hi." She smiled back. "Want some lemonade?"

"No thanks. Just had a soda."

She set her own half-empty glass of lemonade on a nearby patio table and waited for him to get the ball rolling. For once, she didn't feel very comfortable with Brad, and she sensed that he was feeling the same way.

"Cassie—"

"Brad—"

They laughed. "You go first," she offered.

"Maybe you should go first since you're the one who invited me over to talk. I can't believe we haven't managed to get together since I drove you home from the airport."

"I've kept busy at work...on purpose, I guess. But I figured you deserved an explanation about why we went to Alaska. I knew you didn't buy that sudden urge to go on a vacation bit."

"No, but I figured you'd tell me in time. I figured it had something to do with Tyler's father, and I knew that was something you've fretted about over the years."

Cassie smiled wryly. "Yes, but I'd have been better off if I'd just kept on frettin'."

Brad got an understanding look in his eyes. "I know."

"You do? Did Dad—?"

"No, it wasn't your father that told me the whole story...."

"Then who? The only other soul I confided in was—"

"Susan," he finished for her, looking chagrined.

"Susan?" Cassie repeated blankly.

"Yeah, Susan. She said you didn't swear her to secrecy, so she figured it was okay to fill me in. Especially since you were going to tell me sooner or later, anyway."

Cassie shook her head in confusion. "But I didn't realize you even knew Susan. I mean, to talk to her and all."

Brad fidgeted a little, looked off toward the road as she'd done earlier while talking with her father. "We both like to eat lunch over at B.J.'s now and then. It seemed silly to sit at different tables." Gazing at Brad's profile, Cassie could swear she detected a blush on those high cheekbones. "At first we just talked about *you*. Then, after a while..."

Suddenly Cassie was getting the picture. Instead of cuttin' Brad loose, Brad was cuttin' *her* loose! "Brad, are you and Susan—?"

His self-conscious look told all.

She couldn't help an astonished laugh. "You *are* talking about my Susan, the Susan who works for me? The perky brunette?"

"The same."

"Well, why didn't you tell me? Why didn't you *say* something?"

He stared at her as if he weren't sure whether she was happy or mad. At first Cassie wasn't sure, either. It was such a shock!

"In the beginning there was nothing to tell you. Just an innocent little lunch now and then with a nice girl. And, as I said, we talked about you mostly. I think she felt sorry for me 'cause you couldn't make up your mind about us."

Cassie suddenly remembered about Susan's eager defense of Brad on the day they'd found Adam's picture in the magazine, not to mention her eagerness to get Cassie to consider a hot hunk from Alaska in the first place!

"It was a gradual thing, Cassie. I was pretty confused for a while. I've always cared for you, you know that. But I've come to care for Susan, too, and it's...it's *different*. It made me realize that you and I just weren't meant to be." He reached over and took her hand. "But I think you've known that for a while. And this trip to Alaska just made it more obvious to you, didn't it?"

Cassie smiled. She couldn't believe that she was getting off the hook so easily, and, in the process, two people she cared a whole lot about were going to be supremely happy. Well, she was certainly glad her father had made her see sense before she'd made a fool of herself with Brad by sending marriage signals to a man already taken. Sometimes things actually *did* work out.

Cassie squeezed Brad's hand. "I'm happy for you, Brad. And Susan, too. Are we going to be hearing wedding bells any time soon?"

He got a dreamy look in his eyes that made Cassie just a little bit jealous. Not of Susan, but of the happiness she and Brad had found with each other.

"Not *real* soon. Maybe...I don't know... Christmas."

"You make a great couple and I'm sure you'll be very happy."

"Thanks, Cass." His brow furrowed. "But what about Tyler? What will he think about all this?"

Cassie chewed her bottom lip. Brad had asked a very good question. Was Tyler going to miss more than Jolly Ranchers if Brad wasn't in his life?

FOR ONCE in his life, Jasper was taken completely by surprise. "You're kiddin' me."

"No, I'm not."

"I don't believe it."

"Believe it."

"Brad and *Susan?* Hell, I thought he was in love with *you.*"

"He thought he was, too, till recently. Susan changed his mind about that."

Cassie and Jasper were in the dining room. Dinner was over and Ty and Sylvie were in the kitchen getting ice cream and cookies for dessert.

"Why didn't he say something to *me?*" Jasper wondered.

"Come on, Dad, you're the last person he'd tell that he was falling out of love with your daughter. No…he was never *really* in love with me in the first place. Too bad Tyler somehow got the idea that Brad and I were destined to marry."

"Cass, I never actually *said*—"

"I know you didn't, Dad. But Tyler's smart. He picked up vibes from all of us, and he probably heard other people talking, too."

"Well, just because Brad's gonna be married doesn't mean they can't still be buds."

"Over time things will change. It's inevitable, Dad. But Tyler's growing up anyway and he'll be going to school soon. Besides, he'll always have you."

Jasper smiled and patted Cassie's hand resting on the table. He didn't say anything, but Cassie knew what he was thinking. No, Tyler wouldn't *always* have him and it was too bad Ty didn't have a father. But he'd never dream of expecting Cassie to marry simply to supply Tyler with a father. And she had *finally* come to realize that she would never dream of settling for anything less than what she and Ty both deserved—a man they both loved, a man that loved them both.

Funny how Adam suddenly came to mind...

Tyler and Sylvie returned with chocolate ice cream scooped into bowls and homemade oatmeal cookies. After settling Ty in his chair and handing around the bowls, Sylvie headed back to the kitchen.

"Stay and have some ice cream, Sylvie," Jasper called. "There's only a few hundred grams of fat and a cup of sugar in each bowl." Sylvie was as slim as a reed and had the energy of an army, but she refused to eat dessert because she was sure it would make her fat. Jasper loved to tease her about it...among many other things.

"It'd all go to my hips," Sylvie informed them, bustling away. "Besides, I've got dishes to do!"

"I'm glad I don't care about fat 'n sugar," Tyler said complacently as he ate another spoonful of ice cream.

"Me, too, bud," Jasper said.

Cassie watched Tyler eating his favorite dessert and wondered if this might be a good time to break the news about Brad. She telegraphed her intentions to Jasper and he nodded his head in agreement.

"Did Granddad tell you I was going to have a talk with Uncle Brad today?"

Tyler peered at her over his bowl, his nose tipped with chocolate ice cream. He scooped in another bite and mumbled, "Uh-huh."

"Granddad said you were sort of expecting Uncle Brad to ask me to marry him."

Ty's eyes got big. "Did he?"

Cassie shook her head. "No, Ty, he didn't. In fact, I think he's going to marry my friend, Susan. You know the nice lady who works with me at the bookstore?"

"Really?" He seemed momentarily arrested, but not disappointed or unhappy. Then he asked, "Can I have some more ice cream?"

Cassie exchanged a surprised look with Jasper. "So, you don't mind if Uncle Brad marries Susan? You weren't hoping he'd be…you know…a part of *our* family?" She purposely left out the word *daddy*.

Tyler screwed up his face, considering. Finally he said, "I like Uncle Brad a lot and I wouldn't mind if he was my daddy. But I figure there's other uncles you can choose from, Mommy, someone *you* might like better, like Uncle Adam. *I* really like him, too. But don't marry Uncle Alex, 'cause he wouldn't make a good daddy at all."

For a moment, Cassie was speechless. How could such a small boy be so perceptive, so wise? He'd easily picked up on the fact that Alex wasn't daddy material, and that Adam was. And that *she* liked Uncle Adam, too…against her better judgment.

Tyler didn't know the whole story. He didn't know there were chinks in Adam's armor. He didn't know that to pass muster Adam had to be as good at being a husband as he was at being a daddy.

Cassie fought the dull and dreadful ache that crept into her heart every time she faced the possibility of her and Tyler's dream never coming true. Adam might easily fit the bill as a daddy, but the husband part was extremely doubtful. Even if she could bring herself to forgive him, to trust him again, he might not have the slightest intention of committing himself to such a permanent arrangement as marriage.

So her whole Hamletesque agony over "to forgive or not to forgive" might be a moot point. Maybe Adam didn't care either way. After all, it had been a week since she left Alaska and he hadn't bothered to call or write or—

"Well, Mommy?"

Cassie blinked. "What, honey?"

"*Can* I have some more ice cream?"

Feeling foolish for drifting into her own tortured little world, she smiled and said, "Sure, hon. But just half a bowl. Go on into the kitchen and tell Sylvie I said it was okay."

"Thanks, Mom!" He was gone in a flash.

"No childhood angst troublin' that kid," Jasper said proudly. "Don't worry about 'im, Cass. He'll take whatever's dished 'im."

"Especially if it's chocolate flavored," Cassie said wryly.

LATER, AFTER Sylvie went home, Cassie, Jasper and Tyler put an old forties cowboy movie in the VCR and settled in the cozy family room at the back of the house to watch it. When the phone rang during

an especially loud barroom shoot-out, Cassie said to
Jasper, "That might be Susan. If it is, I'll probably
be a while." Then she went into the kitchen to answer it.

"Hello?"

"Hello, Cassie. Don't hang up...*please*."

Chapter Thirteen

"Kelly, is that you?"

"Yeah, it's me. Please don't hang up!"

"Why would I hang up on *you?*" Cassie gave a nervous little chuckle. "You didn't lie to me."

"No, but you might think I'm a traitor. I forgave Alex for lying to me and we went ahead and got married on Sunday."

"You *did?* Oh, Kelly, I'm so happy for you!" And she really meant it. "I felt so bad about showing up at the worst possible time and causing so much trouble for you."

"Well, that wasn't your fault. If Alex had told me the truth—told us *both* the truth—right at the beginning, things would have been so much easier. We could have dealt with it together. It was his lying that made things so complicated."

"And Adam's lying," Cassie added quietly.

"Well, I think that Adam, at least, has learned his lesson," Kelly said in an aggravated tone. "But Alex is on his way to your house right now with another scheme up his sleeve."

Cassie's eyes widened. "What do you mean, another scheme? And why aren't you two on your honeymoon?''

''Alex cut the honeymoon short, if you can believe it.''

''But why?''

''He's been too worried about Adam.''

Cassie's heart seemed to leap into her throat. ''What's…what's wrong with Adam? He isn't hurt or sick or—''

''Just lovesick over you.''

Faintly Cassie said, ''Oh.''

''Before we left for Hawaii, Alex tried to talk Adam into calling you to try to work things out, but Adam didn't think you'd give him the time of day. But Alex can't be happy if Adam isn't, and since he blames himself for dragging Adam into this in the first place, Alex decided this morning to fly down there to Montana and do Adam's talking for him. And I mean that literally.''

''Literally?''

''I mean, he's going to pose as Adam.''

Cassie was stunned. ''He actually told you he was going to do that?''

''He doesn't lie to me anymore, Cassie. He told me exactly what he planned to do. And he promised me that it would be the last time he'd ever do anything like this again. He justified it because he wants to help Adam. Sound familiar, only the other way around?''

Cassie gave a helpless chuckle. ''Those two get in more trouble that way. Why didn't you tell Adam so he could stop Alex?''

''I called his house all morning, no answer. Then

I went over there and saw the plane was gone, so I figure he went to Anchorage or something. When I couldn't get hold of Adam, I decided at the last minute to call you."

"What do you mean the last minute?"

"Alex could show up there any second. I just thought you should be prepared."

"Well, thanks for calling, Kelly, but I don't have a clue what to do."

There was a pause, then, "Can I give you some advice?"

"Er...okay."

"Give Alex a lecture for trying to scam you and send him home with his tail between his legs. The only way we're ever going to tame the brothers Baranof is by putting them in their place whenever they try something crazy like this. *Then...*"

Cassie laughed. "Then?"

"Then send Alex home with a message for Adam. Tell him you forgive him. Believe me, Cass—" Her voice got soft and dreamy "—forgiveness has its rewards."

Cassie sobered. "I don't know, Kelly. I'd *like* to forgive him, but—"

"You care about him, don't you?"

"Yes, but—"

The doorbell rang and Cassie nearly jumped out of her skin. "Oh m'gosh, he's here," she whispered into the phone.

"Call me later, Cass," Kelly said. "And good luck."

Cassie nodded into the phone as if Kelly could see her, then hung up. Suddenly her palms were sweaty and her heart was beating out of her chest. It was only Alex at the door, but he *looked* like Adam, and that, apparently, was enough to get her all worked up. And the very idea that he thought he could pose as Adam and actually fool her into believing him…! She was going to do exactly what Kelly advised and send him home feeling as low as a scolded puppy.

She hurried through the dark living room, not bothering to turn on lights. She opened the door and, barely looking at him, grabbed Alex's arm before he could say a word and dragged him across the porch and around to the side of the house. Under the thick branches of a huge old elm tree that blocked most of the moonlight from getting through, Cassie faced her foe.

"Alex Baranof, how *dare* you?"

The dark outline of a man shaped alarmingly like Adam spread his arms wide. "Cassie, it's me. It's Adam!"

She shook her finger in his face. "Don't try to pull that stunt on me, Alex. I know what you're up to and you should be ashamed!"

"*Cassie—*"

Cassie glanced nervously at the house, at the lighted window of the family room. "Keep your voice down, Alex. I don't want Dad or Tyler to even know you're here. When will you ever learn your lesson? You should never have gotten Adam to take your place as Tyler's father, and you taking his place now isn't right, either! I know you think you're only trying to help, but Adam should be here speaking for himself!"

Alex grabbed her shoulders. "But, Cassie, I *am*—"

Cassie wriggled out of Alex's grasp and turned her back on him, crossing her arms over her chest. "Not that speaking for himself would do him any good, either. I mean, how could he have lied about something as important as Tyler's paternity?"

"That was terrible and I'm sorry."

"It's not enough that *you're* sorry, Alex. Adam needs to be sorry. Sure, Kelly says he's sorry. You say he's sorry. But I need to hear it from *him*."

Cassie kept her back to Alex, stewing, while he remained silent. There was a soft breeze in the air, gently rustling the leaves in the branches overhead. Finally Alex spoke again in a low, measured tone. "So, are you saying that if…if Adam had actually come down here to see you, to say he was sorry, to promise never to lie to you again even about something as silly and inconsequential as a parking ticket, you might…forgive him?"

Cassie kicked at a tuft of grass. "I *might*. But he didn't."

"What if he did?"

Cassie shrugged. "I don't know. He really hurt me."

Alex gave a long, shaky sigh. "I'm sorry about that."

"But is *he* sorry?"

When he spoke again, he was standing so close to her Cassie actually felt his breath on her neck. An unexpected chill went down her back. "Cassie, I *am* Adam."

She whirled on him, furious. "Alex, quit pretending!"

His head fell back and his hands came up in a frustrated pose. "Why do you persist in thinking I'm Alex?"

"Kelly called me. I *know,* Alex. You don't have to keep putting on a show. Besides, you're wasting your time. If Adam really cared you wouldn't be here in the first place."

There was a pause, then he said, "Wait, let's go back to that first part. You said Kelly called you?"

"Yes, but don't be mad at her, Alex. She was just trying to keep you from messing things up again."

"Kelly said that Alex was coming *here?*"

Cassie couldn't help it. She was reluctantly impressed. "You know, you really *are* good at this. Maybe you should have gone into acting instead of marine geology. But save your theatrics for community theater, Alex, because this audience isn't buying your act."

Again Alex fell silent. Cassie couldn't quite see his face in the dark, just the occasional glint of moonlight reflected in his eyes, but she could feel the intensity of his emotions. She decided he must really be guilt-stricken over the situation. But you couldn't fix a bad situation created by lying by telling more lies!

"Can I ask you something, Cass?"

Alex's tone of voice gave Cassie a flutter in her stomach. He sounded almost tender. He sounded *so* much like Adam.

"What?" She knew she was being sulky, but she

couldn't help it. Having Alex there just made her miss Adam all the more.

"What makes you so sure Adam doesn't care about you?"

"Well, to begin with—"

"I know what you're going to say...*he isn't here.* But think back to the time you spent with him in Alaska."

That's all Cassie had been thinking about for the past week! She shook her head firmly. "There's no point in—"

"Do you remember the way he looked at you?"

"What do you mean?"

"The way he couldn't take his eyes off you? The expression in his eyes?"

Cassie thought about Adam's eyes and the way he used to look at her. She was lost in delicious thought until Alex brought her back to reality, then sent her floating on a cloud again with his next question. "What about the way he kissed you? You could tell how he felt about you then, couldn't you? It was different with him, different than it was with...with me, different than it was with any other man."

"All two of them," Cassie admitted with a sigh, then added wistfully, "Different than it would have been with any guy, I suppose."

"Then maybe this will convince you."

Before Cassie knew what was happening, Alex grabbed her shoulders and pulled her against his chest.

"Alex, what are you doing?"

"For the last time," he growled as he wrapped

his arms around her so tightly she could barely breathe, much less struggle out of his embrace, "I am *not* Alex, and I am going to kiss you!"

"This is crazy! This isn't right! This is—"

Despite turning her head from side to side and trying to kick him in the shins with flailing feet, Alex's lips captured hers. It took about two seconds to realize that, once again, she'd confused one Baranof brother with the other.

This is Adam, her heart told her.

She quit fighting and started participating. The kiss combined the excitement of coming home and the thrill of taking off on a wonderful adventure at the same time. The familiar feel of Adam's lips, Adam's arms around her, Adam's thick, silky hair to weave her eager fingers through, was heaven.

They parted at last, both spent of breath, both still clinging to each other like survivors of a catastrophe. But, in a way, that's what they were.

"Now, before either of us say another word, before we kiss again...tell me, Cassie, *who am I?*"

Cassie was tempted to tease, but she could tell how important this was to him. "You're Adam Baranof," she said softly, one finger tracing the slightly stubbly line of his jaw. "The man with the smooth chest. The man who preceded his troublesome twin brother into the world by three minutes."

He pulled her into a fierce, joyful hug. "Oh, Cassie, I've missed you so much! But I was afraid to call. Afraid you wouldn't talk to me."

"I've been so confused and hurt, I might not have," she admitted.

He grasped her shoulders and peered into her

face, struggling to see in the dark. "But you'll talk to me now?"

She dropped her forehead against his chest and chuckled deep in her throat. "Well I suppose we can't just kiss twenty-four hours a day."

He cupped her chin with his hand and gently urged her to look at him. In the dark she couldn't see, but she knew his eyes glowed with love. It radiated from him. "We could try," he teased.

She laughed, then he said, soberly, sincerely, "I *am* sorry, Cassie. We do need to talk. I'll tell you everything. I won't leave a detail out. I never want anything between us again but the truth."

She snuggled closer. "I never want anything between us again, period," she murmured.

They kissed again, and time stood still...until they heard a car approaching the house.

"I'll bet that's Alex," Cassie whispered. "What should we do? Read him the riot act for pretending to be you?"

"No, he hasn't done that yet. Maybe we should just wait and see what he does. Hurry, Cass! You go and meet him before he rings the doorbell. Don't let him know I'm here. Just play along for a while."

Cassie didn't have time to think about whether or not what Adam was proposing was a good idea. She heard the car door slam and knew Alex—if it really was him—was already headed to the house. She hurried around to the front—yeah, it was Alex, all right—just as he was climbing the three steps to the porch. Standing clear of the tree, the moonlight shined on her fully.

"Cassie?" Alex said, a little startled. "Is that you?"

"Yes, it's me. What are you doing here?" Cassie decided she wouldn't address him as Alex or Adam. She'd let him dig his own grave.

Cassie had stopped about fifteen feet away from Alex, crossed her arms over her chest and frowned. He started toward her, then stopped, as if discouraged by her unwelcoming pose. She could see him clearly in the porch light. All trace of the black eye was gone now, or hidden by makeup.

"Were you taking a walk?" he asked her in a meek and cajoling voice. He was stalling, of course. Maybe he was having second thoughts. Or maybe he was just easing into his "Adam act" slowly.

"Yes, I was walking. It's a beautiful night."

He nodded, licked his lips. "I guess you're pretty surprised to see me."

Interesting. He seemed just as reluctant to give himself a name as she was. She decided that maybe he was waiting for her to identify him one way or the other, taking his cue from her.

She wasn't about to make it easy for him, so she said, "Of course I'm surprised to see you, *Adam.* You haven't called or written since I saw you last weekend."

Your move, she thought.

By Alex's troubled expression, Cassie could tell he was having a mental struggle. Maybe his conscience was finally making itself painfully known. *About time.*

He released a long sigh. The struggle was over. "Cass, it's not Adam. It's me, Alex."

"Alex?"

"Don't sic your dad on me yet, Cass. Just listen to me."

"Why should I listen to you? You've done nothing but lie to me."

"Not anymore. I was going to tell you one more lie tonight, *one more* lie just to fix the mess I've made, but I couldn't do it. God, I'm so sorry! About everything!"

Cassie controlled her urge to smile. He sounded so contrite, so sincere! And it made her so happy! It was particularly gratifying to hear Alex's apology since Adam was hearing it, too, from his hiding place around the corner of the house.

When Cassie didn't answer, Alex continued in a more desperate tone. "If you can't forgive me, Cass, at least forgive Adam. That's really why I'm here. I came to plead my brother's case. I was actually going to pretend to be him, try to say all the right words to win you back."

"But why would you do that, Alex?"

"Because *I* was the one who dragged him into this mess in the first place! He's been digging *my* rear out of jams since we were kids, but this time I asked too much and he's paying for it. Cass, he's miserable without you. I've never seen him so much in 1—"

"That's enough, Alex. I think I can speak for myself now."

Alex's eyes grew wide as Adam stepped out of the shadows to stand beside Cassie and wrap his arm around her shoulder.

"Adam! What are *you* doing here?"

"Little brother, I can ask you the same thing."

That silenced Alex for a minute, but only a minute. "You must have heard me just now! I haven't got ulterior motives, bro! I'm here to save your butt, just like you've saved mine a million times."

"I told you I could take care of my own business, didn't I, Alex?" Adam reminded him. "I told you not to interfere."

This was irrefutable, so Alex stuttered for a minute before blurting out, "You sure looked like you needed my help. You and your problems were all I could think about while Kelly and I were in Hawaii."

Adam grinned. "Well, then maybe you've been punished enough. The last thing a man wants to think about on his honeymoon is his brother. I sure as hell won't be thinking about *you* while I'm on *my* honeymoon!"

This announcement sent Cassie's circulatory system into overdrive. Her heart was racing, her head was pounding as blood surged through her body at the speed of light. Was Adam speaking hypothetically, or was this honeymoon something he planned for the near future with—dare she hope?—the likes of her?

Alex was wondering the same thing, but he had no trouble putting it succinctly into words. "Bro, are you and Cassie getting married?"

Adam's arm tightened around Cassie's shoulder, and it was a good thing because her knees got weak suddenly when he answered, "If she'll have me. But since I haven't yet asked, do you think you could give us a little time alone, Alex?"

Alex grinned from ear to ear. "I'd do a hip-hip-hooray, but I might attract coyotes. Or something even fiercer...like Cassie's dad."

"I've already been...er...attracted," came Jasper's voice from the front door. Cassie had forgotten that she'd flown out of the house so fast she'd left the front door open and only the screen door swinging closed behind her. How much had her father heard? And where was Tyler?

Alex looked horrified, but Jasper only laughed. "You look about as comfortable as a mongrel dog caught in the henhouse with feathers 'tween his teeth, Alex." He pushed open the screen door. "Come on in, son. You heard your brother. He wants a little private time with Cassie and, by damn, he's gonna get it. Ty's in the kitchen pourin' root beer and waitin' on me to pop some corn. We've got the second half of a shoot'em-up to watch. Care to join us?"

Alex knew this was not just an invitation, but a command. Still a little leery, but obviously without a choice in the matter, Alex gave a polite, nervous smile and preceded Jasper into the house.

"Straight down the hall to your right's the kitchen," he instructed Alex. "I'll be along in just a minute." Then he turned to Cassie and Adam.

"Since this might come up, Cassie," he began matter-of-factly, "I want you to know that I've got no problem with you and Ty moving to Alaska as long as I can spend part of each year there—the summer months, of course. The boy'll miss me and I'll miss him. Christmas you can come here. When we visit up there, you can give me and Sylvie the guest cabin.''

"You and *Sylvie?*" Cassie was stunned. How long had this been going on?

"Now that you're gonna be settled, Sylvie and I'll get married, too. I'll sell half the ranch to Brad and hire Jed Barlow as full-time manager to handle the other half. Me and my bride plan to travel quite a bit, y'see. So, now that you know how things'll be settled in *my* life, you go ahead and settle *your* life just exactly the way you want it…hear?''

"I—I hear, Dad," Cassie said in a quavery voice. She couldn't believe what was going on! It seemed as though everyone's lives around her had been in limbo until her own life had shifted into high gear and now they were *all* on paths to happiness! Brad and Susan, now her father and *Sylvie?* Boy, where had she been while all this was going on?

Jasper nodded with satisfaction. "Good. Now, take your time, you two. I'll keep the young'uns busy.''

Cassie and Adam laughed at the way Jasper lumped Alex and Ty into the same category. Fortunately Alex was too far away to hear. After Jasper went in, closing both doors behind him, Cassie turned to Alex. "I'm in shock," she said incredulously. "For so many reasons.''

"You didn't know about Sylvie and your dad, I gather?''

"Not a clue.''

"Well, your dad's a cagey guy. If he didn't want you to know, you wouldn't know.''

"But have *I* been the reason he hasn't married her already?"

"I don't know." Adam gave a crooked smile. "But I doubt either of them have been suffering...if you know what I mean. Marriage is probably just a formality for the wonderful, fulfilling relationship they already enjoy."

Cassie blushed and grinned ruefully. "Is that your way of hinting that they're sleeping together?"

"Like I said, your dad's a cagey guy. But let's not talk about Sylvie and Jasper, anymore. Let's talk about Cassie and Adam." Cassie was more than willing.

Adam took her hand and led her to the porch steps. He helped her to a seat on the top step, then lowered himself to the next step down. In the porch light, Cassie could see his handsome face clearly, see every expression, every tender gleam in his eye or smile on his kissable lips. If she hadn't dragged him into the shadows earlier, she'd have recognized him as Adam immediately.

But now he could see *her* just as clearly. Could he tell how nervous she was, how full of wonder and hope and surprise? Could he tell that she was about to burst with happiness, burst into tears, or both?

His smile was gentle, his eyes full of love and tender curiosity. "What are you thinking, Cassie? Have I bowled you over? Have I gone too fast? Talk to me, Cass. Tell me how you feel."

"I feel scared and nervous and happy and confused and never more sure of one thing..."

"And that is?"

"That I love you, Adam Baranof."

His smile stretched from ear to ear. His eyes glowed. "And I love you. In fact, I'm crazy about you. Does this mean…?"

He left the question dangling, but Cassie wouldn't settle for anything but a full proposal. With a teasing sternness, she said, "Adam Baranof, you sent your brother into the house with my father so we could be alone, so you could ask me a question. I've heard plenty of questions, but none of them particularly struck me as needing this kind of privacy. Maybe you'd better get to the point before Jasper and Ty hit the hay. You'll have to ask them *both* for my hand in marriage, you know."

Adam laughed. "I think your father already gave it."

"Adam!"

"But I'll get to the point, anyway." He got very serious, his mouth curved in the sweetest, sexiest smile. "It would give me the greatest pleasure— It would make me the happiest of men— Ah, hell, Cassie, *will* you marry me?"

Cassie's heart filled with joy. Sure it happened fast. But when it was meant to be, did that really matter?

Blinking back her tears, she answered, "Yes, Adam. I'll marry you."

They kissed to seal the deal, but Tyler's voice startled them apart. "Mommy?"

Cassie and Adam looked up to see Tyler standing at the threshold, one hand propping open the screen door, a very serious expression on his face. Jasper and Alex hovered in the background. Suddenly Cassie was nervous. What if, even after what he'd said earlier that night, Tyler didn't approve of her marriage to Adam? She could never do anything that made Tyler unhappy.

"What is it, honey?" she asked.

"Granddad said I wasn't supposed to bug ya, but I couldn't wait to ask Uncle Adam somethin'."

"What did you want to ask me, bud?" Adam said. By the way he was squeezing her hand, Cassie could tell he was nervous, too.

"I was just wonderin'…if you and my mommy get married, will you be my daddy for real or still jus' an uncle?"

"What do *you* want me to be, Ty?" he asked carefully.

Tyler shrugged. "Well, I want you to be my daddy, o' course."

Adam looked at Alex. Alex nodded and smiled. Adam looked at Cassie. She smiled, too, with tears in her eyes. "In that case, Ty, I'd be happy to be your daddy."

Ty's serious expression disappeared. He was beaming. "Good! When can we go fishin'?"

Epilogue

A year later

It was a crystal-blue June morning in Seldovia, a perfect day for fishing. Cassie wiped her wet hands on a dishcloth and looked out the back door toward the boat dock. Adam promised to have everyone back by eleven, time to clean the fish and cook it for lunch.

It was going to be a very special lunch for Cassie, not just because Dad and Sylvie had arrived from Montana the evening before, but because she had an announcement to make.

Cassie propped the heels of her hands against her lower back and stretched like a cat, pushing her bulging stomach out until it looked like a basketball. Cassie was only six months pregnant, but she felt as if she was ready to deliver any minute!

Incredibly, despite her extremely round middle, Adam still found her sexy. He didn't just say so, he showed her frequently. Cassie treasured their long, tender nights of lovemaking. But even when they just held each other and planned their family's rosy future, it was heaven just being in his arms. Cassie still felt like a honeymooner. She had never been so content.

As for Ty, after initially missing his Granddad to the point of a few teary episodes, he took to living in Alaska like a fish to water...the clichéd analogy entirely appropriate. Christmas in Montana did a great deal to speed the adjustment. It had been a wonderful holiday and a sort of confirmation to Tyler that his old home would always be there, complete with Granddad, his horse, Buster, and an especially glowing Sylvie these days.... It seemed marriage also worked a charm for the older generation. Cassie was grateful that Sylvie was filling a void for Jasper that her mother had left behind.

While in Nye for the holidays, they'd attended the wedding of one of Ty's "uncles," Uncle Brad and Susan. Susan now managed Cassie's bookstore and conferred with her via long-distance and E-mail on a daily basis. As long as Susan wanted to manage the store, Cassie would hold on to it. If Susan decided she wanted to buy the store or move on to something else, Cassie would sell.

By retaining ownership of the store, she had a ready excuse to talk to Susan frequently. It was so much fun to share anecdotes of marital bliss—and even to occasionally compare notes and give advice about the very rare not-so-blissful moments—with another newlywed. They were both happier than they ever thought possible.

Brad missed Ty, but he and Susan were working very hard at making a baby so Brad wouldn't be without a "bud" for too awfully long.

Christmas in Montana held special memories for Cassie in another respect, too. That's where she conceived her pregnancy, right there in her old bedroom where she used to have girlish dreams about the kind of man she was now actually married to, a man whom she enjoyed waking up with every morning and lying down to sleep with every night.

Well, except when he went out on two-to-three-week-long research treks, or was a guest speaker for some professor at Fairbanks University. Those occasions were difficult for Cassie, especially when the nights grew endlessly long in the winter. But she kept busy with Tyler, doing all kinds of indoor sports at the local gymnasium, as well as teaching him to read. There was no preschool in the area and he'd be attending kindergarten in the fall, so Cassie was making sure he was as prepared as every other child. Tyler was smart, so that was certainly no problem. He was just like his daddy in that respect.

Nowadays, Alex didn't even cross her mind when Cassie thought about Tyler's father. In every way except biologically, Adam was Tyler's dad.

They were so close, those two. Ty and his dad spent lots of happy times together, and not a day passed that Cassie didn't thank her lucky stars and a gracious God in heaven that Susan had forced her to look through that *Single Men of Alaska* magazine. It was definitely a blessing in disguise for all of them.

Speaking of Tyler's brilliant father, Adam had taken a full-time position at the new aquarium in Seward, overseeing all affairs from business—Adam hadn't mentioned that he had a minor in business, as well—to each animal's environment and food.

Looking around Adam's formerly spartan house now, she decided that she'd succeeded pretty well with their own environment. The feminine touches made a big difference. Even the table she'd set for their special lunch with her own pretty new china, a sunflower-printed tablecloth and napkins she'd made during a surge of energy one night when Adam was gone, added so much to the room.

Looking at the table with the salads she'd made already set out in serving bowls and the plump loaves of crusty brown bread just waiting to be cut, made her ravenous...not an uncommon occurrence lately.

Impatient for the fishing party to return not only because she was hungry, but because she was dying to make *the announcement,* she decided to walk the half mile down the road to the mailbox.

Cassie was staying as active as possible during her pregnancy because she knew it would make her delivery and recovery easier. She smiled her secret smile as she walked under a canopy of aspen trees, the smooth, round leaves flashing like silver dollars in the sun. It was the smile she'd been trying to hide ever since she got her ultrasound results late yesterday afternoon. Yes, she'd definitely need to be in good health come September.

Cassie opened the mailbox and was immediately assailed with the telltale scent of some exotic perfume. Pulling a thick stack of mail out, she knew what she'd find. Thumbing through bills and junk mail, she ran across the suspect envelope. It was powder-blue and addressed beautifully.

Yes, even after a year, replies to his *Single Men of Alaska* ad still came through. Cassie held the envelope near her nose and took a cautious sniff. That's what was stinking up the entire contents of the mailbox, all right.

Cassie admitted to a bit of jealous curiosity about the contents of these letters, and how they compared to her letter to Adam a year ago. But Adam had a very honorable method of handling his "fan mail." He sent them back unopened with a politely phrased apology printed neatly on the back, reading, "Thank you for your interest, but I'm happily married now. Good luck in your future endeavors. Adam Baranof."

Cassie knew that Adam was perfectly correct in handling the letters in this way, because it would be unkind to indulge their curiosity or entertain themselves at the expense of the letter writers. Cassie reminded herself of this as she firmly tucked this tempting morsel of a missive behind the stack she was sorting through, and found another interesting letter on top with international postmarks and colorful stamps. The return address was Brazil—it was a letter from Alex and Kelly.

With a quicker step, Cassie returned to the house just in time to meet the fishing party in the kitchen.

"Beautiful!" exclaimed Sylvie, her dark eyes sparkling, her cheeks glowing with health and happiness. "This state is *so* beautiful! And I've never seen so much wildlife. So many fish!"

"Sylvie, you just wait," Cassie warned her.

"You just got here. You haven't even scratched the surface of this incredible place."

She worked her way down the line of the three most important men in her life, all of them smelling of wind and water and just a teensy bit of fish.

She got on her tiptoes and kissed her father on the cheek. "Hi, Dad. Ummm. What's the aftershave?"

"It's called Fish Musk," he deadpanned, swatting her on the fanny as she passed.

She bent down to rub noses, Eskimo-style, with Tyler. It was a new thing with him. "You catch your limit, bud?"

"Not this time, Mommy." He leaned close to whisper, "I let Granddad catch the most 'cause he's a guest."

She laughed and tousled his dark hair. "Good sport, Ty."

Straightening up again, she found Adam waiting for her with open arms. Moving into that familiar yet always exciting embrace, they kissed with the restraint dictated by a roomful of people, but with tender looks that said much more.

"Feeling okay, hon?" he asked her.

"I feel fabulous."

"All ready for dinner?" He raised his brows in that particular way of his. A double meaning was implied and understood.

She smiled that secret smile. "Ready as I'll ever be."

"Did you get hold of Mom and Dad?"

"Yes. They'll be here in time for dessert. Your

dad couldn't get here sooner. He's coming between charters, meeting your mom at the docks.''

He nodded and they parted reluctantly. It was time to be host and hostess.

The men made quick work of cleaning the fish outside and Adam cooked them while Cassie passed out crackers, cheese and iced tea. Everyone was hungry. The great outdoors did that to you. So did pregnancy.

The meal was delicious, the conversation lively. When Cassie lifted the knife to cut the chocolate cake, the doorbell rang. Adam got up to let in his parents. There was general confusion as greetings were exchanged, then the group settled again in the living room with coffee and cake handed around by Adam and Cassie.

"Sit down, Cassie," Peter finally ordered as she started to collect empty plates. "We should be waiting on you."

Peter had proven to be a wonderful father-in-law, even a little protective. Monica was like a best friend.

"I can't sit still. I think I'm a little nervous," Cassie admitted, stealing a meaningful glance at Adam.

"Why are you nervous, sweetie?" Jasper asked her, always alert to anything that might be amiss in his darling daughter's life.

Adam got up to stand next to his wife, his arm around her nonexistent waist as they faced the suddenly very attentive group. Even Tyler was bugeyed as he sat happily squeezed between his two grandfathers.

"What's wrong, Mommy?" he demanded, not afraid to get right to the point.

"Nothing's wrong, Ty," Cassie told him. "Something's actually very, very right." She felt her eyes well with happy tears. She hated how easily she got emotional these days, but hormones usually had their way with you no matter what you tried to do about it.

Adam handed Cassie a handkerchief and asked a question with his eyes. She nodded. "What my wife is trying to tell you," he said at last, "is that she and I are the proud parents of twins."

"Twins? Well, I'll be damned!" Jasper declared.

Tyler was elated. "You mean I'm going to have two baby brothers! Wow!"

Peter exclaimed. "I can't believe it! Well…yes, I guess I can! I *should!*"

Monica was teary-eyed. "I'm so happy I could cry!"

"Lordy, girl, you're going to have your hands full! In a good way, of course. But *really* full." Sylvie concluded for everyone.

After the initial, spontaneous remarks were made, Adam's hand was pumped and they were both kissed to within an inch of their lives.

"Cassie, when did you find out?" Monica asked her as she wiped her eyes and blew her nose.

"Just yesterday afternoon. Believe me, I wouldn't hold out on you on something this important. We're both so excited!"

"If you wouldn't mind a little advice, I could tell you quite a bit about raising twins!"

"I know," Cassie said. "And I'm counting on

your sharing your wisdom. Only I think it might be a little bit different for me than it was for you."

"How's that?" Peter asked. "Believe me, Cassie, two boys the same age in the house is always a powder keg."

"That's the thing...." Cassie smiled down at Tyler and rested her hand on his head. "I hope you don't mind, Ty, but we're not getting two boys. We're getting a boy and a *girl*."

This caused another commotion that took some time to quiet down. By now Cassie was nearly exhausted from all the excitement. Seeing this, Adam made her sit down and gave everyone in the room a meaningful look. They quickly understood and bottled up their own excitement to explode like an uncorked champagne bottle at another location.

"We'd better go," Monica announced tactfully. "I have some errands to run and Peter has another charter in fifteen minutes. Don't you, dear?"

Peter followed his wife's lead and they were soon gone, smiling like lottery winners as they waved goodbye from the porch. Sylvie and Jasper left, taking Tyler with them for a walk into town. They looked like happy gamblers, too, so full of riches they could burst. Even Tyler was okay with the "girl" surprise. He was sure he could teach the female part of the pair to like fishing, too.

Left alone, Adam sat on an ottoman at the end of Cassie's chair and put her feet in his lap. He tenderly massaged her aching ankles and tired feet until Cassie thought she'd swoon from pleasure.

"Why are you so good to me?"

"Because I love you. And because you're the mother of my three children."

Cassie smiled. He always said the right thing.

Suddenly she remembered Alex's letter. Picking it up off a nearby table, she handed it to Alex. "All this talk of twins and I still forgot to tell you that you got a letter from your duplicate sibling."

He neatly opened the envelope with his thumbnail. "Shall I read it aloud?"

"Yes. Do. I want to hear how the happy couple likes Brazil."

Adam read the letter, which was written by Alex, the bulk of which was a vivid narration of their travels and activities for the past couple of weeks since leaving for Brazil from Florida to work for an oil company there for a few months. It all sounded so exciting, so adventurous, so perfect for Alex and Kelly. They were very happy together and very happy with their lives and jobs. It was again obvious to Cassie that Tyler was meant to be Adam's son, just as she was meant to be his wife.

"Listen to this, Cass," Adam said suddenly after puzzling over the last few sentences of the letter. "This is just too weird."

"'Life is great, bro and Cass. I never thought I'd ever be this happy. But even more important to me is how happy you two are. Or should I say you four, counting my nephew, Ty, and the new little nephew you're carrying? Or is it *five?* Somehow, considering family patterns and all, I can't help thinking that maybe Cassie's carrying twins. But maybe heredity has nothing to do with it. Maybe when you're twice as deserving as the next couple, twice as nice, twice as happy as most, you get twice as many bundles of joy.'"

Cassie got teary-eyed again, grabbed a tissue, and mumbled defensively, "I can't help it. It's the hormones!"

Adam grinned and leaned forward to take his weeping wife in his arms. "It's okay, Cass. I'm happy enough to cry, too, and it's not hormones. *My* hormones are telling me to do something entirely different."

She smiled through her tears. "What's stopping you?"

He laughed. "Nothing," he said as he rested his hand on her stomach. "Nothing at all." Then he kissed her very tenderly on the lips.

HARLEQUIN®
AMERICAN ◆ ROMANCE®

*They're handsome, they're sexy, they're
determined to remain single.
But these two "bachelors" are about to
receive the shock of their lives...*

OOPS! STILL MARRIED!

**August 1999—#787 THE OVERNIGHT GROOM
by Elizabeth Sinclair**
Grant Waverly must persuade Katie Donovan to
continue their newly discovered marriage for just two
more intimate weeks....

**September 1999—#790 OVERNIGHT FATHER
by Debbi Rawlins**
Matthew Monroe never forgot the woman he'd once
married for convenience. And now Lexy Monroe
needs the man from whom she's kept
one little secret....

Look for the special *Oops! Still Married!*
duet, coming to you soon—only from
Harlequin American Romance®!

The honeymoon is just beginning...

Available at your favorite retail outlet.

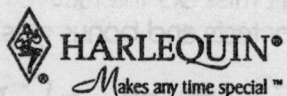

HARLEQUIN®
Makes any time special ™

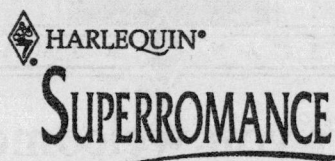

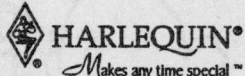

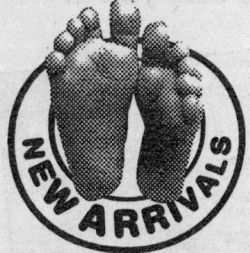
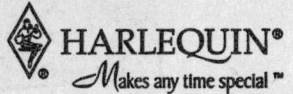

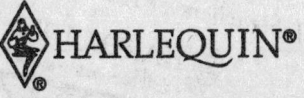

COMING NEXT MONTH

#785 THE LAST STUBBORN COWBOY by Judy Christenberry
4 Tots for 4 Texans
With his friends married and in a family way, Mac Gibbons thought the bet was over, and he was safe from the matchmaking moms of Cactus, Texas. That is, until he stopped to help a lady in distress and looked down into the blue eyes of new doc Samantha Collins...and her baby daughter. A daughter who looked amazingly just like Mac!

#786 RSVP...BABY by Pamela Browning
The Wedding Party
The last thing Bianca D'Alessandro needed was to be a bridesmaid at a family wedding. Especially since she'd be bringing a pint-size guest no one knew about. She could pass off the whispers, but she couldn't avoid the best man, Neill Bellamy—the father of her secret baby....

#787 THE OVERNIGHT GROOM by Elizabeth Sinclair
Oops! Still Married!
Grant Waverly's career was his mistress...until he found out he was married! Kathleen Donovan had been his one true love—and apparently his wife for the past seven years, though neither one knew it. But now that Grant had a wife, he intended to keep her!

#788 DEPUTY DADDY by Charlotte Maclay
Lawman Johnny Fuentes didn't know what to do with the beautiful but very pregnant woman with amnesia who was found wandering in town—except take her home. Trouble was, soon she began believing he was her husband!

Look us up on-line at: http://www.romance.net

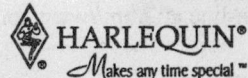

"There's som...
Her eyes held h...
but you make me...
waiting for you forever."

Had she waited? He had no right to expect her to have. He had no right to ask.

"Have you been?"

"I don't know." Her brow crinkled. "What is it that people wait for, Clark?"

He crushed her mouth with a kiss.

He whispered, "Lilleth..." in her ear. He kissed her again, this time slowly savoring her.

"Well," she murmured at last, when he allowed her a breath. "You've just made it clear to me that in some ways I am still a virgin." She curled her fingers into his shirt. "Come with me into the bedroom, Clark."

* * *

Rebel with a Heart
Harlequin® Historical #1160—November 2013

Author Note

Are you like I am? Does your heart beat a little faster for a mysterious hero?

When I was eight years old I sat in front of the television set and fell madly, completely in love with Zorro/Don Diego. The humor of the Don made me laugh, but when the dashing protector emerged I melted. I carried that torch for a few years and, to be honest, there's still a bit of the flame left.

Who can resist the lure of Superman/Clark Kent? Or Batman/Bruce Wayne? For me, the hero in disguise is an irresistible character.

For the longest time I've wanted to create one of my own. I hope you enjoy reading about Trace Ballentine/Clark Clarkly, and that just maybe your heart will beat a little faster.

Three cheers for heroes in disguise!

Best wishes and happy reading.

REBEL WITH A HEART

CAROL ARENS

ISBN-13: 978-0-373-29760-3

REBEL WITH A HEART

Copyright © 2013 by Carol Arens

All rights reserved. Except for use in any review, the reproduction or utilization of this work in whole or in part in any form by any electronic, mechanical or other means, now known or hereafter invented, including xerography, photocopying and recording, or in any information storage or retrieval system, is forbidden without the written permission of the publisher, Harlequin Enterprises Limited, 225 Duncan Mill Road, Don Mills, Ontario M3B 3K9, Canada.

This is a work of fiction. Names, characters, places and incidents are either the product of the author's imagination or are used fictitiously, and any resemblance to actual persons, living or dead, business establishments, events or locales is entirely coincidental.

This edition published by arrangement with Harlequin Books S.A.

For questions and comments about the quality of this book, please contact us at CustomerService@Harlequin.com.

® and TM are trademarks of Harlequin Enterprises Limited or its corporate affiliates. Trademarks indicated with ® are registered in the United States Patent and Trademark Office, the Canadian Trade Marks Office and in other countries.

Printed in U.S.A.

HARLEQUIN®
www.Harlequin.com

Did you know that these novels are also available as ebooks? Visit www.Harlequin.com.

To my daughter, Jennifer Lynne, because sometimes life takes a turn and grants you a miracle.

CAROL ARENS

While in the third grade, Carol Arens had a teacher who noted that she ought to spend less time daydreaming and looking out the window and more time on her sums. Today, Carol spends as little time on sums as possible. Daydreaming about plots and characters is still far more interesting to her.

As a young girl, she read books by the dozen. She dreamed that one day she would write a book of her own. A few years later, Carol set her sights on a new dream. She wanted to be the mother of four children. She was blessed with a son, then three daughters. While raising them she never forgot her goal of becoming a writer. When her last child went to high school she purchased a big old clunky word processor and began to type out a story.

She joined Romance Writers of America, where she met generous authors who taught her the craft of writing a romance novel. With the knowledge she gained, she sold her first book and saw her lifelong dream come true.

Carol lives with her real-life hero husband, Rick, in Southern California, where she was born and raised. She feels blessed to be doing what she loves, with all her children and a growing number of perfect and delightful grandchildren living only a few miles from her front door.

When she is not writing, reading or playing with her grandchildren, Carol loves making trips to the local nursery. She delights in scanning the rows of flowers, envisaging which pretty plants will best brighten her garden.

She enjoys hearing from readers, and invites you to contact her at carolsarens@yahoo.com.

Chapter One

Riverwalk, South Dakota
November, 1879

A splinter jutting from the boardwalk pierced Trace
Ballentine's trousers. He cursed his luck. He growled
at fate. How could it be possible that he was facing
one of the most pivotal moments of his life with a
piece of wood stabbing his rump?

Admittedly, he hadn't slipped by accident, but he
hadn't intended to take a woman down with him, either. Still, here the lady was, sprawled across his lap
in front of the ticket counter at the train depot, with
the contents of her valise scattered near and far. Un-
dergarments and shoes, ribbons and hatpins littered
the boardwalk, mostly crushed under the stack of
books he had been carrying.

He snatched his shattered spectacles from under
his knee and plopped them on his nose.

Even through a spiderweb of broken glass he knew this woman. Even after sixteen years of foggy memory and change he recognized his one true love.

"Why, you big…" She seemed to be searching for the nastiest word in her vocabulary.

"Oaf?" he supplied.

"Dolt."

The accusation didn't sting; she'd called him worse dozens of times in playfulness. Still, that didn't mean he wasn't wounded to his soul.

Lilleth Grace Preston stared straight into his eyes without knowing who he was.

In every fantasy he'd ever had of their miraculous reunion they had showered tears and kisses all over each other.

He had vowed to love her forever, and damned if he hadn't. He'd cherished her memory since he was fourteen years old, yet not a twitch of her eyebrow or a blink of her lashes revealed that she recalled him.

To be fair, how could he have expected her to? The last time they had been together he had been gangly, whereas now he was tall and filled out. Over the years his hair had darkened from blond to brown. These days he wore a beard, trimmed short and neat. Back then he had barely sprouted peach fuzz.

He was nothing like the boy he had been, while she looked very much the same. With her red curls, snapping blue eyes and mouth that went from a grimace to a smile in a flash, he'd have known her even if he hadn't been cursed with a mind that remembered nearly everything.

"Kindly remove your person from under me, Mr.…?" She arched one brow.

It's me. It's Trace.

"Clark," he declared. He wrinkled his brow, then added a hiccup.

"Mr. Clark, your—"

"Clarkly, that is. Mr. Clark Clarkly, at your service, miss."

"Mr. Clark Clarkly, kindly remove your knee from my bustle."

"Your…? Oh, my word, I beg your pardon." He straightened his leg and reached for her hand, desperate for just one touch, even if that touch was through a leather glove.

She allowed him to help her to her feet. He then made a show of being a buffoon by attempting to straighten her skirt.

Curse it, he *was* a buffoon, and he didn't even have to act a part. Of all the disguises he could have chosen for this assignment, why did it have to be Clark Clarkly?

Had he ever dreamed that he might run into Lilleth Preston he'd have made himself a lawman or a cowboy. Anyone but good old Clarkly, the bungling, bookish librarian.

But Trace was good and stuck now. Most of the citizens of Riverwalk had made the acquaintance of

Clarkly—run into him, quite literally. He couldn't change identities midassignment. Too much was at stake. The innocent inmates at the Hanispree Mental Hospital depended on Clarkly.

He ought to thank his lucky stars that Lilleth hadn't recognized him. It broke his heart, but it was for the best.

Hot damn, he was stuck in a muddle of his own making with no way out. There was nothing for it but to dive in headfirst.

Lilleth slapped his hand where it attempted to straighten that fascinating, if tweaked, little bustle behind her skirt.

"Mr. Clarkly! Have you no shame?"

Good girl, Lils, he thought, *you still hold your own against anyone.*

"Why…yes. Usually, that is. Miss, you pack quite a wallop." He shook his slapped hand, then stooped to gather her belongings from under his books.

She would think he was an idiot for plucking up her lacy, pink-ribboned corset, but that was as close to intimacy as he was likely ever to get with her.

Lilleth crouched beside him, her hand already in motion to deliver another swat. He shoved the garment at her, but not before he noticed that it smelled like roses.

"Don't you lay a finger on those bloomers." Lilleth leveled a glare at him, snatched up her belongings and stuffed them into her valise. She snapped it closed, then stood up.

November wind, blowing in the promise of the first snow, swirled the hem of Lilleth's skirt. Her toe tapped the boardwalk with the one-two-three-pause, one-two-three-pause rhythm that he remembered. She was struggling with her temper.

He gathered up his books and, in true Clark style, layered them in alphabetical order. He'd intended her to notice that, and she had. She rolled her eyes and sighed.

"It has been a pleasure, truly." He offered his hand. "I'm sorry about the little knock-you-down. My deepest apologies, and welcome to Riverwalk."

Most women wouldn't accept his apology, given that he'd been clumsy upon stupid upon rude, but he left his hand extended just in case.

Lilleth stared at his face for a long time, studying, weighing, judging.

"I'm ever so sorry, Miss…?"

"Well, accidents do happen, after all." She shook his hand. The smile that had haunted his dreams pardoned him. "I'm Lilly Gordon."

Gordon? Married? No! Sixteen years ago she had taken his hand, pressed it to her twelve-year-old heart and vowed to marry him and only him.

"Hey, Ma, Mary's getting hungry."

A boy, no more than ten years old, walked up to Lilly Gordon carrying a baby.

"Cold, too," the boy added, frowning and shooting Clark an assessing look.

The baby didn't appear to be hungry or cold. In fact, it was bundled against the chill so that only a pair of blue eyes—Lils's eyes—and a pert little nose peeked out.

Trace admired the boy for stepping up. Some big galoot had just knocked his mother down.

"Make Mr. Clarkly's acquaintance, Jess." Lilleth took the baby from the boy's arms. "Then we'll be on our way. There's the hotel, just up ahead."

"A pleasure to meet you, young man," he said. And it was, too, now that the shock was wearing off. He extended his hand.

The boy cocked his head, studied his face as his mother had done, and then, like her, made up his mind in an instant. He shook Clark's hand.

"Well, good day, then, Mr. Clarkly," Lilleth said.

A spray of red curls tumbled out from under her hat. Her smile warmed him in places that hadn't been warm in forever.

Jess picked up his mother's valise, his own, and carried a smaller one tucked under his arm.

Trace watched Lilleth and her little family walk toward the Riverwalk Hotel. It was a good thing it was so close, for the temperature seemed to be dropping by the minute.

He was proud of Lils. She had grown to be a fine and beautiful woman. Even with a baby riding her hip the sway of her gait would be enough to catch any man's eye.

It was a lucky thing for him that she was married.

He had his mission, one he was dedicated to. Mrs. Gordon had her family. Life would go on.

Yes, it was very lucky that she was married. He hadn't really thought Lilleth would remain his Lils forever. Everyone grew up, everyone changed. No one remained a child forever. Not him, and most certainly not the lovely woman walking away from him.

Lilly Gordon glanced back. She arched one brow and smiled with the shadow of a question crossing her face.

He gripped his armload of alphabetized books tight.

It's me, Lils. It's Trace.

Blessed heat poured from the fireplace in the lobby of the Riverwalk Hotel. Lilleth walked past the check-in desk, pointing Jess toward the big hearth.

November in South Dakota was a beast.

"Sit there, Jess." She pointed to a big padded chair, one of a pair flanking the fireplace. "Get your sister out of that blanket so the warmth can reach her."

Lilleth removed her coat and gloves. She stood before the fire, letting it warm her, front then back. It took a few moments, but the bitter cold finally quit her bones.

She glanced about, relieved to see the hotel lobby

empty of patrons. Through an open door to her right she heard the ting of utensils against plates. An aroma of fresh warm bread swirled throughout the lobby, mixing with the scent of burning wood.

The moment she checked into her room, she would take the children to the dining room for dinner. They had to be hungry. The strenuous travel they had been forced to endure left little time for leisurely meals.

Riverwalk in November was not a place she would choose to be, but choice had been taken from her some time ago.

The hotel clerk bent down behind the tall counter. Lilleth took that moment to attempt to straighten her bustle. It had been crushed and bent beyond repair. No amount of yanking or pulling made a whit of difference to its appearance.

By all rights Mr. Clark Clarkly ought to pay for it. The man was beyond clumsy. Thank goodness it hadn't been Jess he had bowled over. He and Mary might have been injured. Mr. Clarkly ought to take his stroll with a warning to fellow pedestrians tied about his neck.

But there was something about him…something almost familiar. She couldn't at this very second imagine what it was, though.

"I'll be back, Jess. I'm going to check in, then we'll get something to eat."

Frigid wind huffed against the windowpanes, but

the hotel lobby was lovely and warm. Thank the stars that she had been able to wire ahead and get reservations on short notice.

"Good afternoon, Mr. Green." Lilleth read his name from the plaque on the counter. "My name is Lilly Gordon. I'd like to register for my room, if you please."

Mr. Green looked her over with interest, as men tended to do. It was a fact of life that nature and her mother had bequeathed her a figure that attracted men's attention. She had quit taking offense to their reactions years before. Men were men, after all, for good or ill.

"Mr. Green?" she asked, returning his attention to her face. "My room?"

The man blushed, ran his thumb down a list of names on the hotel register and then frowned.

"That's Mrs. Gordon," Lilleth said, feeling uneasy. The clerk ought to be smiling and handing her a key by now. "Mrs. Lilly Gordon."

He clicked his tongue against his teeth, then ran his forefinger over the register one more time. Halfway down, his finger stopped. He withdrew a pair of spectacles from his pocket, placed them on his nose, then bent low to peer at the page.

Lilleth tapped her foot.

Mr. Green closed the book and pressed his long, thin fingers on top of it. He cleared his throat.

"I do apologize, Mrs. Gordon. There appears to have been a mistake."

"Kindly check again." Tap tap, tap. "My reservation was confirmed."

"I see that, yes." The man shifted his weight. "But it appears that your room has been given to someone else."

Lilleth took a breath, slowly and calmly. She let it out, drawing deep down for a smile. *You catch more men with lace than you do with homespun*, she reminded herself. This philosophy was also something bequeathed by her mother.

"I'm sure you can provide them another room. Certainly they will understand once you explain the mistake."

"I'd like nothing more, Mrs. Gordon, but the couple in question are the elderly parents of the owner of this hotel. I can't rightly send them out in the cold."

Tap, tap…"I'm not asking you to do that. I'm simply asking that you give them another room."

"There are no others. I'm sorry."

"No other rooms?" There had to be another room; she had reserved one! "Do you see my children over there, Mr. Green? Mary's only a baby. Would you send her out into the cold?"

He truly did appear remorseful. She brightened her smile and forced her toe to be still.

"Not by choice, no, I wouldn't. But it's out of my hands."

"Whose hands would it be in, then, Mr. Green?" This error would be corrected or she was not Lilleth Preston. "We'll wait right here in the lobby until you find the person who can correct this error."

"It won't do any good. No rooms means no rooms. The hotel is booked up long term. There won't be a room here or anywhere else for a good while." Mr. Green reopened the register and flipped through a few pages. "Look for yourself. There's the Grange meeting in town. All the farmers and their families are here for it."

She would not take the children back out in the cold. They had only now quit shivering.

"Be that as it may, I do have a reservation." Lilleth looked about. There was nothing for it. "We'll take the lobby, then. The chairs by the fire will do well enough for now."

It served Mr. Green right to be choking on his Adam's apple.

"Come along, Jess," she called toward the fireplace. "Let's have a bite to eat before we settle into our chairs for the evening."

"May I be of service in some way?" said a low voice from behind her.

A deep breath, hands planted on her hips and a slow pivot brought her about to face a well-dressed man standing beside Mr. Green.

"And you would be?" She arched a brow. This had better be someone who could fix the situation.

"The owner of this establishment. Is there a problem?" he asked.

"There most certainly is, Mr. . . ." She shooed her hand between them, since he hadn't felt it necessary to reveal his name. "My reservation has been given away. According to Mr. Green, my children and I have no place to go but out in the cold to freeze to death."

"There is the meeting of the Grange. The whole town is booked."

"And I am one of the people who booked."

"I understand your frustration, ma'am. Let me think on it a moment." The hotel owner frowned and twirled his mustache between his thumb and forefinger. "There is Mrs. O'Hara's. She might have a room."

For some reason this made Mr. Green's eyes go wide as dollars.

"Very well, I suppose that will have to do." If it didn't she'd be back to camp out in this lobby. "And where will I find Mrs. O'Hara?"

"A few streets north of here will be a saloon. Make a right and go three blocks. That will take you near the edge of town. You can't miss the place. It's the only building around."

She'd rather not walk the children past a saloon, but there appeared to be no help for it.

She bundled Mary up tight. Jess took the bags.

"Give my regards to Mrs. O'Hara," Mr. Hotel

Owner called as she hustled the children out into the first snowfall of the season.

"Auntie Lilleth," Jess said, his shoulders hunched under the burden of the bags. "I hope Mrs. O'Hara's place isn't far. It's so cold I can't rightly feel my toes."

"Careful, Jess, ears are everywhere."

Trace opened the front door to Clark Clarkly's Private Lending Library, stumbled inside and then closed the door with the heel of his shoe.

He shivered from the chill lingering in his coat and dumped the load of books on his desk, letting them fall out of order. He tossed his broken glasses on the pile.

Ordinarily, he would light a fire in the big hearth that took up most of the wall behind his desk, but not this afternoon. Snow drifted past the window, growing heavier by the minute, and he needed to get to Hanispree Mental Hospital.

Unless he missed his guess, the staff wouldn't venture away from their cozy quarters to make sure the inmates were warm. It was back out into the cold for good old Clarkly.

Over the years, as an investigative journalist for the family paper, Trace had uncovered plenty of nasty secrets. Hanispree Mental Hospital had some of the worst. It was a stink hole of corruption. The more he poked around, the more determined he was to expose the malignant soul of the place.

To the casual observer, Hanispree looked like a resort where the wealthy might come to relax. Its gardens were manicured and the marble staircase inside gleamed. Expensive wood floors reflected layers of polish.

The truth that he had discovered ate at his gut. Polished floors and gleaming marble were a facade. Hanispree Mental Hospital was little more than a prison for the cast-off members of wealthy families. He was certain that some of them had no mental illness whatsoever.

A movement beyond the window caught his attention. He figured he'd be the only one foolhardy enough to go outdoors with a storm blowing in. He walked to the window and pulled aside the filmy curtain.

What the devil? Lilleth and her little brood were making their way down the boardwalk, their bodies leaning into the wind. He'd assumed they would be settled into the hotel by now.

He started to reach for the doorknob, to run after her and find out if there was something amiss.

But she had a husband, no doubt a fine man who was at this moment coming to her aid. Trace would do well to remember that he was not himself at the moment, but Clark Clarkly.

If she discovered who he was it might spell disaster for the exposé he was writing. If his true identity was revealed, what would happen to all the folks at Hanispree? He needed to keep his distance.

Trace peered after Lilleth, his eye to the window-pane trying to see up the street, where Mr. Gordon no doubt waited with open arms.

The investigative journalist in him began to gnaw at something. It was trivial, really. But Lilleth detested being called Lilly. He'd witnessed her wrestling half-grown boys to the ground for teasing her with that name.

A knock low down on the front door brought his attention and his eye away from the window.

He opened the door to let in a flurry of flakes and young Sarah Wilson.

"Little Sarah." He closed the door behind her, then brushed an inch of snowflakes from the brim of her hat. "What are you doing out in this weather?"

"Good day, Mr. Clarkly. I've come to borrow a book."

Bless her heart, coming out in the elements. He was familiar with Sarah. She was a nine-year-old bundle of curiosity, as well as a dedicated reader. Her mother was in frail health, and Sarah escaped into stories as often as she could.

Clark Clarkly and his lending library did have their uses in the community. He wasn't a complete waste.

"As luck would have it, I picked up a shipment of new books just an hour ago." Trace lurched toward the desk and snatched one up, along with his shattered spectacles. "I've just the thing for a girl your age, Miss Sarah."

He opened the ledger on his desk and Sarah signed her name in it, her promise to return the book.

"I'll bring it back real soon," she said.

"Not until the weather clears." He would give her the book to keep, along with a few others, when his assignment was finished and he went back home to Chicago. "Come along, I'll see you home."

Trace put on a heavy coat, picked up his collection of new books and gathered Sarah's mittened hand in his.

Outside, he closed the door behind him and glanced in the direction that Lilleth had gone, but she and her family had vanished.

Met up with her husband, no doubt, the lucky man. In his mind's eye, Trace saw the pair of them snuggled in front of a snapping fire. He wished his Lils and her man the best, truly he did.

"You're going to like this story, little lady." Trace walked in a direction away from Hanispree Mental Hospital, but there was no help for it. "It's the tale of a girl just your age."

Main Street was deserted, the silence profound. Only the shuffle of Lilleth's and Jess's footsteps on the boardwalk disturbed it.

Wisely, the folks of Riverwalk had withdrawn

into their homes. Tendrils of smoke curling out of fireplaces made the cold outside seem that much worse. Only yards away, people were tucked into houses and fully booked hotels, enjoying warmth and companionship.

With any luck, Mrs. O'Hara's place, whether it be a boardinghouse or private home with an extra room—Mr. Hotel Owner hadn't offered that information—would be warm and have food for the children.

Biting cold wasn't the only thing troubling her about Main Street this afternoon. The utter stillness was almost spooky. Out in the open, with no one else about, it seemed that eyes observed her every step. It was silly, of course, as she'd been careful.

A block back, she had been startled by a curtain being drawn aside. Her gasp had nearly woken baby Mary, who slept sweet and warm, against her breast.

"It's all right, Auntie Lilleth," Jess had said. "It's probably Mr. Clarkly. The sign over the door says that place is his lending library."

"It makes sense that Mr. Clarkly would be a librarian, the way he stacked those books in alphabetical order." For some reason it didn't bother her that he might be watching. Funny, when for the last two weeks she'd done nothing but live in fear of folks who stared too intently at her family.

"And Jess, don't forget, call me Mother. Anyone might hear you."

"Uncle Alden won't come to Riverwalk." Jess

shifted the small valise under his left arm to his right. "He's too afraid of ghosts."

True, Alden Hanispree had an unnatural fear of them. It was probably the very thing that had spared her sister's life. Had he not been such a fearful little man he might have murdered Bethany instead of having her committed to his haunted mental hospital.

Still, just because Alden Folger Hanispree was a cowardly man didn't mean that he wasn't dangerous.

Dangerous, and greedy for their inheritance, he was a powerful enemy to her niece and nephew.

"He might send someone, though." Lilleth stopped. She lifted her nephew's chin in her fingers and looked him in the eye. "I'll protect you, I swear it. But Jess, we can't be too careful. Watch every word you say and don't trust anyone but me."

"I wish my father was still alive. Uncle Alden couldn't hurt us then."

"I wish that, too." Lilleth traced the curve of Jess's cold cheek. It had been only six months since his father's death. Too little time to keep Jess's eyes from becoming moist. "But he sees us from heaven, I'm sure of it."

"Do you think, somehow from way up there, he can help us sneak Mama out of the mental hospital?"

"Well, if he can, you know he will, and if not, maybe he'll send someone our way who can help us."

She couldn't imagine who that would be, since she wouldn't allow anyone close enough to be able to help. She wouldn't say so to Jess, but it would be she who would have to figure a way to get Bethany away from Hanispree.

"Everything will turn out fine, Jess, don't you worry." Lilleth shifted the baby in her arms. She was small for a twelve-month-old, but nonetheless the weight was beginning to take a toll on Lilleth's back. "We'd better get to Mrs. O'Hara's before we freeze."

"Sure, Ma." Jess stepped forward with a long stride.

If her brother-in-law was watching from above, as she firmly believed, he would be proud of his only son. Jess was a brave and intelligent boy.

Praise the saints, they were nearly to the saloon, then only a few more blocks to sanctuary.

"Jess, come walk on the far side of me."

Things went on in a saloon that a ten-year-old didn't need to be privy to. It would take a heavier snowfall than this to keep men of low morals and women of loose values from their amusement.

Despite the cold, the front door was open to let out the choking smoke that built up in those places. If it were up to Lilleth, Jess would never be old enough to witness mostly exposed bosoms and the men ogling them.

"When we walk past the front door of the saloon, squeeze your eyes closed."

"Yes, ma'am," he agreed, but a grin crossed his face. And weren't his eyes cracked open a slit?

Well, a grin was better than tears. Blooming adolescence would be something for Bethany to deal with once they set her free.

All would be right when she was Auntie Lilleth again, free to spoil and coddle.

They had taken only a few steps around the corner of saloon when the wind began to howl. Cold air bit through their wool coats. Mary whimpered in her sleep. The three blocks to Mrs. O'Hara's couldn't come soon enough.

It became difficult to see through the swirling snow.

Just in time, Lilleth spotted a house in the distance.

"That way, Jess." She pointed through the shifting white veil.

In another moment a front porch came into view. A front porch with a red lantern hanging from the eves!

It couldn't be. Mr. Hotel Owner would not have sent her here…he couldn't have. Maybe Mrs. O'Hara simply liked red lanterns.

In any case, there was nothing for it but to knock on the door. The children couldn't take much more of the cold. Lilleth's own feet were becoming icy stubs.

The door opened after the third knock. Dim light and warmth spread over the porch.

"Is there something I can do for you, missus? Are you lost? And in this weather!"

Jess didn't bother to hide his grin or squeeze his eyes to respectable slits. Clearly, he was bedazzled by the woman with nearly purple hair, clown-red cheeks and eyes lined with black. Or more likely it was her mostly exposed bosom that made his eyes pop wide in wonder.

"No, not lost." Lilleth took Jess by the shoulder and turned him to face the street. "The owner of the Riverwalk Hotel directed me here after he gave away my room."

Well! Mr. Hotel Owner would not insult both her and Mrs. O'Hara by his little joke. This would not be the last he heard of it.

"On occasion I do rent upstairs rooms. But this wouldn't be the place for you and your children. It wouldn't be seemly. I'm sorry."

"I understand, Mrs. O'Hara. We'll find another place."

"I hope you do. I wouldn't turn you away, but there's the children, you see."

Yes, there were the children. Lilleth hustled Jess down the steps. Mr. Hotel Owner would be well aware of them before this night was through.

Chapter Two

One mile outside of town, Trace opened the gate of Hanispree Mental Hospital and walked through.

Apparently neither Dr. Merlot nor Nurse Goodhew had braved the weather to come outside and lock it for the night. Good luck for Trace—it saved him having to scale the tall stone wall surrounding the place.

The grounds of the hospital looked like a winter playground. The pristine snow covering everything resembled a sparkling blanket. Now that the storm had blown away, the moon shone down to make the area glisten.

But the wind was cold as needles.

To anyone who didn't know better, which would be nearly everyone until he finished his exposé, Hanispree was a lovely place to house the mentally ill. Benches and flowerbeds, bare at this time of year, were connected by a series of winding paths. The building itself was made of the same stone as the wall, with three stories of windows overlooking the elegant park.

To Trace's knowledge, no inmate of the hospital had ever set foot on the paths or sat upon the benches, even when the park was at its loveliest in the spring.

A shiver took him from the inside out. One day soon he would have this place shut down. The patients would be better off away from here, housed in institutions where their well-being was important to the caregivers.

Trace walked across the grounds toward a wide front porch, leaving a trail of footprints in the snow. The verandah, lined end to end with rocking chairs, welcomed him forward.

Through the front window the glow of a fire in the hearth cast golden light into the night. Too bad the aura of comfort was a lie.

Unseen in the dark, he watched through the window for a moment. Nurse Goodhew dozed in a fireside chair with her stocking-clad feet stretched toward the flames.

To call Mrs. Goodhew a nurse was like calling a grade-schooler a professor. From what he had learned, she was there for appearances only. Well, also to keep Dr. Merlot entertained of an evening.

Ah, here came the good doctor now, tiptoeing toward the snoring Mrs. Goodhew and touching her where a gentleman shouldn't.

Spy time was over; if Trace didn't get inside now, he might be shivering on the porch until they finished their tawdry business.

He rapped on the door. When a few moments later Nurse Goodhew opened it, she was wearing her shoes and a sour-looking smile. Dr. Merlot was nowhere to be seen.

"Good evening, Mrs. Goodhew. I've come with a delivery of books." He stepped inside, then stomped the snow from his feet. He took off his hat and thumped it against his thigh.

"Mr. Clarkly! Really, this floor was spotless. Who do you think will clean it now?"

"Why?" Trace lifted his spectacles an inch off his nose and peered at the floor through the broken glass. "I do beg your pardon, Nurse Goodhew. I didn't mean to create a mess."

He shook his head, adding a few more splatters to the floor.

"You must be a madman, coming out in this weather to bring books to people who can't even understand a word on the page."

"Yes, but I'm certain they will enjoy the pictures." He pulled the book on top of the stack from under his arm, opened it and extended it for her to see. "Look, we've got animals of every kind, frolicking in water." He turned the page. "Or nibbling grass."

"Give them here, then." Nurse Goodhew took

the stack. "I'll see them delivered first thing in the morning."

She wouldn't, of course. She never did.

"Thank you. I'm sure your patients will be grateful for your kindness." Trace shook his shoulders, dropping more globs of melting snow on the floor. "Oh my, beg pardon again. If you'll allow me, I'll clean this up before I go. It'll just take an instant."

"See that it does. That water will leave a mark if you're not quick about it."

"To be sure, Mrs. Goodhew."

"I'll be back with cleaning rags." She frowned at him authoritatively. "Don't move from that spot."

"Oh no, not an inch, I swear it."

Half a second after she stepped out of the room, Trace slipped off his boots and coat. He hurried to the desk where the key to the back door of the inmates' cells was kept. The second drawer down, he recalled, under a bottle of whiskey.

Tonight, there was only the bottle of whiskey.

He hurried back, stepped into his boots and put on his coat, and waited two full minutes for the nurse to return with her cleaning rags.

She shoved them at him with another frown. He made quick work of drying the floor. He'd lose some time now, having to figure a new way into the patients' wing.

He walked toward the gate in case anyone was

watching, then followed the brick wall around the back of the building.

His first stop was the woodpile. He shoved his useless glasses in his pocket. He loaded his arms with firewood, then made trip after trip to a window that he knew had a broken latch.

The trouble was, the window was eight feet off the ground. The snow was only a foot high. While scaling something seven feet tall wouldn't be hard, scaling and opening at the same time would be impossible.

The only thing to do was stack the wood under the window, climb the pile, then open the window. After that, he could go in and open the back door and bring the wood in that way, or he could avoid all those steps by tossing the wood through the open window, then climbing in after it. Tossing and climbing would take more effort, but going though the door would take more time.

Since the folks inside were probably shivering, he decided on tossing.

In all it took twenty minutes, but he didn't fear being discovered. Inmate care was more of an afterthought here, especially at night, with only Goodhew and Merlot in attendance. From Trace's experience, they tended to disappear from their shifts between the hours of seven and nine.

It was now seven-ten, giving Trace the time he needed.

He scooped up a load of wood and carried it to old Mrs. Murphy's room. There was a bolt on the outside of the door to insure she did not get out.

He slid it open and stepped into her room.

"Good evening, Mrs. Murphy." The old woman lay on her bed, curled up and shivering under a thin, dirty blanket.

Anger burned hot in him to see her treated so carelessly. Because she was frail and forgetful, her family paid Alden Hanispree a huge amount every month to keep her here. Chances were they were not aware of her meager conditions.

His research had uncovered a miserable truth. Visits by family and friends were by appointment only. An hour before the call the patient would be transferred to a luxurious suite for the duration of the visit. If a few patients did complain to a visitor, well, they were mentally ill. Who would believe their word over a doctor's?

Lies and secrets were the shadows darkening these halls. Soon Trace would have all the evidence he needed and the truth about Hanispree would be told.

Trace lit a fire in the old woman's fireplace, then watched to make sure it burned good and hot.

"Good night, Mrs. Murphy. I'll see you again soon."

The gray head nodded under her cover. "You are

quite considerate for a ghost, young man. I'm sorry you passed before your time."

He had told her many times that he wasn't a ghost, but it was just as well that she didn't remember. The lighting of unexplained fires and the appearance of extra food were easily blamed on the supernatural.

In under an hour he had brought warmth to every room but one. That door didn't have a bolt. A heavy lock made it impossible to get inside.

The investigator in him wanted to know what was in there. He'd heard stories of other institutions where the inmates were actually tortured in the name of research. One of these days he'd find a way into that second-story room.

Having done everything he could for the inmates, he went outside. He stepped beside his own footprints going away, thinking that it was a good thing for the old ghost stories. A spirit would be credited with all manner of strange happenings.

Had she not been homeless, freezing and responsible for two children, Lilleth would feel quite pleased.

Dinner at the hotel could not have gone better. In the end they had been kicked out of the restaurant, but she and the children had caused a bucketload of complaints to be served up to Mr. Hotel Owner.

Mary, having been confined to Lilleth's arms for much of the day, wanted to crawl about on the floor.

She wailed and carried on because she was not allowed to do so.

Jess accidentally spilled his milk on the tablecloth three times. Naturally, Lilleth had insisted on fresh linen with each accident.

And, by the saints, why could the kitchen not prepare her steak correctly? The waiter had to return it several times before it was cooked just so.

As annoyed as the other patrons were at her little family, they were aghast when the owner, with his own hands, escorted them out into the elements with orders not to return. Surely the fellow deserved every frown cast his way.

But what to do now? It was not that Lilleth couldn't afford a room, there simply were none to be had. Perhaps the livery would have a stall, but wouldn't that cause a stir? It might be fodder for gossip from one end of town to another. Poor frazzled mother of two, denied rooms at both the hotel and the brothel, ending up in a pile of straw?

She had slept in worse places than a clean pile of straw before, but she couldn't afford the attention that it would draw to her. She needed to remain in the shadows.

Oh, dear, she should have considered that during dinner.

While delivering Mr. Hotel Owner his just rewards had been deeply satisfying, the little show had drawn the attention of every diner in the hotel restaurant. She would have to be more discreet in the future.

"At least the snow has quit," Jess said, fitting his sister into the curve of his elbow.

The poor little thing continued to squirm and fuss. She hadn't been out of her or Jess's arms in ever so long.

Pain cramped Lilleth's fingers. They felt like frozen claws clutching the handles of the valises. "That's a mercy, but the wind! Make sure to keep the blanket over Mary's head."

"She keeps pulling it off."

It wouldn't take long for her tiny ears to freeze, even covered by a hat. They needed shelter and they needed it now. The dark and the cold were swiftly becoming mortal enemies.

A church, then. Perhaps they would find sanctuary there, if only for this night. Lilleth scanned the rooftops of town, looking for a steeple. Where could it be?

Every town had a church! Hopefully, she'd find one with someone in attendance.

"Look there." Jess pointed down the street. "There's a lamp on in Mr. Clarkly's library."

"Hurry, Jess, we've got to get there before he puts it out and turns in for the night."

Doing so took longer than she dreamed it would. The boardwalk had grown icy. Jess half slipped a dozen times. In the end, she abandoned the valises in front of Horton File's Real Estate, Homes for Sale or Rent. She took Mary from Jess's arms and steadied him.

"The lamp's just gone off!" Her brave young nephew sounded truly alarmed.

"We're nearly there. He'll hear us when we knock."

She prayed that he wouldn't turn them away. For all that he was a stranger, Mr. Clarkly seemed a decent fellow.

It took forever, but at last they stood in front of the door of Clark Clarkly's Private Library.

Lilleth knocked. Stabbing pain shot through her frozen hand. She bit her lip to hold in the agony and keep the tears out of her eyes.

Footsteps sounded inside, coming toward the door. Lilleth would simply faint into his arms if he attempted to turn them away, and it might not be an act.

The door opened.

"Mrs. Gordon!" Mr. Clarkly gaped at her without his spectacles on. Even in her desperation, she noticed that he had uncommonly appealing eyes, blue with green flecks. Bless the man for a saint, those eyes reflected more than a bit of concern.

He reached for Mary and tucked her in the crook of his arm. With his free hand he touched Lilleth's shoulder and drew her inside.

"Come in, young man," he said to Jess. "You look frozen through."

"I'll just go back," Jess said with chattering teeth, "f-for th-the bags."

"Well now, that won't do." Mr. Clarkly poked his head out the door and peered at the bags lying on the boardwalk a block down. "They'll be safe enough until I get a fire going. Here, take your sister and sit on that chair. There's a book beside it on the table. That should keep her distracted until she's warmed through."

Clark Clarkly knelt beside the fireplace, urging a small flame to life. He performed the chore quickly. His shoulders flexed and contracted under his shirt with his brisk movements.

Praise everything good that the man built a fire with more skill than he displayed walking.

He stood up after a moment, seeming taller than she remembered, straighter of form.

"Thank you, Mr. Clarkly." That simple phrase didn't begin to express her gratitude. "I can't think of what might have happened if—"

"No thanks needed, Mrs. Gordon." He took her cold hands in his big warm ones for an instant while he led her toward a chair by the fire. "Sit tight while I fetch your bags."

Mr. Clarkly hurried out the door and closed it behind him before the wind could sweep away the warmth beginning to hug the room.

His gait had been quick, efficient. Judging by his swift return, he hadn't taken a single tumble while he was fetching the bags.

He dropped them on the floor, and then instantly forgot he had put them there. His first step forward brought him stumbling across the room, where he careened off his desk and landed at her feet, with one hand caught in her skirt.

"So sorry…I beg your pardon. My glasses." He glanced about, blinking hard. "Blind as a bat without them."

"Mr. Clarkly." She untangled his hand where it gripped her ankle through her skirt. "I am the one indebted to you."

One could almost wish, however unkind it might be, that he wouldn't find his glasses. He had eyes a woman could look into and get lost.

Silly, Lilleth, silly, she chided herself. Getting lost in a man's eyes. What nonsense!

Clark Clarkly had come to her aid and nothing more.

Still, it was disappointing to see him find his broken spectacles. He frowned at them, tossed them aside and rooted through a desk drawer until he found another pair.

The man did need to see, after all. She'd be a silly goose to believe that staring into a man's eyes would result in anything more than heartache, even if he did seem uncommonly kind.

Relief eased the iciness from her bones as much as the flames did.

Mr. Clarkly sat on the floor, playing with Mary and speaking to Jess in low tones. The fire crackled, sounding like music in the cozy library. A teakettle in another room began to whistle.

What she wouldn't give to be able to sing the rest of the tension from her body. But no, that might not be wise. The chances were slim, but her voice might be recognized.

But humming, now that would be a comfort. Anyone could hum and sound the same. So she did. She hummed her favorite tune, one that had comforted her since she was a little girl.

For some reason, that made Mr. Clarkly quit talking to Jess and stare at her with the most peculiar expression on his face.

There was something almost…but not quite, familiar about it. Well, that was silly. She'd never met Mr. Clarkly until today.

"This ought to warm you." Trace grazed Lilleth's hand, passing her a cup of steaming tea.

He didn't think her fingers looked as blue as they had.

What wouldn't he give to be the man with the right to hold them to his heart and warm them thoroughly.

After half an hour beside the fire she had only now quit shivering.

Her husband couldn't be worth much, allowing his family to become wandering icicles.

"I can't think of how to thank you, Mr. Clarkly." She closed her fingers about the teacup and shut her eyes for an instant. "I thought I'd never be warm again."

Trace crouched beside her chair. He had a mind to stroke the ringlets that strayed from under her hat. He'd give up a lot to be able to loop his thumb through one of those red curls, to touch it in the familiar way a man would touch his woman's hair.

In any event, she wasn't his woman. Even if she were free, he wouldn't risk his assignment by revealing his identity. He couldn't. The patients at Hanispree depended on him.

His family was counting on him to deliver an exposé by the New Year. Being employed by one's parents added extra pressure to deliver. Not only that, there was sibling rivalry to be taken into account.

All his brothers and his sister worked for the *Chicago Gazette*. Although, since his sister had become a mother, she had quit the investigative side of the business. On occasion the job became dangerous.

That was one of the reasons that the Ballentines sometimes worked in disguise.

The other reason was that several of their investigations were sufficiently well known that the Ballentines were often recognized. When a case involved secrecy, as this one did, a disguise was called for.

He had picked Clarkly because the character was as unlike his real self as could be. No one could possibly recognize him.

It wasn't easy living in the skin of someone who wasn't real. It was lonely, not being able to let anyone close.

Still, his job was deeply rewarding and made the temporary isolation worthwhile. Over the years his investigations had improved the lots of many people. They'd put swindlers out of business and criminals behind bars.

He couldn't imagine doing anything else for a living.

Trace watched Lilleth sipping from the teacup. He'd always found her mouth to be pretty, but now, as a woman full grown, her lips were a man's fantasy. Moist with hot tea, they glistened in the glow of the fire.

"Mrs. Gordon." Crouched down as he was, his eyes met hers over the rim of the cup. Her mouth stilled over a porcelain rose. "There's something troubling me. I hope you don't consider this forward of me to ask, but Mr. Gordon...oughtn't he be—"

Her pretty lips puckered, as though they had tasted something sour...or needed to be kissed.

For the hundredth time since he had run Lilleth down at the train station, he cursed the decision to become Clarkly. He ought to have adopted his favorite identity, Johnny Kaid, fastest cowboy with a rope or a gun.

Curse it! Johnny was daring, but Clark was safer, and safe was all-important at this moment.

"Here? By my side, you mean?" Lilleth set the cup on her lap and stared down at it. "My husband ran off. I don't know where he is."

"It was nearly a year back," Jess said, hugging his sister close. "Mary was only a newborn."

Poor, brave Lils! On her own with two young children.

"I can't tell you how sorry I am." He couldn't help it; he reached over and held her fingers where they gripped the cup.

"No need to fret, Mr. Clarkly." Lilleth shrugged. She sighed and looked into his eyes. "It's been a while now, and to tell you the truth, my husband was a worldly man. In many ways life is easier without him."

"Pa liked his spirits." Jess covered Mary's ears. "More than most."

Trace's world bucked and shifted beneath him. Having Lilleth within touching distance had been temptation enough, with a loving husband standing between them. Without him things had become complicated.

He let go of Lilleth's hands. The man was gone, and no good, but that didn't make her any less legally wed.

"If I can help you, all you need to do is ask."

"You've been kindness itself already. You did no less than save our lives tonight." She set the cup aside. "Please, won't you call me Lilly."

He forced a smile when he wanted to frown. She hated that name. What had happened to make her use it?

"I'd be pleased if you would call me Clark." He pursed his lips, about to offer something improper, given that she was someone else's wife. But he couldn't see any help for it. "I've a room upstairs. I'd be pleased if you and the children would sleep there tonight."

She took off her hat. Whorls and curls reflecting the fire's glow broke free of a bun that would never be able to confine them.

"You are our very own angel, Clark, sent straight down from heaven."

That comment evidently pleased young Jess. He suddenly grinned so widely that the freckles on his cheeks appeared to dance.

Trace was no angel. Not by a yard. An angel wouldn't be glad that her worthless husband had run away.

A heavenly being wouldn't fidget in his chair all through this long, blustery night, wondering if the virtueless rogue was dead so that he could kiss his wife. A woman he had no business kissing even if she were free.

Chapter Three

"Say your prayers, Jess." Lilleth listened to the wind whistle around the dormers of the tidy upstairs bedroom. Mary and Jess lay side by side in a cozy-looking feather bed that Mr. Clarkly had put fresh linens on before retiring downstairs to sleep, presumably, in a chair. "And don't forget to mention Mr. Clarkly."

"Do you think my pa might have sent him to us?"

"Who's to know? I can't say that he didn't." To see the children safe and snug did seem a miracle. If it hadn't been for Mr. Clarkly's generosity—well, that outcome didn't bear thinking of.

She hadn't had a reason to be truly grateful to a man since she could remember. Not since she was a little girl and believed that princes, knights and cowboys rode to the aid of ladies in need.

In those days she'd had a hero. He was her champion and she'd seen her future in his smile. They'd been as close as berries on a vine the summer that she was twelve years old.

She had loved him with all her young heart, and he must have loved her as well, for he had defended her against a pair of bullies and become seriously injured. Then, to her everlasting horror, before his wounds had begun to mend, her mother had shattered her world.

In the dead of night, she had woken Lilleth and Bethany, packed them up and moved three states away to be with the latest in a constant string of inappropriate beaux.

It wasn't that her mother was a whore in the normal sense, as her reputation suggested. It was more that she was needy. She let men take care of her in exchange for her affections. Unfortunately for Lilleth and Bethany, their mother's affections latched on to the wrong sorts of men.

As little girls they had become skilled, yes, even creative, at keeping one step ahead of groping male hands. Because of Bethany, what might have been a harrowing lot became a game. Lilleth's older sister never let her feel less of herself because of the behavior of men. Together, they practiced ducking, dodging, stomping and pinching. At night they would whisper in bed, recounting tales of near escape and retaliation. Some girls might have withered under such an upbringing, but she and Bethany dodged and ducked through it all.

But life was what it was. Lilleth had been formed by it and so had her sister. Bethany escaped into marriage, while Lilleth took her voice on the road with a traveling show.

Since Bethany loved her husband and Lilleth loved to sing, it had all turned out well enough.

Until six months ago, that is, when Bethany's husband had died suddenly of a fever.

Lilleth kissed Jess good-night and stroked the curly hair at Mary's temple. Her nephew would be a good man. Bethany would raise him to be like his father.

"Uncle Alden can't get to us here. Mr. Clarkly is downstairs." Jess yawned and turned on his side, facing the blaze that Clark had laid in the small upstairs fireplace. "We'll get Mama out of that place, just see if we don't."

"We will, I promise we will," Lilleth said. Firelight cast shadows on Jess's face, making him look like a miniature of his father, Hamilton.

How Alden and Hamilton could be twins was a mind-twisting mystery. Hamilton, older by a few moments, had been a good man, as honorable as he was handsome. Alden was a nervous little fellow who, unless surrounded by a group of fawning minions, was frightened of his shadow. And of ghosts...especially ghosts.

It was understandable that the wealthy Hanisprees, upon their deaths, had willed Alden a monthly allowance and Hamilton their entire fortune.

For a man as greedy as Alden, an allowance was not nearly enough. He coveted his brother's inheritance, which now belonged to Bethany.

Lilleth was certain that, had he not been petrified that she would haunt him, Alden would have killed Bethany to take control of the fortune. But now, having incarcerated Bethany, all he need do was control her children.

That he would never do. Lilleth vowed it on her life. Why, she would tear him to shreds with her bare hands if he got within arm's reach of them.

All at once the wind stopped and snow swept past the dormer window, silent and beautiful. She took a cleansing breath to banish Alden from her mind.

She walked to the window, unbuttoning the bodice of her gown and watching snowflakes sailing past. Sometimes when she was stressed she would try to bring her childhood hero's face to mind. But time had blurred his image; she couldn't see him anymore.

It didn't matter, really. He would have changed a great deal. Even if she ran into him on the street he'd be altered beyond recognition, and so would she.

Yes, life was what it was. All those years ago she had cried for weeks, before tucking Trace Ballentine into a precious corner of her heart.

Aside from her brother-in-law, Trace had been

the only bone-deep good man—boy, really—that she had ever met.

Until Clark Clarkly, that is. So far he seemed to be quite decent.

The poor man didn't know he was sheltering a criminal. For his own good, she would have to be out of his house as soon as she could get her bearings. Hopefully, tomorrow morning.

Lilleth Preston didn't like being on the wrong side of the law. She was a singer, a sister and an auntie. Three things that she adored and had built her life around.

Curse Alden Hanispree for forcing her to kidnap her sister's children.

It was late. On any other night Trace would have been asleep hours before. Early to bed and early to rise and all that. But Lilleth was upstairs, abandoned and unprotected.

He lurched out of his chair for the tenth time in under an hour to pace before the dying fire. The fact that she was, for all accounts, unmarried was a torment and a temptation, but he would deal with that.

Unprotected! Now that was a problem more difficult to cope with.

Yes, she had grown to be a capable and resilient woman.

And no, he was no more able to leave her to the

whims of fate now than he had been when she was a child.

"Well hell, Lils," he muttered. "What am I supposed to do?"

He stomped to the front door and snatched it open. Icy air bit his nose and chilled his ears. It did not, however, do much in the way of clearing his head.

He couldn't give her safe harbor without compromising the secrecy of his mission. He couldn't send her and the children out into the elements.

He could try to get some sleep. Occasionally, the answers to perplexing problems came to him while he slumbered. More than a few puzzles had knit together in his dreams.

He closed the front door, shook off a shiver and tried once again to fold his body in a too-small chair.

Knees up, shoulders hunched, neck twisted, with eyes closed and sheep counted…this time he would make it work.

"Stars shine bright, sleep tight tonight," he whispered. His eyes popped wide-open.

From what dusty part of his brain had he remembered that? Years ago it had been Lilleth's nightly farewell when, far past the time when most girls were allowed out, she would peck his cheek and dash through the trees toward home.

"Stars shine bright, sleep tight tonight," he repeated, dusting off the phrase and polishing it. Amazingly, he began to get sleepy.

Behind his eyelids he saw young Lilleth in the woods.

Summer heat shimmered off the ground even though it was hours after sundown. Leaves on the trees drooped, looking wilted under the light of a full moon.

She ran toward Red Leaf Pond holding the hem of her white nightgown in her fists.

She didn't appear to see him sitting on the rotting tree trunk at the edge of the pond. She must have been trying to escape the heat, just as he was.

His own ma and pa didn't mind their boys running loose after dark. His sister complained to high heaven, but she was a girl, and therefore confined to the safety of home.

But Lilleth didn't live by those rules. Her mother wouldn't care that she was out, even if she knew.

Just now, Lils ran barefoot and free. Her red hair streamed out behind her, winking at the moon.

At the water's edge she waded in past her ankles, then began to lift her shift, clearly intending to draw the thin, worn fabric over her head.

"Hey, Lils!" He stood up quickly and strode into the moonlight. "Mind if I come in, too?"

She dropped the hem of her nightgown and grinned at him. "I'll race you to the middle," she called.

She waited for him to strip to his underdrawers

before she dived in. She didn't need a head start, for she swam like a tadpole.

They met in the center, circling around each other and laughing. Moonlight dappled the surface of the pond where they kicked and splashed.

"Oh." Lilleth ducked under the water, then surfaced again. "The day's been blistering. This feels so good."

"Yeah, but Lils, you shouldn't be out by yourself at night. It's not safe."

"Safer than home, I guess." She brushed her hand across her face, sluicing water from her eyes and nose. "Mama has a new man and Beth and I haven't got him figured out yet. Besides, I'm not alone, you're here."

"I might not have been." He ducked under the water and came up blowing out a mouthful, pretending to be the spout of a fancy fountain. "What if Horn and Pard Higgins are slinking about?"

"Well, they aren't. And you *are* here."

With that she flipped beneath the water and grabbed hold of his feet. She yanked him under. He caught her around the middle, feeling ribs under cotton, and then hoisted her up. He surfaced in time to see her flying through the air, laughing and sputtering.

They played like that for a long time before Lils began to shiver and they swam for shore.

He put his clothes on while she wrung out her hair.

"I'll walk you home," he said.

"I'm going to run." She flashed him a grin with pond water still speckling her lashes. "You won't be able to catch up."

"My legs are longer."

"Mine are quicker." She bounced up on her toes and pecked his cheek. "Stars shine bright, sleep tight tonight."

Then she was off, a streak in the moonlight. He laughed out loud. His longer legs never were a match for her quicker ones, but at least he'd get there in time to see her close her front door safely behind her.

Trace twitched in his sleep. He groaned and woke up.

That night, he never did see Lils open her door. He heard her scream.

Bursting out of the woods, he saw the Higgins boys push Lilleth to the ground. Horn knelt over her, pinning her wrists to the parched earth. Pard laughed and called her obscene names.

Lils spat back oaths that would have sent ordinary mischief-makers running, but Pard and Horn weren't ordinary. The twins fed off each other, one disrespectful and the other mean. Even adults kept out of their way.

Running full speed, Trace plowed into Horn, but didn't see the jagged stick that Lils had gripped in her fist, ready to jab her assailant with.

He knocked Horn over. The bully slammed into his brother. Blood spurted, some from Horn's ear and some from Pard's nose.

It looked as if the boys didn't care for having their own blood spilled, because they ran away crying and cursing. And a good thing, too, because Trace couldn't have moved a muscle to protect Lilleth.

The stick that she had intended to jab Horn with now stuck out of his own chest. Blood pulsed from a long gash across his ribs. Lils looked like a blur leaning over him, pressing his wound and yelling at him. After a moment even her screams sounded like whispers.

Trace sat up in his chair and let his feet hit the cold floor. He'd been sick—close to death, he'd been told. Mostly, all he remembered was a visit from Lils.

She had come to his house weeping, and blowing a kiss at his scar. He told her he didn't mind it, that the scar was bound to heal into an *L*, for Lils. She'd laughed and dried her tears.

That's when she gave him a quick, sweet kiss on the lips, pressed his hand to her heart and vowed to marry him and only him.

Then, suddenly, she was gone, and no one knew where or even exactly when her mother had packed them off.

He'd been right about the scar. From that day until now, all he'd had of Lilleth was her initial across his heart.

* * *

Lilleth stepped cautiously onto the boardwalk. Ice crunched under her feet. Early morning sunshine peeked under her hat and gave the illusion of warmth even though her breath fogged in front of her face.

The storm had blown away with the dawn, and so had some of her worries. She couldn't help it; she had to sing, if only under her breath.

Horton File, Realtor, had been the most agreeable of men. But then, who wouldn't have been, receiving such an excessive amount of money to rent the only vacant house in Riverwalk?

Lilleth felt agreeable as well, even though she had been all but fleeced. She and the children had a place to live. A place that Mr. File had assured her was a lovely, furnished cabin tucked into the woods only steps from town.

The privacy of a cabin hidden among the trees was more than she had hoped for. The rent wouldn't be a problem for the brief time they would live in Riverwalk. With luck, it would be only a month, maybe less, just until she figured out a way to free Bethany.

With sunshine smiling upon the town, Riverwalk appeared to be a charming place. Like many communities in South Dakota it was growing fast, filling with families and their commerce. Between the Realtor's office and Clark's lending library she had passed a dress shop, a barber and a baker.

It was only a couple of hours past sunrise and already the sign on the bakery door read Open for Business.

Clean morning air nipped her cheeks and filled her lungs. Lilly Gordon thoroughly enjoyed the quiet hours just after sunrise.

Lilleth Preston had performed her songs late into the night. Mornings typically found her with her head buried beneath her pillow.

She would miss seeing the sunrise once she returned to her life with Dunbar's Touring Troupe.

Even more, she suspected she would miss the first fresh pastries of the day. She opened the door to Martha's Baked Goods and was greeted by the aromas of cinnamon, vanilla and yeast.

She purchased four cinnamon buns drizzled with honey. The children would be thrilled with the treat.

Bethany would have provided her children with a healthy breakfast of eggs and milk.

But Lilleth wasn't a mother, just an indulgent auntie who had never learned to cook. Life on the road, living from hotel to hotel with a group of traveling performers had never presented her the opportunity to learn.

Well, then, that would be one of her goals this month. By the time they rescued Bethany, the children would be eating meals that she had prepared with her own hands.

Lilleth warmed her fingers about the bag of baked

goods and hurried the three doors down to Clark's place, slipping, sliding and wobbling.

Clark had started a fire while she had been out. Warmth wrapped around her as soon as she stepped inside. Upstairs, she heard Jess's footsteps and Mary's good-morning coos.

Clark sat at his desk, head down on folded arms and fast asleep with a pair of glasses clutched in his fist. The poor man must be exhausted. He couldn't have done more than doze in a chair all night.

"Clark," she whispered. The familiarity of using his first name felt a little awkward, and a lot nice. "I've brought breakfast."

He didn't wake up, but his mouth lifted, revealing the barest hint of a dimple at one corner. My goodness, the man was appealing.

There was something about him that didn't quite make sense. He was a complete bumbler, as likely to trip over his own feet as walk a steady line. Once in a while, though, he wasn't.

Lilleth bent over to peer more closely at his face. She shouldn't; he was nearly a stranger. She leaned another inch toward him. Something about him called to her. Why didn't he seem like a stranger?

She had spent the night in his bed. That must be the reason.

He appeared to be dreaming. She watched his eyes move behind his lids. His lips compressed, then relaxed. Thick dark lashes twitched…they blinked.

Sleep-misted eyes opened wide and blue, then blinked again.

"Good morning, Lilly."

By heavens, there was a dimple. And could she be any more of a ninny, staring and blinking back?

She straightened and backed up, holding the bag of cinnamon rolls between them. "I've brought breakfast."

"Martha's?" He rolled one shoulder, then the other, stretched…grinned and sat up. "I'm starved."

An apology would have been called for, could she have found one appropriate to the situation. But just then Jess came downstairs with Mary in his arms.

"Morning, Ma, Mr. Clarkly. Is that sweets?" His eyes grew wide in anticipation. There were some things that Bethany would have to set straight later on. Her children's diet being the first. "I'm starved."

"Sit down there on the rug in front of the fire," Lilleth told him. Jess did so, placing himself between the hearth and his baby sister. "Careful with the crumbs."

Lilleth sat on the rug and broke off small pieces of cinnamon bun, feeding them to Mary. Clark, with his glasses perched low on his nose, completed the circle. He sat beside her with his ankles crossed and his knees sticking out. He didn't seem to notice that his left knee bumped into her right one.

Any other man would get a swift boot in the…

But this was Clark, and chances were he was oblivious to where his limbs ended up.

"I have good news," Lilleth announced, scooting beyond reach of Clark's knee. "I've found us a place to live!"

"Why, that's… Well, it's…" For some reason it took an instant for his smile to reach his eyes. "Truly wonderful news. Where?"

"We'll be neighbors, Clark. I've rented the cabin in the woods, just down the path behind the lending library."

He choked on cinnamon and honey.

"That's just…" He managed to catch his breath despite the crumbs still lodged in his throat. "I'm pleased as can be."

But he wasn't. And that was as *clear* as could be.

Trace stood on his back porch watching Lilleth and her brood, valises in hand, walking down the path that led into the woods. Cold sunshine winked on the snow and glinted off his fake glasses. He'd have to keep them on, though, even though the glare was making his eyes sting.

At the tree line, Lilleth turned and waved. The confident smile on her face wouldn't last long. In another five minutes she would discover that her cozy, furnished cabin was barely fit to live in.

Trace waved back, but watching while she vanished among the trees made him feel off-kilter. As if something precious had been given, and then snatched away before he'd even had time to blink at the wonder of it.

Trace was a man grounded in reality. Facts were what he lived and breathed.

Still, it couldn't have been an accident that his long-lost Lils had spent the night under his roof. It couldn't have been pure chance that put them both on the same train platform at the same instant in time.

Letting her walk away now felt like an act against their common destiny.

Or could it be that their destinies weren't common? Maybe letting her walk away was fulfilling that.

It was all just a bunch of fancy thinking, anyway, fate and destiny.

Facts, on the other hand, were what they were, no guessing or wondering involved. It would serve him well to keep them in mind.

Here was a hard and cold fact: Lils was walking into a bad situation and taking her children with her.

Another fact was that Trace was honor-bound to protect the inmates at Hanispree, and the safest way to do that was to let Lilleth take that path into the woods and deal with her problems on her own.

And the last fact on his mental list…he would not do it.

Trace picked up the ax leaning against the woodpile beside his back door and followed Lilleth's footprints into the woods.

He grinned, considering a fact he had just added to his mental list. It didn't have a thing to do with fancy thinking; it was as hard as facts go.

Clark Clarkly was going to kiss Lilly Gordon.

Chapter Four

A ray of sunshine filtering through bare tree branches dappled fingers of light on the roof of the small cabin. Close by, Lilleth heard the welcome rush of a creek.

In the event that the cabin did not have an indoor pump, it would be an easy task to fetch water.

"What do you think, Jess?" Lilleth went up the stairs with Mary in her arms. The third step cracked under her weight. "Be careful, this one might need to be replaced."

The broken step was a minor problem, but for the rent she was paying she would make sure the landlord had it repaired by this afternoon.

"The place seems safe, Auntie Lilleth, way back here in the woods." He grinned up at her. "Maybe I can explore later."

Looking safe and being safe weren't necessarily the same thing, but the boy needed to be out, running and playing. Poor Jess had been confined to trains and secrecy for much too long.

"Let's settle in now, and we can explore together."

"You like to climb trees and stuff, Auntie Lils?"

"Let me tell you, when I was your age, you couldn't keep me out of a tree." Not that anyone had ever tried to. "I suppose I can still manage."

Blazes, if she wouldn't make this time as easy on the children as she could. Hiding out in the little cabin for a month might be made into an adventure.

She turned the key in the lock and opened the door.

The very fingers of sunshine that dappled the roof dappled a broken kitchen table. It shone on a floor with layers of dusty things scattered about. It filtered over a lumpy bed where a family of raccoons was suddenly startled from sleep.

Mary squirmed and reached for the floor, but there was not an inch of space that was clean enough to set her down.

"Take Mary outside, will you?" *Tap, tap, tap.* Lilleth fought the urge to kick a crushed pail that she had come close to tripping over. It was best to get the children outdoors for a moment. It wouldn't begin their cabin adventure well to see Auntie in a fit of despair.

"Stay close by," she called after Jess.

He, at least, seemed happy enough, galloping

around to the back of the house with his sister giggling in his arms.

But what was Lilleth going to do? Dusty spiderwebs sagged across shredded curtains at the windows—which, by God's own grace, were at least not broken. The bed was not fit for the raccoons that had just scurried into a back room.

There was a nice stone fireplace, if one ignored the giant mound of ashes spilling out of the hearth. Hours of scrubbing from now, it might be cozy with a couple of chairs set before it.

Naturally, there were no chairs.

No chairs, no indoor pump, not a decent bed. There was the dining table, but one would have to sit on the disgusting floor to make use of it.

And thanks to the family of raccoons, the place smelled. No doubt it also had fleas.

She gathered the hem of her skirt into the crook of her arm.

"We're going to the creek, Auntie Lilleth," Jess called through a cracked board in the wall. "It's real close by."

That was a mercy. It would take endless buckets of hot water to make the place decent enough even to put Mary down.

"Blasted raccoons." Lilleth would start by getting rid of them. "You better have found an escape hole back there. I'm coming in!"

She'd need a weapon, though. There! In the corner

of what used to be the kitchen area, beside a rusted cookstove, was a broom. Too bad no one had ever seen fit too use it.

She held it before her, business end first, and entered the back room with a sweeping motion.

Sure enough, there was a hole. She made contact with a striped tail just as the tip squeezed through.

This apparently was a storage room, stacked from ceiling to floor with buckets, rugs, dishes, more broken furniture and some things she could not identify.

Horton File might believe that this trash counted as furnishings, but he was about to discover that their opinions on what was livable lay miles apart.

Before that, though, she would have to strap Mary to her back in order to clean a spot big enough to set her down.

A faded red blanket lay on the floor. Lilleth picked it up, sneezed, then wadded it up and stuck it in the raccoon hole. She dusted her hands.

If only the cabin didn't smell like old things and wild animal fur.

Night, along with temperatures below freezing, would be here too soon. She would need to clean the fireplace first thing. Then have Jess gather wood.

"Dear Lord, how will I get it all done?" she murmured. Already, grime caked her skin and she hadn't even begun.

The first thing she would need was light, then fire. She walked to the window and yanked on the curtain, which dropped on the floor. Dust billowed out of it and sent her into a full sneezing fit.

She rubbed the window with the hem of her petticoat. A small clear circle appeared on the glass.

Within that circle appeared a man. Clark Clarkly was striding forward with an ax gripped in his fist.

Clark Clarkly was not a bumbler. Well, he was, but not always. Not now. For the past thirty minutes Lilleth had been peeking at him through the window while she passed back and forth, sweeping the floor.

He stood by a woodpile, one stacked from fallen limbs that he had dragged out of the woods. Through the open cabin door she listened to the steady blows of his ax.

As far as she could tell he hadn't come close to chopping off his foot, even though the pile of cut logs now stood thigh high.

One time, when he looked up to see her watching him, he stumbled backward and dropped the ax.

What a puzzle he was. One moment falling all over himself, and the next, as capable a man as she'd ever met.

One would expect a bookish man, one who stacked volumes in alphabetical order, to be fragile in his bearing. Not so Clark. Trip and stumble as he might, beneath those clothes she suspected he was muscle upon muscle. How could he not be, the way he swung his ax.

Passing the window once more, she paused. He didn't notice her this time. She watched the ax circle in the air, then hit a log, splitting it down the center. Clark tossed it aside and spilt another, then another, in the same way.

Those were not the shoulders of a slightly built man. They flexed beneath his shirt with a regular rhythm. Even in the cold, sweat dampened his shirt between his shoulder blades.

To add to his mystery, he was a take-charge kind of individual. One would expect a librarian to be comfortable in the sanctuary of his library, his life as predictable as the next printed page.

But Clark, as soon as he'd glanced about at the rubble-strewn cabin, had taken control of the undertaking. He'd sent the children back to his place, putting Jess in charge of lending out books for the day.

Now here he was, getting her cabin tidy and shipshape. Later she was to come back to his place and spend another night tucked safe under his roof, and no arguments about it.

Truly, she wouldn't tell him no even if she had a choice. There was something about Mr. Clark Clarkly that drew her to him, and it wasn't just a common love of books.

Clark looked up and spotted her at the window. He grinned, wiped one sleeve across his forehead, then waved the ax at her in greeting.

To all appearances, he liked nothing more than to cut and stack wood. Any other man she had known would want something in return for his kindness— which in her mind didn't make it a kindness in the end—but so far Clark hadn't made an improper move toward her.

Still, hadn't it been only a day since he'd snatched her off the boardwalk? She'd known men who hid their true natures much longer.

The light streaming in through the window and the front door suddenly dimmed when the sun passed below the tree line. Time to quit trying to figure out Mr. Clark Clarkly. Whatever tugged at her about him would have to wait.

There was enough work here to keep her busy for a week, and at some point she needed to figure a way to make a secret visit to her sister.

Bethany must be frantic with worry over the children. She had no way of knowing that Lilleth had kidnapped them from their unsavory uncle.

"All finished out here." Clark strode through the door, carrying a load of wood in one arm. Just inside, he stopped abruptly, set the load on the hearth and touched his face. He rooted through his shirt pocket. "Must have lost my glasses someplace."

"I'll help you look." She leaned the broom on the fireplace. "They're probably near the woodpile."

She walked toward the front door, but he stopped her with a hand to her elbow.

"No need to bother, Lilly. It's easier to work blind than have the things slipping off my nose, anyway." He let go of her. "What's next?"

"I'm going to scrub the floor, and you have done enough." Clark looked like a different man without his glasses. It wasn't only his face that seemed different, it was the way he moved. "Go home, Clark. I've taken up way too much of your time."

"A librarian finds himself with an excess of time on occasion." He shuddered and glanced about the cabin. "This is a nightmare for just one person. I'll take care of the holes in the roof."

"You don't have to, really. You've done too much." That was the polite thing to say, and having said it, she hoped that he wouldn't leave.

He took her shoulders in his hands and looked her square in the eye. No doubt this was where he would seek repayment of his kindness.

"I don't have a single thing to do that's more important than helping you, Lilly." He let go of her suddenly, rooted through his pants pocket and pulled out his glasses. "Imagine that! They were there the whole time."

He spun about, crossed the room and stood in the open doorway, with afternoon shadows outlining his silhouette.

"I'm going to stay and help, because that's what

decent folks do." When he turned she thought he
might trip on the threshold, but he didn't.

So far, Clark Clarkly was not like any other man
she had ever known.

Walking up the path toward the cabin, Trace
watched moonlight twinkle in icicles hanging from
the eaves. The day had warmed, but tonight the temperature was dropping in a hurry.

He hoped the cabin was as warm inside as the
firelight shining out of the newly cleaned windows
indicated.

Lilleth had swept, scrubbed and polished herself
to exhaustion. In a few more days the place might
be habitable.

He opened the door and stepped inside.

Lilleth, facing the rusty stove, spun about. Alarm
flashed in her eyes. She clutched the soapy dishrag
that she had been using on the stove to her bosom.

"My word, Clark. You startled me."

Maybe, but that fleeting fear in her expression
seemed more than startled. Maybe she was afraid
that her husband might have suddenly returned. If
the expression on her face was anything to go by, he
could be worse than she or her son had let on.

"I should have knocked." Clark glanced around
the cabin in surprise.

In the few hours that he had been gone she had
accomplished quite a bit. Six chairs, two of which

were placed before the fire, had been wiped clean of the layers of grime that had caked them.

The crate of dishes that he had dragged from the back room earlier were now scrubbed and drying on the table which he had repaired. He wouldn't have believed that the wooden table had a shine left in it, but there it stood, gleaming as it surely had in its glory days.

"You must be starved," he said, placing the pair of napkin-covered plates that he had carried from town on the hearth. "Hope you like steak and potatoes. They're from the hotel."

Lilleth dropped the sudsy rag in the sink and wiped her hands on her skirt. She closed her eyes and took a slow, savoring breath.

From under the cloth wrappers, the aroma of herbs and spices floated on the air.

"Clark Clarkly, I do believe that you are an angel fallen straight from heaven."

Lilleth crossed the room in a hurry. Instead of collapsing into a fireside chair, she stood before him. Hands on hips, she studied him, cocking her head to the right. Then she wrapped her arms about his ribs in a hug.

For the briefest instant her breasts pressed against his chest. His reaction to that was anything but angelic. Lucky thing she couldn't tell what her embrace had done to him. Things stirred that had no business stirring for a married woman.

He stumbled backward, then hiccuped to cover his reaction.

"I'm sorry," she said, clapping her hands to her cheeks, probably trying to hide a blush. "That was forward."

"I'm hungry. Let's eat." What else could he say? He was starved, had been for sixteen years. No plate of food was going to solve that.

"How are the children doing?" Lilleth sat down and placed a dinner plate on her lap. She uncovered the food, tucked the cloth into the bodice of her dress, then sighed and ate a mouthful of mashed potatoes. "I've neglected them dreadfully today."

He followed her example. "Mary's asleep and Jess is reading. They've both had dinner, the house is warm and the door is locked." There, just now, relief shifted in her eyes. He'd thrown that last out just to see how she would react.

Lils was troubled. Trace's gut told him it was not only her living situation that was the problem. He wondered if her husband had run out not just on his family, but also his debts.

This cabin tucked away in the woods might be an attempt to hide from unscrupulous debt collectors.

Outside, the wind began to blow. It huffed against the windows and rattled the door. It moaned under the eaves and prowled around corners, as if searching for a way inside.

Let it do its best. He'd sealed the place up tight,

even though he'd had to finish by the light of the rising moon.

"Mary misses you, but Jess is doing a fine job of tending her." Trace chewed a bite of steak. "You are not neglecting your children, Lilly. You've worked yourself to the bone for them today."

"So have you." She watched him for a long moment, as if trying to see something deep inside him. She blinked, then seemed to give herself a mental shake. "I can't think of how I will repay you."

He set his plate aside, bent toward her with his elbows on his knees. She crossed her arms over her chest and leaned back in her chair.

"I'd like to get to know you." He already did, of course, and he was a cad for not explaining how. If duty did not stand in his way he'd confess right now. "How did you come to be in Riverwalk?"

He shouldn't have asked, not with weariness shadowing her eyes and dragging at her mouth.

"Oh...well." One of the things he loved about Lilleth was that her face was so open. He'd always been able to read her expression. Just now a flash of relief shaded her eyes. "I wanted a fresh start, for the children. I thought this might be a nice place."

"It is." Finished eating, Trace snapped his napkin from his collar and dropped it on his plate. "I've seen that much in the couple of months that I've been here."

"You're a newcomer, too?"

Giving up that little bit of information about himself couldn't hurt, but he'd better switch the conversation back to her.

He nodded. "Do you have family nearby?"

"My sister." Lilleth turned her face to gaze at the fire. Her cheeks, blushed by the heat of the flames, looked soft…kissable…and not his to kiss. "She's not far away."

Bethany. He remembered her well, of course, even though his attention years ago had been absorbed by her little sister.

"Where did you live before you came to Riverwalk?"

"Here and there. We traveled a lot." She snatched her gaze away from the fire and looked him full in the face. "What about you?"

"Chicago." It was a big town; he could be honest about that, too.

"I spend two weeks in Chicago every year for—" Lilleth's eyes widened for an instant before she looked down, to pick at a spot on her skirt. "My husband had meetings there, so we all went."

It might be angry business partners that she was hiding from.

And she was hiding. Trace was all but certain of it. He wished she would confide in him, even if it would be tough to know her secrets without revealing his own.

Lilleth stood up. She turned her back to the fire,

then sat down on the raised hearth. More curls sprang out of her bun than were contained by it. They clung to her neck in whorls.

He had to look away. It wasn't right to want to put his lips right there, to taste her smooth, fair skin.

"I understand there is a mental hospital here, just outside of town," she said, picking at that spot on her skirt again.

"Hanispree."

He turned his chair so that it faced her.

"Have you been there?" she asked.

He nodded. "I take books to the inmates on occasion."

"Is it a safe facility?" Judging by the look on her face, his answer appeared to be important to her. "To raise the children nearby, I mean. They don't ever escape, do they?"

"Not to my knowledge." He needed to be off this subject. "I don't think the inmates are dangerous so much as unfortunate."

"Well, then…" She let go of her skirt and folded her hands in her lap. She smiled. "That is a relief."

"Let me see your hands."

"Whatever for?"

He didn't answer, just reached over and took them in his. He turned them palm-up.

"You aren't used to this kind of work."

She curled her fingers inward, hiding blisters.

"What needs to be done, needs to be done." She shrugged her shoulders.

"This ought to help."

He reached in his back pocket and withdrew the balm he'd brought from home. Some patients at Hanispree got sores, so he kept it on hand.

She opened her mouth to say something, but in the end did not. She uncurled her hands.

He unscrewed the jar lid. A flowery scent wafted out. He scooped up a dollop of salve with his thumb and rubbed it over her left palm.

Work had taken its toll on her delicate skin. Flipping her hand over, he stroked the lotion from wrist to fingertips.

Her sigh, sounding weary to the bone, made him look up. Her eyes had drifted closed, but half a smile lingered on her lips.

Kissing her would be easy. All he had to do was lean forward two feet and ignore his conscience.

Maybe he should ignore it. A runaway husband didn't deserve the respect of a marriage vow, in Trace's opinion.

He bent closer, just a foot, and stared at her mouth.

That's as close as he got. Until he knew how she viewed her broken wedding vows he couldn't lean forward that further twelve inches and claim what he wanted.

Damn! He couldn't kiss her regardless, not with his own secrets standing in the way.

A sudden gust of wind shook the cabin. Lilleth opened her eyes.

"Clark?" Naturally, she looked astonished to see him so close.

"You've got a smudge of dirt, just there." He wiped her cheek downward to the corner of her lip with his thumb. Its path left a glistening, rose-scented trail on her skin. "That's better, all clean."

She arched a brow, and then closed her eyes once more.

By the time he finished treating her right hand, her breathing had slowed. She'd fallen asleep sitting up in the chair.

"Time to go home, Lils." He whispered. "Stars shine bright...."

He choked back the rest. What if she wasn't deeply asleep? She might recall their nightly farewell even if she didn't remember him.

Lilleth felt as if she was being rocked in a hammock. The hammock smelled like Clark.

The hammock *was* Clark. He carried her, wrapped in his coat, through the woods toward his house. Cold air bit her face where the wind touched it, but she was warm under the wool. Hot, even, where one side of her was tucked tight against his body.

Branches scraped and cracked in the trees overhead. Ice crunched under Clark's boots. His breath turned to fog close to her nose, where she rested her head on his shoulder.

She had been correct about muscle upon muscle. She was not a featherweight, yet he did not appear to be winded.

She ought to walk; her legs were perfectly capable. Somehow, though, she didn't want to.

No one had ever made her feel cherished and protected. Right this moment, Clark did.

He made her feel safe. At last, here was a man who stepped in to help when he didn't have to.

His manner wasn't bold or brave. He didn't have a dozen traits that gallant men had. What he did have was a deep sense of honor.

A woman could trust him.

He'd proved that only moments ago when she had closed her eyes, oblivious to anything but the blissful treatment he was giving her hands. He could have kissed her. In fact, he had wanted to.

She knew enough of men to know when one wanted a kiss…or more.

The strange and startling fact was that she had been disappointed by Clark's gentlemanly behavior. She admired him for it, to be sure, but in truth, she'd wanted his kiss.

She ought to have claimed to be a widow. Now she was stuck as a married woman. If she encouraged a kiss, she would appear a regular trollop. Which she most certainly was not.

A sudden gust spun up from the ground, ripping the coat from her shoulder. Clark turned and walked backward against the wind, tucking the fabric up around her ears as he went.

"Breathing's easier when you back into the wind," he told her.

She touched his face. His cheek was cold, her fingers warm from being sheltered in the coat. The scent of roses lingered on her hand.

He stopped suddenly. Sincere blue eyes blinked at her, both brows arched. His icy breath clouded, mingled with hers, then wisped away.

"Would you think I was wicked if I wished that I was no longer married, so that you could kiss me?"

He looked startled.

"That was bold. I shouldn't have asked." What was wrong with her? What she wanted was not what could be. Even if it could, she had not come to Riverwalk to dally with a man. She was not, and never had been, the dallying type. "Please forgive me."

His arms, firm with rippled muscle, tensed and drew her closer.

"Do you think *I'm* wicked?" he asked.

"No, far from it."

He touched his nose to hers. She tasted his breath on her lips, felt his warmth.

"I've wanted to kiss you since the day I bowled you over on the train platform. And that is the truth. If you think you are wicked, I'm more so."

Something inside her melted. Her bones, certainly, and her flesh.

Even though his lips drew away without ever touching hers, she was quite certain that she had never been so thoroughly kissed in her life.

Chapter Five

Alden Hanispree felt eyes staring at his back. He whipped around, searching the hallway behind him. As always, there was nobody there. At least nobody who could be seen. He hated being alone. Even in his own home, dead people's stares followed him everywhere.

"Go away!" he yelled.

He'd heard that if you asked, they might leave you in peace. Since asking had done no good in the past, he was reduced to screeching.

The lifeless souls following him probably belonged to his parents, and most certainly his brother. He'd never been able to please his parents in life and saw no reason why it should be any different now.

His older brother, Hamilton, born only moments before him, had always been the favorite. He was the son who did everything right. Even on the rare occasion that Alden felt a need to please, his own efforts turned sour.

Poor Alden had taken up with the wrong kind of friends, his parents used to say, trying to excuse his behavior. But Hamilton, with the right kind of friends, got commendations.

His brother's friends were a stuffy lot, though. Alden enjoyed his own companions, wrong kind though they may have been.

Damn them all, where were they now? They knew he hated being alone.

Alden slapped something from his shoulder. An unearthly touch, he supposed.

He pressed his back against the wall, where the tender spot between his shoulder blades didn't feel so vulnerable…so watched.

With a clear view of the hallway he saw that no ghostly presence lurked in the shadows. His tension eased.

Someone would be along shortly and the fear would go away. He wasn't a coward, even though he'd heard it whispered in phantom tones from behind curtains, or coming from closets.

Not a coward, but a sociable person, most comfortable in the presence of others, as many others as he could be with.

Just as soon as he had his hands on what should have been his inheritance, he would have the funds to attract a devoted social circle. Friends who would fawn over him day and night.

All he needed was control of his niece and nephew, and the fortune was his. Their mother would give him any amount of money to see to their well-being.

Footsteps tromped on the long stairway that curved from the grand foyer past the second-floor garden room, then up to the third story, where the bedrooms were.

"Where the hell have you been, Perryman?" Alden snarled, even though he was relieved not to be alone any longer.

"Where do you think, Hanispree?"

Perryman looked like a hawk, with a long, beaked nose and small eyes that were dark, nearly completely black. He was tall, thin, and walked hunched over because he was constantly scanning the ground for bugs. Perryman liked to eat bugs. Any kind would do.

He was the most "wrong kind" of his friends, and the one Alden liked the best.

"Whoring?" He peered up into Perryman's gaunt face.

Alden resented being short and having to always look up to other men. He had spent his life doing it. Naturally, Hamilton had been tall.

"As if I have the time." Perryman glanced about, scanning the floor, which was insulting, since Alden took pains to make sure the servants kept Hanispree Mansion immaculate. "That reward you promised better be a big one. Abstinence is wearing on me."

"It's not even been two days since we visited Willow's." He and Perryman did share a taste for the fallen woman. No messy affections involved with the sordid sort. When passion bordered on barbarity, a whore was happy with an extra coin. "What did you find out?"

"The brats are missing. No one knows anything."

"Especially you!" Alden shouted at his stupid friend, before forcing his voice to a more congenial tone. "I know the brats are missing. There will be no fortune for either of us unless you find out where they went."

"Like I said, nobody knows anything. Maybe we should call on a mystic?" Perryman fluttered his bony fingers in front of Alden's face. "Oo-o-o!"

"Maybe we should use logic." He stepped away from the wall, out from under the taunting fingers. "Use your brain. My nephew and niece are gone. Who would have taken them? Not their mother."

"Nice work hiding her away in Bedlam." Perryman chuckled. "Everyone swallowed that crap you spread about her going to France to grieve."

Nice work indeed, that. Hamilton had planned to spend a big chunk of what ought to have been Alden's inheritance on that Paris trip, before he took ill.

It was pure providence that Mother and Father had given Alden the lunatic house to run. Mistakenly, they had hoped that the responsibility might make him a man like Hamilton.

"So, who else, then?" he asked, thinking out loud.

"Don't know." Perryman irritated him by once again glancing at the floor.

"Her sister, you idiot." His friend was an imbecile.

"Ah, the pretty one who sings?" Perryman's gaze shot up. He licked his lips. "I like that one."

"And where might she have gone?"

"Don't know, Alden. Ask the mystic."

All at once, Alden's hand shot out and upward. He slapped Perryman in the face. He hadn't intended to react that way, but Perryman had disrespected him.

"Sorry, Perryman." But he wasn't sorry. The fool would believe he was, though; he always did. "Think about where she would take them."

Perryman shrugged and rubbed his cheek. "Maybe she didn't believe that Bethany went to France."

"That's smart. I bet you think she took the brats to their mother."

"I was just about to say so."

"Then you need to look for them in Riverwalk. You can be on the next train out of here."

"Or you can. I'm for Willow's."

"I've hired you for the job." He would never admit that he couldn't go near the mental hospital. He'd heard the stories of the ghosts that hover in the halls. "And think about this. Once we get those kids back, you and I will be able to buy Willow's. What do you think about that?"

"I think I'm on the next train to Riverwalk."

* * *

Lilleth blessed the person who had built the cabin with a raised hearth. He must have had babies that needed protecting.

Just now, Mary stood on wobbly legs, watching the flames eat up kindling and logs. Had the hearth been floor level, Lilleth would not get a single thing done, with having to move her away from danger all the time.

As it was, Lilleth found it to be a continual task keeping the child out of harm's way. Small items found on the floor were a fascination to her. The pocket in Lilleth's apron was quickly filling up with items she hadn't noticed before Mary began to creep about on the floor. So far the collection included a cork, a button, a wheel from a broken toy and a triangle of broken glass.

Her respect for Bethany grew by the hour. Raising a toddler took more skill and patience than she could have imagined.

This afternoon, though, her patience was being strained. There was so much she needed to get done to make the cabin livable. But only a moment into a task, Mary would fuss or need to be pulled away from some danger that she found to be fascinating.

Naturally, this made the baby unhappy, so another moment passed while Lilleth tried to make her smile and forget her frustration at not being allowed to injure herself.

This was not easy, since Mary was teething. Her rare bouts of contentment lasted for only a moment… unless she was being held.

How did mothers get a blessed thing done?

Jess helped, but he was a child himself and shouldn't be burdened with the care of his sister. He did spend a great deal of time playing in the woods, but fear of Alden kept him within sight of the cabin.

When he tired of exploring, he helped out at the lending library under the watchful eye of—she sighed and felt silly for it—of Mr. Clark Clarkly.

"No, no, Mary." Lilleth uncurled the chubby fingers from the fireplace poker, then cleaned the ash off an instant before the baby plunged them into her mouth. "That's not for you, sweetie."

Evidently, fireplace pokers were one more thing that had to be stored where Mary couldn't get to them. The cabin would soon be dotted from one wall to the other with hooks holding dangerous objects out of Mary's reach.

"Please, Lord, keep this child safe until I learn mothering," Lilleth whispered, looking up.

Mary's eyes watered, her lip quivered. She plopped down on the floor, crying.

"Poor dolly, come here, then." Lilleth set aside the washrag she had been using to scrub the table, and picked Mary up. "How about if Auntie sings to you?"

She shouldn't sing, but really, it was all she knew to do to comfort the unhappy child. She hadn't the motherly skills that Bethany had, but she had been known to quiet fretful beasts and belligerent theater-goers with her voice.

She sat in the chair beside the fire, the very one Clark had sat in a few days before, when he had rubbed lotion on her hands. She imagined that the scent of him still lingered on it.

What was happening to her? She had never longed for the scent of a man. No indeed, she'd kept males as far away from her person as she could without appearing uncivil.

For some reason, she wanted to be civil to Clark... very civil.

There was something about him that set him apart from other men. His kindness, to be sure, but there was more than that.

She liked the way he smelled. She was sure to like the way he tasted, were she given the chance.... Also, there was the way he looked at her when he wasn't aware that she noticed.

"Auntie's becoming muddleheaded." She settled Mary in her arms. The baby stuck her thumb in her mouth. Lilleth stroked the moisture from her niece's round, pink cheek. "What can Auntie sing to soothe you?"

Baby songs weren't in her repertoire, but she remembered a few that her mother used to sing before unfaithful men had snatched away her joy.

"I see the moon and the moon sees me," she sang.

It felt good to let her voice out. The odds were remote that anyone would hear her, even more remote that they would recognize her by it. "The moon sees somebody I'd like to see. God bless the moon and God bless me, and God bless the somebody I'd like to see."

She barely finished the short verse before Mary fell asleep. "And God bless your momma, little one," she whispered into Mary's delicate ear. "I'm going to see her very soon."

Not much could feel better than holding this precious bundle, soothing her, watching her sleep. Still, there was work to be done, and sitting here listening to the fire crackle while she watched Mary's peaceful breathing wasn't getting it done.

Outside, the sun shone. Water dripped from icicles; chunks of snow slid off the roof and hit the ground with a soft splat.

In town folks would be taking advantage of the respite in the weather to scurry about their business. Here in her little cabin the woods, though, Lilleth would take a moment to feel the warm, sleepy weight in her arms and steal a second to daydream.

It was true what she had confessed to Mary—she was becoming muddled. She never daydreamed, at least not much, and not about men.

Clark's near kiss had certainly changed that. Not only did she daydream about his mouth, his scent and the feel of his beard stubble against her fingertips, at night she dreamed about things she should never be pondering with a baby on her lap.

With a sigh, Lilleth looked for a place to set Mary down. The sooner she had the cabin cleaned up, the sooner she would be out of Clark's home and the sooner she would get her emotional balance back.

Life was about the practical. For instance, where would she lay Mary down? The hearth would be warm but dangerous. The table was clean but a bit slanted, and Mary might roll off. The bed was unthinkable.

A quiet knock sounded on the front door. The latch lifted and the door opened wide.

Silhouetted by sunshine stood the object of her muddleheadedness, carrying the answer to her prayer in his arms.

Clark closed the door with his foot, then set a wood cradle beside her chair.

Trace stared at the blank sheet of paper on his desk. He tapped his idle pen on the blotter.

In his mind's eye he saw Lilleth in the moonlight, wrapped in his jacket. He felt again the way her weight fitted into his arms, the curve of her hip and the shape of her thigh.

Had she not been married, he would have kissed her…and thoroughly. He'd enjoyed some kisses in his life, but not a single one compared to the one he'd nearly had with Lilleth. In his mind's eye he saw her lips again in the instant that she touched her fingers to his face.

He had fully believed that moonlight brushed her lips and that starlight frolicked in her eyes. That time had turned back on itself.

The very last thing he had expected was to be resisting her kiss.

Now nothing would be the same until he had one in the flesh.

He'd never been a man to enjoy a parade of meaningless lovers, but he'd hadn't lived a monk's life, either. He had known a few women. Two had been foisted upon him by his ever so helpful brothers, another by his sister. One had been his own choice.

Four women, and all of them lovely. It was just that somehow he could never commit his heart to them.

He suspected that the reason for that was at this very moment soaking in his bathtub in a room just off the kitchen. Her pretty wet body could only be forty feet and a closed door away.

No wonder the blank sheet of paper stared up at him. His pen could do nothing but smear a black blob on the blotter.

Trace shook himself. He'd sat down at the desk with a purpose, and that purpose had not been to imagine what Lilleth looked like lying naked in his bathtub.

It had been to make note of his latest findings on

Hanispree Mental Hospital, and wire them to the family. Three days had passed since his last correspondence, and they were bound to wonder. It was a long-standing company rule to wire daily.

He needed to be able to tell them something other than that there was a woman in his bathtub, though.

Lilleth aside, he'd broken another cardinal family rule: never become personally involved in a case. His job was to observe and report. Anything more than that created problems.

He had come to Riverwalk to uncover secrets and write an exposé that would shut Hanispree down. The inmates could then be sent to institutions where they would be cared for.

The trouble was, how many of those inmates would even survive the care given at the asylum long enough to be transferred? When old ladies shivered in their beds, when previously vital human beings looked to be bones more than flesh, and when otherwise intelligent brains began to rot, someone had to step in.

Clark Clarkly was that someone.

If a cardinal rule was bent, the family would survive. The victims of Hanispree might not.

Darkness pressed upon the library windows, and the temperature was falling. Tonight, he would be bringing food and lighting fires.

Fortunately, he would no longer have to waste time sneaking keys from the nurse's desk. He'd configured one of his own that would open every door in the place.

The Ballentines were gifted with skills that most families were not. Making a universal key was something he had learned to do at the age of fifteen. He could do it in his sleep, if he were getting any.

Trace stared down at his paper...still blank. The stain on the blotter had grown to the size of a silver dollar.

From the back of the house, Clark heard the bathroom door open. Feminine footsteps padded up the rear stairs.

What would his houseguest be wearing? Trace set down his pen to prevent accidentally bending the tip.

A practical flannel gown that covered her from neck to toe? Something filmier that stroked the curve of her breast and caressed the line of her thigh?

Or just a short towel that left her legs and arms bare? If so, drops of scented water might linger on her skin, catching the light of the lantern that dimly illuminated the stairs.

If that was the case he'd be astounded, since she had just tiptoed into a room she shared with two sleeping children. When it came to Lils, apparently his imagination had no sense or reason.

Flannel then. But he had never once, in the last sixteen years, ever imagined that she would be here with only that one layer of fabric between her flesh and his dreams.

Trace stood up. He shook himself, which seemed to be becoming a habit. Lilleth would go her way soon and he would go his. That's how it had to be.

He went to the kitchen, put on the heavy coat that hung beside the back door, and picked up the bag of food he had prepared earlier.

He stepped out into the cold.

Lilleth heard the back door close. She tiptoed past the bed where the children slept, and looked out the window into the small yard below.

Just as he had on previous nights, Clark made some kind of excursion into the dark and the cold. The full moon cast his shadow on the snow. Once again, he carried a big bag. Tonight he took his ax.

Lilleth hugged her robe tight about her and tapped her foot.

It didn't take a lot of figuring to know where he had gone. Off to chop firewood for some woman, unless she missed her guess.

"Lilleth Preston, you are a mountain of a fool," she mumbled, frowning as Clark's long and…no mistake about it…confident strides took him around a corner.

Who was Clark Clarkly, really?

He was a puzzle, and it was no business of hers to try and figure him out. She had no claim on him. Whether there was or was not a woman in his life, it was no concern of hers.

A ninny was what she was. Without knowing his attachments, she had mooned over him. Had come close to kissing him! She had let herself ride a magic carpet of wishes, imagining that he was her hero. That she might be special to him.

But then again, from what she knew of Clark, everyone was special to him. Maybe the woman he was carrying his ax for was just someone in need of charity.

In the end, Lilleth could not guess where he was going tonight. What she did know was that her hair was wet and she was going downstairs to sit by the fire and let it dry.

She kissed Jess on the cheek. He stirred and smiled in his sleep. Maybe he thought it was his mother's kiss. Lilleth did the same to Mary, inhaling the sweet baby breath that grazed her nose.

Downstairs, she picked a book from the library shelf, then settled in the chair that Clark slept in at night.

This chair did smell like him. There was no denying that he was her hero, spending night after night on spindly legged furniture while she and the children snuggled in his bed.

She spread her hair over her shoulders so that the heat of the flames could reach it.

She opened the book. Maybe she ought to have been more selective rather than taking the first volume she touched.

"'*Miss Fairhaven and the Dashing Blade,*'" she read out loud. "The title is featherheaded." Certainly she would be bored to sleep by page two. She ought to get up and select another, but she was settled and her hair arranged just so.

In time, she did get sleepy. Just when the Dashing Blade had cornered Miss Fairhaven in a convent closet, after having rescued her from brigands, losing her in a creepy forest, then discovering her again in a deserted town and chasing her into the nunnery, Lilleth's eyes grew too heavy to continue.

Drat! What was Miss Fairhaven going to do?

Meet the Dashing Blade at the county fair, naturally. There he was; she saw him behind her closed eyelids. He found her crouched behind the kissing booth. She had been hiding from someone, but probably not the Dashing Blade.

He offered her a slice of peach pie and she came along quite willingly.

"Hey, Lils," he said. "Let's go sit on the bridge and watch the fireworks."

Miss Fairhaven must have thought that was a fine idea. She skipped along beside him, looking much younger and happier than she had hiding in the closet of the nunnery.

They sat down on the bridge, hip to hip, eating pie and listening to the creek gurgle under their feet. Miss Fairhaven couldn't remember ever feeling so content, sitting here with Trace and watching fireworks burst over the fields like a million fairies dancing in wild abandon.

Trace held her hand.

"Be my king," she whispered to him. "And I'll be your fairy queen. We'll swirl away into the night and live blissfully ever after."

Trace bent his lips to her ear to whisper something.

"Lilly?" A big warm hand touched her shoulder.

Hazy, half in and out of sleep, Lilleth opened her eyes.

"Trace?" She blinked, stared, then sighed. "Oh, Clark, it's you."

"Disappointed?" He straightened his glasses on his nose, then pulled up a chair and sat across from her, knee to knee.

"Not at all...just surprised. I was dreaming."

"Your robe." He cleared his throat and tipped his head in the direction of the garment. "It's slipped."

"Oh!" She bolted up in the chair. Miss Fairhaven and her oh so Dashing Blade fell out of her lap and onto the floor. Lilleth tugged gray flannel over her shoulder and hugged it tight to her neck. The lace gown she wore under it covered her as thoroughly as a shadow. Clark had just been privy to a sight not seen by any other man.

Heat blazed in her cheeks. Her face must look aflame. She was disconcerted, flustered, by what she had exposed to him.

But it was her immodest mind that turned her crimson with mortification. She studied his face, watching for a reaction.

Did he like what he had seen?

"Who is Trace?" he asked, shoving his glasses to the bridge of his nose, as though her charms had gone unnoticed.

"Clark." She let go of the robe choking her throat. It sagged open, but more modestly this time. "You've just seen more of me than…never mind."

She'd nearly forgotten she was married, and not a woman who had experienced only one, exceptionally brief, encounter with a man. She would have to be more careful in the future.

"You thought I was him, just for that second." At least he had the decency to be fighting a grin. "Just wondering, is all."

"I didn't think you were him. You woke me from a dream."

"You were dreaming…of him?"

"I was not. The Dashing Blade was flitting in and out of my dream, if you have to know." How odd that for a brief second he appeared disappointed. "Trace was a boy I knew a long time ago. We were childhood friends, that's all."

"Childhood friends make the longest-lasting impressions. Mine did. What about this Trace fellow? He must have been darn special, since you dreamed about him after all this time."

"He was." What could she say? He had been her everything and it had devastated her when she had been dragged away in the night, crying her heart out. The tears had gone on for weeks. She'd become physically ill. As a result, she hadn't allowed herself to have a friend that she cared for so deeply again. "He was my first and dearest friend. He was also my last."

"I'm sorry, Lilly." Clark reached for her hands and held them in his. He rubbed her palms with his thumbs.

The robe gaped open another inch, but he probably didn't notice.

Chapter Six

Trace walked toward the mercantile with sunshine warming his shoulders and slush soaking his boots.

It had been three and a half days since he had wakened Lilleth from her dream. Seventy-four hours of joy and torment.

Lace under flannel!

Trace felt off balance with that revelation. It was becoming a challenge to his self-control to remain Clark Clarkly.

Luckily, Lilleth and the children would be moving into the cabin tomorrow. Maybe then he'd be able to concentrate on his exposé instead of constantly watching Lilleth out of the corner of his eye. Maybe then he'd remember that a blank sheet of paper required words to be written on it.

Deep in his thoughts, Trace nearly ran down a stick-thin man walking past the front door of the Riverwalk Hotel.

This time it had not been intentional. The man was not watching where he went. He gazed down, scanning the boardwalk, side to side. Maybe he'd lost something.

"I beg your pardon," Trace murmured, passing by the stranger and glancing down to make sure he didn't trample the thing that the man was searching for.

A beetle, lured from his autumn hiding place by the warm day, scurried over a cracked wood plank, so Trace stepped wide of it. The thin man cocked his head in apparent interest in the bug.

Strange man.

A moment later Trace spotted Lilleth with the children a few shops down, at the milliner's. She carried Mary on her hip and pointed to some lacy object in the window. The baby reached for the glass and Lilleth smiled. She said something he was too far away to hear.

Jess knelt beside his mother's skirt, trying to coax a stray cat to come and smell his hand. Lilleth went into the store, but Jess remained outside, while the cat inched toward his fingers.

What wouldn't Trace give to have them as his family! He'd give everything, everything but his calling. And that was only because innocent lives depended on him.

Well, then, since he couldn't give her Trace Ballentine, he would give her what he could. Just now, as Clark, he bumbled his way to the mercantile to buy her a bed, one for Jess, too.

Having provided the Gordons with plenty of firewood and a place to sleep, he would be free to continue his quest to shut down Hanispree. He could not allow anything to be more important to him than seeing each and every one of the inmates transferred to a respectable institution.

With his hand on the doorknob of the mercantile, Trace turned moon-eyed, to see if Lilleth had come back outside. At some point he'd have to learn not to do that. Watching her smile, studying the arch of her brow and discreetly watching her bosom rise and fall with her breathing could only end in misery.

His Lils was no longer his Lils.

He began to step over the threshold of the store, but stopped dead still. Warm air from inside washed over his face while the cold knob chilled his fist.

The narrow-faced stranger was staring at Jess. The man had gone into the alley between the milliner and bakery. He peeked his head around the corner of the building, blatantly spying on the boy.

Strange man…strange behavior.

Trace closed the door on the warmth. He hurried down the steps to get between the stranger and Jess.

All at once an arm snaked around Trace's shoulder and a man's weight sagged against him. Alcohol reeked from his jacket but not on his breath.

"Brother, can you spare a fellow a dime?"

* * *

Cooper Ballentine leaned against Trace, draping his full weight across Trace's shoulders. Cooper was the most dramatic of his brothers, and the only one to have been born with blond hair and brown eyes. Had he not taken up the family calling, Trace was sure that Cooper would have made a life for himself onstage.

"Abner's hitting the swill a little early, don't you think?" Trace spoke to his brother, but kept his eye on the man watching Jess.

"Never too early for good ole Ab." Cooper slurred his speech to perfection. "'Sides, I like Ab."

Cooper tripped and Trace hauled him back up. As boys, they had perfected various falls and landings. If one looked closely, Clark Clarkly and Abner Welchtin reacted to gravity in an identical manner.

"Tell me what you're doing here later, Coop." From across the street Clark watched Jess tip his head to one side, unaware of the watcher, being absorbed as he was in the slow progress of the cat. "There's a man watching the boy over there, the one with the cat. I need you to follow him, see where he goes."

"Need a drink in the worst way, mister," Cooper said in a loud voice, and all but drooled on Trace's shirt. "Jus' a dime."

"Find your own dime, you swillbelly."

Cooper detached himself from Trace, then stumbled in the direction of the stranger.

"I ain't no swill…swill—whatever that was." Cooper dropped to the dirt, got up and dusted off his knees, then stumbled toward the alley. "Might be for a dime, though."

Not likely. His brother couldn't drink, ever since he'd gotten sick from it as a kid. Cooper cursed that day as much as their mother blessed it.

"Hey, mister!" Cooper weaved his way toward the watcher. "Can you spare a dime…just one?"

The man disappeared down the alley, trying to evade Abner Welchtin, who stumbled behind him, determined in his pursuit of a coin.

As much as Trace didn't care to hear the reprimand that Cooper had most likely come to deliver from the family, he was glad his brother had arrived. Cooper could sniff out a man as reliably as Jess's stray cat was likely to sniff out fish.

Jess stood up. The cat dashed off. The boy stretched his arms over his head, looking young, carefree and ignorant of potential danger. With a slow pivot he went into the milliner's.

One thing was certain. The Gordons would not be walking home alone.

Chances were, the stranger was just a man interested in watching a boy catch a cat. But what if there was more to it?

Trace had had a niggling feeling that Lilleth was

frightened of something. Now, with someone watching, the odds were not good enough for Trace to keep his distance.

"I got a creepy feeling, Ma," Jess whispered while Lilleth switched Mary from one hip to the other. "Couldn't look up to see anything, but the itchy twitchy was there, right in the middle of my back. And the cat was skittish."

"Cats are naturally skittish, especially around strangers."

And Alden may have deduced that it was she who had taken his wards. Where would he look but Riverwalk, even if he did fear being stalked by the restless dead?

She intended to free Bethany if it took her last breath. Alden would know that. With his fortune at stake, he might be bolder than Lilleth had expected.

"He didn't seem like a stranger to me. Ouch!" Jess untangled his hair from his sister's chubby fist. "It was like the cat's known me all along. Do you think I might keep him?"

That would be unwise. Life was in such an upheaval now, how could they offer shelter to a cat?

They couldn't possibly. No, the appropriate answer would be no.

"If you catch him, Jess, you can keep him."

His eyes lit up in a way she hadn't seen in some time. True happiness radiated from them. For all the world, they looked like Bethany's used to, before her life fell apart.

"No" would have been the appropriate answer, but "yes" was the right answer. Jess still needed to catch the creature, after all. In her heart Lilleth hoped he did. It might distract him from his troubles for a little while.

"Thanks, Ma!" Looking like the happy boy he ought to be, Jess dashed from the store.

"Don't forget to be—" she called after him. She caught herself from saying "careful."

A child shouldn't carry the burden of watching over his shoulder for danger. She would do that for him, although if it came to it, all Alden had to do was complain to the law that she had kidnapped his wards. They would be taken from her, all neat and legal.

She would have the devil of a time getting them away again.

"Good luck, Jess," she said to the slamming door. "I hope you catch the kitty."

Lilleth purchased earmuffs for Mary and followed Jess outside. The cat had vanished.

"You'll find him. Maybe tomorrow." She glanced about, pretending to search for the feline, scanning shadows and doorways for someone who might have been watching Jess.

To her relief, the only one watching was Clark.

As luck would have it, they seemed to be headed in the same direction at the same time.

"Good afternoon, Mr. Clarkly." Gracious, but when was the last time her smile had ever felt so warm? "It's lovely in town this afternoon."

His smile in return was sweet, sincere, and if she was not mistaken, just a little bit wicked.

"May I walk you home, Mrs. Gordon?"

There it was; just the slightest blush gave away his thoughts. He wanted more than the kiss they had nearly shared.

"I'd be delighted." And didn't she want more than that, as well?

"It looks like there'll be snow before morning." He glanced at the sky, then down an alley. "We'll have to build a big roaring fire for our last night together."

"Indeed, Mr. Clarkly. I can't think of anything I'd like more."

She blushed. He blushed. They looked away from each other, while Jess watched for his cat to come out of hiding.

As it turned out, it did snow and they did build a fire. A huge raging one…that they shared with Cooper.

No fewer than ten times in the past hour—Trace counted every one of them—Cooper turned his head and arched an inquisitive brow at him.

Luckily, Lilleth hadn't noticed. She seemed absorbed by her thoughts while she stared at the fire. Once again she seemed troubled, and he doubted that it was because of Cooper's charming presence.

Trace had outright lied to her about who his brother was. He'd introduced Cooper as the cousin of a friend from far away. While it was unlikely that she would remember him, one never knew what might spark a memory.

Cooper flirted with Lilleth the same way he did all women. His behavior was more annoying than ever, since the object of his attention was Lils.

Lilleth countered his advances as expertly as a tennis player returning a volley. Her interest in Cooper's game lasted only a few minutes before she went back to quietly staring at the flames.

A skilled flirt! There might be more to his Lils than the sweet child she had been and the abandoned woman she had become. The less Trace knew the better, really, but there was a puzzle here. Puzzles tended to eat at him until he solved them.

"Gentlemen, if you'll excuse me," she said all at once, standing up and smoothing a fold in her skirt. "All of a sudden I'm done in."

Not with weariness, Trace guessed, but done in with something. Could be Cooper, but he doubted it. Ladies usually enjoyed his attention.

"Do I need to ask why you're here?" Trace asked, after he heard the bedroom door close. "Hope you've found a place to stay. I've got the chair."

"Damn Grange meeting," Cooper grumbled. "Guess I've got the kitchen table."

"Tried it. Don't envy you, little brother."

"Younger by eleven months hardly counts."

"Younger is always younger." Trace shrugged, grinned, and stretched his boots toward the fire.

"The folks sent me to check on you. You know how they get when no work is sent in. It's been a more than a week since we heard anything from you. Mother is sure you're lying helpless in a ditch. Pop thinks you've taken up the fast life."

"This case is complicated. It's going to take some time."

Cooper leaned forward, his elbows on his knees. "So, why am I the cousin of some distant acquaintance?"

"Didn't you recognize her?"

"No." Cooper shrugged. "Real pretty, though."

"That's Lilleth Preston."

Cooper sat up straight in his chair. "Your long-lost little girlfriend? The one you were so sweet on it nearly killed you?"

Trace nodded.

"What the blazes is she doing in your house?"

"Hiding, I think." Trace kicked off his boots and let the flames warm his socks. He glanced out the front window. Snow drifted past in lazy, swirling flakes. Too much of it might prevent Lilleth from moving tomorrow. "Don't worry, Coop, she doesn't know who I am."

"Wouldn't expect her to. It's been a long time." Cooper flexed his fingers between his knees. "Besides, you're uglier now than you were as a kid."

Trace ignored the comment, because he didn't feel like spending fifteen minutes exchanging barbs.

"I knew who she was the second after I knocked her over."

"Not everyone remembers every detail of their lives.... Really? You knocked her down?"

"Had to. I was Clark."

Cooper kicked off his boots and tossed them beside Trace's. "You better be careful. The folks are counting on you to get things done here. Hanispree is important."

"I haven't forgotten. Rescuing the innocent and saving the family from financial ruin...I get all that."

"Maybe not quite ruin, but times have been hard. This exposé means a lot to us. That's why they gave the job to Clark Clarkly."

"I'm not in trouble. You can relay that to the folks."

"Why'd you have me trail that ghoul?" Cooper yawned and stretched. "Is he involved with Lilleth Preston?"

"Can't be sure. I saw him staring at her son and it gave me a bad feeling."

"Creepy fellow ate a bug." Cooper shivered. "He

finally tossed me a dime before he went into Mrs. O'Hara's. I left it in the dirt. Pity the poor working girl who has to service him."

"Thanks, Cooper. I don't know if he is a threat to Lilleth, but at least I know where he is."

"I'll tell the folks you didn't die in a ditch or become a libertine. Just send them something so I don't have to come back and sleep on your table again." Cooper stood up, stretched and rubbed his eyes. "I'm getting some shut-eye. Make sure you don't snore."

Trace stood up in turn. "I'll get you a blanket."

He mounted the stairs, his steps muffled by his socks, while Cooper went into the kitchen and closed the door.

A lucky thing for Trace, as his brother was the one who snored like a freight train.

He glanced up the staircase and saw a shadow drift across the hall. Not a creepy bug-eating creepy one, though.

This one had hair that tumbled halfway down her back. Masses of red curls glowed in the dim light of the hall lantern. Bare pink toes peeked out from under the flannel robe that she hugged tightly across her chest.

She didn't see him standing on the steps because she was gazing out the window, watching the snow fall. He stood still for a full minute, taking in the sight of her. His very own miracle, or curse, depending on how one looked at it, standing in his hallway, wearing a lacy shift under her worn flannel robe.

Her breath fogged the glass and she wiped it away with her fist.

"Can't sleep?" he asked, letting her know he was there. "Is something wrong?"

She turned to look at him and shook her head. Lantern light caught the pretty line of her jaw, the arch of her brow and the slight upward curve of her lips.

"What could be, really?" She flipped a tumble of curls away from her eye, and her robe fell open. "The snow's coming down and the children and I are safe and warm inside, thanks to you."

Lilleth grasped her hair and began to braid it. Trace suddenly adored braids. Their creation involved both of a woman's hands and left her robe to part completely.

"I love a snowy night," she said, her fingers moving slowly through her hair. "The quiet, the stillness… It's pristine. Everything is snug inside, so very peaceful."

Not only did Trace adore braids, he now thought highly of snow. But lantern light moved to the top of the things he admired most.

When Lilleth turned sideways to gaze out the window again, flickering shadows licked at her lace gown and dappled delicate flower etchings on her skin.

For Trace, the world narrowed to a single point. He could hardly catch a breath, watching Lilleth in profile—more exactly, watching one breast in profile. Illuminated softly, it moved with her braiding. Up and down with the twisting of her hair, followed by a jiggle when she yanked the tresses tight.

Her nipple pressed against the confining lace. The lamp's glow lathed the firm little bud, gold over pink.

"It's beautiful, don't you think?" she asked.

"I've never seen anything quite like it." He thought his voice actually croaked. He ought to do the noble thing and point out the problem with her clothing.

Didn't want to, but if he stood here much longer, drooling like a hungry dog, he'd do something he'd regret…a little bit, at least.

"The snow, that is." He made a Clarklike gesture with his hands. "Your robe. It's come open again."

"It seems to have a mind of its own sometimes."

Lilleth closed it up, but not before he caught a glimpse of both lush breasts.

Wind howled in the shutters outside, rattling them. Common sense abandoned him and he rushed forward.

He lifted Lilleth up, his thumbs and fingers supporting where her underarms met the tender curve of her torso. Her breasts skimmed his chest. The scents of flowers and flesh filled him. Her cheek rested against his for half an instant, smooth against the stubble of his beard. She turned her face, her mouth nearly grazing his lips.

"There's a very good chance that I'm a widow," she gasped.

He kissed her gently, reverently...for a respectable second. Then heat flashed through him, burning him with the ache of the empty years he had longed for her.

He nipped at her lips, then devoured them, because he was starved. Hunger that had not begun to be satisfied made him senseless to the snow, the wind, the sleeping children and his snoring brother.

Life narrowed to this one moment, where Lilleth returned his passion, heat upon heat. Where pure, white-hot lust made anything else irrelevant and convinced him that she was, in all probability, a widow. No man would ever leave this woman willingly.

He backed her against the wall and slid her slowly down the front of him. Through his worn flannel shirt, her heavy breathing pressed her to him, heart to heart. Her plush breasts with tight, swollen buds grazed a path downward.

He nuzzled her neck, inhaling the scent of her skin, of the spirit of Lilleth.

She moaned and whispered Clark's name. That alone should have been enough for him to let go of her. Damn it, she didn't even know who he was.

But he couldn't because his gray life had suddenly

burst into color, confetti that flew about his mind in wild confusion.

He buried his face in the softly twining curls at her ear.

"Lils," he whispered.

She stiffened and shoved his shoulders.

Oh, damn, had he said that out loud? Clearly he had. She blinked at him in confusion.

"What was that you called me?"

"It doesn't matter." He stepped away from her, feeling sick at heart.

He had wanted her so badly that he had been willing to believe a lie. Her husband might well be dead...but he might not.

"Forgive me, Lilly, I hardly know what to say. My actions were not gentlemanly...but it won't happen again."

Not gentlemanly? They were cowardly and weak. They were the actions of a selfish idiot.

"I do beg your pardon." He turned, taking the stairs down two at a time.

She groaned. He was certain of that.

"No need to be all that sorry," he thought she said.

No doubt he had misunderstood.

Chapter Seven

Lilleth had moved out of Clark's house as soon as she had forced down her last bite of breakfast pastry.

Now, four hours later, she drew aside the curtain over the window beside the front door of the cabin. She gazed out at last night's dusting of snow. Two sets of footprints led away from the porch, one large and one small: Clark's and Jess's.

Clark had come by earlier to pick up Jess and help him catch his cat. His offer to accompany her nephew had been beyond welcome, since she could not have allowed the boy to go to town alone, and she didn't want to take Mary out in the cold.

Things were as awkward between her and Clark this afternoon as they had been this morning. At breakfast, she couldn't quite meet his eye and he couldn't quite speak a coherent sentence.

It was almost as though the air between them pulsed red with embarrassment. To suggest that maybe she was a widow made her sound like a desperate strumpet. He must think she was ready to spring upon him at any moment.

There must have been some kind of spell lurking in the hallway. What other explanation could there be for what had happened?

She'd wanted his kiss. Only a born and bred fool would deny it. How was she to guess that it would ignite the way it had? That it would burn up her good sense.

Last night Lilleth had not been very smart. Had things not fallen apart when Clark called her Trace Ballentine's pet name for her, he'd have soon discovered that she hadn't the knowledge of intimacy that a widow would have.

While not a virgin in the true sense of the word, her one, exceptionally brief sexual experience, born out of pure curiosity, had left her with more questions than answers. Barely out of her teens, she had wanted to know what drove her mother to take man after man into her bed. After the twenty seconds Lilleth had allowed a handsome young fellow under her skirt, she was more baffled than ever.

Last night, Clark had cleared up a great deal of the mystery.

Living in his house had been a sanctuary, and she would be forever grateful. But she had moved out not a moment too soon.

There were things about Clark Clarkly that puzzled her. There was something just below the surface of the man that she should be able to grasp but could not.

Here in her own home she would regain her balance.

"Mary, isn't this dandy? A place all our own."

The toddler, sitting on the newly polished floor, banged a spoon on top of a pot. Lilleth sat on the floor beside her. It seemed impossible that it had been little more than a week since the floor had been covered with grime instead of polish.

Lilleth picked up a ladle and banged it on the pot in time with Mary's spoon.

"Here, like this." She captured Mary's round little fist and helped her tap the pot. "I used to open my show with this tune."

The tempo of the spoon and the ladle made Lilleth tap her knee on the floor to the rhythm. It couldn't hurt to sing the song softly, just under her breath.

"Mamma," Mary announced.

"Soon, little lambie. You'll see your mother soon."

Tonight, in fact, after she had the children bedded down for the evening, Lilleth intended to venture out. There had to be a way to get to Bethany.

Walking, bold as brass, into the hospital was out of the question. If Alden did suspect that she was in Riverwalk, he would have the staff watching for her.

More than a dozen times, she had longed to ask Clark if he had come across Bethany when he delivered his lending books to the hospital. It would be a comfort to know that he had seen her, that she was coping.

"I can't ask him that, though, can I, little Mary? Our safety depends upon keeping our secrets." Lilleth touched Mary's short curly locks. The hair was so soft she could barely feel it swirl about her fingers. "It's not that I don't think Clark is trustworthy, but this is something we'll have to do on our own."

"Ba...bo," Mary cooed, and smiled.

"I know I can you trust to keep silent." Lilleth stood up and walked to the fireplace. She picked up the poker and urged new life into the flames.

It would be bone-chilling tonight, but probably not snowing. There would be no help for it but to bundle up and venture out into the darkness.

This particular night would be ideal, since there would be no moon. She would be able to poke about the hospital grounds with slim chance of being seen.

Poking about was her only goal for tonight, though. As much as she longed to burst inside to free her sister, like a dime novel gunfighter with weapons blazing, she would have to wait. First, she needed to study the building and the grounds, and then she would figure a way in and out.

Lilleth sat down on the hearth and warmed her back.

"Don't you worry, baby, you'll be in your mama's arms in a bang and a thrash."

An hour later, the front door burst open, blowing in Jess, Clark and a rush of frigid air.

"The cat got this close, Ma!" Jess tugged off his hat and shimmied out of his coat. He tossed them on the hearth and then spread his arms wide. "Clark says he'll come to me next time, sure. I can't rush him, though. It needs to be the cat's own choice, else he'll only run away first chance he gets. I'm hungry. Clark brought dinner from the hotel."

Clark stood beside the closed cabin door, holding several items wrapped in cloth. Steam and the aroma of fried chicken, along with other enticing scents, wafted out of the linens.

She would have to learn to cook, and soon, or the children might starve. She couldn't expect Clark to feed them every day.

When she took the food from his hands, he looked as nervous as any man she had ever seen.

Or maybe not. Thinking back on last night, which she had done dozens upon dozens of times today, frightened was about the last thing he had looked. Had he not called her Lils, they might have done things in the hallway that were meant for the bedroom.

In the end, that name, that endearment, had startled her out of her haze of passion. Clark's voice had sounded like an echo of Trace Ballentine's, older to be sure, but an echo all the same.

"Will you join us for dinner, Clark?" she asked.

"No, but thanks. I've got sorting to do in the library." He straightened his glasses on his nose and shrugged his shoulders, one then the other.

Lilleth set the food on the table.

"Go ahead and eat, Jess. Feed Mary, too, will you?" She settled the baby in a chair and tied her in place with a strip of cloth.

"Clark, I'd like a word with you on the porch."

"Oh, yes. I suppose the sorting can—yes, Lilly, to be sure." He followed her outside and she closed the door behind them.

A gust of cold wind ruffled the hem of her skirt. It tugged Clark's hair and snapped a wavy strand across his forehead.

"It's about last night," she said, and wrapped her arms about her ribs for warmth. "What you must think of me. I acted the regular trollop."

"You were lovely, Lilly, and I was an unprincipled devil." He shoved the hair back from his face to reveal arched brows pushing rows of lines to his hairline.

"The trollop most sincerely apologizes to the devil."

"The devil most sincerely apologizes to the trollop." He smiled. A dimple winked at her. "But seriously, Lilly, you are no trollop."

"Perhaps there was just something in the air."

"Something that took us both by surprise." He blinked and nodded.

"We'll have to be on guard for surprises from now on."

"Diligently, so they won't surprise us again."

"Well, I do feel better, now that we've set things straight," she said, but wondered about the sad little ache in her heart. "Won't you stay for dinner?"

"The good thing about sorting is that it never complains about having to wait."

He opened the door. Heat rushed out. Lamplight spilled over the porch to point a finger at the setting sun.

She walked inside and he came in behind her, closing the door on the falling night.

Trace picked up his ax, swung it over his shoulder and stepped off the back porch of the lending library.

Damn, it was cold. His clothes all but crackled with it.

He wished that he could have remained in Lilleth's cabin, where heat from the fire, good conversation and a full belly made him linger far later than he should have.

Unlike the night before, where the thing that was in the air had spun him like a top and then smashed him on his head, where passion had beheaded common sense and nearly exposed him, tonight had been a night for comfort and quiet friendship.

And really, friendship had been his and Lils's bond way back when. Their attachment had been between hearts. Until last night, passion had been an innocent dream of the future. As children, they hadn't even begun to understand it.

In those days they had shared romantic vows and promises along with one sweet, chaste and heart-wrenching kiss.

Lilleth Preston was his past. Lilly Gordon was his friend. That's all there could ever be, and he would learn to deal with it.

By damn he would.

Cooper had left this morning before breakfast and agreed to report to the family that Trace had been bedridden with some illness or another. In return, Trace had vowed to write all night and day. So far his ink bottle remained corked and his page blank.

He and Jess had made good progress with the cat, though.

Clark shook himself. He had a calling and a goal. He would do well to remember that he was first and always an investigative journalist.

That's exactly why he walked to the mental hospital by way of Mrs. O'Hara's. The skinny bug-eater presented a mystery…a mystery that Trace had every intention of investigating.

With an icy breeze pushing from behind, it took him only a few minutes to reach Mrs. O'Hara's. Her red lantern swayed and cast shifting shards of light over the porch and out onto the road.

This late at night most of Riverwalk's citizens

were asleep. The brothel appeared to be just warming up. Music from an untuned piano plinked out a window that was cracked open an inch. Squeals and laughter spilled out as well.

Trace wasn't sure what crouching in the shadows beside the porch would reveal, but he bent his ear, listening.

Nothing came through the window crack, but it did through the front door.

Mrs. O'Hara's burly protector, Sims, held the subject of Trace's investigation by his shirt collar so that the toes of his shoes scraped the porch. He gave the skinny man a shake, then a toss.

The thin man landed bottom-first in the street, a tangle of long legs and awkward arms.

"We don't take to your sort around here, Perryman," Sims barked. He slammed the door.

Lantern light swayed back and forth across the man getting up from the dirt.

Trace had discovered some things, after all. One, the man's name was Perryman. Two, he wasn't even fit for a brothel. Three, he was a physical weakling. But four, he was all the more vicious because of it.

The swing of light across Perryman's face showed him smiling at the closed, and probably now locked, door. The next shift of light revealed him snarling, with unnaturally sharp, yellow teeth grinding, top against bottom, back and forth.

After a moment, he clenched his fists, turned and

growled as he walked away. Growled not like a dog, or even a wolf, but like a threatened cat, a sick cougar.

Cooper had been right—the man was creepy. What, if anything, could he want with young Jess? Possibly it wasn't Jess he was interested in; maybe he wanted to devour the poor feline.

In any case, Perryman needed watching.

Trace let him get a good distance ahead before he stood up from his hiding place. He followed him, hugging shadows and watching from behind trees.

Hell and damn! Perryman was taking a back trail through the woods that led to Hanispree.

With the children asleep in their beds and the fire banked low, Lilleth stepped onto her front porch and closed the door behind her.

The night was black, deep with shadows and secrets. There was one secret that would give itself up tonight: Lilleth would find a way to get to her sister. She might not get close enough to attempt a rescue, but she would figure a way to go about it.

She stepped off the porch and walked through the woods veering off on a trail that split from the path to town. She had never been frightened of the night before. As a child she'd run free in the moonlight, as an adult she entertained audiences by lamplight.

This night, though, was deep, cold and silent. The only sound was the wind scratching bare branches together, with a rasp here and a crack there. If a person believed in the other world, she might see a ghost slip past a tree or a goblin pop up from behind a fallen log to bare his wicked teeth.

Luckily, Lilleth Preston did not believe in those things. If she did she would have been forced to take the wide, level road to Hanispree. Since she could not risk being seen, she took the back road that her landlord had mentioned. She suspected that the timid man's ears still rang with the lecture she had given him on honesty.

He had been forthright about the trail that twisted through the woods. By day it was easy walking, but by night it was brimming with shadows and imagined threats.

She stepped quickly, anxious to be off the path. Even without supernatural beings spying from the shrubbery, the night air was snapping cold. The wind's icy fingers continually yanked back the hood of her cloak. After half a mile she gave up on keeping it in place and used her hands to clasp the front of her cloak closed.

"Who-o-o—" A sudden rush of cold air pushed from behind.

"Who-o-o yourself, you old wind."

One time she imagined she heard footsteps to her left, just off the path. When she looked all she spotted was a bramble bush ticking against a tree.

She hurried down the path, careful not to peer too closely behind trees or fallen logs.

At last she spotted Hanispree. The huge building appeared, then vanished beyond a dense growth of bare-branched cottonwoods. In only a few hundred more yards she would be out of the woods and onto the main road.

All of a sudden, she heard footsteps again. No spectral shuffle, no lithe-footed gremlin; this was a very distinct crunch of boots on the path…following her.

Very well, then. She hadn't spent her life avoiding the lecherous groping of men to simply be caught in the woods.

"Oh! Ouch!" she exclaimed, sounding helpless, injured. She bent over and grasped her ankle with both hands. "My foot!"

Crunch, step, crunch, silence. A shift of fabric warned her that the man was at her back and reaching forward.

By the saints, this was too easy. The idiot had presented her with a perfect target.

She clasped her fingers together, forming one big fist, and in the same instant locked her elbows. She spun about. Swinging upward, she landed a blow to the man's throat.

"Ugh!" He toppled backward, landing in a prickly bush. The miscreant grasped his neck, gasping for breath.

"Why you…you great—" She drew back her boot, aiming for every man's tender spot. "Clark?"

"Ugh!"

"Clark!" She dropped to her knees beside him. "Are you hurt?"

"Yes." His voice sounded it, all raspy and raw. She helped ease him to a sitting position, then plucked a burr from his jacket.

"Well, you were about to get hurt a whole lot worse." She loosened his fingers from his throat and looked at the red welt she had left. "Just give it a minute or two. You'll be all right. What were you doing out here, anyway?"

"Protecting you." That sounded a bit better, a wheeze instead of a gasp.

"From what? Things that go bump in the night?"

"You were being followed." He stared at her oddly, while he rubbed his throat. She couldn't quite tell if the look was reproach or admiration. At least his voice was nearly normal now.

For an instant his remark about her being followed shook her. Not a soul knew she was coming out tonight. And Jess thought he had been watched the other day.

Still, anyone on the path might look like a stalker to a librarian.

"So, you just happened to be on this path at midnight, carrying your ax, and by chance, happened to be behind me. And saw someone else following me?" She shook her head. "Really, Clark, that seems a tall tale."

"Not tall enough." He stood up, yanking a sticker from his trousers. "Lilly, are you in some kind of trouble?"

"No, of course not!" This was a conversation she was not going to have.

"What are you doing out here at this time of night, then?"

"That was my question to you."

"Fair enough. I'll tell you what I'm doing if you tell me what you are doing." He stuck out his hand to confirm the deal with a handshake.

She accepted the shake. To be fair, it turned out to be less a shake than an embrace of hands. It lingered too long and his fingers caressed her wrist.

"You first," she said, to break the spell that might be once again ready to lead them to risky behavior.

He let go of her hand.

"I've noticed, when I deliver books, that on occasion the inmates of the hospital go without fires to warm their rooms. I'm on my way to light them."

Lilleth glanced at the cold, dark windows of the huge building. Was poor Bethany shivering inside even as they stood outside? Worry made Lilleth's stomach sag within her.

"How often is 'on occasion,' Clark?"

"As far as I can tell, nightly." He turned and retrieved his ax from the ground. "Your turn."

"You, Clark Clarkly, are a very good man."

"I hope you're not trying to flatter your way out of your confession."

"There's really not much to confess. I couldn't sleep." That was the truth. She'd barely had a solid night's slumber since Bethany had been incarcerated. "I went for a walk."

He squinted at her. Well, here was something odd. Clark was not wearing his glasses, and yet he seemed to be seeing just fine.

"Just for the record, Lilly, I know you are making that up." He swung the ax over his shoulder. "Come on, I'll walk you home."

"You most certainly will not!" And she was not the only person making things up. She would keep quiet about those missing glasses and just see if he bumped into anything. "I'd never live with myself if those poor folks inside froze while you walked me home."

"You can't walk all that way alone."

"That may be, but I'm not going home. I'm going with you."

This was the most unbelievable luck. When she'd stepped out of the cabin she hadn't dreamed that she might actually get inside the mental hospital.

"They say it's haunted," he warned.

"They say that someday we won't need horses to pull our wagons." Lilleth looked him in the eye, hard. She pointed her finger past him toward the hospital.

"I'm going in that building with you, Clark Clarkly, and that is that."

To prove her point she turned on her heel and walked toward it. For a moment she didn't hear his footsteps following. She did feel his gaze frowning at her back.

"Suit yourself, then," he said, catching up in a few long strides. "Just make sure you keep quiet."

"You'll hardly know I'm there."

So far, Trace found Lilleth to be true to her word, and useful in the bargain.

She was careful not to speak above a whisper. She helped him carry wood. She smiled at the inmates, fawned over them and charmed them. When the ancient Mrs. Murphy would not believe that Lilleth was not Trace's ghostly bride and the reward for his good deeds, she simply patted the old woman's hand and thanked her for her good wishes.

After he had warmed the last hearth, and motioned toward the door to leave, Lilleth tugged on his sleeve.

"That can't be all of them?" She glanced at the closed doors up and down the hall. "Are you sure we haven't missed someone?"

She tapped her foot…one, two, three.

"What's wrong, Lilly?"

"What could be wrong?" Her foot tapped faster. "I

think we might have missed someone, is all. What's up those stairs?"

"A bolted door."

At once she ran for the steps, lifted her skirt and dashed up them two at a time.

"Lils, what's going on?" She didn't hear him; he'd known she wouldn't in her haste to reach the door at the end of that long dark hallway.

When he caught up with her, she had reached the door and pressed her ear to it.

"If someone's in here they're going to be cold as stone."

He prayed that no one was in that room, but instinct told him there was. He'd never heard a cry or a plea for help, even though he'd pounded on the door.

"Let's go. It's late," he said.

Trace walked down the hall, even though he sensed that Lilleth hadn't followed. He stopped with one foot poised over the first stair heading down.

From down that long, dark hall came the most beautiful voice he had ever heard.

He pivoted about and saw Lilleth leaning against that closed door...singing a lullaby. Even at this distance he saw tears shimmering in her eyes.

He opened his mouth to warn her that someone might hear. But then, a ghost could sing a lullaby as well as anyone. He let her finish, then walked back down the hall and turned her away from the door.

"Why were you singing? What's going on?"

"There could be someone trapped inside." She wiped her eyes on her coat sleeve. "I thought a song might help."

"Come on, let's go." He slipped his arm about her shoulder and she let him lead her out of the building. He closed the door and picked up his ax from beside the woodpile.

She huddled under his arm, allowing him to hug her close to his side all through the sleeping woods, along the winding path.

There was more going on than she was admitting. He ached to ask her what it was, but she wouldn't tell him. He knew that for a fact.

So they walked in silence, leaning into each other until they reached the cabin's front steps. By then her tears had dried to frozen, salty tracks.

Tiptoeing up two stairs, she turned and faced him eye to eye.

"Will you come for Thanksgiving dinner?" she asked.

"Yes."

She went up the rest of the steps. She turned and sent him a subdued smile before she slipped inside and closed the door. He heard the lock shift into place, then jiggle as though she was checking its security.

He wondered at what point she would remember that she couldn't cook.

Chapter Eight

"Auntie Lils, you've got flour on your nose." Jess scanned her powdery appearance, hair ribbon to boot toe. "And your elbow."

"I'm well aware of that, young man, but biscuits don't magically appear on the table."

"They used to, back home."

Jess ducked when she flicked a pinch of flour at his nose.

"Back home you had someone trained in the art of biscuit making to set them before you."

"I never saw Mrs. Farmer with white stuff all over her…and the kitchen."

Lilleth scanned the cooking area of the cabin's main room. White dust covered nearly every surface. The only reason Mary wasn't covered in flour was that she was ten feet away, tied to a chair at the dining table, merrily banging a tin cup on the wood planks.

"I don't suppose you ever saw Mrs. Farmer dip her fist, fingers and all, like this." Lilleth smeared her hand in the heap of flour on the small table beside the oven, where she'd set out the mixing bowl, eggs and lard. "I don't suppose she ever did—"

Lilleth lunged, patting her hand on Jess's small rump. "This!"

The boy squealed. He dashed for the biscuit bowl and scooped out a fistful of his own.

He was quick. Lilleth didn't have time to dodge the white cloud coming at her face.

She blinked through powdery eyelashes, then wiped her face with both fists.

Jess doubled over, laughing. Bethany would want that. It's why Lilleth had begun the biscuit fight, even though her own heart was weighted with worry.

"You look like a raccoon, Auntie!" he said, trying to catch his breath.

"And you look like you got a—"

A loud knock sounded at the front door.

"That's Clark! Come to help me catch the cat." Jess dashed in that direction.

"Don't you dare open that door!" she called after him.

Oh, mercy, all powdered in white, she looked like Clark's ghost bride.

Jess opened the door wide. Clark stepped inside, pushed along by a gust of wind.

He straightened his glasses, peering wide-eyed at

her through the lenses. How interesting that today he needed them.

"Good day, Clark." She tried to straighten the blue bow binding the loose hair at her nape, but it was hopeless.

"Lilly?"

Blame it, half a smile tweaked his lips. She must look incompetent to the bone.

Her plan had been to impress him with her new-found skills, not make him laugh. Which he was doing, and quite hardily, even if he did manage to keep it inside.

"Ma's practicing biscuits," Jess announced, while he grabbed his coat off a peg by the door. "She'll be better at it by Thanksgiving."

"Oh, without a doubt. Let's go get your cat."

Jess dashed out the door.

Clark followed, but before he closed the door behind him he turned.

He winked!

"Well!" She slammed her hands on her hips, smiling in spite of herself. "This will be the tastiest Thanksgiving dinner that Mr. Clark Clarkly has ever eaten, mark my words, little Mary."

She had three days to make it so. Seventy-two hours to go from novice to queen of the kitchen.

Snow was on the way, hard and heavy. She'd heard the prediction while she walked down the boardwalk. Not by speaking with anyone about it, naturally. The fewer people she socialized with, the safer it would be.

In passing, she'd caught a word here and a sentence there, enough from each conversation to know that, along with the turkey, the good folks of Riverwalk might have a blizzard for Thanksgiving.

Lilleth stepped into the mercantile, grateful for the stove in the middle of the floor that invited icy shoppers to warm their backsides. This afternoon, she was the only person warming herself at the grate.

With only one more day until Thanksgiving, she had expected a crowd.

Lilleth stretched her gloves toward the fire. She skimmed her mental list of things she needed to purchase. Somehow those things would come together to provide a feast. Other women cooked; they did it daily. Blamed if she wouldn't do it, as well. It was simply a matter of mixing flour, and such, then there you had it. Somehow.

She put away wondering about the mysteries of gravy when thoughts of Clark crept into her mind. The man was perplexing, fascinating even. What was it about him that had tugged at her since the very first time she'd met him?

And what kind devilment had gotten into her, inviting him for a feast cooked by her own hands?

He made her feel safe, was what.

Had it not been for the pit of lies and deceit that

she lived and breathed on a daily basis, she would have asked him not to take the short walk home the other night.

Clark was the kindest, most decent man she had ever met. And honest on top of all that. In case those things were not enough, she wanted him in a most carnal way. Somehow, the librarian had gotten under her skin, burrowed himself into her heart.

Her bedroom walls were thick, made of solid logs, and the children were sound sleepers. Had life been different, she would have invited him for more than dinner.

She'd never met a man she wanted in that way. It could be because she'd never met a man she completely trusted.

She trusted Clark.

Walking home from Hanispree, tucked under the shelter of his arm, she had wept against his chest and found sanctuary.

Even though that moment of refuge felt good and right, she was not entirely comfortable with it. Being her own guardian had served her quite nicely her whole adult life.

In the end, she could not deny that having someone watch out for her gave her that extra bit of courage.

Right now she needed courage. Clark believed that someone had been trailing her in the woods, at midnight no less. All afternoon while she shopped in town, she had felt creepy crawlies itching between her shoulder blades, just as Jess had described.

She was surer than ever that he hadn't imagined he was being spied on the other day.

Thank the stars that she had come to town alone today and left the children in the warm safety of the cabin. The cabin with the sturdy lock that Clark had insisted on installing with his own, not so bookish hands.

Lilleth shook off a shiver. No one was watching. Her nerves were getting the best of her, what with the pressure of cooking a holiday feast. Not a feast for just the children and Clark, either; she'd make enough food for all the folks locked up in Hanispree. *I'll find you, Bethany.* She sent the thought for the thousandth time.

The mercantile owner came out from behind the curtain of the storeroom, wiping his hands on his long apron.

"What can I do for you, missus? Hope you don't want a turkey—sold out of those yesterday. Folks came in early, stocking up for the storm. No one wanted to get caught without a bird for Thanksgiving."

Luckily, she didn't need a bird. Clark was supplying that, although she would still need to cook it. From what she had been able to learn from the cookbooks that Jess had sneaked home from the lending library, turkey was the easiest part of the meal to fix.

"I don't need a turkey. Just some green beans, a dozen cans of milk." If a blizzard was coming she would need to have extra milk on hand. "Make that two dozen cans, along with potatoes and a big bag of flour."

"You go through all that flour you bought the other day already?"

"My biscuits are renowned." Hopefully, he didn't see her blush at her womanly failing to prepare the perfect bun. "I can't seem to make enough of them. They disappear almost before they are out of the oven."

That might be the case at some point in time, after she practiced a few dozen more batches. Hopefully, Jess wouldn't turn into a lump of dough for all the sampling he'd been doing.

"In fact, let me have two bags of flour. They are that good."

She laid money on the counter to pay for the food.

"You'll need help with all that. I'll send my boy over in the buggy."

"Thank you. Here's something for his trouble." She placed a quarter on top of the bills.

"You take care, Mrs. Gordon. That blizzard's going to be a killer." He scooped up the money and slid it in his apron pocket.

Lilleth turned to walk toward the front of the store. A man, his hat tugged so low it flopped over his ears and nearly hid his eyes, peered through the window. Ice crystals frosted the glass where he breathed on it. He grinned at her, then licked the pane with a long narrow tongue.

Just as quickly as he'd appeared, he vanished.

"Did you see that?" She spun about, but the mercantile owner had gone into the back room.

Had the apparition even been there? She'd like to hope that it was merely stress getting the better of her. Just in case, though, she'd ride home in the wagon with the storekeeper's son.

The turkey had nearly frozen while Trace went from the lending library to the cabin. So had he. The five minutes it normally took to walk that distance stretched to fifteen.

Wind howled past his ears, swirling snow every which way. He knew he was on the path only because he didn't bump into a tree.

Predictions of a blizzard had been underestimated. This storm was a violent force that breathed menace down turned-up collars, and foreboding up pant legs. Pity anyone who got caught out in it.

At least his family in Chicago wouldn't be expecting him to wire them his tardy progress report on the investigation.

A lamp glowing in the cabin window reassured him that he was going the right way. He leaned into the wind and pressed toward it.

The Gordons must have been for watching for

him. As soon as his frozen boot touched the porch the front door was flung open and Jess rushed out to take charge of the turkey.

"Ma thought you wouldn't come," he said. "But I knew you would, Clark."

The boy looked up at him, grinning. The gladness illuminating his eyes made Trace want to go down on his knees and embrace him.

It was plain to see that Jess missed having a father, one who would be around no matter what. Apparently, without meaning to, Trace had stepped into the role. He shouldn't have let that happen, but it had come about so naturally that he hadn't noticed until this instant.

Besides, this was Lilleth's son, her own flesh and blood. He could no more turn away from him than he could the boy's mother.

Jess crossed the room, carrying the bird to Lils. He almost staggered, tipped to one side with the weight of it. She lifted it from his arms, her face flushed from the fire she had just built up in the stove.

"Wait till you see my surprise, Clark!" Jess dashed toward his mother's bedroom and disappeared around the corner.

"He's been on pins all morning with excitement. I didn't expect you'd make it in this weather. You must be frozen through." Lilly brushed a spot of snow from his shoulder.

"It would take a worse storm than this one to keep me from this meal. I'd have crawled through the woods if I had to." He shrugged out of his coat, then hung it on a peg on the wall beside the fireplace.

Lilleth smiled at him, bright and pretty. Something about her was different today. She looked at him with softness in her eyes. Or maybe it was simply holiday cheer.

He'd give thanks today for that, even if what he should be giving thanks for was that she hadn't discovered who he really was.

Jess came around the corner, walking carefully and carrying a big cat in his arms.

"He finally came to me, just like you said he would." The boy's small chest seemed to puff up with pride while he carried his prize across the room. "Just in time, too."

As if to emphasize the point, a screeching wind grabbed hold of the cabin. It pounded, as though it wanted to blow the place down, but being made of good solid logs, with all the holes repaired, the structure held without a creak.

"He's a fine cat." Warmth from the fireplace on one end of the cabin and heat from the stove on the other chased the chill from Trace's clothes, then his bones.

He bent down to gaze closely at the cat, which purred with contentment in Jess's arms.

"Might be the finest I've ever seen." Trace stroked

the orange head and got a nudge in response. "Maybe he'd like some turkey, later."

"Bet he would. He's hungry as anything." Jess settled in one of the chairs beside the fireplace and snuggled the feline close. "He already gobbled down two eggs and four of Ma's practice biscuits."

"Those must be some good biscuits, then."

Jess arched a brow, then shook his head, long and slow. Luckily, Lilleth was busy sliding the turkey into the oven and didn't seem to notice.

"Where's your sister?"

"Napping." Jess bent his nose into the cat's fur and nuzzled.

Halfway between the kitchen and the fireplace, Lilleth had constructed a bedroom of sorts for the children. By stringing up blankets she had given them a private space near enough to the fire to catch its warmth.

Trace walked over to it. He drew back the curtain and peered inside.

Mary, sucking her thumb, snuggled in the small bed that he had given her. Red ringlets curled about her precious little ears. If the Thanksgiving ever came that he was giving thanks for a sweet baby daughter like this one, he would be a happy man.

"If you wake her up, it will be you who entertains her," Lilleth whispered, standing close beside him. Her breast grazed his arm ever so briefly when she peeked around him to look at Mary. "Why don't you go sit by the fire, Clark? The turkey won't be finished cooking for hours."

"Can't I help with anything?"

"And you a guest? I should say not. Take yourself over to that chair…put up your feet. They've got to be frozen through." She nudged his arm, urging him toward the fire.

He sat down beside Jess, kicked off his boots and crossed his feet on the hearth to let his socks warm. They talked about this and that while snow blew past the window and the wind screeched and moaned under the eaves.

Firelight cast the room in a warm amber glow. Logs snapped, flames hissed and danced, burning fresh sap. One log burned through, then crumbled to a blanket of coals.

Trace added another one. At some point he fell asleep. He couldn't have guessed how long he dozed, but he woke to the sound of Lilleth singing softly in the kitchen and the scent of the bird roasting in the oven.

With the bottom of his socks toasty and his heart simmering in a pot of contentment, he kept his eyes closed to better listen to the voice that he had longed for over too many lonely years.

If he could choose a moment of his life to last forever, it might be this one. Outside, the storm raged like a banshee, but it also isolated this snug little house from the rest of the world. He had a sense of such peace that he doubted anything could intrude upon it.

"Mama...ba," said a small voice at his knee. "Tee."

He opened his eyes to see Mary staring up at him.

"Hello there, ladybug." With pretty red ringlets framing her face, she did look the part. He lifted her into his lap. "Did you have as good a nap as I did?"

She laughed and poked her finger in his mouth. He kissed it.

And that was how the afternoon went. Playing with the children, while he listened to Lilleth sing in the kitchen. Smelling the food while it cooked, and grinning, although maybe he shouldn't be, at the fact that this storm would probably keep him from returning home tonight.

Chapter Nine

Lilleth joined hands with Jess and Mary. Across the table from her, Clark did the same.

She closed her eyes and listened while he gave thanks for the food and the company, then asked for blessings upon distant family and friends.

"Amen," she murmured, praying for a loved one not so distant at all.

While they ate, she gave silent thanks for three more things.

One was that no one had gagged on her biscuits. Clark had eaten two of them, and while that may have been due to the good manners of a guest, Jess had gobbled down three. After enduring all her practicing, her nephew might have politely set one aside after the first bite. Perhaps her culinary future held more surprises than she might have dreamed.

Another was that Clark Clarkly had been thrown

into her life's path, perhaps by fate or by the spirit of her late brother-in-law.

Clark was not a dashing dandy of a man. Not the kind to make a woman's heart skip at the sight of him, and truly, she praised the heavens for it. Men like that, she had learned time and again, were not to be depended upon.

Clark was a good, upstanding librarian, a man that a woman could trust her heart to…and possibly even her secrets. Maybe Lilleth ought to consider telling him who she really was. Given what he was doing at Hanispree, he was in a position that he might be able to help her.

Then again, it had been said that silence was golden.

The last thing…and maybe she ought not to give thanks for something scandalous…was that the blizzard would prevent him from going home tonight.

She was very thankful for that, because even though Clark might not make most women swoon, he most certainly did it to her.

It made no sense. He made no sense. Men did not make her heart skip. More often than not they were cads who needed outwitting. Clark was as sincere and reliable as the printed word on a page.

Just here was where he made no sense. He was everything safe and yet…not. He was temptation and seduction sitting right across the dinner table from her.

Reliability didn't make knees weak and breasts long for touching. Trustworthiness did not turn a high-principled woman into one who sat across the Thanksgiving table from a man and lusted after him.

Who was Clark Clarkly, really? Now and again a feeling of familiarity passed between them in a glance or a word. For that instant it seemed that they had known each other in another lifetime, which was silly, since she did not believe in other lifetimes.

Still, when he laughed, as he was doing now at something that Mary had gurgled, it sounded like an echo.

"What is it, Lilly?" Clark asked, arching his brows and shoving his glasses up the bridge of his nose with one finger. "You look a thousand miles away."

"Pie," she answered, mentally drawing her attention back across those thousand miles. "It's pumpkin, but I purchased it from the bakery. Would you like it now or later?"

"I'd like some now *and* later, if it's no trouble."

"Me, too, Ma! Some now and some later, just like Clark!"

"Some now, and bedtime later," she declared, because that was what Bethany would say.

Jess took his time eating his pie, long enough for Mary to fall asleep in the crook of Clark's arm.

It was well past Jess's bedtime when he finally swallowed the last bite and patted his belly.

"Off to bed with you now, young man."

"But, Ma, I never got to discuss with Clark what to name my cat." Jess walked to the hearth and scooped up his feline.

"It might be that something will come to you while you sleep," Clark suggested. He stood up and carried Mary to Lilleth.

"Could be." Jess lugged his cat toward the blanket that partitioned off his room from the rest of the house. He lifted the flap. "We can discuss it at breakfast, then, since it's snowing too hard for you to go home."

Bless Jess for so innocently bringing up the subject that Lilleth didn't know how to, without a dozen inappropriate visions filling her mind.

Her nephew disappeared behind the curtain. She watched it fall, and felt Clark's hands brush hers, lingering a moment longer than would be required to pass Mary to her.

It wouldn't be wise to look up at him this very instant and risk him seeing her expression. If she didn't, though, she would not know what he was thinking.

She took a breath and glanced into his eyes.

"Please do stay," she managed to say quite politely, given that his thoughts very clearly had taken the same imprudent path that hers had. "It's far too dangerous to walk home."

"I appreciate the offer," he answered just as politely. "And I accept."

She hugged Mary close, then followed Jess behind the curtain.

Well-mannered words had disguised what was truly going on between them. She wanted him to touch her in all the ways a man touched a woman... her heart and her body. He wanted to touch her, but she knew he wouldn't.

A make-believe marriage stood between them. A man who didn't even exist kept her from knowing Clark more intimately than she had ever known anyone.

She laid Mary down in the little bed that Clark had given her, and kissed her curly head.

Kneeling beside his bed, Jess whispered a prayer for his mother, then hopped under the quilt and tugged it to his chin. Lilleth kissed his forehead, then stroked the cat.

She parted the blanket doorway and stepped into the main room.

Clark sat in front of the fireplace with his back to her and his stocking-clad toes pointed at the flames.

One thing was certain. She could not share her body without first sharing her secret.

Trace knew that he was a villain. Everything about him was a living, breathing lie. To let his Lils, a vulnerable, abandoned woman with two precious children, get caught in the deception that was Clark was unforgivable.

He glanced sideways at her where she sat in a chair beside him, watching red-hot logs crumble into coals.

She seemed distracted.

Telling her who he was would be the right and honorable thing to do. It would also betray his family. No one ever broke character in the middle of an assignment. Not for health, wealth or convenience… and most especially not because of wanting a woman.

So here he sat with a miracle beside him, nearly desperate for more than a kiss from her, and all the while he was being held hostage by Clark Clarkly. Not to mention her miserable husband who might even be dead.

The bedroom curtain rustled. Paws whispered across the floor. The cat, as orange as a pumpkin, brushed his chair then hopped onto the windowsill. He batted one paw at the snow blowing against it.

Beside Trace, Lilleth began to tap her foot.

He turned in his chair, set his feet on the floor and looked her in the eye.

"Is something wrong, Lilly?"

"Why would you ask?" She stood up, walked to the kitchen and a moment later returned, bringing him a slice of pie.

"You're troubled. Tell me why."

"Well, there's all those hungry people shivering away their Thanksgiving at the mental hospital, while we sit here warm and full, for one thing." She paced to the window and stared out, stroking the cat's back in a distracted manner.

Those cold and hungry people bothered him, as well, but there was nothing to be done about it in a blizzard.

"I think it's more than that. Are you worried about your husband?"

"Hardly." She glanced at him and rolled her eyes.

A wave of relief swirled through his belly, further proof that Trace was a villain.

"Talk to me, Lilly. Tell me what's wrong."

"Very well," she said, her blue eyes crinkled in a frown. "I like you, Clark."

"I like you, too."

She shook her head. A lush mane of red curls shivered down her back.

"That's the problem." She opened her hands, palms up. "You can't like me. You don't even know who I am."

"I know who you are."

"You only think you do. The fact is...I'm not Lilly Gordon. I even hate the name Lilly."

"What should I call you then?" Lils...and nothing else would do.

"Lilleth. Lilleth Preston."

"Was that your maiden name?" he asked, pretending to be startled at her revelation.

"Not was, Clark. Is." She wrung her hands in front

of her. "I've never been married. Until lately I've spent my nights singing with a traveling show."

"But the children?" Good Lord! What kind of horrors had she endured, raising Jess and Mary out of wedlock?

Lils tipped her chin up a notch. She took a breath and stared down at him where he sat like a sorrowful lump on his chair.

"Close your mouth, Clark. Unmarried women have children more often than you might imagine. But the truth is that Mary and Jess are not mine. They're my sister's children."

He stood up slowly because the blood had suddenly drained from his head.

No detestable husband? She wasn't a mother? The perfect little girl had grown up to be a liar?

"Why tell me now?" He was surprised that his brain and his tongue could work despite the shock.

"I'm in some trouble. I think you are the only one in a position to help me."

This was where he ought to wrap himself up in righteous indignation and storm out of her house. She had lied to him, outright and bold. What else was there her about her that he didn't know? She could be a criminal, or had she grown up to be like her mother, a woman of easy virtue?

"I'm so sorry, Clark." She hurried away from the window and knelt in front his chair, looking up into his eyes. "I don't suppose a man like you would know anything about being dishonest. But the children's safety was at stake and in the beginning you were a stranger. Please forgive me."

He wanted to crawl in a deep hole and cover himself with dirt. Forgive her? The only difference between them was that he was a worse liar than she was. She at least had the decency to finally admit the truth.

He did not.

If he blurted out now that she was his long-lost love, she would hate him. He wouldn't blame her.

And if she hated him she would not allow him to help her out of whatever trouble she and the children were in.

Just as on the day he had knocked her over on the train platform, he was stuck being Clark Clarkly.

A tear glistened at the corner of her eye. Lils never gave in to weeping, so he let that tear tremble on her eyelash without wiping it away with his thumb.

"What is it? Ask me anything."

It might take time away from his investigation, but family be hanged, he was going to help.

"I'm breaking someone out of the mental asylum. I need your help."

He hadn't expected that. To break an inmate out of the hospital wouldn't postpone his investigation, it would ruin it. The place would be locked up so tight after that he'd never learn another dirty detail.

He'd be the first son to be dismissed from the family business. The rule not to become personally involved in a case was taken so seriously that it might have been the eleventh commandment. Already he'd crossed the line by taking care of the inmates.

He'd be exposed. He was stuck on a high wire with no way down.

"Who?" he asked, and sounded like an owl more than an intelligent human.

"My sister, Bethany."

It was odd. The Bethany he remembered was as sound of mind as anyone.

The tear at the corner of Lilleth's eye slipped down her cheek and broke his heart. He would do anything for her.

It meant continuing to live as Clarkly. But he knew this as well as he knew Clark would stumble when he stood up…Lilleth thought he was an honest man, and if she found out he wasn't she would not accept his help.

Here it went, blast it. He sat down on the floor beside her.

"Tell me everything."

"Bethany's husband passed away six months ago and left her a fortune. His twin brother, Alden, figured the inheritance ought to have been his, so he locked my sister up." Lilleth shook her head and pushed a wispy curl away from her cheek. "He believes that by controlling her children he can make her give him whatever he asks. Since he owns the place, there's no one to tell him no."

One more horror to be noted when Trace wrote his exposé. How many more victims were there like Bethany?

"Before you say yes…or no, Clark, you should know that I'm a criminal. Alden is the children's guardian. I kidnapped them."

He didn't know what to do. He had to help Lilleth. Innocent children were in danger.

Still, he couldn't sacrifice all the inmates in order to save one. The mental hospital was no more than a prison. It was his job to write about it, expose it and have it shut down.

For the first time in his life, Trace honestly did not know what to do. He felt half-sick at his options.

A log crumbled to coals in the hearth, sizzling and popping. The cat stood up on the windowsill and growled. It arched its back, a ridge of orange fur peaking along its spine.

Lilleth rose and hurried to the window. She snatched the cat to her chest and peered out at the blowing white.

Trace reached the window in two long strides, placing her firmly behind him.

Anything might spook a cat, most likely the crumbling log in the fireplace. But it could be a vile bug eater that spooked this one.

There was no longer any doubt that the man had been spying on Jess.

Just in case the fool was crazy enough to be skulking about in the storm, Trace yanked the heavy curtain over the window. He reached out and tugged at the lock on the front door to make certain it held fast.

Lilleth carried the cat back into the children's bedroom. A moment later she came out and went to the kitchen area, silently wiping the stove down with a damp rag.

"I saw a man in town," Trace said, watching her hair sway with her scrubbing.

She dedicated her attention to a stubborn spot and attacked it. The fabric of her skirt shimmied over her hips.

"He was watching Jess," he said.

She dropped the rag and turned to face him, her hands braced on the countertop behind her. "Jess noticed him." Her expression was tense. "I believe he was leering at me through the window of the general store yesterday, too."

"His name is Perryman. Alden's spy, he has to be. He was following you in the woods the other night." Trace would take care of the spy. That was one thing he knew he would do.

She moved away from the counter, crossed the room and stood before him.

"I'm trusting you to keep my secret, even if you can't help me. Please say that you will."

"You can trust me with your life, Lilleth."

"I thought as much," she murmured, and touched his wrist when he folded his arms across his chest. "I knew you would be a friend that very first day, when you took us in."

"Anyone would have." He needed to step back, not take her shoulders in his hands.

"No one else did. There's something about you." Her eyes held his. "I can't explain it, and surely I sound like a ninny, but you make me feel like…like I've been waiting for you forever."

Had she waited? He had no right to expect her to have. He had no right to ask.

"Have you been?"

"I don't know." Her brow crinkled. "What is it that people wait for, Clark? Not what men gave my mother, not what one gave me behind the—"

He crushed her mouth with a kiss, and half a second later all he cared about was the press of her plush breasts against his chest.

He whispered "Lilleth" in her ear, but Lils in his heart. He kissed her again, this time slowly savoring her and afraid that if he lifted his mouth she might reveal what that cad had given her.

"Well," she murmured at last, when he found the courage to allow her a breath. "He didn't give me that."

"I can't claim to be sorry."

"You've just made it clear to me that in some ways

I'm still a virgin." She curled her fingers into his shirt. "Come with me into the bedroom, Clark."

"The children?" He nodded toward the blanket wall.

"Sleep like rocks." She smiled up at him. "Even when I try to wake them, I can't."

"You mean a great deal to me, Lilleth. I think you should know that."

She let go of his shirt, took his hand and tugged on it. "Come along, Clark. I intend to mean a great deal more."

Firmly, resolutely, he dumped the voices of his parents, his siblings and his own nagging conscience into a deep mental well in his brain. He covered it with a lid.

Whether Lils was put in his path by a remarkable twist of circumstance or something more marvelous, here she was. He could no more turn away from her than he could the obligation he had cast into the bottom of his moral well.

He picked Lils up in his arms and carried her into her solid-walled little bedroom.

Chapter Ten

Lilleth had never been one to believe that blood could hum. Or if it could, it was a dull and dirty tune.

And yet notes that she had never known existed trilled through her.

She tried to sing them, which made Clark nuzzle her neck and quicken his pace.

"You sound like an angel, Lilleth," he whispered against her neck. He set her down, but slowly, so that her belly slid over his hips and his…my word, but a man's anatomy could go through some remarkable changes.

"I don't feel like an angel." She leaned across the bed to light the lamp on the night table. She turned the wick low, then straightened and reached behind Clark to close the door. "I feel rather wicked."

Amber light flickered over his face. It lapped his shoulders and caressed his thighs where he stood at the foot of her bed. The bedroom was a small space, which made him seem taller, broader in the chest and more virile than any male she had ever met.

Something curious had come over her. This fanciful yearning for a man was a thing she had never expected to experience. Flighty women felt fanciful, not her. But there was no denying the fact that she wanted to be the lamplight, kissing the line of Clark's cheek and stroking the curve of his lips.

Now, being well past the age of blushing maidenhood, she did just that. She reached up and felt the masculine shape of his jaw and the scrape of beard stubble under her fingertips. She pressed her thumb to his lips and traced his smile.

"You've never had a wicked day in your life," he murmured against her flesh.

"You only just found out who I really am." She lifted the glasses from his nose and set them beside the lamp. "You can't possibly know that."

"I told you…I know who you are." He touched her hair and cupped the back of her head in his hand.

The gold flecks in his eyes seemed to swim in the blue, which had to be a trick of the bedside lamp.

"We've known each other such a short time," she said. An old shadow began to take shape in her mind, then drifted away like a ghost.

He shook his head. "We were in love, a very long time ago."

He didn't know her, not really, but for this one night she would allow fancy thinking because she felt fancy...and dreamy, with a connection to this man she could not explain.

"You read too many books, Clark, but it's a sweet game...pretending once upon a time." She sighed and closed her eyes. "What were we like way back when?"

"So young that falling in love was the most innocent thing in the world." She felt him kiss her cheek, and smelled his warm breath close to her mouth.

Suddenly the fabric of her dress felt heavy, the air in her lungs too thick to breathe. Clark pressed her palm over his heart. Beneath the woven cotton, it thumped against her fingertips.

Clark took a step back. She opened her eyes.

He reached for his glasses, but she plucked them up from the nightstand and hid them behind her back.

"I have secrets, too, Lilleth. Secrets that I have to keep."

"Everyone has secrets." Whatever they were, they couldn't be as awful as hers were. It was unlikely that he was a kidnapper.

"I'll sleep in the other room."

She shook her head and reached her free hand toward him. There was so much about life that she didn't know. At her age, she ought to know.

"Clark, show me why grown men cry when I sing a love song."

He gripped her fingers, then sat down beside her on the bed.

He turned her face toward him, grazing her cheeks with his thumbs. He stroked her hair from root to tip, pausing for a moment over her breast. Her heart danced like a whirligig under her ribs. She wondered if he felt it against his knuckles.

"They cry for things that used to be. For things they can never get back."

He kissed her sweetly before he stood up and walked backward three steps, looking perfectly miserable.

"Good night, Lilleth," he whispered, then went out.

"Stars shine bright," she murmured to the closed door.

The ghost in her mind took the shape of a boy for the space of one heartbeat.

"Good night, Trace," she whispered, then rolled onto to her side and turned off the lamp.

Trace opened the cabin door and stepped outside. Snow swirled in circles.

He took a lantern with him down the stairs, scanning the ground for footprints. He breathed the cold air deep into his lungs. It stung, but that was nothing compared to the pain in his soul.

Everything he'd ever wanted had just been handed to him, and he'd turned his back on it for the sake of duty.

He didn't know if he'd be able to help Bethany.

For one thing, she might be in that room with the mammoth lock. Truthfully, the way the weather had been lately, and denied the warmth of a fire, would she have survived? He'd never heard even a whimper coming out of the cell, even though he'd called through the door.

The frightening truth was that it might be too late for Bethany.

The one thing he could do was take care of the spy.

He lifted the lantern and looked again.

Nothing. Any footsteps that might have been left behind by a prowler had been filled in with snow.

Back on the porch, Trace swiped the snow from his face, brushed it from his shoulders. He went back inside and bolted the door.

He didn't think it likely, but there might be a prowler with the stamina of a polar bear.

He dumped another log on the fire, then sat down on the hearth with his rump toward the flames.

He tapped his fingers on his knees and wondered what Lilleth was wearing on the other side of the bedroom door.

He stood up when his backside grew hot. He strode to the window and drew back the curtain to watch the snow fall. After a few moments, the cat hopped up on the ledge, pacing and turning, and drawing its tail across his shirt.

"I reckon you need to go out." The cat nudged his

palm with its head. "Not a chance of that, sport, for you or for me."

The cat purred, so he carried it to the chair in front of the hearth.

Trace settled into it. He ought to be used to spending the night in chairs by now. One would think the wood wouldn't feel so hard on the bum.

With a stretch and a flex of its claws, the cat snagged the weave of his pants. Then, with a flip, it offered up its furry belly for stroking.

"You've never been in love, have you? You don't look miserable enough."

"Clark, wake up," Lilleth whispered. A feminine hand shook his shoulder.

Trace cracked his eyes open a slit.

His back ached. When he had decided to sleep on the children's bedroom floor the wood hadn't seemed as hard as it did now.

The cat, which had been sleeping blissfully on Trace's belly, stood up, stretching and arching. He leaped off and strode out of the blanket room, tail swishing.

"I'm going out." Lilleth leaned over Trace wearing a heavy coat and a furry hat. She clutched a canvas bag to her chest that was clearly stuffed with food.

He struggled to his elbows and groaned. "Snow's too deep to go anywhere."

"Snowshoes." She lifted her foot and brought it

down on the floor with a clunk. "They were with all that junk in the back room."

"Snowshoes or not, it isn't safe to go out, even if the snow did let up."

"That may be, but I won't allow those poor people in the hospital to miss their Thanksgiving meal." She shook the bag at him.

It was difficult to argue with Lilleth while she was hovering over him. He stood up, stretching the stiffness from his muscles.

"I'm going with you."

"There's only the one pair of snowshoes. Besides, I was hoping you'd stay with the children. If there is someone lurking about…"

He had to admit, it wounded him that she could launch into a mercy mission so wholeheartedly only hours after the intimate moments they had shared last night. It was almost as though she had dismissed the kiss and the fact that they had come within a heart-beat of making love.

"I'll take care of Mary, Ma," Jess said, popping his head out from under his blanket. "I'll lock up good and tight after you leave."

"You can call me Auntie now, Jess. I told Clark all about us."

The boy sat up and blinked. "Are you going to help us get Ma out of that place, Clark? We've been won-dering if my pa put you in our path so you would."

Lilleth tilted her head to the side, staring up at him. She arched her brows, echoing Jess's question.

He sat down on the bed beside Jess.

"Son, there's nothing I'd like better than to break into Hanispree and get your mother out. The fact is, I…well, there's—"

"Jess, Clark is a librarian," Lilleth said. "Breaking folks out of mental hospitals isn't what he is used to doing."

"But he knows lots of things."

"Well yes, that's true. Perhaps if he has read about a breakout, he can advise me on how to go about it."

All right, he deserved that unmanly observation of his skills, but it rankled.

"Give me your foot," he said to Lilleth.

She backed up a step, shaking her head, narrowing her gaze at him.

He grabbed her ankle, untied the rawhide lacings of one snowshoe and yanked it off. He did the same to the other.

"What do you think you are doing?" Lilleth bent to grab them back, but he strapped them to his own feet.

Since it would have been useless to tell the Lilleth of old to stay safely at home, he didn't tell the grown-up Lilleth to stay home, either.

"Come with me," he said, stuffing his arms into his coat, then buttoning it up.

He opened the front door and turned to see Lilleth staring doubtfully at the one and only pair of snowshoes. Turning around, he motioned for her to hop on his back, piggyback style.

"Last chance." There was something about watching her perplexed frown flash into a grin that made him want to laugh. Little Lils had accepted the call to adventure with that very same smile.

Holding the canvas bag in one hand, she dashed across the room and leaped upon his back. He hooked his arms under her knees and stepped outside. He turned to look at Jess, who appeared perfectly, delightfully, scandalized.

"Lock that door up good and tight, pal," Trace said, and then trotted down the steps.

He felt like a boy again, cavorting with his Lils. It was easier than he would have thought to let the years fall away and remember how it had been to be happy and innocently in love.

Lilleth pressed her nose into Clark's upturned collar. Even though the storm had passed, the weather remained bitterly cold. She took a deep breath, savoring the warmth, inhaling the scent of his skin where it permeated the wool.

Something had become perfectly clear during the half hour trek through the snow. Clark had not always been a librarian. To the casual observer he might appear clumsy, but nothing, she had come to discover, could be further from the truth.

A bookish man would not be able to carry a full-bodied woman and her bag of food all this way without wheezing and groaning. And for a man who claimed to be nearly blind without his spectacles, he hadn't tripped over a single fallen log.

She'd be a flat note in a perfect melody if he needed them at all. Just as soon as he pulled those glasses out of his breast pocket was when he would begin to stumble about.

It was as clear as the icicles hanging from the eaves of the mental hospital, just coming into view, that Clark Clarkly was not the man he portrayed himself to be.

He had claimed to have secrets, but she hadn't paid his confession much attention.

She'd been so caught up in wanting him that she hadn't noticed much else. Even now, when the heat had cooled and a new day begun, she still wanted him.

Clark was handsome and virile, everything a man ought to be…and she wanted him to be the one to teach her things she had always considered foolish. To show her why a woman would surrender good sense, lay it at a man's feet and be glad for it.

"It's such a beautiful building," she murmured, while Clark carried her past the big iron gate, held ajar by two feet of fresh snow. "It must cost Alden a good sum to keep up the appearance."

"Appearance is all this place is. At its core, it's ugly."

"I'm curious about something, Clark. How did you discover how awful this place is? I wouldn't think Hanispree's secrets are something that a librarian would just stumble upon."

"I'm nosy." He shrugged.

She adjusted her weight against him. While he might not be showing signs of stress, her legs were becoming tingly where they hooked through the crooks of his elbows. "Is it safe coming here in broad daylight?"

"It's not safe. But this was your choice, if you will recall." At the back door of the inmates' quarters, he set her down. "You were right, though, Lilleth. There's no telling how cold and hungry the people inside might be."

"Who are you, Clark?" She stared at him while she stomped the tingling out of her legs. A flicker… a shadow crossed his eyes. "Who are you really?"

He didn't answer. He turned the knob on the back door, but it was locked. Last time they had come it had not been. Walking inside had been as easy as entering her own front door.

"Follow me," Clark said. The snow under the eaves of the buildings was not too deep. She was able to walk over it without needing his help.

He pointed to a window a few feet above his head.

"We can get in this way if the sash isn't frozen to the frame. Can you stand on my shoulders?"

"I grew up freer than most boys." Clark looked away from her all of a sudden. Clearly, he didn't believe her. "Stoop down."

She stepped on his shoulders, crouched, then braced her gloves on the wall.

"Okay, stand up slowly." She climbed the wall with her hands, stretching taller as he elevated her. She and Bethany had used this trick on a few occasions.

Level with the window, she tried to slide it open. "It won't budge."

"We'll have to try and jar it loose."

She hit it with her fist, but it held firm.

"How's your balance?" he called up.

"Better than yours."

She thought she heard a curse, but she must have misheard. This was Clark, after all.

His shoulders shifted. She held on to the window frame. A moment later he handed her a snowshoe.

It took a few whacks, but she freed the window and shoved it open. She scrambled inside, then looked back. Clark reached up to give her the bag and the other snowshoe and then jumped, gripped the sill with his fingers and pulled himself up and inside.

Very interesting, she noted. It took a good bit of strength to do that. Most men wouldn't have managed it.

He went to the back door and leaned the snow-shoes against it. If anyone came in that way they would clatter to the floor.

Very clever, Clark. You are more than you seem. Her thoughts came up short when she heard a voice.

"Everyone is cold, Mrs. Murphy." The speaker sounded edgy...more than impatient.

"We wouldn't be if you'd use the fireplace for its intended purpose, Nurse Fry."

"Hush your mouth, you old hag. Be grateful that you aren't out in the snow."

"I'll be grateful when I pass to my Maker and leave your nasty personage behind."

"Those belligerent words will get you tied to your bed without your breakfast."

"For all the good that will do you." Mrs. Murphy's aged voice crackled in laughter. "The ghost will set me free the moment you leave here."

"You've done it now. It's the ropes for you."

Bedclothes rustled. The old woman tried to stifle a grunt.

"You are a bully, Miss Fry. The ghosts don't take kindly to bullies."

"Ghosts? So there's more than one now?" Nurse Fry snorted in derision.

"Why yes, the specter has got himself a brand-new bride. A pretty thing, too, and so kind."

"It's no wonder you're locked up in here, you crazy old loon."

"In my time, I was as sane as you are, and prettier by far."

"I'm going to have to slap you for that. Insulting the staff is against the rules. Let your ghost friends help you now."

Clark lunged forward, but Lilleth touched his arm, stalling him and drawing him around the corner, where the stairwell led to what she feared to be Bethany's frigid cell.

She cupped her hands over her mouth and started to sing. Her voice trilled up the scale and down, sounding eerie as it echoed through her fingers. She held long high notes, then moaned over low ones.

Miss Fry screeched. Her heavy footsteps pounded down the hallway. The door to the pleasant part of Hanispree opened, then slammed closed. The key in the lock snapped, its echo whispering down the hallway.

Clark dashed ahead of Lilleth into Mrs. Murphy's room. By the time she rushed in behind him, the frail woman was sitting upright with her bindings on the floor.

"You shouldn't anger the nurse, Mrs. Murphy," Clark told her.

"Oh, I feel quite safe having my say." She patted Clark's hand when he traced the red welt the rope had made on her arm. "I knew you were close by."

"But I might have been in another realm."

"Oh, and there is your bride! What a lovely voice

you have, my dear. Please do sing again, but something more cheerful than the melody you sang the other night."

"I'll do that." Lilleth knelt beside Mrs. Murphy and arranged the thin nightgown across her shoulders. "I sang that one for my sister. She's locked up here. Her name is Bethany. Maybe you know something about her?"

"Would she be Mrs. Hanispree?"

Lilleth nodded, her voice trapped by the lump in her throat.

"Well, she'll need your help. I haven't seen her, mind you, but I do hear things."

"What do you hear, Mrs. Murphy?" Clark asked.

"That nasty doctor tries to get money from her. Every few days they take her out of her room for short periods of time. When they bring her back they are mad as hornets. I reckon she's not giving them any."

"Do they hurt her, do you think?" Clark covered Mrs. Murphy's knees with a thin blanket.

Panic cramped Lilleth's stomach while the woman appeared to consider her answer.

"Not as far as I can tell. Her spirit doesn't sound broken yet." Mrs. Murphy touched a strand of Lilleth's hair that curled out from under her fur cap. "I used to have pretty hair. Maybe I will again when I pass over. That's something to look forward to."

"Thank you, Mrs. Murphy, for telling me about Bethany. What can I sing for you?"

"Something that I can tap my toe to, if you please. In my time I could dance with the best of them. My dance card was always full." A distant smile crinkled her lips. She appeared to look inward, perhaps watching that lively girl whirl once more about the dance floor with a dozen hopeful beaux looking on. With a blink and a sigh, she returned to her cold, dark room. "And dear, for Mrs. King in the next room, perhaps a lullaby. Sometimes I hear her talking to a baby. The poor thing doesn't guess it's only her pillow."

For nearly an hour Lilleth went from room to room, singing, while Clark passed out food and warmed cold hearths.

The last door she stood before was Bethany's. Just as before, it had a special lock that looked impossible to breach. No food for her sister, no warmth for yet another night.

"The children are safe. I've got them tucked away in a cabin in the woods not far from here." Lilleth spoke quietly, digging her fingers into the dirty, splintered door. "Don't give up, Bethany. I'll get you out of here."

Something in the room hit the floor with a thud. It shattered. No doubt her sister was tied and gagged, with no way of communicating but that. Only a heavy door and a miserable lock separated them.

It was enough to make Lilleth want to scream in despair.

She didn't, though. She didn't even whimper, because Bethany needed to know that everything was under control, that there was a plan to set her free.

"I hear you." She pressed her forehead to the wood and stifled her grief. "I'll be back for you, just as soon as I can."

Clark touched her shoulder and drew her away from the door. He supported her down the creaky stairs.

She sniffled into his coat collar while he carried her on his back through the icy woods, all the way to the cabin door.

He set her down on the first step of the porch and cupped her cheeks in his hands.

"Please excuse me, Clark. I'm not a weeper, not usually."

He wiped a smear of icy tears from under her eyes. He kissed her cheek, grazed her lips, then kissed her other cheek.

"What would you say if I told you that you might be the woman I've always dreamed of?"

Without waiting for her answer, he turned and sprinted down the path toward the lending library.

Chapter Eleven

She would have told Clark that dreams were all well and good. They were the stock and trade of librarians, after all.

Just now, leaning back against the front door, she watched him tromp homeward over snow that glistened in the cold morning sunshine. The brilliance nearly blinded her eyes, but not her common sense.

This man was not a librarian, not in the usual sense, at least. Further, she did not want to be the object of his dreams. She wanted to be the object under his fingers, under his lips. What she wanted was to know him through and through, and for him to know her.

All of a sudden the door opened. A pair of fists grabbed the back of her coat and yanked her inside.

"Don't stand out there, Auntie." Jess slammed the door and shoved the bolt in place. "He'll see you!"

"Clark has seen me for the past two days," she

said, wandering to the window and lifting the curtain to watch him disappear around the bend in the path.

"Not Clark." Jess yanked the curtain closed. "The man in the outhouse."

Lilleth gripped Jess by the shoulders, staring down at him.

"Are you certain there's a man in there? You haven't gone out, have you?" She tapped her boot toe on the floor.

"Didn't need to, Auntie. Until you and Clark walked up he was hollering and thumping against the door."

"Serves him right, getting trapped in the privy." She lifted the curtain again and watched the outhouse. Even from fifty feet away she saw an eye peering out of the moon-shaped cutout in the wood. It might be days before the snow that had accumulated in front of the door melted enough for him to get free. "I suppose I'll have to let him out."

"He's the one who was watching me that day. It has to be him. Don't go out, Auntie Lilleth, he's probably dangerous!"

"Considering where he got himself stuck, I don't believe he's overly bright." She dropped the curtain.

"I'll go for Clark." Jess reached for his jacket.

"You most certainly will not, young man." She cupped his face with gloves that were still crusted with ice from her trek home perched on Clark's back. Worried eyes blinked at her. They looked equally like his mother's and his father's. "I'd let that miserable wretch freeze before I'd allow you to risk yourself in the cold."

"You might get hurt."

"Don't you worry." She ruffled his hair and wiped the frown from his forehead. "Your mama and I have been outwitting mean, stupid men from the time we could crawl."

"I can help."

"Well, naturally, I'll be depending on you." She tugged at her gloves and flexed her fingers. "First, go check on Mary to be sure she's still sleeping, then stand by the window and watch. If anything goes wrong, take your sister out the back door and run for Clark."

While Jess checked on Mary, Lilleth got a shovel and a rope from the back porch. She wrapped the rope around the shovel's handle, then gripped it in both hands.

She grinned at Jess to show him that he didn't need to be afraid.

She was, though. Over the years she'd learned that a woman needed that edge to keep the upper hand. Have confidence, but never underestimate your opponent.

Jess grinned back at her, and she was certain he was also hiding his fear.

She went outside and closed the door behind her.

"Lock the door, Abigail," she called loudly, going down the front steps.

The outhouse was fifty very long steps from the cabin. Snow nearly reached her knees. She high-stepped and struggled every inch of the way to the little wood building.

Wind whispered in the treetops and a beating of bird wings ruffled the air. Only silence came from the outhouse now. The eye no longer peeked from the moon-shaped cutout.

No doubt the moron planned to rush out at her, a helpless woman, and take her by surprise.

At least she hoped that was what he planned.

"Oh, my word, this trek to the privy is exhausting! Soon as the ground thaws I'm going to have my husband move it closer to the house." She stopped to wipe her brow and appear winded in case Alden's minion might be spying on her through the moon. "Next time my four little girls need to visit the privy, he is the one who will carry them all this way."

She rested her hand on her breast to make sure the man had time to plan his assault on her helpless self.

At the outhouse door, she began to shovel the snow away.

"All this shoveling is too difficult for poor little me. I may just squat right here in the snow, then holler for Harvey to come out and carry me back."

With most of the snow cleared away, she removed the rope from the handle of the shovel. She glanced up to make sure the eye was not watching while she wound the rope about the outhouse and across the top step. She tied a knot, good and tight.

"Only another minute until I have this door free. I doubt if it will be soon enough, though."

In fact, the door was completely clear. She took a few seconds to strike a helpless pose, while gripping the shovel behind her back.

Thirty seconds later the door burst open and the same face that had been leering at her through the mercantile window glared at her, blue lips snarling and teeth chattering.

He lunged and she stepped to the right. One of his shoes snagged the rope. He toppled. She swung the shovel and walloped the back of his head before he hit the ground.

Sprawled, with arms and legs pointing north, south, east and west, he lifted his head. She whacked it again, but not hard to do enough to do lasting harm. He would need some strength to stumble back to town, after all.

And really, had she wanted to kill him she would not have gone to this trouble. She would have simply left him in the privy to freeze.

"Harvey! Come quick," she called. "There's a stranger in the outhouse!"

She poked the shovel at his nose, while making sure to stay well out of his reach, just in case he was not as dazed as he appeared.

"You'd best not have been planning harm to me or my little girls, stranger." She walked backward toward the cabin with the weapon in front her, at the ready. "If I were you, I'd run away quick before Harvey comes out. My man is half bear and half cougar, and he eats strangers for breakfast."

She backed up the stairs and across the porch. The door opened behind her and she stepped inside.

Jess slid the lock closed, then hugged his arms about her middle.

"I almost felt sorry for him, Auntie Lilleth." He squeezed hard. "We didn't need Clark at all."

Hopefully, Jess didn't notice her trembling. Alden's spy had been weak because he was so cold, but the rage boiling in his eyes had all but burned her.

The men she had dealt with in the past were greedy leches, but none of them had such an aura of malevolence about them.

Had she been able to convince him that she was not the person he had been looking for? That a woman with four little girls and a beast of a husband lived in this cabin?

Or would he wire Alden and report that he had found Bethany's children? Worse, was Alden here already?

They did need Clark, more than young Jess knew.

On occasion, Trace's pen got him into trouble. Luckily, a fact reported incorrectly could be easily revised, or apologized for in the next edition of the paper.

This morning, as he'd dropped Lilleth at her front door, the trouble had come from his mouth. He had blurted out the truth. Lilleth was the one he had waited for all his life.

Luckily, she couldn't have known what he really meant by that admission.

There was that part of him, though, that wished she had. That she would toss her arms about his neck and tell him she knew exactly who he was and that neither time nor distance had changed her love for him.

With slush soaking his boots, Clark marched through the twilight toward the cabin.

The day had warmed and melted much of the snow. Come dark, when the temperature froze again, he'd probably be able to slide all the way home on the ice.

He carried the snowshoes over one shoulder and a bag of meat pies from the hotel slung over the other. Chances were Lilleth had taken every bit of food from her pantry this morning to give to the inmates at Hanispree.

As soon as he rounded the bend in the path, the front door flew open and Jess rushed outside.

"You should have seen it, Clark!" The boy waved and shouted from the porch. "Uncle Alden's spy got caught in the outhouse and Auntie walloped him good!"

Fear cramped Trace's gut. A picture flashed through his mind—of a young Lils on the ground, a pair of ruffians hovering over her and intending to do her harm. The scar on his chest began to throb with the memory.

Lilleth stepped onto the porch with Mary riding her hip.

"You should have come for me," he said. Why would she, though? No doubt she considered bumbling Clark too inept to handle the situation.

Jess answered first. "Auntie wouldn't let me. Said she would let that no-good fellow freeze to death before she'd allow me out."

She should have let him freeze. The man could only be Perryman. Mrs. O'Hara was not all that discriminating about her customers. If the purpled-haired madam tossed him out, he must be as vile as he had seemed that night.

"The fellow was a dimwit," Lilleth told him while he came up the stairs. "Baby Mary could have ousted him with ease."

Young Lilleth had never asked for help in dealing with her mother's unprincipled men. There was no reason to think she would now.

It hardly seemed possible that he could love her more now than he did then, but he was a man of facts and this was a fact.

"I brought dinner, since you must have emptied the cabin of food this morning." Trace went inside and set the meat pies on the dining table.

"Nearly," she answered.

"Auntie made biscuits for lunch." Jess opened the bag and drew in a lungful of aroma. He sighed over it. "Not that they weren't grand, mind you."

The four of them sat at the table, Jess beside Trace, hip to hip, and Lilleth across, with Mary on her lap. They asked a blessing for those shut up in Hanispree before they ate.

During dinner, Jess recounted how his auntie, armed with only a shovel and pretending to be helpless, had made the villain flee.

Trace asked if she'd ever done any acting with the traveling troupe and she replied no, but she'd been exposed to actors long enough to learn a few things.

They spoke of this and that while the fire snapped and the full moon cast a beam of light through the window.

This might be his world if he told Lils the truth… and if she forgave him.

With the four of them snug and safe, life had never seemed so right. Villains might be cavorting on the streets of towns across the country, needing to be written about and exposed, but for this one night, in this peaceful cabin, he would put that away. Troubles would still be waiting tomorrow.

For tonight life was as he had only dreamed it could be.

In time, the fire grew low. The beam of the moonlight crept across the cabin floor and Mary fell asleep in Lilleth's arms. Jess yawned and stretched.

"It's off to bed with you, young man."

"But Auntie, I'm not tired."

"Nonetheless, it's bedtime." Lilleth stood up and Jess followed her into the blanket bedroom.

Trace added another log to the fire and stirred the coals.

If Lils invited him to her bed again tonight, would he be able to walk away? Not very likely. Alone together, it would only be a matter of seconds before clothes came off.

How would he explain the scar that cut an L across his chest? Even though it had been many years, she might recognize it.

"Have you ever been swimming at midnight, Clark?"

He looked away from the orange glow of the coals to see her walking toward him with a bright, mischievous smile on her face. She truly was an exceptionally beautiful woman with her full bosom, her tiny waist and that mane of red curls shimmering over her shoulders.

"A long time ago," he admitted. With her.

"I had a friend once." She reached her fingers toward the flames. "We used to do that."

"Is he the one you mentioned in your sleep?" Trace wanted to cover his shirt so she wouldn't see how his racing heart made the fabric shiver.

She nodded. "Can you believe that I still miss that boy? His name was Trace. For some reason I've been thinking of him more often lately."

She gazed into the flames. He was grateful that she did, because he wasn't sure how he would react if he saw the memory of the young man he had been in her eyes.

"We thought we'd marry one day."

"What happened to him?"

"I don't know." She sighed, shrugged and glanced up, spearing him with her gaze.

And there it was. He saw it in a blink. After all these years she still hurt over their separation. Then as quickly as he'd glimpsed that sadness, it vanished. She grinned.

"What do you say, Clark? We might not have a pond, but there's a slick of ice outside and a full moon."

"I say, first one to land on their bottom owes the other a favor."

"Challenge accepted." She dashed out the front door ahead of him, down the steps and onto a patch of snow that had melted and refrozen into a large, smile-shaped ice sheet.

"I have to warn you, Clark. I'm a wizard on skates."

Cold air nipped her cheeks and moonlight glinted in her hair. If he didn't know better he'd swear that the great bright ball in the night sky was laughing along with her.

"That may be, but we're not on skates." He slid across the ice on his shoes, windmilling his arms and spinning in a fancy circle. "I've had lots of practice walking on ice."

"That was impressive, I do have to admit."

Lilleth demonstrated her own abilities by lifting the hem of her skirt in one hand and reaching toward the stars with the other. She twirled about twice on one foot without falling.

He'd have to work to gain that favor.

"Copy this, then," he challenged, and ran three steps, then glided thirty feet.

He nearly fell at the end of his slide, but he caught the glint of victory in her smile and managed to keep himself upright.

Lilleth shrugged. "You don't walk that well on dry ground."

That stung! It was Trace competing in this game, not Clark. If he wanted to keep his secret, and he was beginning to wonder if he could, he would be forced to take a tumble…but not just yet.

"Let's see what you've got, Miss Preston."

This time she lifted her hem high, anchoring it in both elbows so that her stockings flashed white to her knees.

He'd never known Lils to allow maidenly modestly to stand between her and victory.

She ran four steps, looking like a fairy tiptoeing over the ice, then slid past him with a laugh.

He reached for her hand, intending to keep her from gaining more ground than he had. When his fingers closed around her wrist, she lost her balance. She went down with a screech and a flounce of lace and wool.

"That, my friend, was cheating," she announced, reaching one hand up to him for help.

"Down is down." He shook his head, happy for the victory, even though she was right about the cheating.

He clasped her cold palm to pull her up, but she yanked, catching him off guard. His shoes grappled for purchase. He thumped down beside her.

"Down is down," she echoed.

"You took the first fall."

"Only because you played unfairly. As I see it, we ought to grant each other favors."

"I'll have a song," he said, wanting a kiss.

"And I'll have a waltz in the moonlight."

"Agreed." He stood and helped her to her feet.

He took her in his arms. She looped her hands around his neck and clasped her fingers together. He slid half a step to the left and she followed, her ribs shifting under his fingertips. He guided her in a circle. As it turned out, this slow dance over the ice was not a waltz so much as a moving embrace.

She looked up at him with her eyes reflecting moon glow and his smile. An instant later he swore that she looked into him rather than at him. She must know who he was.

Slowly her hand slid from his neck to his chest. She had no way of knowing that her fingers traced the shape of a heart over his scar.

Then she sang for him. Her beautiful voice told the story of a love, long lost but never forgotten.

It was about the two of them, many sad, long years ago.

He dipped his head to her shoulder. To keep up the appearance of a dance, he spun them in another slow circle.

He knew why grown men cried when she sang a love song.

When she finished, he lifted his head from her shoulder, took her cheeks in his hands and brushed his lips across hers.

What he wanted was to delve into her mouth in a seduction that would end with him delving lower. What he wanted couldn't be.

Even if he did admit the truth, it wouldn't solve his problem. Lilleth would hate him. The deception that he had played upon her was beyond forgiveness.

"I want to know why that song brought a tear to your eye," she whispered.

"I loved a girl a long time ago. Your song reminded me of her."

"Tell me about her."

He couldn't help it; he looped a red curl about his finger and felt it wrap his calloused skin in a caress.

"She was just like you."

She was you!

Lils frowned. Starlight winked a crimson crown in her hair. A gentle breeze washed the air with the scent of crisp, cold cedar. "You ought to try and find her, Clark. I think you still care for her."

She was wrong about that. He didn't simply care for Lilleth. He loved her more now than he had years ago.

"I care for her very much."

The time had come to choose. His career and the poor folks at Hanispree? Or the woman who was bound to hate him regardless of what he decided?

Without warning, his foot caught in a bank of snow. He toppled, carrying Lilleth down with him.

He landed on top of her, but she didn't struggle to be free of his weight. She touched his hair and wiped a smattering of snow from it.

"You fell," she whispered. "I get another prize."

"I hope you want a kiss." He felt her breasts rise in a sigh against his chest.

She shook her head. His hopes were dashed.

"I want you, Clark…all of you."

"Do you know who I am?"

"You're not a librarian." She plucked the glasses from his nose and tossed them somewhere. "I know you don't need those."

Her breath touched his and spun to fog in the inches that separated him from the kiss he wanted.

"Close your eyes," he whispered, and she did. "Listen to me, to the sound of my voice. You know who I am."

He kissed her. He touched her throat and her waist, wanting to give her all that she wanted. But he had to give it as Trace, not Clark.

"Don't you know me, Lils?" he asked. "It's me... it's Trace."

Chapter Twelve

"Ballentine?" She shoved at his chest and wriggled out from under him.

She knelt beside him, gazing down at the man lying in the snowdrift with his hair tumbled over his forehead in disarray. Slivers of ice clung to the dark tips and began to melt against his face.

This was not Trace Ballentine. He had disappeared into the mists of time. A boy cherished and hidden away in a secret, precious part of her heart.

This man looked nothing like her Trace. Her Trace had cheeks as smooth as her own. This was a grown man with hair on his face.

She peered hard at him while he pushed up on his elbows then sat up.

"It's me, Lils. It's Trace."

No, he was not. Trace had been slim. This man was lean, ripped with muscles. The boy had laughing, friendly eyes. This fellow stared at her, somber-eyed.

Something about his voice, though, made her listen closer instead of stomping on him where it would hurt the most.

Her Trace's voice had just begun to deepen when her mother had torn them heartlessly apart for the sake of her new, soiled love. But there was something…there in the tone. It was the same in the man and the boy.

"Say something," she demanded.

"Stars shine bright, sleep tight tonight."

Her heart slammed against her ribs. Blood throbbed in her ears.

"You might have heard me say that in my sleep."

"It's me, Lils." His gaze bored into her, clearly pleading with her to look back over the lost years and see him.

A rush of emotion flared in her chest, tightened her throat. It couldn't be true. This was impossible!

And yet it seemed that her lost love sat beside her with snow melting in his hair and dripping down his nose.

She stared into the face of a miracle and nothing short of it.

"Trace!" She tossed her arms about his neck and squeezed. "My Trace…" Now she began to sob. She felt like a little girl whose fairy king had returned. The boy had become— "Clark!"

Trace recoiled when she shouted in his ear. "That

fool doesn't exist." He reached for her, but she stood up and backed away. "I can explain if you'll let me."

"I will not. Not another word, you…you deceiver."

This stranger gazed up at her, pain clearly etched over his handsome features. "If I'd ever guessed I would run into you, there would have been no Clark," he declared.

Of course there had been a Clark. He had been as real to her as Trace had been. She had admired him…trusted him.

She had been ready to share her bed with him!

"Clearly, you are no longer the Trace I knew. That boy was honest and a good friend."

Or so she remembered. She'd thought the same of Clark, who was all of a sudden nobody.

"I think you are an impostor." She didn't, not really, but she wanted to.

"Do you want proof?"

"I certainly do not!"

But the stranger on the ground gave it to her anyway. He opened his shirt and exposed a scar in the shape of Trace's wound.

Words failed. She might deny who he was until she froze out here in the snow, and he would still be Trace Ballentine…or some form of him.

Not the one she had loved, though. Her Trace was dead and gone. Her Clark had never been.

What was she to do? She needed this man's help. Until a few moments ago she had wanted his love.

While she stood in the snowbank, stupidly gazing down, she thought of the girl she had been. Back then, she had always known what to do. She let the child in her out now.

She stooped and snagged a fistful of snow. She pounded it into a ball, then tossed it at the stranger's face as hard as she knew how.

He grimaced and shook his head. Beside his nose a red welt began to swell.

She hoped it turned black-and-blue by morning.

"Go back to your library, Mr. Ballentine." She gazed down her nose at him. "Or Mr. Clarkly, whoever you are at this particular moment."

With her heart feeling as heavy as the low note in a tragic song, she mounted the cabin steps.

She held her head high, though, while she lifted the soggy hem of her skirt.

Trace was not the only one who could put on an act. If she looked aloof and uncaring in the face of his confession, so be it. He didn't deserve to know to know how much he had hurt her.

Once inside, she shot the lock home, then tripped over to the fireplace, where she crumpled to her knees. She folded her arms on the hearth and buried her head in them. She wept, silently and bitterly, for the loss of her fairy king…and her librarian.

* * *

Alden Hanispree's collar grew tight. Anger pooled in his throat until he felt that he was choking on it.

He stood outside a rear window of the whore-house, shivering in the night air. He would have come in the front door, but Willow would have charged him something. Thanks to Lilleth Preston, his bank account was not as big as a man like him deserved.

There was no sense in paying the madam for noth-ing, for the privilege of stepping on her carpet and looking at her girls as he passed.

The word was, Perryman had returned. He'd slunk back into town and had been hiding and whoring for two full days.

If he didn't need Perryman, Alden wouldn't hesitate to strangle him. That the fool could come straight here without reporting what he had learned was beyond maddening.

Alden pounded his fist on the icy windowpane. This wasn't the first time he had been left outside Slender Sadie's window waiting for Perryman to finish his business. She was the only whore who allowed the idiot to indulge in his favorite, disgust-ing vice.

"Open up, Perryman!"

"Not now," his voice grunted in reply.

"Don't make me break the glass."

Just as he'd figured, Slender Sadie's skinny hands

lifted the window. She wouldn't want the cost of the glass to come out of her pay.

Perryman sat at a table beside the window in his long johns, with Sadie sitting across from him. A crimson shift hung off the whore's shoulder revealing one small, sagging breast. A bowl of bugs, some dead and some still squirming, sat between them.

"Want one?" Perryman asked, retrieving a live worm from the bowl and sucking the slimy creature through his lips.

"What I want is to know if you found the brats."

"Don't know. Could be."

Alden breathed frigid air through his nose, but it didn't help cool his roiling temper.

Too enraptured by his feast to notice that he was about to be slammed by a blast of anger, Perryman licked his lips. He poked his squirming feast with one long, bony finger.

Sadie stood up, walked quickly to the door. Her hand shook when she went out and closed it behind her. Someone, at least, remembered the last time Alden had been unable to hold his temper in check.

He took three deep breaths. He couldn't afford to lose Perryman as an ally.

"Climb out the window and tell me what you know."

"I'll climb out once my balls warm through."

Not a soul on earth could rile him like Perryman could.

"I'll rip them off you and bury them in the ice if you don't tell me what you found out."

Perryman blinked his eerie-looking, coal-black eyes. "I found out that you don't hide in an outhouse if you want to keep your man-parts healthy."

Alden reached through the window and slapped Perryman's face. He couldn't help it. The only reason he regretted it was that now he'd have to have act snivelly and sorrowful or Perryman might close his mouth on any information he had gained. The man could be stubborn as a rock and just as dumb.

"I'm sorry," Alden grated through his teeth. "I appreciate that you were nearly unmanned. Please sit inside where it's warm while I stand out here and freeze my balls off."

"Nothing to keep you from crawling through the window."

Nothing but a revolting bowl of bugs, an idiot, and a fee he didn't feel he ought to pay. He clenched his fingers into fists and shivered. "Please…do tell me what you found out."

"I saw a lady, figured she was the one, since she had the kid and the baby with her. I followed her home one night, but then it snowed. That's when I got trapped in the latrine."

"It could happen to anyone," Alden lied.

"After all that, it turned out not to be her." He bit a dried roach in half. "When she came out to do her business, it was some other lady. This one had a passel of little girls and a big husband."

"How do you know that?"

"She said so, after she knocked me over with a shovel."

"Did you see the girls? Did the husband come out when she discovered a stranger in her outhouse?"

"Only thing I was seeing were stars from when she walloped me. If I'd been myself I'd have given her what for and left the remains for her husband to scrape off the snow."

Idiot! Idiot! Idiot! Alden bit his lips to keep from shouting it out loud.

"From what I've heard of Lilleth Preston, she can get the better of a man. No need to feel too bad about it."

"This woman weren't her. She had a voice like sand."

"Only one way to make sure." This was the very last thing Alden wanted to do, but maybe he could handle it if he wasn't alone. "I'm going to Riverwalk to see for myself, and you are coming with me."

"I'm staying here."

"Remember what I said? When we get my brother's money we'll buy this place."

Perryman's head snapped around. He got up to investigate something crawling in the corner.

"Don't mind things the way they are," he said. "Sadie let me eat bugs off of her—"

"I'll give you the singer," Alden said quickly. He truly didn't want to know about the insects. "I'll put her in the room with her sister. You can have them both. Eat bugs from between their toes, for all I care."

Perryman stood up and snatched his clothing from the floor. After he dressed, he folded his long frame through the window and stepped outside.

"Get me a warm room at the Riverwalk Hotel and it's a deal."

They would both stay in the hotel. There was no way Alden was going to go anywhere near his insane asylum.

Ghosts probably drifted over every inch of those grounds.

Three days had passed since Trace Ballentine's betrayal. Plenty of time to dry her eyes and decide that she did not need his help in rescuing Bethany.

She would do it on her own. That had been her plan from the beginning, after all. She hadn't spent all her life depending on herself only to rely on someone else to do something so important.

A great deal of heartache might have been avoided had she done so all along. She would still be Lilly Gordon and Trace would have remained Clark Clarkly, strangers who could bid each other good day and never give the other a second thought. Ships that pass in the night.

So here she was this fine sunny morning, sailing her lone ship up the steps of Hanispree Mental Hospital.

She opened the front door and walked up to a desk with a name plate on it reading Nurse Goodhew. A bored-looking woman glanced up at her.

Lilleth wondered what secrets she kept behind her indifferent gaze. Did she know about Bethany? Did she care?

"I'm here to see Mr. Alden Hanispree."

The nurse came to attention with a start. "He isn't here."

Lilleth glanced about the room, looking casually at this piece of art and that velvet chair, hoping that the nurse would not notice the relief that had to show on her face.

The room was a disgrace. Alden had to have spent a sinful amount of money on it, while those left in his care froze and starved.

She didn't want to think about the things that Trace might have uncovered about this place.

"That, Nurse, is quite impossible," she stated. "Mr. Hanispree and I have an appointment."

"You may call me Nurse Goodhew." She picked at a strand of her dark hair and glanced toward a side hallway.

"Very well, Nurse Goodhew, I'll wait by the fire for Mr. Hanispree. I do hope he won't delay me overlong."

"I don't believe you have an appointment. Mr. Hanispree rarely visits. What are you up to?"

With any luck the miserable creature would know soon enough.

"I beg your pardon?" Lilleth set her face in what she hoped was an incredulous look. "I have a signed contract. He is supposed to be here to pay me after I perform."

"Perform what?"

"Songs for the inmates, naturally." Lilleth opened her coat. She had put on a red satin gown—low cut, with glass jewels adorning it. It was the only professional gown she had brought with her when she'd come to Riverwalk. And only because a woman never knew when she might need to sing herself out of a situation. "Be sensible, Nurse Goodhew. Why would I come wearing this if I were not intending to perform?"

"Show me the contract."

Lilleth opened her reticule and withdrew the paper that she had forged last night. She showed it briefly to the nurse, then folded it neatly and put it back in the bag.

"Mr. Alden has agreed to pay me twenty dollars. In exchange I am to sing for each and every patient, one at a time."

"I don't believe you." Nurse Goodhew stood up. "Mr. Hanispree wouldn't hold with such nonsense. He certainly wouldn't pay for it."

"In any event, he isn't here to pay me my due." Lilleth sighed, shook her head. "I will perform an act of charity."

"Be on your way, miss, before I have you removed."

"I, Nurse Goodhew, will not be budged."

"Dr. Merlot!" she called. "I need some assistance."

A man strode into the lobby, looking well turned out, with a stethoscope about his neck. His eyes glittered brightly at the nurse, until he noticed Lilleth standing there in her red gown.

His glittering gaze settled on her, then sharpened in appreciation. Lilleth was well acquainted with the expression. Very clearly, his attention did not sit well with Nurse Goodhew.

"Dr. Merlot, this woman is a cheat and a charlatan. She wants twenty dollars to sing to the patients."

"I was offered twenty dollars by Mr. Hanispree himself. But since he has reneged, I have offered to perform as an act of charity."

"Thank you, miss, but no."

The doctor gripped her upper arm and propelled her to the front door. She felt a shove at her back and was suddenly on the outside, with the door locked behind her.

She had held out slim hope that singing would gain her entrance. Anyone who worked for Alden knew that he would not allow the inmates such a treat, that he would not want anyone to see their paltry living conditions.

Lilleth cursed and didn't care. She marched around the back of the building and stared up at the window Trace had hoisted her into. It seemed fifty feet up rather than nine…and it was closed. There was no way in.

She wanted to cry, but she wouldn't. She swallowed her tears and her pride and took the wide road to Riverwalk and Clark Clarkly's Private Lending Library.

Trace sat at his desk with his pen in his fingers, his mind blank.

His lone customer sat on the rug in front of the fireplace, reading and warming the chill from her young bones. Little Sarah never hesitated to venture out in search of a book, no matter how cold she got in doing so.

"What do you think, Mr. Clarkly?" She glanced up at him with freckles dotting her cute nose. The shadow of a frown crinkled her brow. His heart squeezed. "This one about the beautiful horse sounds good, but this other one about the drummer boy in the Civil War seems important. I can't decide."

"Don't decide. Take them both." The window rattled with a sudden gust of wind. "You'd better hurry home, miss. It looks like the weather might turn."

Sarah stood up. She slid her arms into her coat,

tugged on her hat, then scooped up the books and hugged them close to her heart.

"I'll bring them back real soon, Mr. Clarkly."

"Those are yours to keep."

Since he'd committed the cardinal sin of exposing his identity to an outsider, he didn't think Clark would be in business much longer. It couldn't hurt to give the books away at this point.

Even in the event that Lilleth did not expose him, his family was bound to find out. Keeping even a minor secret from a clan of sleuths was impossible. Each and every one of them knew each and every thing about the others.

Trace picked up his pen and stared at it. He could buy some time by doing one of two things. Number one, he could make up yet another story about why he hadn't reported his progress on the investigation. Or two, he could tell the truth…he had met a woman and revealed who he was. That might keep the family in an uproar for a day or two while they considered what to do about it.

He set the pen down and put the cork back in the ink bottle. A decision of this magnitude took more thought than he could give it with Sarah beaming at him.

"Truly?" The little girl's grin warmed the room more efficiently than the snapping fire. She stroked the leather spine of *Black Beauty*. "I'll take the best care of them forever."

The front door opened. Icy wind whooshed inside, along with an even icier looking Lilleth Preston.

Sarah dashed around the desk and hugged his neck. "Someday I want to be a librarian, just like you."

Lilleth folded her arms across her bosom. She rolled her eyes toward the ceiling.

"Good day, missus," Sarah said in greeting, and then hurried out the front door.

Trace stood up, hoping against the odds that Lilleth would rush into his arms. He had held on to a pin-size flicker of hope through the dragging hours of the night that she might have forgiven his deceit. That she had remembered the tender feelings they had once held dear between them.

He removed his glasses and set them beside the ink bottle, staring for a moment at the dark liquid under the label.

When he looked up, Lilleth's expression was neutral. She didn't appear angry, but she didn't appear warm. She seemed a stranger. They might have had no more history between them than a librarian and his customer.

"Mr. Ballentine." To his surprise, she addressed him without a shred of rancor in her voice. "I've come to ask something of you."

"Ask me anything, Lils." At least she was not shutting him completely out of her life.

"Two things, then." She tapped her toe one time,

then took a breath. "First, do not call me Lils. Second, I would like to hire you to free my sister from Hanispree."

"Hire me?" He locked his knees to keep from plopping down in his chair. "I would never take your money."

"You'll understand if I cannot accept a favor." Color rose in her cheeks, but her voice remained in stoic control. "After all, favors are performed between one friend and another. Even though you and I knew each other long ago, we are nothing more than acquaintances now."

He strode to the window and flipped over the sign from Open to Closed. He crossed the room to Lilleth in three long strides. He gripped her shoulders and stared into her eyes. Private thoughts remained secret behind her indifferent gaze.

After a moment she glanced away. He took her chin in his fingers, turning it up so that she had to look at him…to listen to him.

"I'll give you that," he admitted. "What was between us as children was a very long time ago. You probably forgot me."

She nodded her head and broke his heart.

"But this is now," he said. "What is between us has nothing to do with years ago. Casual acquaintances don't feel what we do when we kiss."

"I kissed Clark, not you."

Fair enough. He understood how she might feel that way.

He slid his free hand up her spine to the curve of her neck, then bent his lips to hers. To his relief she didn't bite him. To his joy she softened her mouth and leaned forward, close enough that the front of her coat grazed his shirt. He wanted to unbutton the heavy wool garment, to reach inside the bodice of her dress and show her that what they had had never gone away.

"Clark never kissed you," he murmured across her mouth. "It was always me."

"Who are you?" She pushed out of his embrace and strode to the fireplace, facing the flames. "Very clearly, you are not the friend that I remembered over the years."

"I've always been him. That night you disappeared, I didn't want to recover from my wound. But my mother cried, my father threatened. They were not about to let me slip quietly out of my misery. They pestered me until I had no choice but to get well. You've got to know—I never forgot you, Lilleth."

She seemed unmoved by his story. Still, she hadn't marched out the front door, so he continued to explain.

"Once I grew strong enough, my family moved to Chicago. My parents started a weekly newspaper that focused on exposing corruption. When we were of age, all us kids became involved. The paper prospered and became well-known. On occasion, we had to go undercover, and that meant taking on fictional identities. There was also an issue of safety since we made plenty of enemies along the way."

She glanced over her shoulder, then back to the flames. It took only that one peek to encourage him. Her countenance had softened toward him, if only a little.

"And what secret assignment are you on now? Are there villains running the hotel? Gouging guests and giving their rooms away? Or maybe the baker is using inferior products in his tasty creations? Tell me, Trace, what is so very important that you would deceive me?"

"The villains we are after are very real. Very dangerous."

"I suppose it must have something to do with unscrupulous landlords who lease splintering cabins to unsuspecting renters."

"Lilleth, it has to do with Hanispree. I've come to shut it down. To have the inmates moved to respectable facilities."

That made her spin about. She pointed her finger at him in accusation. "You will not move my sister to another institution, Mr. Ballentine!"

"No, I won't. I'll get her out of there."

And there it went, his career with the family gone. He should have known from the beginning that he could not turn his back on Lils. Even if she never forgave him, he didn't regret this decision.

She lowered her arm, but lifted her chin. "Very well, then. Come by the cabin this evening and we'll devise a plan."

What he needed was a plan for the rest of his life. He had just turned his future over to a woman who walked casually past him, bidding him goodbye with nothing more than a curt nod, while she dropped a hundred dollars on his desk.

"Take the money back or the deal is off."

She turned and plucked it up.

"I'll see you this evening, then."

Maintaining an attitude of indifference toward Trace was nearly impossible. In spite of everything, the very last thing Lilleth felt for him was indifference.

In a matter of minutes he would walk around the bend to the cabin. She still hadn't decided whether she wanted to dump fireplace ashes all over him or kiss him.

Preparing for his arrival, she had brushed her hair into a lovely coif, frowned at her reflection in the mirror, then ripped out the pins and fluffed the curls into a royal mess. Whichever way she wore her hair, it wasn't right. Too fancy made it look as though she was trying to cover the pain of his betrayal. Too messy made it look as though she was wallowing in it.

In the end she stuffed the unruly mass into a single braid. This was as poor a choice as the others had been, since stubborn ringlets popped out with every twist and tug.

With the children asleep, Lilleth stepped onto the front porch, a shawl drawn about her shoulders and a lantern gripped in her fingers. The beam cast its light as far as the top step of the porch. The path that trailed into the woods was invisible. She, on the other hand, was completely visible.

The prudent thing to do would be to go inside. Trace might not be the only one walking the trail on this moonless night. While there had been no sign of Alden's spy, that didn't mean he was not lurking, waiting to do the children harm.

Going back inside would be the wise thing to do, but at this very moment she needed the bite of the cold wind to rush about her. She breathed in deep, trying to settle on the side of anger or of forgiveness. As things stood now, she was dizzy from the constant tip of emotions.

Curse Trace for tossing her into this turmoil.

"Don't give up, Bethany," she whispered into the night. "I'm coming."

"You shouldn't be standing in the open like that, Lils." Trace's voice shot out of the darkness.

An instant later his boots creaked on the stairs and he stepped into the lantern's circle of light.

Kiss or kill?

"I'm no longer Lils, and I was perfectly safe on my own front porch." She strode into the cabin ahead of him.

"Better to be careful, though. Perryman might have left town, but if he did you can bet he went straight to his boss." Trace placed a burlap bag in her hands. "Apple pie. It was warm a few moments ago."

She removed the pie from the bag and set it on the fireplace hearth to heat.

Clearly, she could not kiss or kill until they had discussed how they would free Bethany. The pie would help keep her mind on business and off her long-lost friend.

She watched him place his coat on a peg near the door. He was tall, his shoulders broad, and his hips... that was something to consider another time.

He turned to smile at her and all of a sudden she saw years fall away. Without the librarian to confuse her, she recognized Trace. She tried to fight it, but memories and old feelings bubbled to the surface.

That one man could cause such upheaval to a woman's heart was beyond distressing. For an instant, she understood her mother.

She would never be like her mother, though. Understanding and making the same mistakes were far from the same thing.

With the pie and her guest finally warmed through, she brought a pair of plates and forks from the kitchen area. She set them on the dining table along with a knife that glittered in the softly glowing lamplight. She sat down, then motioned for Trace to sit across from her.

She watched the pulse in his throat tap against his skin.

"I reckon you'd like to use that knife on me," he said.

To her mortification, she would rather feel that throbbing bit of flesh under her lips. When she was young she had dreamed of a lifetime of sweet, tender kisses from Trace. Just now, the kisses she tried so hard not to imagine were not sweet or tender, but wild and wanton.

"If you have a plan to free my sister, I'll wait."

She sliced a piece of apple pie for each of them.

After they ate Trace got up and walked to the wall peg where his coat hung. He reached in the pocket, then returned with a short saw. He set it on the table.

"This is your plan?" She picked it up and turned it this way and that in the light.

"And what would you do?" He closed his hand around hers on the saw handle. She ought to have yanked free, but his fingers felt warm, strong and slightly calloused. She ought to have known he wasn't a librarian.

"I'd pick the lock." She set the saw on the table

with his hand still covering hers. "It would be quicker and much quieter. Please don't touch me."

Lifting one finger at a time, he released her hand.

"I've tried to. That one can't be picked." He shook his head. "All I can do is hope to cut it off."

"Let's go, then." She stood up and swatted her fuzzy braid from her shoulder to her back.

"I'm going alone."

She marched to the peg, plucked down her coat, then shoved her arms inside. "If you remember me as well as you claim to, you know that I will not be left behind."

"You wouldn't be my Lils if I could make you stay home safe and warm."

It would be good to wipe the hopeful smile off his face with a well-deserved slap, but the truth was, she wanted to see that smile. More than see it, she wanted to kiss it.

"I am not your Lils."

She walked into the cold, windy night before he could read in her expression that just maybe she was.

Chapter Thirteen

Lilleth stood in the open doorway of what she had believed was Bethany's cell. Trace stood behind her, holding the lantern high.

The room was empty. Not a bed or a blanket indicated that anyone had ever been incarcerated here.

"Not even dust to leave footprints," Trace observed.

"I know Bethany was here." Lilleth squeezed her eyes shut.

She would not weep. Fainthearted women came to sorry ends. Her sister would not come to a sorry end. Lilleth would not allow it.

She stepped inside the room, while Trace hoisted the lantern behind her. He carried it to each dim corner while she knelt on the floor looking for... anything.

"They won't have harmed her, Lils." Trace knelt beside her and placed his big solid hand on her shoulder.

Apparently he was not going to give up calling her that pet name, and just now she didn't have the heart to argue the point.

She would not tell him so, but at this very moment it felt good to be his Lils, to know that his strength was there to bolster her.

A loose shutter banged against the side of the building in the wind. Even though the gust didn't penetrate the thick wall, cold radiated from the stone as though it were a block of ice. Wherever they had taken Bethany, it must be warmer than this.

"Not all clues are seen," Trace said, standing and drawing her up with a hand under her elbow. "Let's pay Mrs. Murphy a visit."

Trace took off his shoes and indicated that Lilleth should do the same. She nodded in understanding and bent to untie the laces. To Mrs. Murphy they were ghosts who could drift about unheard.

In the unlikely event that a fainthearted caregiver was working at this time of night, spectral silence would be crucial.

Trace turned the lantern wick to low. His face took on an eerie glow. Hers would appear just as frightening. They must look like visitors from the underworld.

Lilleth opened Mrs. Murphy's door. The old woman sat on her bed, gazing out the window, but turned when she heard the squeal of the hinge. She gave them a crinkled smile.

"I was watching you just now. I didn't know spirits would have to walk all the way across the yard. I thought you could pop in and out at will."

"We can do that," Trace answered, while he squatted in front of the fireplace to stir life into the embers of the weak blaze. He placed a log on top and watched while it kindled to life. "But my bride and I enjoy a stroll after dark now and then."

"How lovely to be newly wed." Mrs. Murphy's smile turned inward.

Lilleth sat down on the bed beside her. "We have become concerned about my sister. She is not in her room and it's been swept bare. Did you hear anything? Any little thing that might help us find where they've taken her?"

The old woman's gaze shifted, her attention returning to the reality of the dank cell she lived in.

"Oh, yes, dearie. I did hear something." Mrs. Murphy looked at her with clear, sharp eyes. Lilleth was sorry to have yanked her from her vision of happier days, but it couldn't be helped. "It was the doctor. He came himself this time, and only an hour ago. He and Mrs. Goodhew both. I remarked to myself that it was odd. They never come here after dark."

"Did they say anything? Any little detail that might tell us where they took her?" Trace asked, still poking at the log.

"If they did, I couldn't hear it. Mrs. Hanispree was raising quite a fuss."

Lilleth thought she might be sick. A struggle meant that Bethany could have been harmed.

"Did it sound like they hurt her?" she asked through her tightening throat.

"Don't you worry about that, missus," Mrs. Murphy said, patting Lilleth's hand. "What I heard was the doctor grunt and Nurse Goodhew screech. Mrs. Hanispree got the best of them, she did."

"Maybe she escaped on her own?" Lilleth said hopefully to Trace, who was now standing and peeking his head around the doorway into the corridor.

"I doubt that," he said, glancing back inside. "This place is a fortress."

"That's certainly true." Mrs. Murphy shrugged. "The only ones who come and go freely are the ones who have passed on, like you two lovely young shades."

"They won't hurt her, Lils. They can't afford to."

"If you call me that one more time I won't be responsible for what I might do!" she snapped, letting her frustration take aim at him. He had to stop this. It was difficult enough to be near the man without him trying to resurrect her affection by calling her Lils.

Mrs. Murphy's hand flew to her mouth. "Do lovers spat even on the other side? I was so hoping things would be different there, being a place of goodness and love."

Lilleth felt terrible. Mrs. Murphy looked forward

to her journey to the other side with such optimism. It was heartless to dash the frail woman's hopes in order to express her own annoyance.

"Oh, it *is* a place of love," she explained quickly, and patted her hand. "But even there we are human, and sometimes harsh words are spoken. You needn't worry, though—lovers always kiss and make up."

"That's a relief." Mrs. Murphy smiled brightly at her, then at Trace. "Go ahead, then, kiss and make up."

"Well, no, not right—"

Before she could protest, Trace stepped forward and drew her up from beside Mrs. Murphy. He braced his arm around her back and tugged her close.

Since there was no way out of this situation without disillusioning the dear old woman, Lilleth lifted her face to allow one chaste, dry kiss.

She ought to have known that would be impossible. This was Trace, and she was, despite the intervening years, his Lils.

She should have pushed away when she felt the first flash of heat roar through her veins. That would have been proper. It would have been wise. But this was the kiss she had imagined forever…her fantasy flaring to red-hot life.

Mrs. Murphy would have no worries about a cold hereafter now.

Dawn came with heavy clouds breathing down on the earth. Clark sat at his desk and dipped his pen in the ink bottle.

This time, words would not fail him. The telegram to his parents would be short and to the point. Finally, with his feelings settled, his goal determined, he knew what to write.

Lilleth had kissed him. She had kissed him as Trace, not as Clark. In that instant his world had shifted and fallen into place.

Afterward, just as he had expected, she fought what she was so clearly feeling. On the way home through the woods she had seemed as icy as the frozen tree limbs they walked beneath.

Even so, he couldn't help but sit at his desk grinning at his pen. His imagination flared to life, picturing the ways that he would thaw her. In the end she would be his Lils again. He wrote with a firm, bold hand.

Mother…Father, cannot complete assignment. Have become personally involved. Have broken character. Understand that this will end my career.
Always, your son,
Trace
Postscript: Marrying Lilleth Preston.

That last would be a shock. Over the years he had been encouraged by one family member or another to forget her. The past was the past and best forgotten, they would preach. That would have been sound advice for most people, but it was different for him. His memory was such that he remembered things most people forgot.

He recalled that little girl in detail. He saw the spark of mischief in her smile, and even today he clearly heard her giggling laugh in his head. What his family could never understand was that the scar of their separation would be with him forever, not just the one on his chest.

With his decision finally made, Trace stood up with a stretch and a grin. He put on his coat and went outside.

One block into the two-block trek to the post office, it started to snow. He caught a drifting flake on his tongue.

He enjoyed the stab of cold on his flesh. It felt fresh, just as life did right now.

It was true that challenges lay ahead of him, but he was not without hope.

Lilleth had kissed him.

He struggled to adjust the weight of the alphabetically layered books in the crook of his arm, because that was what Clark would do, and he couldn't put the character away just yet. He strode, less than sure-footedly, the last block to the telegraph office.

He sent his wire without the angst he'd thought would go along with such a life-changing decision. Just because he quit the family business, something that no one else had ever done, did not mean that his life would be empty.

Just then, the reason that his life would not be empty stepped out of the bakery. Lilleth was bundled against the blustery day in a heavy coat. The wind nipped her cheeks with a pink blush. A few red locks streamed out from under her hat, to bounce and frolic about her face.

Only a thoroughly smitten man would think poetic thoughts of frolicking red curls. If she glanced up and saw him, would she be thinking poetic thoughts, as well?

He stood beside the telegraph office door and watched to see.

Coming out of the bakery, Lilleth shivered even under her heavy coat. She would have attempted to make flapjacks for the children's breakfast—they were kin to biscuits, after all—but her thoughts were distracted in so many ways she barely knew how to feel.

She'd lain awake most of the night trying to gather her thoughts into some kind of order.

First, where was Bethany? Lilleth would scream in frustration if she could. Where once there had been only a wood door and a very impressive lock keeping her from her sister, now she did not know where she was. Lilleth prayed one more time that Trace had been right when he said that Alden could not afford to hurt her. That she had been stashed in a fancy room at the asylum that was used to trick families into believing their loved ones were being luxuriously cared for.

Lilleth only hoped that someone had laid a fire in Bethany's hearth just as Trace had done for each of the inmates last night, before the two of them made the brisk walk home.

One more thing that left her sleepless was that the inmates were not the only ones to have had fires laid in their hearths. Trace had done a fine job of igniting one in hers.

Of all the wicked timing. She couldn't consider romance while her sister was in peril.

Even though, walking home, she had put on a brilliant show of iciness toward Trace, the truth was that his kiss had claimed her. It had nearly claimed poor Mrs. Murphy, too. The dear soul was looking forward to the other side more eagerly than ever before.

Lilleth couldn't afford to dwell on her feelings for Trace. But only a born and raised fool would deny that something life-altering had shot between them with that kiss.

Just in case this kettle of turmoil was not enough, she had Alden to consider. There was every chance that he was in Riverwalk. That could be the reason they had moved Bethany. Alden might have an apoplexy if he had to visit the inmate quarters.

Enough time had passed for that squirmy Perryman fellow to have reported to Alden about her and the children. Alden might be watching her from a window or an alley this very moment. The hotel was close to the bakery. She and her bag of quickly cooling pastries would be in full view of anyone caring to look.

All along, she had feared a visit from the marshal. Alden could have easily wired him and had her arrested at any time. Since he hadn't, it had to mean that he intended to deal with her in a more personal way.

She had met the man only a few times, but in private, Bethany had told her things about him. He was a wicked little man with filth in his heart. Greed was his core value.

With her husband alive, Bethany had had no need to fear him. He had simply been an unpleasant relative to be tolerated on holidays. In her grief, she hadn't recognized the danger he had become to her and the children.

Frowning, Lilleth glanced behind her at the boardwalk. On this side of the street no one had ventured out into the cold. But on the other side, she saw Trace standing in front of the telegraph office, grinning at her.

She glanced away with an insincere huff.

All of a sudden her heart tripped, stalled, then tripped again.

There was no one staring at her through the hotel

window because they were staring at her from the hotel porch.

Two doors down from where Clark stood, Alden Hanispree stared past Perryman's raised and wagging finger. He looked her in the eye and recognition flared.

It was too late to run. In any case, Perryman knew where to find her—where the children were at this very moment!

She returned their glares, stalling and frantically figuring out how to get the children away before the men could reach them.

She glanced at Trace for half a heartbeat, and in that second saw his expression harden.

He nodded back at her and all of a sudden Clark appeared.

She didn't stay long enough to see what he would do, but she knew. He would bumble his way down the boardwalk and no doubt bowl them over.

Even with his help, she might not have enough time.

She dashed around the back of the bakery, passed the library and ran up the trail that led through the woods to the cabin.

Maybe she would always love Clark Clarkly, just a little bit.

Lilleth raced toward the cabin, taking just a moment to glance at the path behind her. She prayed that

Trace had been able to keep Alden from following her. She would need ten minutes to get the children out of here and to the lending library.

The library was the logical place to go. It was the only place to go.

Every second mattered, because there was no other trail between here and there. She hiked up her skirt and ran with her head down, forcing her legs faster with each step.

She went down, hitting the frozen ground hard on her hands and knees. The impact jarred all her joints, but she forced the pain from her mind. Already the fall had cost her seconds that might change the fate of her family forever.

Still a hundred feet from the cabin, she began to yell, "Jess…Jess!"

When he opened the door, it was with a frying pan gripped in his fist.

"Put on your shoes and coat," she rasped, the harsh breathing nearly closing her throat. "Your uncle is on his way here."

"Holy cats!" Jess exclaimed, leaping away from the doorway as she charged through it.

She snatched Mary off the floor, where she had been playing with her rag doll.

Jess snagged his coat from its peg, shoving his arms inside while he ducked into the bedroom.

Lilleth stuffed Mary into her little jacket, then buttoned the baby up inside her own coat.

All the way home the wind had gained in intensity and the temperature had fallen.

She dashed to the kitchen, put the pretty Wedgwood baby bottle in her pocket, then hurried to the fireplace, where a line of clean diapers was strung to dry. She stuffed those in her other pocket.

"Let's go, Jess!" She stooped down and grabbed the rag doll off the floor, then put it inside her coat for Mary to hold.

Jess burst out of the blanket wall with his shoes on his feet, but not laced. Something squirmed under his coat. It meowed and poked its orange head from between the buttons.

He dashed past her toward the front door, not pausing as he reached down and scooped the skillet off the floor.

Once outside the cabin, Lilleth considered taking the children off the path and through the woods, where they would be unlikely to encounter Alden. That would take much longer, though, and they could become lost. With the first snowflakes of the storm already falling, she couldn't risk that.

Mary wailed, probably cold and hungry. Lilleth didn't try to quiet her. If she met Alden on the path, the baby's crying would make no difference.

"Run to the library!" she panted.

She was tired, and with the toddler's extra weight, Lilleth was slowing Jess down. Alone, he might be able to outrun Alden. At least one of the children would be safe.

"Clark will delay your uncle, but I don't know for how long."

"Clark?" Jess slowed his sprint to glance back at her. "Auntie, we could stop and have a picnic along the way."

That might be true. As Clark, Trace could bumble his way through anything...probably.

"Get along!"

Jess turned and dashed ahead of her.

Five minutes later she saw him where the path met the woods behind the library. He was coming back, dragging Trace's heavy ax on the ground behind him.

"Quick! Into the house." She plucked the tool from his hand.

He darted forward once more. While she walked backward, she cradled Mary under her coat and dragged the ax over dirty snow left over from the last storm. She did her best to obliterate their footprints.

It seemed a hundred years later that she reached the front porch and went through the door, which Jess had opened.

She said a silent prayer right there on the spot, a thousand times thankful that they had made it and that the door had been unlocked.

Jess put his cat down and took Mary from her arms. Lilleth hurried to lock the doors as the aches of the fall began to set in.

There was no fire in the hearth and she didn't dare light one. Both Alden and Perryman knew that the librarian was not at home. They were a pathetic pair, but evil-minded and cunning enough to notice smoke coming from a chimney with the librarian not there to light a fire.

Twelve long minutes later a key scratched in the lock and Trace opened the door.

Lilleth rushed to him and he hugged her tight about her shoulders. Jess wrapped his arms about the pair of them.

"I knew you'd come to me," Trace said.

She leaned into his strength. Just this once, it felt good to be able to depend on someone other than herself.

"Did Alden go to the cabin?"

He nodded.

"How did you hold him off for so long?" Jess asked, his voice brimming with excitement.

"Ah...well, it took a while for them to gain their balance." Trace grinned down at him. "Then they had to hold my books while I put them back in order. Turns out they didn't want to borrow any of them, however, even though I showed them picture after picture."

"I reckon I want to be a librarian when I grow up." Jess puffed out his slim chest. "One just like Clark."

"There might be an opening for that job." Trace

ruffled the boy's hair. "For now we've got to get you and your sister out of here."

"I don't know anyone in town we could turn to." Lilleth squeezed her eyes shut, thinking. She opened them and shook her head.

"They'll be safe with Mrs. Murphy," Trace said.

She began to object, but Trace shook his head, clearly set in his decision.

"Auntie..." Jess stood beside Trace, stretching as tall as he could. "Uncle Alden is that scared of ghosts. The last place he'll go is the mental hospital."

"What about the staff?" She wasn't convinced. "They might find the children."

"Maybe, but it's the best we can do. And it looks like another blizzard getting ready to blow. They won't stir from their own cozy fires."

"We'll be closer to Mama there, Auntie." Jess tugged on her sleeve, looking hopeful.

"I can't see that there's a choice, really," she admitted. Even though she didn't like having the children there, the asylum would probably be the safest place for them.

"Let's pack some food and get going. Hanispree might figure out that I was delaying him for a purpose. He could show up here."

Within moments they were rushing through the woods. Lilleth's palms burned, and so did her knees, but it helped that Trace carried Mary.

With half an ounce of luck, they would get to their destination before the heavy snow set in.

They did, but just barely. The walk back to town would be more of a challenge.

When they ushered the children into Mrs. Murphy's room, she clapped her knobbed and slender hands.

"Why, it's children! How I've missed seeing little ones." She motioned Jess forward. "Are you happy, young man? Even though you, too, have passed before your time?"

"Yes, ma'am, me and my sister both are happy as larks." He sat beside her on the bed. "We'd be obliged if we could spend some time with you, though. Our regular granny is busy on heavenly errands for a while."

Lilleth nearly gasped. She had been trying all the way here to figure out what to tell Mrs. Murphy. Her nephew was a clever little boy. Trace arched his brows and gave Jess an approving nod.

"That would be lovely." The elderly woman hugged Jess with a frail arm. "It's nice that you feel so warm and solid."

"That's one thing that surprised me about passing over." He leaned into her hug. "The warmth, even the cat's warm."

After an hour of settling in and seeing to the other inmates, Trace clutched Lilleth's hand and led her down the dark hall toward the back of the building.

She winced and he let go.

"I bruised them a little when I fell, is all." Near

the back door she stopped and glanced up the stairway. "Maybe they moved her back."

Trace shook his head. "I already checked."

"I'm scared, Trace." She didn't want to say those words. In a small way they admitted defeat.

"Don't worry—we'll find Bethany."

Snow fell in earnest now, blowing sideways and in circles.

"Maybe we ought to stay here."

"You can. Maybe you ought to tend to the children."

"What about you?"

"I need to be where I can see what Hanispree is up to. Chances are, he'll remain in town."

"I'm staying with you, then."

Lilleth breathed in the cold, fresh scent of ice and pines.

"Hold on to me, then, Lils. This is going to be some blower." Trace drew her in tighter.

"Say it again," she said.

"Hold on to me."

"Not that…"

Chapter Fourteen

"Lils?"

Maybe he had misheard, with the wind blowing in his ears.

"Lils," he repeated, trying the endearment out cautiously.

Wonder to beat all, she smiled at him. Even though her teeth chattered with the cold, there was no mistaking that she wanted him to use the forbidden name.

He'd like to take a moment to enjoy it, to consider what it meant, but the storm grew worse by the minute and her pretty lips shivered.

Too bad he didn't have time to kiss them warm and rosy. Evidence pointed to the fact that she might allow it.

"Let's get you back to the library before you freeze solid," he said.

"Alden and Perryman might find us there." He'd

never seen fear in Lilleth's eyes before and he didn't now. Still, the concern he read in them was not uncalled for.

"That pair of tenderfeet? The farthest they'll venture is the hearth in the hotel lobby."

Frost-tipped curls peeking out from under her fur cap nodded against his coat sleeve. She tried to walk at the urgent pace he set, but her skirt had become sodden to the knees and dragged like a weight behind her.

He scooped her up. It felt good to have her in his arms. To protect her. This was what he'd wanted from the first time he'd rescued her from a gossip's tongue, way back when.

Wind howled about his head. It blew his hat off. Snow stuck to his face and crusted his eyelashes.

"Almost home, Lils. There's the end of the path up ahead." He said it with more confidence than he felt. With the snow swirling from every direction at once, he couldn't be sure he was even on the trail.

"It's a lucky thing we got the children to Mrs. Murphy when we did." Lils's voice shook. He felt her shivering under her damp coat.

As numb as his lips were, he doubted that they looked as blue as hers did.

"I think I see the back door."

"Praise heaven…" Her teeth clacked.

He did praise heaven a moment later, coming inside and closing the door on the wind. He set Lils on her feet, then knelt beside the fireplace, piling on kindling and logs. He poked and prodded until a single flame burst into full-blown fire.

Two thumps sounded, then one more. Lils's hat and gloves hitting the floor, he reckoned. Glancing behind, he watched her try to unbutton her coat. With her fingers looking as brittle as blue porcelain, all they could do was tremble against the wet wool.

"Come over here to the fire, Lils."

He stretched his hand toward her. She stepped forward, grasped it, then settled down beside him.

"Land sakes, but aren't we a p-pair of i-icicles."

"Let me get those." Even though his fingers were not blue, they were numb, clumsy as an oaf's. The buttons felt like silver dollars that he was trying to push though dime-size holes.

This task would be impossible until his hands were warmer. He reached toward the flames at the same time Lils did. In unison, they shivered in their damp outerwear.

"Why are you letting me call you Lils?"

Damn! He hadn't intended to blurt that out. His plan had been to heat her up first, in front of the fireplace with a few kisses.

"I've decided to forgive you." She arched a dark auburn brow at him. "There is no reason we cannot be friends."

"Humph." With his fingers warmed, he reached

for her coat and slipped the buttons free. "I can think of one."

He slid the wet wool off her shoulders and tossed it somewhere. Removing his own coat, he pitched it in the same direction.

"And what would that be?" She knew what it was. The knowledge flared in her eyes along with the reflection of the snapping blaze.

He didn't speak, couldn't really. Not with his heart in his throat and his fingers moving toward the bodice of her dress.

The buttons parted so smoothly that he feared she would think he was accomplished at undressing ladies.

He had never been that man and now he knew why. There was only one woman for him. Not time, not distance, not even years of living a full and successful life had made him forget her.

He looked into her eyes and she held his gaze.

"You want to be my lover," Lils whispered, answering her own question.

He shook his head.

"No, Lils, I want to be your husband." He traced her jaw with one knuckle, then her throat. He rubbed the lace of her corset between his thumb and finger and felt the heat of her breast. "I'll be your lover, the father of your children. I'll be the man who never goes away."

"This is something for another time. I can't think about this now…not until my sister is safe."

"You're wrong, Lils. This is our time. We can't do a damn thing to help her in this storm—but Hanispree can't hurt her, either."

Trace leaned forward and kissed Lilleth. "This is our time."

She nodded, then kissed him back. "We shouldn't waste it."

She unbuttoned his shirt, then pushed it off his arms, trailing her fingers slowly over his skin, pausing at the muscle of his forearm and the bone at his wrist.

Baring her chest to the lapping heat of the flames, he traced the shape of her, from the full outer curves of her breasts, to the inner swell, then up her throat, where her pulse shimmied in her neck.

She touched the jagged L shape of his scar with the tip of her finger, silent for a long moment.

He squeezed her hand, but she winced.

"From the fall?" He kissed her palm, then lay it gently over his heart. "Will you marry me, Lils?"

"I told you a long time ago." Tears glittered in the corners of her eyes. "I will marry you and only you."

"Tonight. As soon as the snow quits." It had to be now. "Before something happens and someone snatches you away from me again."

"No one will ever do that, Trace. I'm older now. I would fight for you." She nodded, as though settling something in her mind. "I will marry you just as soon as my sister can stand up for me."

Lilleth leaned forward and pressed her breasts to his chest. A pair of hot circles branded his heart just as the scar had done over the years. But the scar had been cold, a reminder of loss.

Lils, crushing her body to the old wound, singed him with another brand. This one erased the past. Oddly, his elation at this moment was greater for having lived the loss.

Only one thing stood between him and his fantasy come to life.

A few pieces of clammy clothing.

In four swings of the pendulum on the mantel he had tossed away his trousers, long johns and socks.

Lilleth made even quicker work of her skirt, numerous underthings and boots.

She knelt across from him, looking like a mythical nymph...a goddess, bare and glorious. Her gaze took him in from shoulder to knee. It ignited a blaze across his flesh and kindled it deep in muscle and bone.

"I always figured you'd grow to be a beautiful woman, Lils, but you are so much more." He watched the fire warm her skin while he memorized each curve and hollow. "You make it hard for a man to breathe."

"And you make it impossible for a woman to have a respectable thought."

He caressed her bare shoulders, then pressed her back until she lay against the hearth rug.

Heat shimmered in her eyes. It sparked in her hair where it tumbled on the rug, wild and enticing. She made him feel feral in a way that he never had, as if he were a beast about to claim his mate.

He straddled her hips, his weight settling hot against her belly. Firelight licked her skin. It flushed her cheeks, her throat and the swell of her chest. It fondled her everyplace that he was about to.

He wanted to jump upon her all at once, to devour her, but this was a moment to be savored.

First, he tasted the curve of her waist.... He stroked the flare of her hip with his tongue and smoothed the fine goose bumps that had risen under his mouth with his hand.

An hour ago the storm had seemed a curse that fought and delayed them, but not any longer. Howling wind and whiteout snow would insure that every soul in Riverwalk stayed indoors. It gave them a precious bit of time before life returned, with a sister to be rescued and villains crushed.

For now, the only reality was his mouth showing her why grown men cried when she sang a love song.

The storm battered the front window, shook it until it nearly broke. At the same time it rattled the front door on its hinges.

With one touch, Trace did the same to her. His fingers moved over her skin, caressing, nuzzling, then settling down to explore that tender spot that had never been explored.

"I've always loved you," she whispered, rising to meet his mouth on her throat. "Even when I didn't want to."

"Good to know." He lifted up to smile down at her, and gently pinched her bottom. "I hope you always love me even when you don't want to."

He turned his attention to the swell of her chest, nibbling and pebbling her flesh with his tongue and teeth. She felt wicked and wonderful all at once. As though she had made herself into a delectable meal and allowed him to feast upon her.

"Trace?"

"Umm?" he answered, sounding husky.

"There's something I used to imagine when you were sitting at your desk." Her breathing came quicker now because his mouth was nibbling a lazy trail down her belly.

"Umm?" He paused.

"It's wicked. You'll be scandalized."

"Nothing between us will ever be wicked."

That couldn't be true when just the musky scent of his skin drove her to envision things that made her tremble.

"Sometimes, when you sit at your desk, I imagine that I am your book. You open me up, then—"

Just like that, before she could finish speaking, he stood up, his muscular thighs bunching and stretching while he lifted her.

With a sweep of his arm, he cleared the desk. Pens and ink bottles plinked on the floor.

He set her bare bottom on the polished wood and spread her thighs with big, firm hands.

"You're right, Lils. This might be a little bit wicked."

He touched his erection to her curls, then pressed the tip past her nether lips. Inch by slow inch he thrust into her. Squeeze by slow squeeze, she enfolded him.

His breathing sounded ragged.

"I love you, Lils," he said, leaning in close to her lips, but not quite kissing them. "Never anyone but you."

Cupping one hand under her buttocks, he climbed upon the table and slid her over the smooth surface without losing the precious contact of their joined bodies. He pressed her flat against the desk.

He drove into her and she met him. She owned him...or did he own her? She couldn't think, or breathe, or speak. With each thrust of his hips he made old heartaches disappear. The future dawned in an explosion of fireworks that shimmered in red and gold behind her eyelids.

"You weren't the only one who fantasized about

what could happen on this desk," Trace panted, while she felt the library fall slowly back into place.

"I wouldn't have guessed that a common book could lead to what we did." She trailed her fingers through his damp hair and rejoiced in the huff of his moist breath against her neck.

"Not any common book, Lils. You are my love story."

"You are a pea-brain, Perryman!" Alden shouted into the wind blowing stinging ice at his face. "You've gotten us lost in a blizzard."

"Never claimed to be a scout." Perryman looked down his razorlike nose and blinked his obsidian eyes. "Hotel's probably a little farther on."

"It had better be," Alden grumbled. "I paid you good money to get me those children and all you've got is us lost in a storm. You are a bungler."

He no longer cared if he hurt the fool's feelings or not. The man was an idiot. An apology later on and they would be friends again. It didn't even have to be sincere. Perryman was a dog in many ways, an insect-munching canine who welcomed the slightest show of approval from his master.

That was a pleasing thought. Alden Hanispree... the Master. And very soon he would be wealthy to go with it. Wealth would give him power; power would draw people to fawn over him. They'd be drooling all over themselves just to do what he wanted, no matter what it was.

All he needed was the brats. Now that he'd found them it would be a simple matter to get them back. Give that sister of Bethany's over to Perryman and he would no longer have to worry about her interfering.

Maybe he'd send Bethany a little gift from Perryman, just to let her know the easy times were over.

"Look!" Perryman shouted, only inches from Alden's ear. "There's a building ahead."

"You colossal moron!" He would have slapped Perryman's face with his glove, but the cold blow would have stung his own hand. "That's my insane asylum. You know I can't go there."

"You're the moron if you'd rather stay out here and freeze to death."

"Take me back to town."

"See those chimneys with the smoke coming out? I'm going there to get warm."

"You're going to get possessed, is what. You know those fires are kindled by ghosts."

"Warm is warm, my mother always said."

"Your mother left you while you were still at her teat."

Perryman shrugged. "Someone's mother had to say it, because it only makes sense."

"Come back here!" he shouted, but the fool turned his back and walked away.

"Stay here and die or face the ghouls," Perryman called over his shoulder.

"You'll pay for this!"

And he would, dearly. But for now Alden had no choice but to follow.

Lilleth stared down at six foot two inches of naked male sprawled midway down the staircase. Half an hour earlier he had been fondling her and she had been teasing him while they descended from the bedroom to the kitchen to get a bite of supper. Suddenly, desire had taken them over, completely and utterly. His kisses and her response had been too powerful to resist, and a deeper hunger than mere food had tumbled them down upon the middle step.

She knelt beside him now, sorry to say goodbye to this cozy nest, but it was time.

Touching his shoulder, she trailed her fingers to his jaw then tapped his nose.

"Wake up, Trace. It's raining."

"Not asleep," he groaned, and tried to pull her down to him. "In a pleasure daze."

"You're bound to be bruised on your backside," she mumbled into the sweat-dampened hair behind his ear. "It was kind of you to take the bottom position."

He popped one eye open, then arched that brow.

"Gallant," he agreed. He patted his belly. "Climb back on and I'll play the hero again. It's a small price to pay for seeing you riding me like a goddess taming her wild steed."

A flush heated her skin. After everything they had done over the past two and a half days, she was amazed that she had any modesty left.

Her blush was not the only thing rising, though. Trace tried to set her on top of him, but she scooted across the stair with more regret than she let on.

With the weather taking an unusual turn, rain of all things, it was time to find Bethany. The road to Hanispree would be passable even if the wooded trail would not be.

"Come on, we've got to hurry." She rushed down the steps to the lower floor, glancing quickly about the library. "Where did we leave our clothes?"

Trace stood up slowly, his muscles flexing while he stretched and groaned. She glanced away, but heard the wood stairs creaking with his weight while he came down.

If he touched her she was done. It might be hours before they made it to Hanispree.

She grabbed her coat off the rack and wrapped it around herself. Out of sight, out of mind.

The wool scratched her breasts and tickled her belly. Before Trace, she'd never paid much attention to what touched her skin. Now all she wanted on it were his hands…and his mouth. What a wicked creature she had become.

"Lils," Trace whispered, coming up from behind. He reached around, pulled the coat open, then slipped his hands between the wool and her belly. "If you want to get to the hospital you'd better at least put on your underclothes."

"You're a fine one to give orders, Mr. Naked Ballentine."

He turned her around and nibbled a trail between her ear and her throat.

"Oh," she moaned, and leaned into his lips. Her intended was dangerous. With his mouth alone he could turn her into a spineless creature who cared for nothing more than coupling with him.

Somehow during these precious days, lying under, beside or on top of Trace, she had come to understand her mother…and to forgive her. They were the same, except that poor Mama had never been able to distinguish a good man from a dissolute one.

Lilleth gathered her wits—or what she had left of them—and pushed away from her trustworthy man, because trustworthy or not, he was temptation incarnate.

"Get dressed." She tapped her toe and Trace sighed. He shoved his fingers through his matted hair.

"Who knows what might be happening at the mental hospital while you and I dally away precious time?" she asked.

"Dally, Lils?" He strode to the fireplace, where trousers tangled with bloomers and coarse red long johns lay beneath a delicate ivory camisole. "Love doesn't dally, it binds. The minute we free Bethany, we're headed for the preacher."

"And I'll lead the parade," she said, crossing her arms over her chest. "Now put on some clothes."

Traveling the main road to the hospital held some risk, but as far as Trace could determine there was no other way to get there. The woodland path was impassable with the snow piled in drifts and broken tree limbs littering the way.

Not only was he concerned about encountering Alden and Perryman, but the weather had taken an odd turn. Rain had switched back into snow almost the moment they'd stepped out of the lending library.

They were still a quarter mile away from the hospital when lightning exploded with a long, muffled crackle. It sounded far-off, but wouldn't be.

An eerie loop of light illuminated the sky. It looked like a static halo. He'd never seen the likes of this but he'd read about it. Thunder snow happened when bitter cold clashed with warm air in some odd and unusual way. Mostly, it happened in the spring, but also in the fall once in a great while.

"That was spooky," Lils whispered, huddling closer to his side.

"Can you still run?"

She nodded. Red curls pulled away from his coat, full of static. She dashed out ahead of him, then turned back to wink. Lilleth put on a brave face, but she had to be frightened.

Hell, he was nearly shaking in his socks, watching her run up the wide road ahead of him. Bolts of electricity hit the ground all around. It etched spiny fingers through bare trees and gave the snow a freakish white glow.

Lils was still a runner, faster than he was by far. She paused at the front gate to wait for him.

When he got there she rose on her toes to kiss him. Then, as they had plotted on the way, she headed round the back, toward Mrs. Murphy's room, to make sure all was well with the children, while Trace—in character as Clark—entered through the lobby to find out what he could.

He was greeted by a merrily snapping fire in the big hearth and the rotund Nurse Fry gesturing wildly to Nurse Goodhew.

The drama between them was intense. They either failed to notice him come in, or downright ignored him.

"I heard it myself," Nurse Fry wailed. "A baby crying, and no doubt about it."

"We have no infants here, Nurse. Pull yourself together."

"No human infants." Nurse Fry wrung her hands. "I won't be going back in those dark halls again, I can tell you."

"If you value your job you will."

"I will not! Not alone, at any rate. It's not just the baby crying anymore. There's a boy, a frightening apparition that pops out from anywhere." Nurse Fry covered her mouth and shook her head. "Not an hour ago it tugged on my apron strings."

"Really, Miss Fry, have you been getting into the drug cabinet?" Nurse Goodhew stared down her long nose at her employee.

Lightning shocked the lobby, making the women appear rather spooky themselves. If Trace didn't know who the ghost child was, he might be frightened, as well.

If one were to imagine ghosts and goblins gliding in and out of walls, this would be the night for it.

"Good evening, ladies," Trace declared.

"Mr. Clarkly." Nurse Goodhew shot him a frown. "Why must you always come when the weather is foul? Do you enjoy dripping all over my floors?"

As a matter of fact, he did. That particular trick had come in useful on a few occasions.

"Why, no. That is, I don't mean to. It's just that the weather is normally foul. It is November, after all." He shook his coat to make sure that the snow splattered on the floor. "I've brought books. Since you and Nurse Fry seem to be engaged, I'll hand them out myself. Won't be but a few moments."

He took several steps toward the hallway where the well-appointed patient rooms were.

"Stop right there!" demanded Nurse Goodhew. "Not one more step."

He continued on for five more. "It's no trouble at all." He meant to get into those rooms. He suspected that's where Bethany had been taken.

When the weather cleared and Hanispree ventured from the hotel, he wouldn't have the courage to confront her in her old cell. That had to be the reason she had been moved.

Nurse Goodhew abandoned her argument with Nurse Fry and ran toward the hallway, cutting Trace off.

"Give me those books and go home, Mr. Clarkly."

"I believe Nurse Fry looks ill. Perhaps if we take her down this corridor and open each of the doors, between the two of us we can convince her that there is no such thing as the wandering dead."

"She will simply have to accept my word on that."

He resolved to get into those rooms even if he had to tie the unpleasant Goodhew to a chair. Lilleth counted on him to free her sister. He would get Bethany out of this hell pit today, before Hanispree got here.

"What if Nurse Fry is correct? Shouldn't we assure ourselves that she is not?"

"Don't blather, Mr. Clarkly. There is no boy and there is no baby. It's bad enough having Mr. Hanis—"

"Mr. Hanispree is in attendance?" Trace's stomach pitched.

He could not have gotten here in the storm. That meant he had come before that and been here three days, and possibly Perryman with him.

No matter what it took, this would end today.

"Perhaps he'd care for a book, if you will point me to his room?" he asked mildly, in spite of the turmoil in his gut.

"Mr. Hanispree is indisposed."

"Terrified of the ghosts is what he is." Mrs. Fry pointed a plump finger at Trace. "He knows the truth."

Mrs. Goodhew heaved a long-suffering sigh. "You are dismissed, Nurse Fry. Take your belongings and don't come back."

A spear of lightning brightened the room at the same time that Nurse Fry opened the door.

An older couple blew inside with the wind. The nurse hurried past them, sailing out into the night.

Trace blinked, Clark style, more than surprised to see the couple about in the storm.

"I'm Mr. Horace Bolt. I've come to commit my wife," the man said, his voice harsh as sand. "She's losing her mind."

"I'm saner than you, you old goat!" Mrs. Bolt said. She gazed at Trace, clearly noticing his alphabetized stack of books.

"I'd like to speak with Mr. Hanispree himself," Mr. Bolt demanded.

"He is not available," Nurse Goodhew answered with a sniff. "I'm certain I can help you."

"I'm rich. I'll pay a lot." Mr. Bolt withdrew a wad of bills from his money pouch. "Go get him."

"You won't lock me up." Mrs. Bolt continued to stare at Trace. "I'll pay Hanispree even more to set me free."

At the sight of the cash, Nurse Goodhew's demeanor softened. "We are not concerned with money here at Hanispree. The well-being of our patients is of paramount importance to us," she said, acting her part so well she might have been a Ballentine. "Perhaps Mr. Hanispree will see you tomorrow."

"He will see me right this minute or the deal is off." Mr. Bolt stuffed the cash into his coat pocket. "Give my wife a room before she drives us all to distraction."

"And who," Mrs. Bolt demanded, pointing her finger at Clark, "is this? You ought to be more careful about who you expose that wad of money to, Mr. Bolt."

"Clarkly," Trace answered. "Mr. Clark Clarkly."

"That ridiculous librarian?" She stepped up close to him, her eyes narrowed in her round, pink-cheeked face. "I heard he'd retired."

"Without a word of warning," Mr. Bolt added. "Just up and quit."

Trace nodded at his mother, then his father. "Sometimes a career won't let you go even when you try to give it up."

"Who would want to be a dreary librarian, anyway?" Mrs. Bolt observed.

"Dreary or not, Mrs. Bolt," her husband replied, "it's a job and someone's got to do it."

"If you think so, ma'am…sir—" he wanted to hug them, but his shoelace made him lose his balance, and he slipped to one knee "—I reckon I'll give the job another go."

Mr. and Mrs. Bolt, the wealthy and overbearing couple, turned as one to face Nurse Goodhew.

"If you value your job, miss, you'll send Mr. Hanispree to the lobby." Mr. Bolt demanded. "If not I'll fetch him myself."

"Get him this very moment!" Trace's mother snapped her fingers at the nurse, then turned and winked. "I find that I can't endure my overbearing husband for another instant. Please show me all your very best rooms."

Chapter Fifteen

Lilleth hustled around the corner toward the back door. Jess was supposed to have made sure that it remained unlocked. He would have been expecting her to return well before now, though.

She was more than a little nervous to know how the children had fared with Mrs. Murphy. She was an old lady and two young ones would be a challenge. Jess was capable, but because of the storm, it had been three days.

Thankfully, the knob turned in her hand. Before she went inside she went to the woodpile and picked up three logs. There was not any smoke coming from the chimneys of the inmates' quarters, so they must have run out.

She stacked the wood beside the door, then returned to get more. On her next trip she tried to carry four logs, but ended up dropping one. She bent to pick it up.

A hand clamped down on her shoulder. It spun her about so that she lost her balance and fell over.

She looked up into the obsidian eyes of the bug eater. He hovered over her as though she were a roach and he was about to chomp on her with those unnaturally sharp teeth.

"You idiot!" she swore.

"Look who's on the ground and who's standing up. Who's the idiot now, pretty lady?"

She was, of course. She hadn't been talking to him at all. To let a man creep up on her unaware was the height of folly.

"You've got me now, I reckon." Reaching for a log to defend herself with would be a mistake. Perryman would disarm her easily. Her only defense would be surprise, so she sighed and gave a helpless shrug. "Whatever will you do with me?"

"That's for me to know. It ain't wise to tell a woman too much."

"You're right, of course." She reached a hand for him to help her off the ground. "It's just that if you tell me where we're going I can walk there instead of you having to drag me."

"Could be I want to drag you." He ignored her hand.

"Could be you'll be sorry for it," she snapped, even if it meant revealing that she was not as helpless as she pretended.

Perryman rubbed the back of his head. Good, it looked as if the two blows she had dealt him with the shovel still smarted.

"Walk, then, but I'm right behind you...breathing down your neck."

"You might want to tell me where I'm walking to."

"You'll see when we get there. Just march your helpless self right through them trees."

Across a frozen meadow and then through a copse of icy-branched trees appeared a gardener's shed made of stone.

Perryman opened the door, gripping her wrist with fingers that felt more like cold bones than flesh and blood. He shoved her inside and shut the door behind them.

Cold air crept up her legs. It nipped and swirled about her. The interior of the shed was too dark to see anything. Metal scraped metal, probably a bolt being shot home.

Perryman was about five feet away from her, judging by the rasp of his breathing. A match hissed, then a lantern flared to life.

"You poor man, is this where Alden makes you sleep?" she asked, spotting a crude pile of blankets that made for a tattered bed in the corner. A shovel and a pick leaned against the wall beside it.

Perryman must have noticed her looking at them.

"I'm no fool, lady." He snatched the tools and

tossed them out the door. To her relief, she didn't hear the lock slide back into place. "I won't forget what happened the last time you had your hands around a shovel. Just since you asked, I sleep in the big house, all warm and cozy. The gardener's shed is for you, for as long as I want to keep you here. The pick and shovel are for when I don't."

The hiss of his bare palms scratching against each other filled the room. He chuckled, obviously expecting her to cringe.

Well, she wasn't ready to cringe, not just yet.

"I hit you because you were a stranger." She walked up close to him, pretending that she was not his victim. "A mother has a duty to protect her little girls."

"S'at so?" He pinched her chin between his stringy fingers. "I know you ain't a mama. Those kids you got hiding in the crazy house belong to Hanispree."

"If you believe that, why are you here and not turning them over to your employer?" She wrenched her chin from his hold and walked to a far corner of the shed. Perryman followed her, his grim shadow crossing the dirt floor.

Thunder shook the building. The lightning must have struck only feet away for it to make stone tremble. For an instant, it rattled Perryman and distracted him.

Lilleth's foot kicked something solid that had been covered in dirt and straw.

"Got me a plan. Guess it don't matter to tell you, though, since you won't be saying anything to anybody anymore." He grinned. In the dim lamplight his sharp teeth glittered with a feral snarl. "I'm not giving those kids to Alden, not for the pitiful price he was going to pay. My pockets won't be big enough for all the cash he'll have to hand over. A man ought to get a fair price for something another man wants so bad."

"You're smart as well as handsome, Mr. Perryman." She sat down on the floor, then fluffed out her skirt. Just under her derriere pressed the cold hard shape of a spike.

"I'm not a fool who can be charmed, so don't you try." He snatched a rope from a hook on the wall. "Take off your coat."

She had no choice; she did it. He tied her hands behind her back and tested the knot with a vicious tug.

Lilleth doubted that her mother's suitors had prepared her for this battle. Not a single one of them had ever gotten close enough to disable her with a rope.

"You are no fool, Mr. Perryman, and I am no charmer."

But her voice was. She settled onto the floor with a sigh, feeling the cold shape of the ten-inch weapon beneath her. She hoped it was sharp.

She smiled up at her captor's black scowl and began to sing.

* * *

Trace watched Alden Hanispree stride into the lobby.

The short, cowardly man glanced fearfully at the door that led to the inmates' quarters, then over his shoulder.

He spotted the money that Trace's father held, and seemed to forget about what might be following him. His hands twitched and his avaricious grin flickered in the stabs of lightning flashing through the windows.

"My word, Mr. Hanispree. Are you well?" Trace's mother asked. "You look as though you've seen a ghost."

Clearly, his parents had been doing some investigation. They knew exactly where to place a dig.

"Or they've seen you," Clark added, peering hard at the man through his spectacles. "Unpleasant business any way you look at it."

Hanispree hadn't appeared pale before his mother fired her jab, but he did now.

"See here." His father waved the cash at Alden. "That's enough rubbish talk. I've come to do business. I want the best room you have for Mrs. Bolt."

"It had better be," Trace's mother declared, then turned her back on the transaction.

She walked across the room to stand beside Trace, who appeared to be warming himself near the big snapping fire in the hearth. In reality, he was studying the situation in the room, figuring how he could use it to get to Bethany.

"What are you doing here, Mrs. Bolt?" he whispered.

"A lucky thing for you, my dear, that your brother is nosy. Cooper smelled trouble, what with that odd Perryman fellow spying on your young lady. Quite naturally, we began an investigation. Alden Hanispree is a greedy twit, I do have to say…separating children from their mother. I hope we are in time to help sort this mess out."

"Look here, Hanispree," Trace's father exclaimed. "I'm not handing over this money until I've seen every room you have."

"Where is Miss Preston?" His mother jabbed Trace in the ribs with her elbow. From across the room, he thought Nurse Goodhew noticed.

He handed his mother a book and opened it.

"Here we have an otter," he said loudly. "Cavorting with its two little babies. Otters are devoted creatures, did you know?"

"I'd like to see one for myself one day, young man."

"They live in dark places," he said, not knowing if that was true or not. "With lots of other otters living in dark places."

He inclined his head toward the door behind Nurse Goodhew's desk.

"Oh, I see." His mother tapped her finger on the

page. "I believe I'll take a trip to the zoo, Mr. Clarkly. I'd love to see a pair as sweet as these two."

"Nurse Goodhew!" she called, when it looked as though the nurse would sink down into the chair at her desk. "If my husband finds a suitable room to lock me up in, I will be bringing a boxcar full of belongings. I'll not even leave him a pair of my bloomers."

She glared at Mr. Bolt, then focused her attention back on the nurse. "Please show me where my goods will be stored. Naturally, I will require access to them day and night."

"We have plenty of room for whatever you bring."

As far as Goodhew would be concerned, the more of Mrs. Bolt's worldly goods she brought with her the better. As part of his investigation Trace had discovered that the nurse sold the patients' personal belongings to add a tidy amount to her already high wages.

"We don't think of our guests as being shut away, Mrs. Bolt. We treat them as we would our own dear families. Hanispree is a resort more than anything else." Goodhew pointed to the door behind her. "There ought to be room for all your things back in storage."

It took all his self-control not to snort at the lie. Behind that door were things far more precious than belongings to be stored.

"I'll have a look. Since my husband is dumping me here, I might as well see to it."

"We'll think of all that tomorrow, after we've seen to your comfort. Let me find you a lovely room down the hall, then your husband can be on his way."

"You'll rue the day you did this to me, Mr. Bolt."

"Mr. Hanispree, my wife is not herself these days. She's a bit addled, if you know what I mean." His father touched his temple, then slipped the money back into his pocket. "I'll see to the room now. Kindly lead the way."

Hanispree gave Bolt what ought to have been a cordial smile, but on his corrupt face it was a mask.

"As it happens we have a few lovely rooms available just down this hall."

"Mr. Hanispree!" Nurse Goodhew hustled out from behind the desk. "Now would not be the time to show our best rooms. Some of the patients are receiving treatments."

There were no patients in there, only a captive. Time was up; Trace needed to get to Bethany before the doctor gave her a "treatment" that she would never recover from.

"I'll come along." Trace walked up to his father and stood shoulder to shoulder with him. "The treatments will certainly go easier with a book to read. I'm sure that Mr. Bolt would appreciate seeing an example of the care his wife will receive at your hands."

Nurse Goodhew shot him a look. She clearly didn't trust him. "I'll be back shortly," she said, giving his mother a nod. "I'm going to find you a nice big storage room."

Trace's mother frowned. The otters were in danger was what she would be thinking.

"Not a single one of these rooms is up to standard, Mr. Hanispree. My wife is used to being pampered in every detail. You do have servants? I haven't seen any."

Hanispree had not hesitated to open each door on the ground floor, and most of them on the second.

Wherever they had put Bethany, it wasn't here.

"I've a capital idea!" Trace exclaimed. "Mr. Bolt, why don't you have the attic remodeled for your wife?"

"Couldn't hurt to see the place, might have some nice views. Are there windows up there, Mr. Hanispree?"

"Not a single one. The attic won't do for your wife at all."

Because that's where Bethany was.

"Nonsense." His father clamped his fist over Hanispree's arm. "I insist on seeing it. Lead the way."

Trace didn't wait to be led anywhere. He dropped the books and dashed toward the back stairs at the end of the hall.

Nurse Goodhew's voice brought him up short.

"Mr. Hanispree!" she shouted from the landing

of the stairs. "I found this heathen child in the storage area. I believe he belongs to you?"

"Indeed he does." Alden Hanispree strode forward and took the struggling, gagged boy from Goodhew. "What about the other one?"

"I'll fetch her right away." Goodhew snorted. "I believe we've found our ghosts, Mr. Hanispree."

"Why is the boy gagged?" Trace asked.

"He is a detestable child with much too much to say." She rubbed her backside as she retreated down the hall.

"Mr. Bolt." Hanispree squeezed Jess's shoulder, making him wince. "If you wouldn't mind coming back tomorrow?"

Trace leaped from the second step of the attic stairway, on the run. He shoved Hanispree to the floor and caught Jess to him. The gag was tight. The more Trace worked at the knot, the harder it held.

A moan drifted down the hallway, sliding along the walls and creeping across the floor.

An apparition appeared bit by bit. She came into view slowly, appearing at the top of the stairs. First her head, then her shoulders, and at last the rest of her ghoulish self.

Trace continued to work at the wet bindings, but couldn't avert his gaze from his sister's performance.

She drifted toward Hanispree, where he lay sprawled on the floor. She hunched her shoulders and stretched out her arms, reaching for him.

"Killer…" she wailed. "Murderer…"

"Keep her away from me," he squealed.

"Her who?" Trace's father asked, reaching down a hand. "Your nurse has already gone downstairs."

Hanispree began to sputter words that made no sense. He wagged his finger at Hannah. "The woman who looks like she drowned," he finally yelped in a trembling voice.

Trace and his father glanced about. They shrugged their shoulders.

"Show me the attic, man. There's no one here but me and the librarian…and this boy who has been treated so miserably."

Clearly, Jess had something to say, but with the gag in his mouth his words were stifled. Trace worked harder at the knot while Jess tried to pull the cloth away.

"Hold still, Jess. It's beginning to loosen."

The boy stood as still as he could, but Trace felt the tension strung tight inside him.

Hannah "levitated" forward, moaning. She drew a web of moss across Hanispree's face. He scurried backward, looking like a crab trying to escape a seagull.

"You killed me!" she moaned.

"I never killed anybody, I swear it!"

"You drowned me in the pond…oooh."

Actually, the pond was frozen, and Alden wouldn't have been able to do that if he had tried.

Luckily, the man was too panicked to notice Hannah's mistake.

"I suppose a murderer might be haunted, don't you agree, Mr. Bolt?"

"It would be hard to avoid that."

Jess stamped his foot.

Hanispree clawed at his collar. "I didn't kill you. You're…"

All of a sudden he lunged to his feet and ran for the attic stairs.

They all followed. Hanispree stopped at one of several doors in the dim attic and fished a key ring out of his pocket, his fingers skittering over the choices. He selected one, then opened the door, banging it hard against the wall.

"There you are!" he shouted. "Sound and hale! I never killed anyone."

Not yet, at any rate. In the center of the room was a chair with straps—a spinner. It was a device that was supposed to spin patients until the blood left their head, and with it their mental illness.

It whirled and clicked as it turned. This was a torture that could go on for hours in the name of treatment.

Jess ran to his mother and hugged her about the waist.

The person in the spinning chair was Dr. Merlot, his face green, and vomit stinking up the front of his jacket.

Served the fellow right for messing with one of the Preston women.

Trace would have laughed had it not been for the fact that Jess's panic didn't subside with finding his mother.

Bethany, apparently more adept at knots than he was, yanked the gag from her son's head in under ten seconds.

"Perryman took Auntie Lilleth!" he shouted.

Bethany folded her boy in her arms and rocked him, wept over him. "Where, Jess?"

"I don't know. That nurse grabbed me before I could find out."

Jess turned to his uncle, but didn't leave the safety of his mother's arms. "Since it wasn't Ma that you killed, you must have let Perryman kill Auntie Lils. There's still the spare ghost."

Trace's sister shook her weeds at Hanispree and screeched.

The man shook his head. Drool pooled in the corners of his mouth and, by heaven, he had peed his pants.

Trace was at Alden's throat, squeezing, threatening, and wishing he could kill the man. "Where the hell is Lilleth?"

Hannah drifted forward. She draped her funeral gauze over Alden's pasty face.

"Gardener's shed…in the woods," he croaked.

Trace didn't feel the stairs beneath his shoes, nor

his lungs aching or his heart beating, but he did notice the inmates gathered in front of the fireplace in the lobby.

He took in the details of the scene as he dashed out the front door.

A dozen people in tattered clothing turning their cold bodies in circles, warming to the flames. Mrs. Murphy blew him a kiss.

His mother smiled and cooed to Mary. Nurse Goodhew cursed out loud, because she had been tied to the chair behind her desk.

The door to the prison rooms stood wide-open.

It seemed that her only weapon would be the stake, if she could even grasp it with her hands tied behind her back.

The very thought of using that metal shaft made her shiver. Last time she had defended herself with something pointed, Trace had nearly lost his life.

If she thought that Trace wouldn't find her, she would use it with barely a breath of hesitation.

But he would find her eventually, once he realized she was missing. The man did follow clues for a living.

She would have to escape on her own—and soon. How could she ever draw another breath if the same thing happened again? History had been known to repeat itself.

Suddenly the sharpened metal underneath her felt as a much a threat as a help.

"You look scared, lady."

"What?" Perryman hadn't spoken in some time, and in her worry over the spike she hadn't noticed that he was staring at her as if she were his dinner. "Well, yes I am. Trembling, in fact."

"I have to punish you." He stood up, awkward limbed, looking like a gaunt scarecrow rising from a pumpkin patch.

"Not if you don't want to."

Oh, dear. The flash of his grin, malicious in the lamplight, told her that he did want to. That he would enjoy it.

"You did bean me with the shovel. It hurt right smart. You insulted me."

"Surely you can understand a mother wanting to protect her children."

"Surely can't. My mother was a slut. Turned me away before I knew how to call her one. Besides, you ain't nobody's mother."

"My mother was a slut, too." Maybe common ground would soothe him. "But I loved her just the same."

"Then you were a fool." He clapped his hands. "Let's eat."

Incredibly, in spite of the cold, Perryman began to undress. His flesh pebbled, but that didn't stop him from removing every stitch.

His naked body and Trace's resembled each other in the same way that a sway-backed nag resembled a wild stallion.

Ribs and hip bones jutting out from his gaunt flesh made him appear a ghoulish creature who might have escaped from the pages of one of Trace's horror books.

While he struggled with the knot on a small black bag, Lilleth thought frantically. How would she outwit him?

"There you are, you pretty little beast," Perryman murmured, drawing something dark and squirming out of the bag.

"Eat it." He squatted before her. "Chew it slow… and smile when you swallow it."

No! No matter what, she would not eat the inch-long stinkbug struggling between Perryman's grimy fingernails.

He pinched it and smeared its guts against her lips. She wanted to gag, to scream, but that would mean opening her mouth. Panic threatened the edges of her control. She shivered with the effort of containing it.

She would not be forced to this vileness, to be a victim of his depravity. If she ate the insect, what would come next? She suspected this was only the first of many wicked things that he planned to force upon her.

Her lips felt slick with the bug ooze that he'd

smeared there. She turned her head, wiped her mouth on her shoulder. She spit.

"That wasn't polite." He dug in the bag again. "Maybe something more moist? More squirmy? I don't like to eat alone. That would offend me."

He stared at her chest, tilting his head this way and that. He licked his lips.

Placing a hand between her breasts, he pushed her down to the dirt.

She struggled, but it was all for show. If she were going to use her weapon, she would need to be lying flat to reach it. If she lay down of her own accord, he would become suspicious.

So she cowered in the dirt, giving a show of fear and submission. And the truth was, she had never been this frightened of a man.

Bent at an awkward angle, her arms hurt. She breathed deeply and steadily in an attempt to ignore the pain.

She gripped the spike, watching for her moment and praying that it would be soon.

History could not repeat. Trace was not here. He couldn't be injured.

Perryman came down upon her slowly, his chest and his hips pressing her against the dirt. He touched her lips with what could only be a giant maggot. It squirmed and so did he.

It was this moment or not at all.

Lilleth clutched the cold metal in her tied fists.

Her elbows felt as if they would pop at the joints. She wanted to vomit.

The memory of the sound of Trace's flesh tearing, the scent of his blood and the stickiness of it on her hands, made her scream. She didn't want to. It weakened her.

She bit Perryman's ear. He screeched and jerked up far enough for her to turn and lift the blade.

To her complete horror, she spotted Trace standing in the doorway of the shed, his face consumed with anger, his teeth clenched in rage.

He lunged. The tip of the spike was pointed at his chest.

Lilleth tried to move it out of the way, but Perryman's weight held her. Just as before, she could do nothing to prevent the disaster unfolding.

This time Trace would die. She would kill him by her own hand.

Lilleth shrieked. The howl filled her head. She heard the crunching of bone. The scent of blood filled her nose.

She managed to lift her knees. She ground them into Perryman's belly, shoving his weight away from her.

Arms grabbed her, held her tight. Someone picked her up off the ground to take her who knew where. Frenzied, she kicked out, gnashing her teeth, seeking his throat.

"Lils." The arms around her began to rock. A

large, firm hand stroked her hair. It cradled her head to a stallion's chest. "It's all right, Lils, I've got you."

Jess rushed forward. He wrapped his arms about her and Trace.

"It's all right, Auntie," he said, out of breath. "You're safe now. We all are, even Ma."

"Bethany?" Lilleth looked about through tear-flooded eyes and saw her sister, clutching her skirt high and rushing through the door of the shed. Trace made room for Bethany in the hug.

Other people gathered in the doorway. A middle-aged woman Lilleth did not know brushed a tear from her eye.

A man who looked like Trace, but a generation older, held Alden in front of him. Hanispree struggled, but the man had his arm locked around his neck.

"Kidnapping carries a hearty penalty," a young woman said. She strode in the door, swiping moss away from her face.

She walked up to Perryman, who was detained in the corner by a big, if thin, man Lilleth recognized as one of the inmates.

"Quit your blubbering, man," the young woman said. "It's only a broken nose."

"Cover that man up. He's perfectly revolting," the middle-aged woman said to Trace.

He kissed Lilleth, then went and plucked a filthy rag from the corner and dropped it on Perryman.

Lilleth hugged her sister's neck, and they both wept. Jess patted their shoulders.

After a moment she looked for Trace. He stood beside the moss-covered woman dressed in gauze, speaking quietly to her. The woman glanced at Lilleth and smiled, then clapped her hands.

When Trace came back to her, she lifted his coat, skimming her hands over his shirt, searching for blood. "I thought for sure I'd stabbed you."

"I thought so, too." He touched his shirt where the old scar was. "Saw the spike coming right at me."

"I couldn't turn it away. I tried.... I don't know how...."

"It was Pa that turned the stake away." Jess looked at his mother.

Bethany cupped his cheeks, then kissed his forehead. "I'm sure it was," she answered. "He watches over us from above."

"Not above, Ma. Right here. I saw him as clear as I'm seeing you. He pushed the point of the spike down. After that he went over to Uncle Alden and kicked him in the butt."

Alden Hanispree fainted. The man holding him let him drop, then anchored him with a boot to the chest.

"I understand, son," Bethany said. "It's been a frightening day. It's only natural that you might imagine your father's ghost was here. But in the light of day, there is no such thing."

"Mrs. Murphy wouldn't say so," Jess answered. "But Pa wasn't a ghost, he was more like an angel."

"I believe you, Jess." Lilleth spoke up for him.

She did believe it. Trace had been coming down on that spike. She was not the one who had moved it out of the way.

"So do I," Trace declared. "Never expected to say so, but the fact is, I'm not dead and I ought to be."

"There's more to the universe than we mortals can understand," the pretty older woman declared. She smiled and she, too, looked like Trace. "I understand there's to be a wedding."

Trace stood before the fireplace in the library, kissing his bride…at last. At long last.

The ceremony hadn't taken place the moment Bethany had been freed, because according to the women of the family, weddings involved more than just the bride and groom being willing.

To his dismay, they had swept Lilleth away an hour after the town marshal had come to escort the criminals to jail, and they had not let Trace near her since.

It had taken four very long days to arrange things to the ladies' satisfaction. Lace ribbons and satin sashes draped the library from ceiling to floor in what he had been assured was a romantic setting to thrill his bride.

As far as he was concerned, a romantic setting

would be Lilleth wearing nothing but blushing skin, soaking in the bath or reclining on the bed...or the stairs.

Since his mother, his sister, and Bethany, too, had their hearts set on all the frills and frippery, the only thing to do was grin through each prewedding task.

At last a feast was prepared and a guest invited. Mrs. Murphy had been confused at first. Wasn't Lilleth already Trace's spirit bride?

Happy events, Lilleth had explained to her, were often repeated in the great beyond, given that folks had eternity to celebrate. This pleased Mrs. Murphy no end.

Cooper had come for the wedding, but had been no help in rushing Trace to the altar. Very clearly, he had taken a shine to Bethany...and Bethany had taken, if not a fancy, at least an interest in him.

With Alden going to jail for a very long time, Bethany had become the new owner of the mental hospital. Seeing to the inmates' comfort and moving them all to the fancy wing of the facility had taken time away from hammering down the wedding details.

The longest delay had been due to the wedding gown. Trace's mother, Hannah and Bethany had fussed over the secret garment for all the four days.

In the end, with the waiting finished, he had to admit it was worth the delay.

His Lils glided toward him looking as if she were

wrapped in the mists of heaven. A lump lodged smack in his throat when she smiled at him.

They stood in front of his brother Jace to recite their vows. Jace was the only Ballentine to not take a position in the family business. His was a higher calling, as he liked to explain.

Finally, the promises were given. Lils was Trace's from this day forward. He was hers for now and forever more.

Cheers erupted in the library. Lilleth and Trace were now "the Ballentines." A couple, man and wife.

After a lifetime of wishing, he was finally kissing his bride. His mind itched with visions of things to come later.

A tap on his shoulder reminded him that this was not later.

"I'd like to welcome my daughter-in-law, son," his mother said.

She wrapped Lilleth in a great hug and whispered in her ear. When his mother transferred her to his father for a welcome, he whispered things, too. Things that made Lilleth grin and nod her head.

If he'd eavesdropped correctly, his father had just given Lilleth a job. Trace would have something to say about her being a spy. He didn't like it. One investigator in the family was treacherous enough.

Trace snatched his wife back from her brand-new father-in-law and tucked her close to his side. She was his, and that meant protecting her.

"There's a rule against working in the field when you become a mother," he whispered in her ear.

"Don't be silly, Trace." She wrapped her arms around his neck, looked him in the eye, then rose up on her toes to kiss him. "That's a weak rule, according to your sister."

"Rules are rules," he recited.

"And yet you broke the biggest one of all, and here you are, employed and forgiven."

"And given a raise," he grumbled.

"Life is going to be grand." She patted his cheek. "Not a dull moment."

"I'm thinking of keeping the library open, right here in Riverwalk." That sounded safe.

"You'd die of boredom and make me miserable in the process."

Lilleth wriggled out from under his arm and dashed across the room to embrace her sister.

That one action told him just what life would be like. He would try and hold Lils to him, to protect her as a man ought to, and she would dash away and do whatever she wanted.

Life with Lilleth Ballentine would not be a sweet and predictable fairy tale. He thanked God for that. It would be earthy, exciting and wonderful. She had been right when she told him he would be bored with the life of a librarian, even if it was in the name of safety.

Candlelight, satin swags and the aromas of the

feast did make for a night of romance. In spite of his impatience to get to this moment, Trace wouldn't have changed an instant of it.

The guests would leave soon. Then the night would belong to him and his bride.

The front door opened. Sarah blew inside on a dark cold wind, carrying the latest books she had borrowed. The little girl shivered in her thin coat. It was well past the time that she ought to be out.

Trace took a step toward her, then stopped when he spotted Jess doing the same. The look on the boy's face was one that he remembered on his own face many years ago.

Jess was smitten. He walked toward little Sarah in a Cupid-induced trance.

Sarah smiled at him. Jess grinned back and lifted the books from her arms.

That just went to show that love was timeless. As far as Mrs. Murphy was concerned it crossed eternity.

Trace caught Lilleth's gaze from where she stood across the room, speaking to her sister. He nodded his head toward Jess, who shifted from foot to foot, looking nervous and enraptured all at once.

Lilleth elbowed her sister in the ribs, then discreetly pointed toward the children.

Bethany covered her mouth with her hand to hide a chuckle. Lilleth whispered in her ear, and whatever she said made her sister's eyes widen in horror.

Lilleth laughed out loud, then looked at Trace, the love in her eyes as tangible as a kiss.

His bride touched her heart. She winked and blew him a kiss.

* * * * *

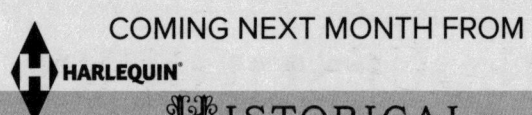

REQUEST YOUR FREE BOOKS!

 HARLEQUIN® HISTORICAL:
Where love is timeless

2 FREE NOVELS PLUS 2 FREE GIFTS!

YES! Please send me 2 FREE Harlequin® Historical novels and my 2 FREE gifts (gifts are worth about $10). After receiving them, if I don't wish to receive any more books, I can return the shipping statement marked "cancel." If I don't cancel, I will receive 6 brand-new novels every month and be billed just $5.44 per book in the U.S. or $5.74 per book in Canada. That's a savings of at least 16% off the cover price! It's quite a bargain! Shipping and handling is just 50¢ per book in the U.S. and 75¢ per book in Canada.* I understand that accepting the 2 free books and gifts places me under no obligation to buy anything. I can always return a shipment and cancel at any time. Even if I never buy another book, the two free books and gifts are mine to keep forever.

246/349 HDN F4ZY

Name _____ (PLEASE PRINT)

Address _____ Apt. #

City _____ State/Prov. _____ Zip/Postal Code

Signature (if under 18, a parent or guardian must sign)

Mail to the **Harlequin® Reader Service:**
IN U.S.A.: P.O. Box 1867, Buffalo, NY 14240-1867
IN CANADA: P.O. Box 609, Fort Erie, Ontario L2A 5X3

Want to try two free books from another line?
Call 1-800-873-8635 or visit www.ReaderService.com.

* Terms and prices subject to change without notice. Prices do not include applicable taxes. Sales tax applicable in N.Y. Canadian residents will be charged applicable taxes. Offer not valid in Quebec. This offer is limited to one order per household. Not valid for current subscribers to Harlequin Historical books. All orders subject to credit approval. Credit or debit balances in a customer's account(s) may be offset by any other outstanding balance owed by or to the customer. Please allow 4 to 6 weeks for delivery. Offer available while quantities last.

Your Privacy—The Harlequin® Reader Service is committed to protecting your privacy. Our Privacy Policy is available online at www.ReaderService.com or upon request from the Harlequin Reader Service.

We make a portion of our mailing list available to reputable third parties that offer products we believe may interest you. If you prefer that we not exchange your name with third parties, or if you wish to clarify or modify your communication preferences, please visit us at www.ReaderService.com/consumerschoice or write to us at Harlequin Reader Service Preference Service, P.O. Box 9062, Buffalo, NY 14269. Include your complete name and address.

HH13R

Visit Edinburgh with Ann Lethbridge and fall for rugged rogue Logan—the notorious Gilvry brothers are the hottest Highlanders around!

"She held still, as if she had not noticed the growing warmth in the room. The heat between them. And then he lifted her hand in his, carefully, as if it could be broken by his greater strength. Eyes fixed on her face, he turned it over and, bending his head, touched his lips to her palm. A warm velvety brush of his mouth against sensitive skin. A whisper of hot breath. Sensual. Melting.

Her insides clenched. Her heart stopped, then picked up with a jolt and an uneven rhythm. She felt like a girl again, all hot and bothered and unsure. And full of such longings. Such desires.

But the woman inside her knew better. She craved all that kiss offered. The heat. The bliss. Carnal things that shamed her. Things she had resolved never to want again. They left her vulnerable. A challenge she could not let go unanswered. To do so would be to admit he had touched her somehow.

"Charity," he said softly, as he lifted his head to look at her, still cradling her hand in his large warm one, his thumb gently stroking. "Never in my life have I met a woman like you."

The words rang with truth. And they pleased her. She leaned closer and touched her lips to his, let them linger, cling softly, urging him to respond. And he did. Gently at first, with care, as if he thought she might take offence or be frightened. Then more forcefully, his mouth moving against hers as he angled his head, his free hand coming up to cradle her nape while the other retained its hold. The feel of his lips sent little thrills spiraling outward from low in her belly. On a gasp she opened her mouth and, with little licks and tastes and deep rumbling groans in his chest, he explored her. The gentleness of it was her undoing.

The way he delved and plundered her mouth as if making the discovery for the very first time was incredibly alluring. If she didn't know better, she might have thought this was his first time. Passion hummed in her veins. Dizzied her mind. Sent her tumbling into a blaze of desire.

He drew back, his chest rising and falling as if he, too, could not breathe, his gaze searching her face. And she melted in the heat in his eyes.

Has this bad boy Highlander finally met his match with English bad girl Charity? This time around, two wrongs could just make a right....

Don't miss
FALLING FOR THE HIGHLAND ROGUE
by Ann Lethbridge, out December 2013,
only in Harlequin® Historical!

Suddenly, Emma had an odd feeling that she was being watched.

Of course, she had this feeling whenever she was in New York, where guys watching girls and girls watching guys was practically a national pastime, but this feeling was different.

Emma shivered. Being watched in New York doesn't have quite the same safe feeling as being watched on Sunset Island, *Emma thought to herself. She turned around slowly.*

"Oh, my God," she breathed.

There was a guy watching her. But he didn't look terribly dangerous to her. He was tall, dressed in sneakers, jeans, and a New York University T-shirt. He had a thick shock of curly dark hair, piercing blue eyes, and a broad smile that spread across his face.

It was Adam Briarly. Gorgeous Adam. Sam's half-brother.

The SUNSET ISLAND series
by Cherie Bennett

Also created by Cherie Bennett

Sunset Glitter

CHERIE BENNETT

Sunset™
Island

SPLASH™

A BERKLEY / SPLASH BOOK

SUNSET GLITTER is an original publication of The Berkley Publishing Group. This work has never appeared before in book form.

SUNSET GLITTER

A Berkley Book / published by arrangement with General Licensing Company, Inc.

PRINTING HISTORY
Berkley edition / February 1994

For J.G.—tender

Sunset Glitter

ONE

"Ah, yes, this is the life. Am I right or am I right?" Sam Bridges sighed blissfully to her best friends, Emma Cresswell and Carrie Alden, as she stretched herself out to full length in the hot tub all three of them occupied. They were in New York City, at Emma's Aunt Liz's loft in Soho.

"You are definitely right," Carrie agreed, luxuriating in the feel of hot bubbles on the back of her neck.

"This is clearly the life I was meant for," Sam continued. "Now all I need is a really cute guy fanning the sweat from my perfect brow—"

"How about a couple of really cute guys?" Emma suggested with a laugh. "Why stop at one?"

"You're right," Sam agreed. "I'll take an even dozen." She let her red hair swirl around in the hot, bubbly water. "Imagine having a hot tub in your own home," Sam mused. She looked over at Emma. "Well, I suppose you do, right?"

"Well, my mother does," Emma admitted. In fact, at her mother's mansion in Boston there was both an indoor and an outdoor hot tub. There was a time when Sam's teasing Emma about being rich really bothered her—but she was used to it now.

"We picked a good time to come to New York," Carrie said, "when your aunt is out of town, Emma. She must miss this place."

"Don't feel too bad for my aunt." Emma grinned. "She's in Paris on business."

"Who needs Paris when we have this?" Sam cracked, waving her hands expansively around the loft they had taken over in Liz's absence. The high-ceilinged, open-design apartment really was impressive—it was huge and was furnished simply and sparsely, so that the overall impression was one of endless space. And space, in cramped and crowded New York City, was an exquisite luxury.

"When did you say your aunt was coming back?" Carrie asked Emma, moving around in the tub so that a soothing jet of water propelled from one of the sides hit her more directly on her neck.

"Soon," Emma replied.

"How soon?" Sam asked.

Emma smiled slowly. "Oh, in about two months."

"Yes!" Sam exclaimed. "I'm liking this more and more. In fact, I'm ready to move in."

Carrie laughed. "I don't think our employers would want to give us *that* much time off!"

Carrie, Emma and Sam had arrived in New York City the day before. By the greatest of luck, all three girls had found themselves temporarily free from work obligations.

"Anyway," Carrie continued, "most New Yorkers do not live like this."

"I am not most New Yorkers," Sam replied regally.

"You're not any kind of New Yorker," Carrie teased her. "You're from Kansas."

"Oh, thank you *so* much for reminding me," Sam snorted sarcastically.

Aunt Liz's loft was, Sam had to admit, pretty grand. Liz was Emma's mother's sister, and while she had an important job with the Environmental Defense Fund that required her to spend a lot of time traveling—often in exotic locales—she didn't earn nearly enough money in that public-interest job to afford this loft.

That's where Liz's family money came into

play. It allowed her to purchase the three-thousand-square-foot fifth-story loft right on Spring Street in New York's exciting Soho district—an area abounding with art galleries, restaurants and culture. And it was the same family money that gave Emma Cresswell a trust fund so big that Sam and Carrie still had a hard time fathoming it.

Actually, all three girls had a hard time fathoming that they had become best friends. They couldn't be more different from one another if they had come from different planets in the solar system. Emma was petite, blond and very rich, and had been educated at a private boarding school in Switzerland before she had begun attending Goucher College in Maryland. She came from Boston money, was an only child, and wanted to go into the Peace Corps. She also had the best manners Carrie and Sam had ever seen.

Sam, on the other hand, was Emma's opposite. Tall and thin, with wild red hair, Sam came from a small town in Kansas and dreamed of being a big-time star. She was an extremely talented dancer, and she attracted guys like bees to honey.

Carrie was totally different from either Sam or Emma. She hailed from Teaneck, New Jersey (a suburb not more than ten miles from Aunt Liz's loft), and had brown hair and a curvy (she thought *too* curvy) figure. Carrie had recently finished her freshman year at Yale and she planned to be a photojournalist. In fact, some of her pictures had been published in *Rock On* magazine.

The three of them had met at the International Au Pair Convention in New York City the previous year, and then had lucked out, all finding summer jobs with families on fabulous Sunset Island, a resort island off the coast of southern Maine. During their time on the island, they had become inseparable friends. "All for one and one for all," Sam had put it many times.

Buzzz! The buzzer for the front door intercom of Aunt Liz's loft sounded.

"It's gotta be the Chinese food," Sam said. "Who's gonna get the door? Not me." She sunk further into the steaming tub.

"Mmmm!" Carrie sighed, as she closed her eyes, pretending to be asleep.

"Hey, that's not fair!" Emma cried, but she smiled as the buzzer sounded again. She got out of the hot tub, slipped a robe over her dripping bathing suit, and went to answer the buzzer.

"Come on up!" Emma said into the intercom, after finding out who wanted to get into the building. She then waited to unlock the double deadbolt until she could see the delivery person through the door's peephole.

Emma paid the young Chinese delivery guy and arranged the white take-out containers on Liz's living room floor.

Sam breathed in deeply. "I'm outta here!" she announced, climbing out of the tub and toweling off. "Only thing better than a hot tub is food!"

"I'm hungry too," Carrie said. "Anyway, I don't think I could sit in there much longer."

"No plates?" Sam asked dubiously, coming into the living room with Carrie.

"Nope," Carrie replied.

"New York tradition," Emma explained.

"What?"

"It's traditional—you eat right from the container, if you want to impress anyone," Carrie added.

"What's that?" Sam asked, pointing to one open container that had a sort of violet-white tinge to its contents.

"Squid," Emma reported. "Prepared in its own salt water ink."

Sam stared at her. "You're kidding, right?"

"Wrong," Emma replied, reaching for that container.

Sam made a face. "Major barf-out! Fish go to the bathroom in the ocean." She reached for a different container—one containing pieces of stir-fried chicken with cashew nuts mixed in—took a fork, and took a bite.

"Heaven," she pronounced. "Hey, how'd they deliver this so quickly?"

"Bicycles," Emma said. "Next time we pass a Chinese place, look in front."

"I can't believe they deliver this late!" Sam exclaimed, looking at her watch. It was well past eleven o'clock.

"The city never sleeps," Emma mumbled, her mouth full.

"Sounds like a great summer job, doing delivery," Carrie ventured.

"Not!" Sam decided. "I've seen the traffic out there. It sounds tougher than babysitting, which is as tough as I want to see my life get."

For several minutes, there was silence except for the satisfied sounds of the girls eating their late dinner.

"Okay," Sam said finally, taking one more bite of cashew chicken and then a big slug of Coke. "I feel human again."

"I feel ready for bed," Carrie moaned.

"We're not going nightclubbing?" Sam asked, a note of disappointment in her voice.

"Another night," Emma said, agreeing with Carrie. "I'm wiped out."

"I'm not," Sam said grumpily. Then her

face lit up. "Well, I guess there's only one thing for me to do. . . ."

"Don't go out by yourself," Emma said quickly. She knew that Sam was not above venturing out solo and getting into all sorts of misadventures.

"I'll find a job," Sam said decisively.

"A job?" Emma repeated, looking at Sam as if she were crazy.

"What are you talking about?" Carrie asked. "We're here to have fun."

"Girlfriend," Sam said quickly, reaching for a newspaper she had stowed in her black backpack, "I am in the show biz capital of the world now, and I intend to make the most of it."

She spread the newspaper out on the floor next to the now-empty Chinese food containers. It was *Back Stage*, a weekly show business tabloid that carried news and articles about the business, along with announcements of auditions for shows, revues, films, and other performing arts events.

Sam started flipping pages and scanning the list of auditions. Carrie looked over Sam's shoulder and pointed at one of the audition notices.

"This is perfect for you," Carrie said, her voice deadpan. She winked at Emma.

Emma started to read the notice out loud.

"Auditions will be held for tall dancers for a tour of Japan—"

"Hold it hold it hold it!" Sam cut her off. "I'm not going through that again!" The previous summer, Sam had been hired to dance in Japan and found out at the very last minute that it was actually a prostitution scam.

"How about this, then?" Emma suggested, pointing to a notice on the next page.

"Ugh!" Sam reacted.

"Why not?" Carrie asked reasonably. "You'd be perfect. It's a childrens' theater that needs dancers."

"It's enough I once had to *be* a child," Sam sniffed. "Now you're asking me to perform for them. No way!" Carrie and Emma left Sam reading *Back Stage*, and started unpacking some of the things they'd purchased that afternoon.

Just then the phone rang. The girls looked at each other, puzzled. It was almost midnight. Who would be calling them at that hour?

Emma shrugged and picked up the phone.

"Liz Barrington's home, Emma Cresswell speaking," she said. Then she listened carefully as the voice on the other end of the phone apparently went on and on.

"Who is it?" Sam finally hissed.

Emma took the phone off her shoulder and handed it to Sam. "It's for you," she said.

"Me?"

"You," Emma said emphatically, a grin crossing her face. No one noticed as Emma reached over and pushed the speakerphone button so that she and Carrie could hear the entire conversation.

"Sam Bridges," Sam said.

"Sam, darling," a male voice blared, "I've been searching all over the country for you."

"Who is this?" Sam asked suspiciously.

"Oh, don't you know?" the voice asked.

"No, I don't know," Sam said impatiently, "So tell me!"

"Temper, temper," the voice said to her. "Must remain calm when the heat is on!"

"Listen, you jerk," Sam yelled, "just tell me who the hell you—"

"Now, Sam," the voice said, "calm yourself. You shouldn't talk to your former employer this way."

"What are you talking about?" Sam asked.

"My name," the voice said, "my favorite redheaded dancer, is Mr. Christopher."

"Mr. Christopher!" Sam exclaimed. "I'm so sorry, I mean, I—"

"No need to go on, dearheart," Mr. Christopher interrupted. "I'm just thrilled that I've tracked you down—I got this number from some hateful child on Sunset Island who said her name was Becky and she hoped you'd stay away until she was old enough to drive, which she informed me wouldn't be for two more years—"

"I babysit for her," Sam explained. "I'm sorry she was rude. She—"

"Not to worry," Mr. Christopher insisted. "Let's talk about why I've been trying so desperately to find you."

"Yes?" Sam asked, gripping the phone hard.

"Sam, darling, I want you to audition for my Broadway show!"

TWO

"Great, just great," Sam muttered to herself morosely.

She looked quickly around the audition hall, and her face fell. It was packed. Overpacked.

"You couldn't wedge one more skinny dancer in here if you tried," she sighed. *I had no idea that there were so many tall, thin, aspiring actresses and dancers in the New York metropolitan area. This sight is megadepressing. There is no way,* she thought, *that I'm ever getting this part. Mr. Christopher or no Mr. Christopher.*

Sam had her first brush with Mr. Christopher when she had worked at Disney World in Florida for a time, and Mr. Christopher was the choreographer of the stage shows there. And while he had fired Sam because her dancing was, as he termed it, "too origi-

13

nal," Sam knew Mr. Christopher really respected her talent.

He proved it some time later, when he needed a replacement dancer at the last minute for a show on Paradise Island in the Bahamas. Emma, Sam, and Carrie were on vacation there together, and Mr. Christopher put Sam into his show for the night with great results.

Sam turned to Emma and Carrie, who had agreed to come for moral support, even though she knew that once she was in the audition room, she was on her own.

"I'm screwed," she said, trying to muster a smile.

"There've got to be a hundred girls in here," Carrie marveled.

Emma tried to cheer Sam up. "But Mr. Christopher called you specially to audition. That should mean something," she said.

"Yeah," Sam retorted. "It means my audition will last twelve seconds instead of the usual ten. Look at how many people are trying for this part. I don't even know why he bothered calling me."

"Because you're a great dancer," Carrie said. "I think you sign in over there." She pointed to a long table at the end of the big room. The girls made their way over, and Sam approached the short, somewhat nerdy-looking guy sitting there. He reminded her a little of Howie Lawrence, one of their friends on Sunset Island.

"Yes?" he said, barely looking up.

"I'm here to audition," Sam said meekly. "For *Helen!*"

"You and the rest of the world," the guy said to her. "You sure you're not interested in another show?"

"Mr. Christopher told me to come," Sam replied, ignoring the guy's snide remark.

"Oh, really?"

"Yes," Sam repeated firmly. "Really."

"Well," the audition monitor said, "I haven't heard that line for at least thirty seconds, so it does appear you're at least average for creativity. What's your name?"

"Bridges," Sam said, "Samantha Bridges."

"Equity card," he said, holding his hand out.

"I don't have one, but—"

"No card, no audition," the guy said. He looked behind Sam at the girl crowding her. "Next!"

"But Mr. Christopher really did call me," Sam began. "I've worked with him before. He knows I'm not in the union, but he said he'd arrange for me to get in—"

"You don't actually expect me to buy that one, do you?" the guy asked Sam.

"Yes, I do," Sam replied, heat coming to her face, "because I'm telling you the truth. And if you don't put my name on that list, I'm going to stomp into that room and interrupt the entire audition and Mr. Christopher is going to come out here and blame it all on you."

"Hey, you can't threaten me—" the guy said.

"I just did," Sam replied smugly.

"All right, you're number ninety-one, Samantha," the monitor said curtly. "They're doing dance first, acting second."

"Thanks," Sam said sweetly. She grinned at the impatient girl behind her and maneuvered to the corner of the room with her friends.

"Way to go, Sam," Carrie cheered.

"Well, I wasn't about to take no for an answer," Sam replied.

"So what do we do now?" Emma asked as she was jostled by a tall girl with long black hair.

"Wait," Sam said, sliding down the wall until she was sitting on the floor. "Don't let anyone step on me."

All around the room, girls were stretching, doing exercises, warm-ups, and other preparations, and Sam decided that was a good idea. She got up and stretched, too. The audition monitor kept calling in girls five at a time. It seemed to Sam that each group of five was in the room for about ten minutes or so, and that most of them left with very long faces.

Sam found out during the wait that this was the callbacks. The really big "cattle call" had been the day before.

"See," Emma said, "Mr. Christopher must really believe in you if he asked you to audition today without even being there yesterday."

Two hours passed. Emma and Carrie read magazines, while Sam simply sat and stretched and got more and more nervous as the room emptied out and more girls left the audition hall looking disappointed. Then, finally, her number was called.

"Dancers ninety through ninety-five!" the monitor yelled out.

Sam jumped to her feet.

"Wish me luck, you guys," she said to her friends.

"Break a leg," Carrie said for luck.

"Break both legs," Emma added.

Sam hitched up the sweatpants she was wearing over her skimpy black leotard and headed into the audition room. She could feel her heart racing a million miles a minute.

"Hey, number ninety-one!" the audition

monitor called to her as Sam entered the room, but Sam ignored him. *If he wants to apologize to me* now *he can just wait,* she said to herself. What was important were the people she was auditioning for, not the little creep who probably hadn't had a date since nursery school, she told herself. She was scared enough without dealing with him.

Who do I think I am, Samantha Bridges from Junction, Kansas, auditioning for a Broadway musical? I must be out of my mind, she found herself thinking. But she forced her long legs to walk across the room with the other four girls, trying to look as confident as she could.

She immediately spotted Mr. Christopher. He gave her a friendly wave.

"Hey, Sam," he said, "glad you could make it. Looking forward to seeing what you can do."

"Glad to be here," Sam said as nonchalantly as she could, noticing that the other four girls in her group were giving her stares of pure hatred.

Sam stripped off her sweats and took a look around the room. Next to Mr. Christopher was a dark, swarthy-looking mustached man in jeans and a cable-knit sweater.

That has to be the director, Sam thought.

And those two guys in the suits, they must be producers.

Mr. Christopher, who was apparently running this part of the audition, got to his feet.

"We'll begin with a simple combination—four patterns of eight," he said. "My assistant, Timmy, will do it for you, and then you'll do it together. Watch closely."

He flipped on a cassette player and nodded to Timothy, a slender, muscular blond-haired guy in dance pants. Timothy whirled through the combinations and Sam concentrated on every step, her mind reeling.

This is very, very tough, she realized, her heart hammering nervously in her chest.

"Simple, isn't it?" Mr. Christopher asked when Timothy finished dancing. Some girls nodded nonchalantly. Mr. Christopher did the combination a second time with Timothy, then he gave a quick look at Sam when he was done. His eyebrows went up into his hairline, and he grinned at her.

Suddenly she realized why. The combination was almost exactly what Mr. Christopher had used at Disney World! In fact, it seemed to Sam that Mr. Christopher recycled this combination at his show in Paradise Island, too!

I was just too nervous to realize it was the same thing! Sam realized, grinning back at

Mr. Christopher. *I can do this*, she thought. *I really can do it.*

When it came time for Sam to do the steps, her hopes came true. She pulled off the combination perfectly. She was great. In fact, she saw the director point directly at her, and whisper something to Mr. Christopher. Then Mr. Christopher stood up.

"You all can go," he said.

Sam's heart fell down to her knees.

"Except for Miss Bridges," he added. "You'll be back late this afternoon to read for us. See the stage manager on the way out, and he'll give you some sides."

Sam tried to stay cool as she thanked Mr. Christopher and was introduced to the director, Laszlo Comfort, but her heart was beating so fast she could barely breathe.

And what in the world are sides? she thought to herself as she closed the door behind her. Then she decided it didn't much matter. One way or another, she was going to find out.

She caught Emma and Carrie's eye and gave them a big thumbs-up sign and an even bigger grin. Then she screamed for happiness and jumped into the air, and she didn't care who saw her.

"Sam!" Emma's voice called to her. "Over here!"

Sam stood on tiptoe and looked over the sea of bodies that filled Washington Square Park in Greenwich Village near New York University, but though she'd heard Emma call to her she couldn't find the body that went with the voice. The girls had agreed that they would meet at the park following Sam's afternoon audition, but they had no idea that the park—only a half-mile around, if you walked all the way around the perimeter—would be such a zoo full of people.

"We're over here!" Carrie called, waving her arms wildly.

Sam looked toward the sound of the voice and finally spotted her friends, sitting with a bunch of people on the wall that ran around the dry fountain in the center of the park. The two of them were listening to a couple of guys playing Beatles songs on their guitars.

Sam ran over to her friends. She noticed how cute both of them looked. Emma had on a white lace vest and white shorts, and Carrie had on jeans and a Yale T-shirt. Sam had chosen a flowing red-and-white flowered minidress to wear to the second part of the audition, and she still had it on, along with her trademark red cowboy boots. "Having a blast, fellow foxes?"

"How'd it go?" Emma asked her breathlessly.

"Yeah, how was it?" Carrie asked.

Sam smiled modestly. "We'll see," she said mysteriously, "we'll see." Then she hooted with joy.

"Oh, my God, you actually think you got it?" Emma cried.

"I've got a really good chance," Sam said. "Mr. Christopher wants me in and I think the director has a crush on me."

"You think everything in pants has a crush on you," Carrie said with a laugh.

Sam grinned at one of the cute guitar players. "Well, they usually do," she replied serenely.

"That's not exactly the best way to get a part in a show," Emma said softly.

"Hey," Sam shot back, "I didn't say I had a crush on *him*. And anyway, he wouldn't give it to me if I couldn't dance and act."

"So," Carrie said, "tell us everything!"

"Let me get a soda first," Sam said, "then I'll meet you over at that bench." She cocked her head toward an empty bench near the grass. "I'm killer thirsty. You want?"

Carrie and Emma shook their heads, and Sam went over to a nearby hot dog vendor and bought herself a Sprite, and while she was at it, a hot dog with everything on it. Then, she went and sat with her friends.

"So?" Carrie urged.

"So," Sam said, biting into her hot dog, "this park is serious babe heaven. Look at all these guys!" As she was talking, a couple of cute guys with great tans walked past them. They were wearing baggy shorts and NYU T-shirts. "You see what I mean?"

"Don't change the subject on us," Carrie commanded.

"Yes, ma'am," Sam said obediently, polishing off her hot dog. "Okay, I was great." She launched into the full story about the rest of her audition, from the time she read from the "sides"—certain pages from the script that involved her character—to the end of the audition, when Laszlo Comfort asked her if he might take her to dinner sometime.

"Unbelievable," Emma exclaimed. "A Broadway director asked you out? So what did you say?"

"I said," Sam produced, "that everything depended on the next twenty-four hours."

"Wow," Carrie breathed. "You have major guts."

"I'm a natural at this," Sam said with glee.

"But what if he puts you in the show so he can go out with you, and then he expects you to put out?" Emma asked.

"Then his expectations will be dashed," Sam said breezily. "In other words, I ain't gonna do it."

"So when do you find out?" Carrie asked.

"About the role, or the date?" Sam responded.

"Both, apparently," Emma qualified with a sigh.

"Really soon," Sam said. "Probably tonight."

Emma and Carrie shared a look. "I just hope you know what you're doing," Emma finally said.

"Come on, you guys!" Sam exclaimed. "I do not have to do the wild thing with this director, I swear! I mean, he's famous! He could get a zillion girls in New York! If I get the part it's going to be because I deserve to get the part!"

"As long as he doesn't think it means he deserves to get you," Carrie replied darkly.

"You two definitely worry too much," Sam pronounced.

At that moment, a thin guy wearing a multi-colored knit hat and an Army-issue jacket walked past them, muttering the words "Smoke, sinse, smoke, sinse, smoke it up," over and over again. In fact, once the girls paid attention, it was clear that there were a lot of people doing exactly the same thing as they walked by.

"What's that all about?" Sam asked.

"Drugs," Carrie hastened to explain. "They're selling marijuana, and sinse means sinsimilla, a certain type of marijuana."

"How would you know?" Sam asked pointedly.

"Hey, I grew up in Teaneck," Carrie responded. "I spent enough time around here to know what's going on."

"Are you implying I don't?" Sam challenged.

"Yep," Emma said, "she is."

"Just checking," Sam responded with a shrug. "Wow! Look at that!"

She pointed to the outer edge of the park, where a couple of New York cops mounted on horseback were racing their mounts toward a couple of guys, one white, one black. They jumped off their horses, grabbed the two guys, who were putting up no resistance, and handcuffed them. Sam, Emma, and Carrie watched in amazement.

"So what's that about?" Sam asked Carrie.

Carrie shrugged. "Could be anything. But I'd say probably hard drugs—maybe speed or cocaine."

"They let the guys sell marijuana but arrest them for selling cocaine?" Sam asked.

"Jail cells," Emma intoned. "There're not enough of them for all the criminals."

"Wow," Sam breathed in reply.

"Of course," Carrie pointed out, "if no one bought the drugs, they'd all disappear anyway."

Sam sniffed the air. A few benches away from them, a couple of kids who looked like college students were smoking a joint together.

"What a waste of time," Emma commented, watching the kids inhaling. She turned back to her friends. "You guys ready to go?" Sam and Carrie nodded agreement.

"What do you want to do now?" Carrie queried.

Sam looked at her watch. "There's this killer movie I want to see at Bleecker Street Cinema," she said. "It starts in a half hour."

"What is it?" Emma asked.

"It's called *Harold and Maude*," Sam said. "My brother Adam told me about it. He said he'd kill me if I didn't see it."

Emma and Carrie nodded. Sam's brother— actually, her half-brother—really knew films. He was studying to be a director at the University of California at Los Angeles. All three girls had met Adam on a trip they had taken to California to meet Sam's birth family after Sam had found out she was adopted and had located her birth mother. While there, Emma and Adam had found themselves almost irresistibly attracted to each other.

"I've seen it," Emma said, with a gentle smile. "But I'll see it again."

"What's it about?" Carrie asked.

"Romance," Emma said blissfully.

"Oh," Carrie replied. "Sam's favorite subject."

"Between a very young man and a very old woman," Emma added.

"Sounds like Sam and this director, only in reverse," Carrie quipped.

"Shut up kindly," Sam commented. "Now come on, or we'll miss the movie."

So with the sound of police sirens, the busy city traffic, the guitar players singing, skateboarders and rollerbladers rolling along, and thousands of people conversing, Carrie, Emma, and Sam started walking south toward Bleecker Street.

THREE

"Let's detour here," Sam said suddenly, as they headed down Sullivan Street toward Bleecker.

"What for?" Carrie asked, "we'll be late. I hate missing the beginning of a movie."

Sam checked her watch. "Nah, we've got a couple of minutes. I'm hungry."

"You're always hungry," Carrie said.

"Can't help it, I'm a growing girl," Sam retorted.

"I wish I had your metabolism," Carrie lamented.

"Yeah, well, I wish I could fill out your bra," Sam replied.

The girls cracked up as Sam led the way to a corner pizzeria. Since the girls had arrived in New York, they'd gotten used to the fact that Sam had turned it into a personal mission to try a slice from every pizza joint they passed—and that was a considerable number already. New York had good pizza.

Sam led the way up to the counter and joined the line. Carrie and Emma followed her.

"You guys want a slice?" Sam asked.

Carrie said yes, Emma no. Sam got to the head of the line, ordered two slices, and the Greek counterman cut them for her from a pie that had just come out of the oven, put them on a double paper plate, and gave them to Sam. Sam paid and then led the way to a corner stand-up table, on which there were napkins and containers of powdered garlic and red pepper.

Suddenly, Emma had an odd feeling that she was being watched. Of course, she had this feeling whenever she was in New York, where guys watching girls and girls watching guys was practically a national pastime, but this feeling was different.

Emma shivered. *Being watched in New York doesn't have quite that same safe feeling as being watched on Sunset Island*, Emma thought to herself. She turned around slowly.

"Oh, my God," she breathed.

There *was* a guy watching her. But he didn't look terribly dangerous to her. He was tall, dressed in sneakers, jeans, and a New York University T-shirt. He had a thick shock of curly dark hair, piercing blue eyes, and a broad smile that spread across his face.

It was Adam Briarly. Gorgeous Adam. Sam's half-brother.

"Hi, Emma," he said easily, walking over to her.

Sam chortled and whooped. "Oh, I am everything!" she cried, in a child's sing-song. "I kept a secret, I kept a secret!"

Adam picked up the slice of pizza he'd been eating and made his way over. He embraced his half-sister, and then hugged both Carrie and Emma. And try as she could to avoid it, Emma felt a special thrill race through her body as Adam hugged her.

"What are you doing here?" Emma asked, unable to control herself.

"And how did you keep your sister's big mouth quiet?" Carrie asked.

Adam laughed. "One question at a time," he said.

"Emma's first," Sam ordered.

"Watch that bossy stuff," Adam playfully warned Sam.

"I'm allowed; I'm family," Sam answered.

"In that case," Adam said, "I'm here at NYU film school for a course in screenwriting. I won it. Full ride. Room and board and everything."

"Wow," Emma said, "that's great."

"You better believe it. I love New York. I come here whenever I can, especially for the film festivals. And as for Sam keeping her mouth shut," Adam continued, "I bribed her."

"With what?" Carrie asked.

"I promised I'd introduce her to Christian Slater if she'd help me surprise Emma and you," Adam explained, taking a bite from the crust of his pizza.

"You're taking a film course with Christian Slater?" Emma queried.

"No," Adam said easily, looking over at Sam. "Sue me. I lied."

Uh-oh, Emma thought to herself, *I can feel it starting. I could fall for this guy again. Only when I was with him in California there was Kurt, and I didn't want to betray Kurt. Now, there's no Kurt in my life. Kurt. Even thinking of him is still so painful.* She shook off the feeling. *Is Sam trying to get me together with Adam?*

While Adam went to get more napkins, Sam looked over at Emma. "You're psyched about this, right?"

"You could have asked me if I wanted to see him," Emma replied.

Sam put her hands on her hips. "Now, what fun would that be? And anyway, the fact that he was already in town made this meeting fate."

"Listen," Adam said, "I really do want to go see this movie. You all up for it?" He looked closely at Emma. "You okay about this?"

Emma stared back at him. She could feel that same intense attraction to him that she'd felt the very first time she'd met him. "I'm okay," she finally said, deciding then and there to not let herself get all introspective, to just have fun.

The four of them left the pizzeria laughing and joking, walked a block south on Sullivan past all the little shops and restaurants that lined both sides of the street, and turned left onto Bleecker.

"What a zoo!" Sam exclaimed, once she saw the narrow street clogged with cars, and the sidewalks jam-packed with tables and chairs from the outdoor cafes, even more restaurants, and even more shops.

"Just a couple of blocks more," Adam urged them on. "There it is, on the south side of the street!"

They made it in just before the movie started.

"Is this theater dark and air-conditioned?" Sam asked as they took out their money to pay for the tickets.

"Of course," Adam answered.

"Good," Sam said, "because once the movie starts I'm gonna beat you up for lying to me."

"What I don't get, Sam," Carrie said, as they made their way into the lobby of the theater, "is how you can stay so calm when sometime tonight—"

"Oh," Sam cut her off, "the part!"

"Yes," Emma said, "the part."

"I'm not worried about the phone call," Sam said insouciantly.

"Why not?" Emma asked.

"Your Aunt Liz has an answering machine," Sam answered. "It'll take the message just as well as if I were there."

Carrie shook her head. "I still marvel at your cool."

"I'll tell you the truth," Sam said. "Inside, I'm a total wreck worrying about the phone call. But you know my motto: Never let 'em see you sweat!"

"I thought your motto was two guys for every girl," Emma reminded Sam.

"Yeah, that's right," Sam agreed. "So, first I don't sweat, then I get in a Broadway show, and then I get the two guys! Life is a peach!"

"So," Adam said to Emma as the two of them stood on the nighttime deck of the Staten Island ferry, which plied the route between lower Manhattan and nearby Staten Island, "what did you think of the movie?"

"I still can't believe you're here!" Emma replied, not answering Adam's question.

Adam's face shone in the moonlight. "Believe it, Emma," he said. "And I'm glad I am."

After the movie, Emma and her friends had split up. Sam could only carry her too-cool act so far—she was desperate to go back to the loft to see if Laszlo Comfort had called. And Carrie had pleaded exhaustion, so she went back with Sam. Which left Emma and Adam on their own. Adam had suggested that the two of them catch one of the many ferries to Staten Island and back just for the fun of it, and Emma had quickly agreed.

"Cheapest thrill in Manhattan," Adam had said. "It's only fifty cents round-trip."

The two of them flagged down a taxicab on Bleecker Street and took the fifteen-minute ride—there was practically no traffic at that hour of the night—down to the Staten Island Ferry building and had taken the next ferry out. Now, they were on the return trip and the dramatic lights of the lower Manhattan skyline were the backdrop to their conversation.

"I never got a chance to really thank you about the wedding," Emma said, as the night air whooshed by them.

Adam laughed. "Don't thank me. I couldn't stand the thought of you getting married."

Me neither, I guess, Emma thought. *Back when I was about to marry Kurt, and had so many second thoughts, it was Adam who showed up on the island and helped me decide not to go through with it.*

Kurt. There was that "ping" of pain in Emma's heart once again. She had hurt him so badly, even though she hadn't intended to. But she just hadn't been ready to get married. And neither had she been ready to get involved with Adam. Not then.

"Let's not talk about it now," he suggested. "There's plenty of time. I'm here for a while."

"Thanks," Emma said with a smile. She wanted to have fun, to not think about anything serious.

"So, what should we talk about?" Adam asked. "Geopolitics? The abstract expressionist movement in modern art? Ruth Gordon and Bud Cort?" Adam named the two stars of the movie they'd just seen.

Emma laughed. She was perfectly capable of conversing on any of the subjects Adam had mentioned, and they both knew it.

That's one of the reasons I like him so much! He's interested in so many things, Emma said to herself. *He knows art, he knows so many more things than Kurt did. But Kurt—* Emma stopped herself before that train of thought went any further. *No. I won't think about him. I won't.*

"Let's talk about you," Emma suggested lightly.

"Moi?" Adam said in French. *"Le rasoir?"*

Emma laughed. Adam had used a slang French expression that literally meant "the razor," but which in slang basically translated to "totally boring."

"Pas du tout," Emma replied. "Not at all."

"My life is movies," Adam summed up, his attention fixed on the approaching skyline of lower Manhattan. It was spectacular.

"Some people would be happy to trade places with you," Emma suggested.

Adam laughed and edged closer to Emma. She could feel the warmth of his body through the thin lace vest she was wearing. "The damn thing is," he said, "I can't enjoy a movie anymore."

"What do you mean?" Emma asked, puzzled. "I thought you loved movies."

"I do," Adam replied, "but now when I watch one, I'm analyzing this, studying that, critiquing this, remembering that—"

"You're just enjoying them on a more sophisticated level," Emma suggested.

"Yeah, right," Adam agreed half-heartedly. "But how much fun can it be when you're watching *Harold and Maude* and trying to figure out the breakdown of the acts of the screenplay."

Why don't you just end this stupid conversation and take his hand in yours? a voice inside Emma said to her. *You know that's what you really want.*

"Emma?" Adam asked, a note of concern in his voice.

"Yes?" Emma replied.

"You were so quiet there," he murmured. "I thought something was wrong."

Emma turned to Adam and smiled. "See?" she said. "Nothing's wrong. In fact, everything's right."

"I'm glad," Adam replied. They were silent for a moment, as the ferry continued to cut across the New York harbor, heading back for the Ferry building. And then Emma felt Adam's hand seek hers, felt his fingers intertwine with her own, and happiness flooded through her.

She rested her head on Adam's shoulder, and they looked out at the vastness of the darkened water.

"So?" Emma said, letting herself into Liz's apartment and spotting Sam and Carrie sitting on the sofa.

"Nothing," Sam said miserably. "Nothing. And it's already midnight."

"He didn't call," Carrie explained.

"You sure he got the right number?" Emma asked.

"Sure, I'm sure," Sam said gloomily. "I may be naive, but I'm not stupid."

"He said he'd call either way, right?" Emma queried, sitting down next to them.

"Yep," Sam answered. "But you know these show biz types. They say that kind of stuff, but they never mean it. He probably hated me. He was probably just being nice because he felt sorry for me. I must have been crazy to think that I had a shot at this!"

"Maybe he'll still call," Emma said gently. "Or maybe you'll hear from him in the morning."

Sam shrugged. "I'm not holding my breath. So, how are things with my brother?"

"I still can't believe you kept Adam a secret!" Emma said.

"That wasn't the question," Sam replied. "Are you in love again, or what?"

"Lust, maybe," Emma admitted.

"So, girlfriend, we want details!" Sam cried. "Since my life sucks, I need to glom on to yours!"

Emma settled back on the couch and started to tell the story of her trip on the ferry with Adam. She had just about gotten to the part where Adam took her hand when the phone rang. Sam jumped up with a start.

"You get it," Sam said to Emma, her eyes wide.

"But why?" Emma asked, reaching for the phone.

"I don't want to look too anxious," Sam replied.

Emma shrugged, picking up the receiver.

"Emma Cresswell," she answered. Then she listened for a moment and put her hand over the receiver.

"It's for you," she said to Sam, "as if you didn't know."

Sam reached for the phone, and Emma gave it to her.

"Hello?" Sam said, trying to be cool, but not doing a very good job of it.

"Okay. Yeah. Okay. Of course! Bye!" Sam hung up. She turned to her friends.

"So, did you get it?" Carrie asked her, her own eyes shining in anticipation.

Sam shook her head. "Nope," she said, "I didn't get it. They gave it to another girl. Damn!"

"I'm really sorry," Emma said, laying her hand on Sam's.

"Oh, I never really thought I'd get it, not deep down," Sam confessed sadly. She tried for a tremulous grin. "Oh well, there's good news, too."

"What's that?" Carrie asked.

Sam shrugged her shoulders and attempted a nonchalant air. "Now I don't have to go out with Laszlo Comfort!"

FOUR

Ring!

Sam reached sleepily for the phone. It was early the next morning, and the bitter taste of disappointment from Laszlo Comfort's call the night before was still in her mouth. Sam was awake, but barely.

"Hello?" was all Sam could muster.

"Hello, Sam Bridges?" the voice said.

Laszlo Comfort. I recognize the voice, Sam thought. *If he's calling me to ask me to dinner, I'll tell him to take a dive off the Brooklyn Bridge, thank you very much.*

"You're talking to her," Sam said evenly.

"It's Laszlo Comfort, the director."

"Is there another one?" Sam mumbled.

Laszlo laughed. "I hope not. Anyway, I'm calling with some interesting news."

Sam's sleepy heart leapt in action. *Maybe I still have a chance*, she thought.

"Yes?" Sam asked noncommittally.

"The girl we offered the part to slipped on some dishwater in a coffee shop this morning," Laszlo said. "It was a freak accident, but her leg is broken. She's in the hospital now."

Sam's heart pounded. But she tried to stay cool.

"So?" she asked.

"So," Laszlo said, "we're offering you the part."

Yes. Sam said to herself. *Yes yes yes yes yes yes!*

"With a Broadway production contract? And an Equity card?" Sam forced herself to ask, as if being offered a role in a major Broadway musical was an everyday occurrence for her.

"Of course," Laszlo answered.

"I'll do it," Sam replied, as evenly as she could, hoping that Laszlo couldn't hear the sound of her vocal cords constricting with excitement.

"Good!" Laszlo exclaimed. "Your first rehearsal starts at noon."

"Noon?" Sam asked.

"Today," Laszlo added.

"Today?" Sam squeaked.

"Yes, you seem to have the gist of this," Laszlo said with amusement in his voice. "Noon today. The show opens in a week."

"No previews?" Sam asked. She knew previews were performances done for a lower ticket price before the critics came to review a show.

"No previews," Laszlo intoned. "That's what the producers want."

"Don't shows usually rehearse for more than a week?" Sam asked, feeling scared at the thought of so little rehearsal.

"Yes, of course," Laszlo replied, "but this cast has already been in rehearsal for quite some time. You're a replacement, remember?" Laszlo said.

"Oh, right," Sam said chagrined. Actually, she'd forgotten all about that. "Well, I'll be on time," Sam promised.

Laszlo then told Sam where the rehearsal was taking place, and what she would need to do about signing her contract.

"Oh," he added, "and one other thing."

I think I know what's coming, Sam thought.

"Do you think you might be able to join me for dinner tomorrow?" Laszlo asked, a bit of wolfishness in his voice. "To talk about your role, of course."

Bingo.

"We'll talk about it at rehearsal, okay?" Sam replied smoothly.

"Done," Laszlo answered. "See you at noon. Don't be late." He hung up.

Sam let out a yell of joy that could practically be heard on Sunset Island.

I'm in a Broadway musical, she thought. *They'll never believe it in Junction, Kansas. Big time, here I come!*

Emma and Carrie dropped Sam off by taxi at the theater at 11:30 A.M. While Sam was rehearsing, the two of them were planning on spending the day at the Museum of Natural History—there was a special exhibition there on primates that Emma wanted to see—and the three girls had agreed that they'd all meet up at Liz's loft later that evening.

Actually, Emma had been hoping that they could all meet up with Adam that night, but Adam had also called earlier that morning to say that he had classes all day and then screenings at night and wouldn't have a moment free. He did promise, though, to do something special with Emma and Carrie the next day—Shannon Berman, the first woman ever to make it to the major leagues, was scheduled to pitch her first game in the majors for the Mets the next afternoon, and Adam had managed to get three tickets. They would get to see history in the making.

Sam found the stage door, took a deep

breath, and went inside. The theater was huge and was a beehive of activity. The set for the show was already in place, and all over the place lighting technicians were hanging lights, sound engineers and stage crew were positioning equipment, and set dressers were painting and arranging things. It was rocking.

Sam looked around for someone who might know what she was supposed to do. She saw a young man, about twenty-five years old, who was wearing a plaid short-sleeved shirt, jeans, and sneakers.

What the heck, she thought, *he's as good a prospect as any to get me steered in the right direction.*

"Excuse me," she said to him, smiling ingratiatingly.

"Yes?" he said impatiently, looking over his glasses.

"I'm Samantha Bridges," Sam continued, mustering up her courage. "I'm—"

"You're Sam Bridges!" the guy said to her, grinning broadly. "Welcome!"

"Thanks," Sam said, "but who are you?"

"Neil Glascow," the guy replied, "stage manager to the stars. Actually, assistant stage manager on this show. But one day I'll be production stage manager, and then I'll be a director, and then I'll be rich and famous."

Sam laughed. "I like the way you think!"

He stuck out his hand, which Sam took and shook.

"You got any idea what I'm supposed to do?" Sam asked Neil.

"Rehearse, I guess," Neil joked. "Not that it'll save this show. Only joking!"

"I mean, what I'm supposed to do now," Sam explained, ignoring his pointed comment about the show.

"Try the green room back there," Neil indicated. "Everyone hangs out there until rehearsal starts. They're expecting you."

"Thanks," Sam replied. "How big a cast is this?"

"Twenty-five," Neil answered her. "Mostly pretty cool."

"Cool," Sam echoed. "Listen, I'll catch you later. And thanks."

Neil gave her a friendly nod, and Sam headed over to the actor's lounge, marked "Green Room" on the door.

She opened the door and, with as calm and collected a look on her face as she could muster, strode inside. The first thing she noticed was that the "green room" was painted white. The second thing was that someone started calling her name.

"Sam Bridges? Holy smokes I can't believe it!" said a muscular and very handsome guy in jeans and a T-shirt, who was sitting on one of the couches, holding a thick novel in his hands.

Jeez, he looks totally familiar, but I can't place his face! Sam thought to herself.

"You don't recognize me, huh?" the guy said to her, grinning widely. "And I'm your favorite actor."

"Well," Sam countered quickly, "you know, there are just so many guys who swarm around me. . . ."

The guy laughed. "You haven't changed," he said. "Let me give you a two-word hint: Paradise Island."

Then it came to her in a shock of recognition.

"Oh, my God, you're Matt Carlton!" she yelled. "How could I be so dense? I'm sorry!" She threw her arms around Matt and gave him a huge hug.

Sam thought back to when she and her friends had met Matt. Emma had won a trip to Paradise Island in the Bahamas and had brought Carrie and Sam along with her. Out on a cruise one day, the girls had met Matt, who was an extremely nice actor from New York. Not to mention seriously cute. Matt had just finished doing a show off-Broadway that had flopped—not because of him, of course. Sam recalled that Nancy Pumpkin had starred in that show, too—something called *Exhaling Darkness* that he said had opened and closed in one night.

Sam also recalled that during their trip to Paradise Island, Matt and Carrie had been an item.

Well, well, well, won't Little Miss Alden be psyched when I tell her Matt is in this show! Sam thought with a sly grin.

"I'm so glad to see a friendly face!" Sam cried.

"Me, too," Matt said with a grin.

"So, you're doing another show with Nancy Pumpkin," Sam marveled.

Matt nodded. "She's Helen. I'm Helen's father."

Sam looked puzzled. "But . . . aren't you both about the same age?"

"Yeah," Matt agreed. "It's the magic of the theater."

"Well, it must be love," Sam cracked.

"It must not be," Matt replied. He looked around to make sure no one could overhear him. "Actually, I can't much tolerate her. Her mood swings drive me nuts!"

"My friend Carrie is in New York with me," Sam said casually.

Matt's face lit up. "Carrie's here?"

Sam nodded. "She's gonna die when I tell her you're in this show."

"Is she still . . . uh, involved with that guy from—what's the name of that place where you guys work?" Matt asked.

"Sunset Island," Sam replied, sitting on the worn couch. "Yeah, she still is. His name's Billy."

"Right. Billy," Matt repeated, looking disappointed. He sighed and shook it off. "So, tell me, have you seen the script to this puppy? And how did you happen to get the part, anyway?"

Sam explained about her audition. "I haven't actually read the script," Sam admitted. "I mean, I just got hired. I guess I'm replacing somebody. Actually, the whole thing is making me kind of nervous—coming in so late and everything."

"Yeah, I can understand that," Matt sympathized.

"So, tell me about the script," Sam suggested, running her hands through her hair.

"It's . . . interesting," Matt said vaguely.

"It sucks!" yelled another actress, who was sitting across the room. She was dressed in a black leotard and black jeans, and had jet black hair and startling green eyes.

Matt grinned. "That's Chili Dumont, who plays Annie Sullivan, Helen's teacher. You'll learn she's always afraid to speak her mind."

"The script sucks and that's all there is to

it," Chili said matter-of-factly. "And the songs are worse. Imagine, a number called 'I Am Not Dumb Now'!"

"Well, if it sucks so bad, why are you doing the show?" Sam asked her.

Chili laughed, her long, wild dark hair cascading from side to side as she chortled. "Boy, you must really be green. It's a paycheck," she said. "I haven't been in a show in six months!"

"Wow," Sam remarked. "I haven't been in one in my life."

"Then pray it runs forever," Chili commented. "Except it won't. Whoever heard of a musical about Helen Keller? She couldn't even hear, for God's sake."

"Maybe it'll work out okay," Matt said, trying to be encouraging.

"Yeah, and maybe monkeys will fly out of my butt," was Chili's retort.

"Chili's just pissed because Laszlo and Sheila cut one of her monologues yesterday," another actor yelled from a far corner.

"Shut up," Chili growled. "You wouldn't know good writing if it jumped up and bit you in the butt."

"Who do you play?" Sam asked her. "Oh, that's right, Matt told me—Annie Sullivan."

"Well, it doesn't matter," Chili surmised.

"Why not?" Sam asked.

"Because we're not staying open more than one night anyway," Chili concluded.

"Five minutes!" Neil Glascow yelled, sticking his head in the green room door. "We'll start with the water dance. Sam, you're in it. Watch it once and then Timothy will block you into the number."

Sam turned back to Matt Carlton. "What's the water dance?" she asked nervously.

Geez, do you think I'm asking enough questions? she thought to herself.

Matt attempted a smile. "It's a fantasy dance Mr. Christopher came up with."

"About what?"

Matt broke into full-fledged grin. "About when Helen first figures out that the letters Annie is spelling into her hand mean W-A-T-E-R."

"You've got to see it to believe it!" the actor in the corner sang out.

"You see what I mean?" Chili queried. "Lemme give you one piece of advice, Sam."

"What's that?"

"Don't count on *Helen!* paying for your college tuition," she said with a smirk, and then turned back to the *People* magazine she'd been reading. Sam turned and looked at Matt, but all he could do was shrug and smile.

"She calls 'em the way she sees 'em," Matt said finally.

"Is she right?" Sam queried.

"Who knows?" Matt asked. "I'm a professional actor. My job is to go out and do the job they pay me to do as well as I can possibly do it."

"Yeah," said Sam, though she knew nothing about the professional theater and had spent even less time thinking about her philosophy of it. When she did take a minute to stop and think, she knew she was damned lucky to even be in this show.

"Okay!" Neil said, sticking his head in the green room again, "let's get started! Sam, go to studio A, everyone else out on stage!"

Obediently, the entire cast of *Helen!*, who'd been filling up the green room for the last fifteen minutes, quickly exited.

"We'll be seeing a lot of each other," Matt said as he and Sam walked out together.

"Cool," Sam replied. She liked Matt.

"So . . . you're really sure that you friend Carrie and this guy Billy are still an item, huh?" he asked Sam.

"They are," Sam replied honestly. "But I guess she could answer that question for herself."

"Yeah, if I could see her," Matt pointed out.

"Yeah," Sam agreed. But she felt kind of

funny. *Billy is a really good friend of mine,* she thought to herself. *And Carrie really loves Billy. But, hey, I'm Two-Guys-For-Every-Girl Bridges, so who am I to moralize to anyone?*

"So, I can call Carrie?" Matt asked.

"I guess," Sam replied. She quickly scribbled their phone number at the loft on a piece of paper and handed it to Matt.

"Thanks," he said, tucking it into his pocket. "Later." He headed off for his rehearsal.

I hope it was okay to do that, Sam thought to herself. *Here I am, fixing up Emma and Carrie, and I am totally solo! Well, that is going to change quick! Later for that!*

"Where's Sam Bridges?" Timothy called out from down the hall.

"Coming!" Sam called back. She fluffed up her hair and headed to Studio A.

Water dance, ready or not, here I come!

FIVE

Sam tossed her dance bag into a corner of Liz's loft and plopped herself down on the couch. As exhausted as she was, she still took note of the fact that Adam was not only at the loft, but sitting very close to Emma on the Oriental rug in the middle of the floor.

"How about a hot tub?" Carrie suggested.

"I'll bring you a Coke," Emma offered.

"And I'll get some of my cuter friends to give you a massage," Adam added.

"Too pooped," Sam said, so wiped out she was barely able to form the words. *I have never been this tired in my life*, she realized. *Broadway dance rehearsal is tough.*

"Everything hurts," Sam moaned. "My hair hurts."

"Wow," Emma exclaimed, "you really are whupped."

"No kidding, Ice Princess," Sam responded.

"No kidding." Sam reached over and, slowly and gingerly, started massaging her right calf. "Lemme tell you this," she said finally, once she had massaged out the worst of the ache. "Those people are good. No, let me take that back. Those people are great!"

"Who do you mean?" Emma asked, crossing her legs Indian fashion on the rug.

"The dancers, the singers, the actors," Sam explained. "I mean, they're unbelievable. I heard them talking about going out night-clubbing tonight. Nightclubbing!"

"This is too hilarious!" Carrie exclaimed. "You've finally found people with more energy than you!"

"You can keep up, can't you?" Emma asked, concerned.

"Yeah . . . for about an hour," Sam cracked. "I mean, these girls are in some awesome shape."

"So," Adam said, "you'll just have to start waking up at six in the morning with me to go running."

Sam looked at him closely. "Since when did you start that?"

"Since never," he admitted with a laugh. "But it sounds impressive, doesn't it?"

"You know, that's not a bad idea," Sam said quietly.

Carrie looked at her askance. "You?" she

asked. "You, who doesn't think the day even begins before noontime?"

Sam shook her head. "You don't seem to get it," she intoned. "These people are amazing. And they've all had tons of training and stuff." She sighed and flopped over on the couch. "I am a total rodent of dance compared to them."

"Hey, you have natural talent!" Emma cried, defending her friend. "You wouldn't be in the show if you weren't good enough!"

"Maybe you really do need some kind of training program," Adam mused, twining a lock of Emma's hair around his finger.

"No kidding," Sam agreed. "But not tonight. Tonight, every single part of me hurts."

"How about some Ben-Gay?" Carrie suggested.

"That means I'll have to get up." Sam grinned slightly as she spoke. "No way."

"What are you going to do about tomorrow?" Emma asked her. "When's rehearsal?"

Sam moaned. "We start at ten o'clock. God, I'll never make it." She managed to turn her head to look at Adam. "Is tomorrow that baseball game you guys are going to?"

Adam nodded. "Gee, you remembered. It's only like the biggest story in the news—the first female in the majors."

"I'm totally psyched," said Carrie eagerly.

"I am totally dead," Sam replied. "How am I going to go through this again tomorrow?"

"You'll be there," Adam warned her. "You have to uphold the family name."

"Your family name isn't the same as mine," Sam noted.

"Details, details," Adam pooh-poohed. "You'll be there."

"So what are you guys up to tonight?" Sam asked them.

"Out to Bradley's on University Place to hear some jazz," Adam replied. "Wanna come?"

Sam answered by burying her face in a pillow.

"What about Laszlo Comfort?" Carrie asked her.

Sam picked her head up. "What about him?" she replied.

Emma measured her words carefully. "I thought you said that you'd tell him whether you'd go out with him," she said.

Sam shrugged. "I did. We're eating lunch together in a couple of days."

"Sam!" Carrie warned. "Don't get yourself into something you can't get out of."

"You think I'm a child?" Sam shot back. "It's lunch, not dinner and not bed. I'll be careful." Then she buried her head back in the couch pillow.

Right now, she thought, *I'm too tired to even get up and go to the bathroom. How can I worry about Laszlo Comfort? And everything really does hurt. How am I going to make it to rehearsal tomorrow? What am I doing, being in a Broadway show? I can't even get through one day of getting ready for it.*

Within thirty seconds, still fully clothed, Sam was fast asleep on the sofa. Emma, Carrie, and Adam left her right there as they tiptoed out of the loft and locked the door behind them.

Though it was an afternoon game at Shea Stadium, it seemed to Emma and Carrie as if all of New York had taken the afternoon off to come to the ballpark. Adam had insisted that they all take the number seven subway— although he said a true New Yorker would call it "the train"—to the stadium ("to get the true flavor of the event," he'd said), so Emma, Carrie, and Adam had endured a packed subway from Grand Central Station out to Shea Stadium in Queens.

"That's the first time I've taken the subway," Emma had intoned as they pushed their way out of the crowded car, "and the last."

"Wrong," Adam had said, "because we've

got to get back to the city. Guess how we're doing it."

One thing was for sure—this was going to be the sporting event of the year. The whole country had been mesmerized in recent weeks by the story of Shannon Berman, the cute, blond-haired, eighteen-year-old pitcher who'd been drafted by the Mets out of high school and now was about to make her debut as the first woman to play in a major league baseball game.

All the way to the entrance to the park, people were frantically trying to buy tickets to see the game. The Mets were playing the Los Angeles Dodgers, which had a special significance, because many years earlier the Dodgers were the team that broke the "color barrier" and allowed a talented man named Jackie Robinson to be the first black ballplayer in the majors.

"You got tickets, son?" a middle-aged man in a porkpie hat with two young grade-school girls in tow accosted Adam and the girls as they walked toward the stadium.

"We do," Carrie said quietly.

"I need three! I'll give you a hundred a piece for them," the man said.

"No deal, man," Adam replied.

"A hundred fifty," the man pleaded.

"Sorry," Adam answered.

"Two hundred and no more!" the man begged. "Please. We've got to see this game. It's once in a lifetime!"

Adam and the girls just pushed on.

"Unbelievable," Carrie said. "Two hundred bucks for a ticket to a baseball game."

"Yeah," Emma said, "and I don't even like baseball."

"Do you know what I could do with that money?" Carrie asked. "I mean, I really need it for school in the fall and—"

"Girls, you cut me to the quick," Adam said, solemnly placing his hand over his heart. "I am out with two women with no soul, no sense of history—"

"How'd you get tickets to this game, anyway?" Carrie interrupted.

Adam grinned. "I have connections," he replied. "Actually, it's pure luck. I won them from a radio station."

Carrie looked behind her longingly at the guy who had offered them two hundred bucks a ticket. "Since you won the tickets anyway, maybe we could just sell one? Mine?" she asked hopefully.

"Hey, I thought you were the great baseball lover!" Adam exclaimed.

"I am," Carrie agreed. "But I'm also in debt up to my eyeballs. Yale costs a mint."

"Hey, you only live once," Adam told her,

taking Carrie with one arm and Emma with the other. "This is going to be an experience you'll be able to tell your grandchildren about."

Adam led the girls through the turnstiles and up to the loge level of Shea Stadium. Though the game wasn't due to start for another half-hour, the stadium was already filled to capacity. Adam found an usher who took the three of them to their seats on the third base side, and the three friends settled in.

"Wow, this is bigger than a Graham Perry concert!" Carrie exclaimed happily.

"See, you're glad you didn't sell your ticket already," Adam pointed out.

"I love it," Emma agreed. "Look at all these people!"

"In the words of Sam, there are some serious fashion errors being committed left and right," Carrie commented, noting a group of older women sitting just to their left, who were dressed in an assortment of polyester pantsuits with puffy animals outlined in glitter paint parading across their bosoms.

Emma laughed. "Hanging out with Sam is really getting to you, Car. You used to be oblivious to stuff like that!"

"I know," Carrie agreed. "I can't figure out if it's good or bad. But sometimes I just hear these Sam-type things coming out of my mouth! Very weird!"

"Maybe that means she'll grow up and start sounding like you," Adam suggested.

Carrie gave him a look. "That was a compliment, right?"

"Right," Adam agreed.

"I wasn't sure," Carrie admitted. "You make me sound so . . . I don't know . . . boring."

"You're not boring at all," Adam assured her. "You just have your priorities together— you know, college, a career—"

"Billy," Emma put in.

"Billy?" Adam echoed.

"Her guy," Emma explained. "Lead singer for Flirting With Danger."

"That's the band you sing backup for, right?" Adam asked Emma.

"Right," Emma agreed. But thinking about the band made her think about Kurt, who had gone out with them on their recent East Coast tour as road manager, so she badly wanted to change the subject. "Too bad Sam is missing this game, isn't it?" she asked her friends.

"Even if she didn't have to be at the theater, Sam couldn't have walked up the ramp to get here," Adam joked.

"I hope she's okay for rehearsal," Emma commented.

"So does she," Adam added with a grin. "You guys hungry? I want to go get some franks."

"I don't eat ballpark franks," Emma said, shaking her head. "Imagine what's in them. Ugh!"

"I do!" Carrie replied. "I'm hooked on mystery meat. Let's go!"

Adam and Carrie headed off to one of the many concessions stands that sold overpriced sodas and food. Emma looked down at the field, where the players were taking fielding practice, and then reached into her bag and pulled out the day's *New York Times*, which had a story about the game on the front page. She rolled up the sleeves of her pink silk T-shirt so she could get a bit more sun on herself and began to read.

**FIRST WOMAN IN
MAJORS TAKES MOUND TODAY**
by Mal Itkins

Baseball history will be made at Shea Stadium this afternoon, when Shannon Berman, the 18-year-old knuckleballing righthander from Perrysburg, Ohio, strolls to the pitcher's mound for the New York Mets to take on the Los Angeles Dodgers. Berman will be the first woman to ever take the field in a major league ballgame.

The article went on for several paragraphs. Emma looked at the picture of Shannon Berman *The Times* was running next to the story.

She is really gorgeous, Emma marveled. *Thick blond hair in a braid—she really does look like a movie star.*

Just then Adam and Carrie got back to their seats. Adam was carrying a cardboard box that contained three hot dogs covered in mustard and relish, and three sodas.

"We brought you a dog, just in case," Carrie reported, as they sat back down.

"Yuck," Emma replied. "Hey, what's a knuckleball?"

"What?" Adam asked.

"A knuckleball," Emma answered. "You know, the pitch that Shannon Berman throws."

"I thought you hated baseball," Carrie observed.

"I changed my mind," Emma said lightly. "Now, what is it?"

Adam spoke up. "It's a pitch that you don't have to throw hard—"

"Because you grip the ball with your nails and try to throw it without any spin," Carrie concluded.

Adam and Emma looked at Carrie, amazed. "What makes you the baseball expert?" Adam asked her. Carrie just grinned slyly.

"I've been around," she said.

"So what's so special about this pitch?" Emma asked.

"Just try to hit it," Adam warned. "It basically floats all over the place, crazy-like. Catchers hate it!"

"So this girl is that good?" Emma queried.

Adam laughed. "You'll see," he said. "Just wait and see."

A huge cheer went up from the crowd. The Mets ran onto the field. There was a uniformed player at every position, except pitcher. The cries from the crowd got louder. Then, a lone figure in a Mets' uniform emerged from the dugout. She walked slowly to the pitcher's mound, her blond braid glinting in the bright afternoon sunlight.

The crowd rose to its feet and roared its approval. The lone figure at the pitcher's mound doffed her hat. Even the Los Angeles Dodgers, standing on the front steps of their own dugout, were clapping. Emma, Carrie, and Adam stood and yelled and pounded their hands together until they were hoarse.

The umpire gave a baseball to the Mets' catcher, who fired it out to Berman on the pitcher's mound. The game was about to begin.

SIX

"Turn up the TV," Adam instructed. "The sports comes on next."

"I am seriously jealous that you guys got to go to that baseball game and I didn't," Sam said. She had actually arrived home from rehearsal before everyone got home from Shea Stadium, and she was prone on the couch watching the TV with the sound turned down. "I can't believe you got to go somewhere that was in the news."

"We certainly did," Emma said proudly. "And I'll never forget it."

"They should have cancelled rehearsal," Sam groused. "I can't believe I missed it! My picture might have ended up in the paper—you know, a cute fan in the stands kind of thing."

"Shannon Berman is so cute and so talented that no one would have been taking your picture, Sam—no offense," Adam told her.

"How'd rehearsal go, anyway?" Carrie asked her.

"I'm here, that's the best I can say about it," Sam reported. "And hungry. Pass me those Doritos."

Carrie reached over and tossed a package of Doritos to Sam, which she grabbed for and dropped.

"Knuckleball!" Carrie joked, and they all cracked up.

"Sssh!" Adam cried as he turned up the TV. "It's the report on the game."

Emma, Carrie, and Adam watched once again what they had witnessed at the ballpark that afternoon. Shannon Berman had shut out the Los Angeles Dodgers, and the Mets had won 5–0. And not only that, she had given up only two hits the entire game— the first one in the fifth inning.

The sports report ended with Berman's final pitch of the game, with which she struck out the Dodger's clean-up hitter. Then, all the Mets ran to the pitcher's mound to embrace her as the fans gave her a standing ovation that didn't quit until she came out of the clubhouse for a curtain call, just as if she were a Broadway actress.

"That's me," Sam cracked, "next week."

"You wish," Carrie said, but with a smile on her face.

"No kidding," Sam replied. "But I don't have a chance. Half the cast openly says the show sucks. And from what I've seen so far, I'm inclined to agree."

Emma reached over and turned off the TV. "You're joking, I hope." Emma reached daintily for a single Dorito, and then Sam snatched the bag back.

"Uh-uh," Sam cautioned, stuffing a handful of Doritos in her mouth. "No one eats these but me. I'm replacing my body's salt levels."

"No, you're pigging out on junk food," Emma corrected her.

"You are such a stickler for details," Sam replied mid-crunch.

"So what's the problem with the show?" Carrie asked.

Sam grimaced, then washed the Doritos down with a huge swallow of Coke. "Everything," she said. "Everyone thinks so, too. The script bites it, and the music isn't much better."

"So how does something that bad get produced on Broadway?" Carrie wondered.

"It happens," Sam said with a shrug.

"What about your part?" Adam asked.

"Well," Sam said, "you'll get to see me do it

on opening night. Then *you* can tell *me* what you think."

"Don't be so sure it's bad," Emma cautioned. "No one can tell for sure ahead of time what's going to be a hit and what's going to be a miss. My parents invested in a couple of shows that they were sure would be really big, and they both closed quickly. But Aunt Liz invested in a little show that started downtown at the Public Theatre—everyone said it would be a flop—and she ended up making a ton of money. It ran forever."

"Hey, maybe your family would like to invest in my career?" Sam asked hopefully.

"Someone in the business once said to me—'in show biz, no one knows,'" Carrie quoted.

"Yeah, who is this show biz genius?" Sam asked, reaching for another handful of chips.

"Oh, a nice guy named Matt Carlton. Who happened to call me before we left for the ball game."

Sam blanched. She hadn't yet told Carrie that Matt Carlton was in the cast of *Helen!*, but she had given Matt their phone number at Liz's. Clearly, Matt had beaten Sam to the punch.

"I meant to tell you we were in the show together last night—" Sam began.

"Last night you could barely talk," Adam reminded her.

"True," Sam agreed. "So what was Matt's report?"

"Same as yours," Carrie said.

"See what I mean?" Sam replied with a sigh.

"But he also said he's seen great shows close in one night—" Carrie said.

"—and crap shows run forever," Sam mumbled. "He told me the same thing. So, how did you feel about Matt calling you?"

Carrie thought a second. "Good," she replied honestly.

"He's a great guy," Sam said. "He's really nice to me at rehearsal—it's nice to know someone in the show."

"How do you know this guy?" Adam asked, stretching out on the rug.

Carrie filled him in on their vacation at Paradise Island and how they'd met Matt.

"And you two became an item?" Adam asked Carrie.

Carrie blushed. "No. No way. I'm in love with Billy," she said vehemently.

"A mini-item?" Adam asked slyly.

"No. A friend," Carrie insisted.

"He was more than that on Paradise Island!" Sam sang out.

Carrie got even redder. "Okay, so I had

temporary insanity. That was then, this is now."

"Are you gonna see him?" Sam asked Carrie.

"I'm having lunch with him tomorrow at two o'clock," Carrie admitted.

"Rehearsal break," Sam said.

"You got it," Carrie answered.

"He really likes you, you know," Sam told Carrie.

"And I really like him," Carrie replied, "but I love Billy. All I'm doing with Matt is having lunch. L-U-N-C-H."

"Speaking of lunch," Emma said, looking over at Sam, "what about yours?"

"Mine?" Sam asked, her voice totally innocent. "Today I had two pieces of pizza and—"

"That is not what I'm asking about and you know it," Emma chided her. "I'm asking about—"

"Oh!" Sam cried. "You're asking about that director, what's-his-name . . ."

"Laszlo," Emma and Carrie said together.

"I've renamed him the Wolf Man," Sam reported. "Because of how he looks at me. And every other girl in the cast, I might add."

"So you're not going to see him," Carrie concluded.

"Did I say that?" Sam queried. "He's my

director, remember? We're having lunch tomorrow. Same time as Carrie."

"Be careful," Emma cautioned Sam.

"Get a grip, Emma. It's lunch!" Sam exclaimed.

"I know you," Emma insisted. "You are quite capable of getting into trouble over a double cheeseburger."

"Thank you for that vote of confidence," Sam said. "If I'm not back tomorrow night," she continued, "send out a search party." Her friends all laughed.

"Listen," Sam asked, pulling out a paper bag she had stowed next to the couch, "can you guys help me with a project?"

"Sure," Carrie said, leaning closer to Sam. "What's up?"

Sam explained that she had some cards made up by the print shop around the corner that announced her debut in *Helen!*, and that she wanted to send these announcements to a list of people she had already drawn up. She pulled out the list of about fifty names and addresses.

"This is pretty organized for you," Emma commented. "You're scaring me."

"I'm a pro, now," Sam chastised. "Pros send out announcements about their shows."

Adam took a quick look at the list. Then he looked at it again. "Pros tend to invite their families to their openings," he pointed out. "I don't see any family on this list."

Emma and Carrie looked at Sam quizzically. They hadn't noticed that Sam had left her birth mother's family, Susan Briarly, off the invite list, and had even neglected to list her mother and father back in Junction, Kansas.

"I'm not inviting family 'cuz the show's gonna stink," Sam cried. "You think I want to be humiliated?"

Adam looked at her closely. "You've got to do better than that," he said. "I mean, I notice you're willing to be humiliated by every big agent in town whose name is on your list."

Sam sighed. "Okay," she admitted. "It's just that, well . . . I don't want to talk about it now."

"Sam?" Carrie said in her reasonable tone of voice.

"Carrie," Sam moaned, "you know when you talk like that I'm helpless."

"So?" Carrie asked.

"Okay," Sam said in a low voice. "It's just that . . . I'm nervous about them all being here at the same time."

"So you're not inviting any of them," Adam surmised.

"So," Sam asked, "does that make me a chicken?"

"Yep," Adam responded.

"Oh," Sam said.

"Not that I blame you," he continued.

"I'd think they'd be as nervous as you are," Emma suggested.

"Right!" Sam concluded, reaching yet again for the bag of Doritos and nervously stuffing a handful in her mouth. "So I'll spare them the pain."

"Are you sure about this?" Emma asked,

"No," Sam admitted. "That's one of my problems in life. I'm never sure about anything. I just pretend to be—but then you guys already know that."

"It's your call," Adam said finally. Emma and Carrie nodded, agreeing with him.

"Are you at least inviting Danny and Pres?" Emma asked. Danny was Danny Franklin, a guy Sam had met at Disney World when she had worked there as a dancer. Danny had been working as the cartoon character Goofy, and the two of them had become really good friends. Danny was always interested in Sam as more than just a friend, but just as Sam was getting romantically involved with him, she pulled back because she thought it was Pres who she really loved. Pres, of course, was Presley Travis, who played bass in the band Flirting With Danger with Carrie's boyfriend Billy

Sampson. Pres was Sam's on-again/off-again boyfriend on Sunset Island.

"Danny I already invited—I left a message on his answering machine. Pres no," Sam said, taking back her list and quickly looking it over. "Remember, Pres is visiting his family in Tennessee while the band is on a break."

"He'll probably want to come anyway," Emma mused.

Sam shrugged. "We haven't exactly been getting along lately," she reminded Emma. "Anyway, his mom's sick. That's why he went home."

"I didn't know that," Emma said. "We should send flowers."

Sam shook her head. "You kill me. You have the most perfect manners in the world."

"So true," Emma joked in a lofty voice. "I even drive a car with my legs crossed daintily at the ankle."

Sam laughed. "An heiress with a sense of humor. I love that. Anyway, Danny will come. I need someone to protect me from the Wolf Man."

"You're pretty confident he'll be there," Adam said slyly.

"To know me is to love me," Sam intoned.

"You'll never change," Emma laughed.

Sam reached over and picked up the Doritos bag. She turned the bag over and shook it. Nothing came out. "Bogus! They definitely shorted the chip count in this bag!"

"Maybe you just ate them all," Carrie said, getting up to stretch.

"Moi?" Sam asked. "I didn't eat the whole bag by myself!"

"Yes, you did," Adam told her. "I saw you."

"Wrong," Sam said smugly. "Emma ate one."

Everyone else went to bed at about 1:00 A.M., but Emma and Adam were still up, sitting close to each other on the couch, watching the movie *After Hours* on the VCR. It was really funny and the two of them kept exploding into laughter, almost always simultaneously.

"We even laugh at the same things," Adam pointed out.

Emma just smiled.

"I want to make a movie like this one," Adam said to Emma, squeezing her a little as he spoke.

She melted into his arms. *This feels so good, so right*, she told herself, blissfully closing her eyes. *I'm getting to like him more and more*. "Then you will," Emma whispered back.

"Nah," Adam said, putting the VCR on pause for a minute. "When I get my chance, it'll be on some low-budget horror movie like *Return of the Bloodsucker, Part Three.* That's how Hollywood is."

"You could go independent," Emma suggested.

"That's true," Adam whispered. "Or I could put you in my movie. Then it's sure to get studio backing."

Emma blushed, and Adam leaned over and kissed her lightly on the ear.

"Not my career goal," Emma whispered back.

"I know," Adam murmured. "You're into monkeys."

"Primates," Emma corrected him. "And Africa. And the Peace Corps."

Adam gave her an appraising look. "You are definitely more than meets the eye."

Immediately Kurt's face appeared in Emma's head. *When we were first falling in love he said almost the exact same thing to me,* Emma recalled. *And I ended up hurting him so badly that he left Sunset Island, the island that he loves more than any place on Earth. . . .*

She shook off her brooding and nuzzled against Adam. *I won't think about Kurt!*

"So what are you planning to do tomorrow?" Adam asked her.

"It's already tomorrow," Emma whispered,

looking at her watch. It was nearly 2:00 A.M.

"So it is," Adam said.

"Anyway," Emma whispered, "I'm planning to go to this modeling agency uptown. My Aunt Liz knows the owner—she gives a lot of money to Greenpeace—and made me promise I'd go up there. My aunt already sent in a bunch of photos of me."

"You want to model?" Adam asked, surprised.

Emma shrugged. "I never really thought about it," she said. "Maybe it'd be fun to try out."

"Well, I know you're cute enough," Adam said, "but aren't models tall?"

"Not petite models," Emma replied.

"It's hard to picture you doing something so . . ." Adam searched for a word.

"Vacuous?" Emma suggested, then she laughed. "Evidently this agency is really special. They do cool stuff, not your usual fashion catalogues—at least that's what my aunt says."

"You want some company?" Adam asked. "I've got the late afternoon free."

"Sure," Emma said happily, "I'd love it."

"I'll protect you from the Wolf Man," Adam said, wiggling his eyebrows in a sinister fashion. "I understand he gets around."

Emma laughed and threw her arms around Adam's neck.

"You are too funny!" she accused him.

Then Emma pulled away just far enough to kiss Adam lightly on the lips, then more passionately.

There was no more conversation.

SEVEN

"Danny!" Sam said with a start, nearly dropping her full coffee mug on the floor in shock. "What are you doing here? Come on up!"

"See you in a sec!"

It was the next day, and Sam and her friends had been enjoying an early breakfast in the loft before Sam had to leave for rehearsal. They'd been interrupted by the front door buzzer going off, and when Sam answered it, she was shocked to find it was Danny Franklin. She quickly buzzed him in, and in seconds, heard the sound of rapping on the front door of the loft.

Sam peered through the peephole. It was indeed Danny. And he was sopping wet—there was water dripping from every square inch of his body. She opened the door right away.

Danny grinned. "It's me," he said. "It's a monsoon out there. Anyone got a towel?"

Emma and Carrie jumped up to meet him, Emma carrying a dish towel along with her so that Danny could at least mop off his head—which he did before he embraced each of them in turn, saving Sam for the last, warmest hug. She hugged him, screaming and jumping up and down.

Danny grinned at Sam shyly, happy to receive such a warm welcome. They hadn't parted very well the last time they'd been together.

"You look fabulous," Danny told Sam sincerely.

Sam grinned. She had on her oldest pair of jeans that fit her to perfection, and a crocheted top that ended just under the bust. "I'm glad you didn't catch me a half hour ago in my ratty robe!" Sam exclaimed.

"Come on in," Emma said, "and sit down. Coffee?"

Danny nodded. "Iced would be good. My favorite weather. Hot and pouring rain."

Sam checked him out. He looked as good as ever. Tall and rangy, with sun-streaked brown hair and green eyes, it looked like Danny had continued his recent regimen in the gym. The last time she'd seen him, he'd added a few pounds of muscle, and now it seemed like he'd added a few more.

Babe-a-licious, she thought, *no doubt about it. Wet or dry. But what am I thinking—the last time I saw him I told him we were only going to be friends. This is seriously confusing!*

"How'd you get here from Florida so fast?" Sam demanded, sitting back down and taking a bite from a buttered bagel.

Danny smiled. "I was here all the time."

"You live here now?" Carrie asked him.

"Nah," Danny said, "but I'm here visiting my aunt and uncle. When I checked my messages last night, I found out you were here, too!"

"It's fate!" Sam cried happily.

"Where does your uncle live?" Emma asked.

"Chelsea," Danny said, wiping a few stray drops of water off his brow with a napkin. "Maybe twenty-five blocks from here."

Unbelievable, Sam thought to herself. *I didn't expect him to come until right before the opening—if at all! Now I've got him here for a while . . . and he has family here. I really like him. As a friend. As more than a friend. Help!*

"So what's your rehearsal schedule?" Danny asked, pulling Sam out of her reverie.

Sam gave Danny a quick rundown on what the next few days were going to be like for her—leaving out the part about her lunch with Wolf Man Comfort later that day.

"Well, I can see that you don't have a lot of free time—you're in a show that's about to open. But we'll still have some time to hang out, huh?"

"I'm into it," Sam replied honestly.

"Then, how about the West End Cafe tomorrow evening?" Danny queried, mentioning a well-known jazz club up by Columbia University. He turned to Emma and Carrie. "You guys up for it?"

Emma said she'd be there, and try to get Adam to come too, but Carrie replied that she was supposed to have dinner with her parents in New Jersey and couldn't make it.

"Okay, but we'll do something else another time," Danny replied.

This guy is so sweet . . . and there's something about him that's so, well, comfortable, Sam thought to herself. I never feel that with Pres. *But maybe comfortable isn't good, maybe comfortable isn't sexy, maybe—*

"Hey, aren't you supposed to be at rehearsal in twenty minutes?" Carrie asked Sam.

Sam looked at her Mickey Mouse watch. "Eek!" she cried, jumping up. "I gotta boogie!"

She kissed Danny, grabbed her dance bag, and flew out the door.

"I'm really glad to see you!" Danny called after her.

Mutual, Sam thought to herself as she hailed a cab—no time for the subway now. *Very, very mutual.*

"So, Sam," Laszlo said to her in his deep, portentous voice over their plate-laden table. "Did you enjoy lunch?"

Sam took a deep breath. Lunch had actually been a pretty excruciating experience, as Laszlo thought that Sam would be impressed by all his show biz stories about famous stars, but when Sam figured out that all the stars were women with whom Laszlo claimed to have "an intimate and passionate relationship," the stories quickly lost whatever attraction they might have had.

"The food was good," Sam said, mustering as much enthusiasm as she could.

"That's Sardi's! Ha ha!" Laszlo chuckled, his imposing mustache bobbing up and down. "I was referring to the company. Oh, hello, Rocco!" Laszlo turned and exchanged a few sentences with a distinguished-looking bearded gentleman who was leaving with an actor who looked vaguely familiar to Sam until she realized it was Michael J. Fox. Laszlo introduced the two of them to Sam, saying that Sam was one of the featured dancers in *Helen!*, and someone that they both should keep an eye on.

Holy Junction, Kansas! Sam thought giddily as she shook Michael J. Fox's hand. *I'm meeting Michael J. Fox. If only Emma and Carrie could see me now!*

From where she was sitting with Laszlo, near the front door of Sardi's, Sam suddenly spotted two even more familiar people walk out of one of the back rooms.

It was Carrie with Matt Carlton. Holding hands.

Gee, they really look cute together, Sam realized.

Carrie and Matt caught sight of Sam and Laszlo, and Matt, who had a pretty big role in *Helen!*, steered Carrie toward their table. Michael J. Fox and Rocco Landesman were still talking with Laszlo Comfort, so when Laszlo caught sight of them, he smoothly introduced Matt, and got Matt to introduce Carrie.

Sam looked over at Carrie. She was in total awe of what was happening. Matt, on the other hand, handled the entire thing with total aplomb. Then Michael J. Fox and Rocco Landesman excused themselves, and Laszlo insisted that Matt and Carrie join him and Sam for coffee.

"Any friend of Sam's is a friend of mine," he said, lasciviously oogling Carrie, not even attempting to hide the lecherous side of his nature.

"So Sam, did you enjoy your lunch?" Carrie asked her friend too politely, a secret look on her face saying that what she was really asking was "Did you survive lunch?"

"Why, yes, Carrie, lunch was lovely," Sam replied, matching Carrie's formal tones. "And how was *your* lunch?" Which really meant "What were you and Matt doing holding hands, girlfriend?"

"Friendly," Carrie replied pointedly.

"I was just about to ask Sam," Laszlo said, checking out Sam's slim figure thoroughly, "whether she might not want to do this again, sometime soon. But in more comfortable surroundings. Get it? *Comfort*-able!" Laszlo Comfort cracked up at his own pun.

I gotta hand it to this turkey, Sam thought with a wry grin. *He may be a total womanizer and lech, but at least he's up front about it, not like most of the slime-buckets running around out there.*

"I get it," Sam said.

"And you're amused, I can see," Laszlo added.

"Oh, absolutely," Sam replied.

"Puns are the highest form of humor, you know," Laszlo explained.

"Ya don't say," Sam marveled.

"So what about it?" Laszlo asked.

"Gee . . . " Sam began.

Laszlo turned to Carrie. "Tell her my intentions are totally honorable—even if they aren't!" He chuckled again at his own joke.

"Sam speaks for herself," Carrie said, trying to keep her distaste for Sam's director out of her voice.

"I want to concentrate on the show until we open," Sam answered. She saw that Matt was nodding—who could argue with that answer?

"Well," Laszlo said, "I'm not deterred easily."

"Clearly not," Carrie said under her breath, but Laszlo, rather than taking offense, just laughed.

"I'll tell you what," he said. "How about you and I go out together the night after our second performance?"

"Second performance?" Sam repeated.

Everyone is saying there isn't going to be a second performance, Sam thought. *This director is not only a lech, but is also a dense lech. At least about his own show.*

"Laszlo," Sam answered, thinking she had

nothing to lose, "if there's a second performance, and I'm in it, we've got a date."

"Now that's the kind of career move I like to see." Laszlo Comfort cackled with glee. "Start making your plans to get comfortable. Real comfortable. Now, let's get back to rehearsal."

As she rose from the table, Sam looked over at Carrie and Matt, who just shrugged. Obviously, nobody thought she had much to worry about. And neither did Sam.

Emma and Adam sat side-by-side in the waiting room of The F-Stop Agency, located on the twenty-third floor of 666 Fifth Avenue, in midtown, listening to the evening rush hour traffic below mix with the sounds of the relentless rain. All around them on the wall were blown-up covers of some of the most famous magazines in the world, including *Paris Match, Elle, Vogue, GQ,* and *Cosmopolitan*. And each of the cover models was an F-Stop client. There were also posters from environmental magazines: beautiful, lush nature shots from around the world.

The waiting room was full of gorgeous and not-so gorgeous young women and men, all checking each other out. At one point, Emma watched a cover model saunter directly through the waiting room and into the private offices.

"I can't believe we're still here," Adam groused good-naturedly. "It's been all afternoon."

"You'd rather be out there?" Emma asked, pointing to the rainy streets below. Her comment was punctuated by a flash of lightning and a brutally loud clap of thunder.

Adam smiled. "I guess not," he replied. "It'll be a trick getting a taxi."

At that moment, a tall, very slender, very striking-looking woman with hair a color not found in nature strode into the room.

"Not to worry, I'll send you home in my limo," she said. "Anything for the niece of Liz Barrington. Come on in."

Emma and Adam followed the woman back to her office, a large corner room decorated with plants, tribal masks, and trinkets from around the globe.

"You're Gillian Garrett," Emma said, still standing.

"The one," Gillian replied, in a wonderful-sounding Australian accent. "I own this place. Now sit down." Gillian sat down across from them and laid a big portfolio she was carrying on the conference table.

"This is my friend, Adam Briarly," Emma

said, introducing Adam. "Aunt Liz told me to tell you she misses you," she added.

"And I miss her," Gillian agreed. "But now I owe her one."

"Excuse me?" Emma asked.

"I said I owe her one," Gillian replied. She opened a portfolio and spread out the photos of Emma that her aunt had sent in. There was also a sheet of color slides Liz had taken the last time Emma was in New York.

"Normally, this takes several days," she said confidentially, "but Liz has been a friend for a long time." She continued to spread the photos out. Then, she flipped on a switch next to her and suddenly the whole table lit up, perfectly illuminating the slides from the back.

"It feels very strange to see so many photos of myself," Emma said uncomfortably.

"You'll get used to it," Gillian said absently. She studied the slides carefully. "Emma, dear, you've got real possibilities. Look!"

"I . . . don't know what to look at," Emma admitted. "I mean, I just look like me."

"Your aunt is a terrific photographer," Gillian stated. "And you were a terrific model—natural, graceful, and what bone structure! See, even in jeans and a T-shirt you look sort of regal."

Emma blushed. "Thank you," she said simply. Adam reached over and squeezed her hand.

"Don't thank me, thank good blood lines and good bone structure," Gillian replied. She looked up at Emma. "You're too short to do high fashion, but maybe for the right print ad—"

"You mean you're saying you can get me work?" Emma asked incredulously.

Gillian smiled. "Isn't that why you're here?"

"Well, yes," Emma said carefully. "I mean, Aunt Liz made me promise to come, but I didn't really think . . ."

"Well, perhaps you should start," Gillian said, appraising Emma. "Do you want to do this?"

"I . . . think so," Emma said hesitantly.

Gillian laughed. "I wish I had a tape of this conversation. Do you know how many girls would kill for the chance I've just offered you? Did you see the girls out in that lobby who are begging for an opportunity?"

"I don't mean to seem ungrateful," Emma said quickly. "I've made a decision that it's time to try some new things." *Especially now that Kurt's out of the picture and the Peace Corps is on hold,* Emma added to herself. "I just . . . honestly, I never really thought much before about becoming a model! It's such a new idea to me, and I wouldn't be in it for the money . . ."

"Yes, I know that," Gillian agreed.

"Pay me instead," Adam joked. Emma grinned.

"I'm in it for the money," Gillian replied, looking closely at the pictures again. "Listen, don't be too far from a phone in the next few days, okay?"

"Okay," Emma agreed. "My aunt told you that I'm going back to Sunset Island soon, didn't she?" she asked.

"Well, let's see what happens before we discuss that, shall we?" Gillian replied.

Emma thought a moment. "Do you think . . . I mean, if I actually get a modeling job, could we just donate the money to Greenpeace?"

Gillian smiled. "Well, you just picked a cause directly after my own heart. You really are Liz's niece, aren't you?"

"I sure am," Emma agreed with a smile.

"Emma, dear, you can donate the money anywhere you like," Gillian said.

Emma thanked Gillian, and she and Adam left the office.

"You're too much, Emma," Adam said as they waited for the elevator.

"What?" Emma asked.

"You almost turned down the hippest modeling agency in New York!"

"Modeling just seems . . . tacky," Emma admitted. "I can't help it."

"Tacky?" Adam repeated, looking amused.

"Oh, I don't know what I'm saying," Emma said, shaking her head ruefully. "That's my mother talking, not me. Doesn't it drive you crazy when your parents' words come out of your own mouth?"

"Actually, Susan's words are generally pretty cool," Adam said. The elevator came and they stepped inside.

"It's amazing that she's Sam's birth mom," Emma mused. "They are so totally different."

"You think?" Adam asked. "I see a lot of similarities."

"Such as?" Emma asked.

But instead of answering her, Adam calmly wrapped his arms around Emma and started kissing her.

They were still kissing when the elevator doors opened at another floor and several surprised people came aboard.

EIGHT

"This place is unbelievable," Carrie muttered, looking around the crowded main floor of New York's world-famous Hard Rock Cafe. Rock and roll memorabilia covered every spare surface, and waiters and waitresses darted around the tables.

"And crowded," Emma added as someone bumped into her chair from behind. A crowd of giggling girls ran past, screeching at the top of their lungs, and Emma winced. "Very crowded." She looked over at Carrie and smiled. "I really like that outfit."

Carrie looked down at herself. She had on a forest-green scoop-necked body suit under a forest-green crocheted mini-dress, with ankle-length black tights and black flats. A black velvet ribbon circled her neck like a choker. She had bought the entire outfit in the village the day before. "Pretty racy for me, huh?" Carrie asked doubtfully.

"But you look great!" Emma insisted.

"I just feel so much more comfortable in baggy clothes," Carrie said with a shrug.

"That's just because you're used to baggy clothes," Emma pointed out gently. "You look completely darling in that. Even Sam would approve."

Carrie laughed. "Well, she'd be giving you major fashion points right about now," Carrie said, taking in Emma's white military-style mini-dress with navy blue piping.

"Maybe," Emma said. "But wearing white in New York is not the most practical choice in the world. Every time I come here, I realize all over again why my Aunt Liz's entire wardrobe is black!"

"I just saw Sylvester Stallone!" a freckled redheaded girl screamed from the next table. "I swear to God! Sylvester Stallone! Right by the front door!"

Emma and Carrie both turned to look and caught a glimpse of someone who looked only slightly like Sylvester Stallone disappearing into the crowd.

"He's short!" the redhead crowed to her friends. "Seriously short!"

"Even your boyfriend is taller than that!" her Asian companion exclaimed. "Oh, my God, I think Tom Cruise just came in!"

"No, that guy has zits," the redhead snorted. "Tom Cruise does not have zits!"

Emma laughed. "It seems like everyone in the world is in here."

"Or at least their look-alikes," Carrie pointed out. She swiveled around to look at the long line waiting to get in. "We got lucky, huh?"

They had arrived at the Hard Rock a little early, and were among the last people to get seated immediately for lunch. A huge line began forming outside the club before it was even eleven o'clock. Inside the Hard Rock, the bar area, a long way from where Emma and Carrie were sitting, was incredibly crowded.

"Yes, really lucky," Emma agreed, although in her head she could hear her mother saying that a Cresswell never waits in line for anything. *But then, no Cresswell but me would be caught dead at the Hard Rock Cafe!* Emma added to herself.

"Hey, isn't that Joey Lawrence over there?" Carrie whispered to Emma.

Emma looked across the room. "I can't tell behind the sunglasses," she said.

"I'm sure it is," Carrie affirmed. "He is so adorable—"

"Tell me that's Cher!" the girl behind

Emma screamed just then, clutching her friend's arm. "Please tell me that's Cher!"

Emma winced.

"Serious celebrity watching," Carrie observed. "Sam is going to go nuts that she missed this."

A gorgeous waitress hurried over to them. "Yeah?" she asked impatiently.

"We haven't seen menus," Emma pointed out.

The waitress sighed and grabbed two menus from a nearby coffee service stand and thrust them at the girls. "So?" she asked, her pad poised.

"We haven't read the menu yet," Emma said.

The girl mumbled something under her breath and disappeared into the crowd.

"Don't tell me," Carrie said. "She's got to be a struggling actress who hates the fact that she's waiting tables for a living."

"Probably," Emma agreed, scanning the menu. "Or else she's just incredibly rude, ill-bred, and a bitch."

Carrie laughed. "You never fail to surprise me," Carrie said, looking over the menu.

Suddenly the jukebox came on and the sounds of U2 filled the air.

"Ready?" the waitress asked loudly over

the music, appearing at their table again a few minutes later.

"Why, yes, how kind of you to ask," Emma said in her frostiest voice. Carrie stifled a laugh. The girls ordered and the waitress took off. Emma and Carrie peered around the restaurant some more.

"So," Carrie said, looking right at Emma.

"So what?" Emma replied, grinning back.

"What do you think?" Carrie asked.

"About what?" Emma queried, though she guessed what Carrie was referring to.

Okay, I'll tell her, Emma thought, *but I want to get the story on Carrie and Matt, too! I mean, fair's fair!*

The waitress came back with their drinks, and Emma took a sip of iced tea before she turned back to Carrie.

"You want to know what's going on with me and Adam," she said.

"Bingo," Carrie replied. "But if I'm prying, you don't have to tell me—"

"Carrie! You're my best friend! How could you be prying?"

"Well, you can't beg for confidences," Carrie explained, sipping her diet Coke.

"I like him," Emma said simply.

"That's obvious." Carrie grinned.

"I mean I *really* like him," Emma qualified.

"Do you love him?" Carrie asked.

"I can't tell yet," Emma replied. She pushed some of her perfect blond hair behind one ear. "I mean, really, I hardly know him yet. It's confusing, you know? And I keep thinking about Kurt . . ."

"You did the right thing by not marrying him," Carrie said firmly. "You know you did."

"I know," Emma agreed with a sigh. "But I just wish I'd figured that out before I accepted his proposal! Before I planned that wedding . . ."

"Don't be so hard on yourself," Carrie said quietly.

"I can't seem to help it," Emma commented.

"Em, do you still love Kurt?"

"It's over," Emma said. "Even if I did, it wouldn't matter. Kurt will never speak to me again as long as he lives. And . . . maybe it's for the best. Maybe he needs a completely different kind of girl than me."

"Well, I do think you and Adam are really well suited to each other," Carrie said.

"Do you?" Emma asked. She grinned. "He's really terrific."

"You sure seem to be spending a lot of time with him," Carrie noted.

Emma smiled. "Wouldn't you?"

Carrie reached for a roll. "He's not my

type," Carrie joked. "I like my guys short, ugly, and stupid."

"Like Billy," Emma cracked.

"Amen!" Carrie laughed.

Emma took a deep breath. "The thing is," she began, "I'm just trying to be really careful about getting too involved too soon. . . ."

"Well," Carrie reasoned, "you can take it at your own pace. No one is making you rush."

Emma pursed her lips. "That's easy to say—theoretically."

"You mean that every time you see him your heart races?" Carrie asked, raising her voice to carry over the jukebox and the overall din in the restaurant.

"No, it doesn't race," Emma said. "It spins out of control."

Carrie laughed. "A lot of girls would love to have that problem."

"They can have it," Emma said with a sigh. "Sometimes I'm sorry I like him so much."

"You're in the driver's seat, Emma," Carrie repeated, raising her voice still another notch. "You're calling the shots."

"I guess so," Emma said.

"There's nothing to guess," Carrie said emphatically.

"Well," Emma responded, "it's not that simple. I mean, when he kisses me I just . . ."

"Melt?" Carrie suggested.

"Something like that," Emma said.

"So what's wrong with that?" Carrie asked.

"But I'm not in love with him!" Emma said. "Maybe I will be—someday—but it's too soon!"

"You think that to hold someone or kiss someone you have to be in love with them?" Carrie asked.

"Well, not exactly," Emma began.

"But you think there has to be the possibility of love," Carrie continued.

Emma nodded. "I only had one boyfriend before Kurt—"

"Trent," Carrie said, recalling that she'd met him the previous summer.

Emma nodded. "Right. And he was more of a companion than a boyfriend. There was never any chemistry between us—not for me, anyway. Kurt was the first guy I really, really wanted. I used to have really wild, sexy dreams about him."

"Sounds like fun!" Carrie replied, sipping her soda.

"But look how everything turned out," Emma reminded her friend. "I can't go through something like that again. I just can't!"

"What's that old saying . . . once burnt, twice shy?" Carrie asked.

"Right," Emma said, nodding firmly. "That's just how I feel."

"Look, Kurt and Adam are two entirely different guys," Carrie said. "What are you going to do, never get involved with another guy because things turned out badly with Kurt? We're still really young, you know. Maybe you two really weren't right for each other!"

"But maybe—" Emma began.

Before Emma could finish her thought, she saw a dark look cross Carrie's face. *What could be wrong?*

"What is it?" Emma asked, concerned.

Carrie was on the verge of tears. "Look!" she cried, pointing to the bar.

Emma looked.

Oh, my God, she thought, *that's Billy Sampson up there, right next to some blond girl who looks like a model. I'd recognize his ponytail and that black leather jacket anywhere. And she's hanging all over him!*

"I thought Billy was in Canada visiting friends!" Emma cried. "What's he doing here?"

"How should I know?" Carrie said angrily. "But obviously he's two-timing me. Look, I think I'd better go." She stood up quickly.

Emma stopped her. "Let me give you some

Carrie Alden advice," she said slowly. "Carrie Alden would say to go up to him and confront him, and then walk out with your head held high."

Carrie grimaced.

"Carrie!" Emma said forcefully. "I'll go up there with you."

Carrie stared at Emma with tears in her eyes. "I can't do this, Emma."

"You can," Emma said firmly.

"Oh, damn," Carrie muttered miserably. She sighed and made a decision. "All right. I'll do it. But if I'm doing it, I'm doing it alone."

She took a deep breath, then Emma watched as Carrie wended her way through the packed Hard Rock Cafe, toward the bar. It must have taken her five minutes to make her way there. Billy and the model were huddled together, their faces hidden. Carrie strode slowly up to Billy's back, avoiding the huge crush of people around the blond girl.

Emma watched in a combination of fascination and horror as Carrie tapped him on the shoulder. He turned around.

Then Emma watched Carrie crack up.

God, that's weird, she thought.

But what was even odder was that right after that, Carrie and Billy exchanged a few sentences, laughing together. Then Billy kissed Carrie on the cheek, and Carrie started back to Emma and her table. It took as long for Carrie to make her way back to Emma.

When Carrie got back, she was still laughing. "What was that all about?" Emma asked. "You let him kiss you! I saw it with my own eyes!"

"That's right," Carrie laughed. "I did."

"But I thought—"

"You thought wrong," Carrie said, still chuckling. "I thought wrong. It wasn't Billy. It was some Irish rock musician named Seamus O'Donnell. God, am I embarrassed!"

Emma started to giggle. And then the giggle turned into a chuckle. And then the chuckle turned into one of the biggest laughs she'd ever laughed.

"Wait'll you tell Billy," she stammered between laughs.

"I gotta tell you," Carrie replied, still laughing. "That Seamus O'Donnell sure looked good. Great, even. I must really miss Billy! When's lunch?"

At that moment, the waitress came back with the two spinach salads Emma and Carrie had ordered. She looked at the girls really strangely because they were laughing so hard, but all she did was mutter "kids" derisively under her breath.

"So that's what happened to Carrie," Emma explained to Adam, Sam, and Danny as the four of them sat in the small jazz listening room at the West End Cafe, located just across from Columbia University, on the upper West Side.

"Incredible," Sam said. "I wish I could have seen it."

"Well, you know," Adam said, "supposedly everyone has a double in this world."

"Wrong," Danny cracked. "No double for Sam. The world couldn't take it."

"I'm one of a kind and aim to stay that way," Sam said.

Sam was dressed in her usual style. She had on a Mickey Mouse-covered bra top with a jean jacket vest, and biker shorts over which she wore a see-through mesh miniskirt. And of course, her trademark cowboy boots. Emma, for her part, wore a short yellow and white flowered mini-dress that she'd purchased on a shopping spree that afternoon with Carrie.

After lunch at the Hard Rock she and Carrie had shopped for a few hours, then Carrie had taken off to go to New Jersey for dinner with her parents. When Carrie had gotten on the bus at the Port Authority, she and Emma were still laughing about mistaking an Irish rock star for Billy.

It was the West End's usual late Friday afternoon jazz session, and the four of them were sitting in the crowded room listening to the Countsmen, who were all alumni of Count Basie's old band. Sam had groused that her grandparents in Kansas were into Count Basie, not her, but after the band did a few numbers, she was bopping along like there was no such thing as rock and roll.

"So, you like it after all!" Danny told her.

"Right now I'd like anything other than rehearsal for the show," Sam said. "Lucky for me there's a problem with the sets and they gave us a few hours off."

"What's the problem?" Emma asked.

"Oh, something about the hydraulic lift for the fantasy dance number. Nancy Pumpkin almost fell into the pool of water this morning. She could have gotten electrocuted. Actually, everyone was kind of hoping she would."

They listened to the next two numbers, everyone tapping their feet to the terrific tunes.

"This is great!" Sam cried, after one of the

musicians finished a particularly hot trombone solo.

And then it happened. All the lights in the listening room suddenly went out. And the amplifiers went out. And even the constant humming of the air conditioner and refrigerator systems went silent. The band quit playing. There was a buzz of conversation as people waited for the lights to come on, but they didn't. Then, after everyone's eyes had adjusted to the faint lighting, the band picked up again, this time without amplification and with an acoustic guitar instead of an electric one.

"Power outage," Adam surmised. "It happens sometimes in San Francisco, too. It'll come back on in a sec. They must have blown a fuse or popped a breaker."

Except it didn't come back on. And because the day was hot, the room got hotter and hotter. The girls and their friends sat there for a while, but some people were already leaving.

"Come on," Danny suggested, "let's give this a rest."

In unison, they got up and left the listening room together. And what they saw when they got outside was unforgettable.

Not only was the power out in the West End Cafe, but all over the neighborhood. And from the rumors that were already floating around, the whole city was blacked out.

Sam and Emma looked around some more. Even though it was only five o'clock and the summer sun was still shining, New York City without electrical power was like a blind man in an unfamiliar place without a guide.

The traffic lights were all out, and the rush hour traffic had already clogged every intersection they could see. Cash registers in the stores had locked shut, so merchants couldn't do business. The underground subway system had ground to a halt, and people were pouring out of a stop near Columbia University with exasperated looks on their faces.

A well-dressed man with stains of sweat around the armpits of his expensive shirt came out of the subway and looked right at Emma. "How the hell am I supposed to get home? Would you answer me that? I live in New Jersey!"

Emma, of course, had no answer.

The man swore under his breath and took off up Broadway.

"What're we going to do?" Sam asked her friends.

Danny wiped his forehead with the back of his hand. "Sweat, evidently," he said.

People were moving around them, looking stunned.

"Basically," Adam said cheerfully, looking around, "it looks like we're screwed."

NINE

"It's a nightmare!" Danny said, looking at the chaos on the streets around them.

"Not yet," Adam commented. "The nightmare starts tonight, if the lights don't come back on."

A dozen cars started blaring their horns in the packed intersection of Broadway and West 116th Street, making it nearly impossible for the friends to hear one another.

"Has this ever happened before?" Sam shouted.

Emma nodded. "I read that it happened once in the late sixties and again in the seventies," she yelled back.

"How long did it last?" Sam asked.

Danny grinned a sick grin. "Long enough that people still ask 'where were you when the lights went out?'"

"Great," Sam moaned. "Just great. That's

all my show needs. A day less rehearsal. How are we gonna get back to the loft? How far are we from there, anyway?"

Emma rolled her eyes. "About one hundred and twenty blocks," she said. "Give or take a few streets."

"How many blocks to the mile?" Sam demanded.

"Twenty," Adam responded.

"And I had to wear cowboy boots," Sam said, looking down at her feet ruefully.

"So, I think we ought to hang here until the power comes back on," Adam shouted over the sound of a particularly loud car horn bleating. "It looks like it's impossible to get a cab, and traffic's not moving anyway."

"What if it doesn't come on?" Danny said.

"Party! Party!" Two guys yelled as they ran into the street and shimmied in front of the backed up cars.

"Great, the lunatics are already coming out of the woodwork," Adam muttered.

"I don't get along well with lunatics," Sam said, eyeing the guys in the street, who were now waving their arms at the cars for no apparent reason.

"Maybe we should try to help out," Danny suggested.

"Yeah, and maybe that would be nuts," Sam shot back as one of the guys climbed up onto the hood of a car that was stuck at the intersection.

"They're leaving," Emma said as they watched the two dancing bozos run across the street and head into a bar.

"I wonder what we could do?" Adam said.

Just then they watched a motorist climb out of his car and stride directly into the intersection of Broadway and 116th Street, which at that moment was a sea of automobiles and trucks jammed together in a classic case of gridlock—vehicles were blocking the intersection from all directions, leaving their drivers with no place to go and nothing to do but lean on their horns.

Sam, Danny, and Emma watched in amazement as the man, holding a red bandana in his hand like the torch in the hand of the Statue of Liberty, began directing traffic in the middle of the jammed intersection. Adam grinned and ran over to help. And, miraculously, though it took a while, the traffic gridlock began to thin out. The street was still a cacophony of blaring car horns, but at least there was some distance between the vehicles whose owners were leaning on their horns.

"Very cool," Danny said approvingly.

"Sort of like bullfighting," Sam quipped. "That's my idea of a good time—two tons of

Ford station wagon bearing down on me, I leap to one side, executing a perfect pirouette—"

"Only you could make a disaster into a dance," Danny said with a laugh. Something caught her eye on the other side of the street. "Hey, that ice cream shop is giving out free cones over there."

"I guess they figure without electricity they might as well give the stuff away, or else they'll end up with soup," Emma said.

"Take advantage of every opportunity, I always say," Sam said, leading the two of them across the street to the ice cream shop. They all got ice creams, and an extra for Adam, who darted between the cars to meet them.

"Here's your reward, you good citizen, you," Emma said, handing Adam an ice cream. They all licked their ice creams quickly before they could melt in the heat.

"Now what?" Sam asked, licking the ice cream off her pinky.

"I hate to say it, but we might as well start walking back to SoHo," Emma said.

"Ugh," Sam replied.

"Maybe we could get as far as your theater and take a break," Danny suggested to Sam.

"God, the theater," Sam said with a shudder. "It must be a total zoo there without electricity."

"Get the hell off the road, you frigging jerk!" a man yelled out the window of his car as a woman tried to maneuver her car through the intersection.

"Make me!" the woman yelled, giving the guy the finger. She beeped her horn, and then the other guy beeped his horn long and hard, and then everyone seemed to join in. The intersection that Adam had helped clear was completely clogged again.

"This is crazy," Danny muttered.

"And the natives are getting restless," Adam added. "Maybe we really should just start walking. It's going to get dark soon."

"We'll vote on it," Danny said. "All in favor?"

"I," Emma said with resignation.

"Me, too," Adam said.

"Me, three," Danny added. He turned to Sam. "You?"

"Me? I'm brilliant!" Sam cried, eyeing a store across the street.

"Is that your vote?" Danny asked, amused.

"I'm a genius," Sam declared. "What's your shoe size?"

"What?" Danny asked.

"Your shoe size, dummy," Sam repeated.

"Ten and a half, but why? Are they giving away shoes?" Danny asked.

Sam ignored him, thinking to herself, *I'm an eight, Emma's a six, and Adam's an eleven—I remember from when I was in California, I asked him.*

"How much cash do we have between us?" Sam asked the little group.

They totalled up their money and Sam motioned to them to follow her. She took Danny by the arm and dragged him to the store she had spotted. URBAN ROLLERBLADE: SALES AND RENTALS. When Danny figured out what Sam had in mind—that they were going to rollerblade back to the loft in SoHo, he started to crack up.

"You really are brilliant," he told Sam, giving her a quick hug.

"Gee, thanks," Sam said happily.

They hurried across the street and rented the rollerblades. Right after they came into the store a deluge of people followed them— but evidently Sam was the first one to get the idea.

"Have you ever actually done this before?" Emma asked Sam as she gingerly tried out the rollerblades.

"No," Sam admitted. "But I rollerskated when I was a kid. How tough can it be?"

"Tough," Adam commented as he almost

fell over. "I don't think I've got the hang of this yet."

"Well, shall we roll?" Danny asked them.

"Here goes nothing," Adam muttered.

And the four of them began the long, long roll home.

"That was the wildest ride of my life," Sam said wearily.

"Columbia University to SoHo in two hours!" Danny laughed, sitting down on the small stoop in front of Aunt Liz's loft building on Spring Street.

"I thought we were gonna die when we came out of Central Park and then landed in Times Square," Adam admitted. "There were people looting stuff from stores!"

"Not many," Emma noted. "And there were lots of cops, too."

"Traffic wasn't moving too fast, but we were. You have to admit it, it was a great adventure," Danny said.

"Only because we made it back here in one piece," Emma said.

"Thank God for that," Sam cracked. "My legs are killing me."

Emma laughed. "You looked like you were born on rollerblades. I thought I'd never make it."

She looked down the long street. "This is so

wild. Everyone is out on the street! People act like it's Mardi Gras or something!"

Sam looked at Emma. "Don't tell me. You've been to New Orleans for Mardi Gras."

"Well, yes," Emma admitted. "Twice."

"Figures," Sam muttered.

"Hey, cheer up," Emma said, nudging Sam playfully. "This is actually more fun!" She reached down and began to unlace her rollerblades.

All up and down Spring Street, neighbors who didn't know each other were hanging out on their stoops, drinking beer being given away for free by the owner of a bar on the corner, and eating desserts being given away by the sweets shop in the middle of the block.

Someone had turned up a battery-powered radio really loud—loud enough so that everyone on the block could easily hear it. WCBS-AM was broadcasting on emergency power, and the all-news station was keeping New Yorkers abreast of the latest developments in the power outage. The announcer was repeating that the blackout was affecting the greater Manhattan and New York City area. Meanwhile, New Jersey, right across the Hudson River, was totally unaffected. And while there were some isolated reports of trouble—like what Sam and Emma had seen in Times Square—the New

York Police Department was reporting actually less crime than normal. The announcer repeated that New Jersey and Connecticut were unaffected.

"Carrie's in the light!" Sam said. "But she's missing an experience."

"She'll be sorry she missed this," Emma noted wryly.

"You're probably right," Sam said, rubbing gingerly at her aching calves. "It could have been a photo opportunity for her. The 90's Blackout—a documentary by Carrie Alden."

All up and down Spring Street, an impromptu party was going on. There was very little automobile traffic—in a blackout, there's really no place to go—so people had mostly taken over the street. Candles were set out everywhere, and people were picnicking on their front steps. Adam went upstairs and brought some plates of food down for everybody to munch on.

"Everyone's so friendly!" Sam commented, watching the candlelit circus. "Back in Kansas, they think New Yorkers are like criminals who have the key to their prison, but they're just too dumb to leave." She thought for a moment. "Of course, that's how I feel about Kansas—so who knows?"

The others laughed.

"I think New Yorkers are great," Danny said. "I'd love to live here."

Sam gave him an appraising look. "You would?"

Danny nodded. "It's the most exciting city in the world."

"Well, I'd love to live here, too," Sam told him.

He gave her a sweet smile. "Huh. Isn't that a happy coincidence."

Just at that moment, a young guy with a long black ponytail, wearing black biker shorts, a Bob Marley T-shirt and a Mets baseball cap came zipping around the corner on his bike. He stopped right in front of them.

"Hey, do you know if there's a Liz Barrington in this building?" he asked breathlessly.

Emma looked at the guy closely. She didn't recognize him at all.

"Is there something I can help you with?" Emma asked, wanting to see what the guy wanted before she volunteered any information.

"Yeah," the guy said, "you can, maybe. I gotta delivery here—for an Emma Cresswell . . . she's in Barrington's apartment."

A delivery? For me? Emma thought. *That's weird. At this hour?*

"That's me," Emma said warily.

"Come on," the bike messenger said. "That's the oldest line in the book. You gotta show me some I.D."

"Hey, maybe she should be asking you for I.D.," Adam suggested in a no-nonsense voice.

"Oh, man, I'm just going back home and getting in bed," the young guy groused. "Do you know what my life has been like today, trying to make deliveries in this crazy city with the power out? I practically got mugged in Times Square. A lady in the East Village went into labor and wanted to commandeer my bike to get to the hospital!"

"Ducky," Sam said. "Now show us some I.D."

"Fine, cool, great," the guy muttered sarcastically as he pulled out his wallet and flipped to a photo I.D. of himself from the Comet Messenger Service. "You happy?"

"Elated," Emma replied.

"You think someone would pose as a messenger in this jungle?" the guy asked. He threw up his hands. "What for?"

"To get near one of the richest heiresses in the country!" Sam exploded, pointing at Emma. All three of her friends stared at her, and she immediately realized her blunder. "Oops," she said meekly.

"Yeah, she's an heiress and I'm Michael Jordan," the messenger snorted. "Can I please see some I.D. so I can go harass other innocent citizens?"

Emma reached in her pocketbook and pulled out her Massachusetts driver's license, and showed it to the messenger.

"Cool," he said. "Sign here. Quick. Tonight's busy because there's no telephone. I'm runnin' five hours behind. My life is a nightmare." Then he handed Emma the package and rode off into the night.

"Thank you," Emma called after him. She tore open the envelope. Adam grabbed one of the many candles that had been placed out on the street and held it by the envelope so that she could read it.

The first thing Emma saw was the F-Stop Agency logo across the top of the letter. Then she read it. It was from Gillian Garrett at the agency.

Emma—I would have called you but obviously tonight that's fairly impossible. However, we New Yorkers are nothing if not resourceful, even if we were born in Brisbane, Australia! Therefore, I am counting on you tomorrow to be at a modeling shoot, which commences at 2:00 P.M. on the roof of 98 East

7th Street. There is no elevator, but what good would an elevator do now, anyway?! We will pay you $150 per hour for a minimum of three hours. There will be other models there. Clothes will be provided for you. Come with freshly washed hair and no makeup. I'll be there because this shoot will be featuring a major new model I just signed.

Love, Gillian

"Wow," Adam said, reading over Emma's shoulder. "Your first modeling job. Are you going?"

"Of course," Emma said. "I mean, I can't very well not go. She's expecting me. And . . . maybe, maybe it'll be fun."

"Yeah," Sam cracked, "and she can give the proceeds of her labor to the Sam Bridges Emergency Show Biz Relief Fund."

"Come on," Danny chided her, reaching for a bagel on one of the plates of food Adam had brought down. "You're making major bucks now! You're in a Broadway show!"

"For about five minutes," Sam replied, swallowing some potato salad. "I'm telling you, this show is a loser. My big break is going to be a big flop!"

"Negative thinking will get you nowhere," Adam opined.

Sam grabbed the note from Emma. "Tomorrow, huh? Maybe I should go with you and try to get some modeling work instead of going to technical rehearsal at the theater."

"Yeah, and maybe you'd get sued for not showing up," Danny told her. "Besides, no one's hiring you to model, they're hiring Emma."

Sam kicked him in the shins playfully. "That's for being so logical."

Danny whacked Sam on the head with the now empty paper plate. "That's for being a pain in the ass!" A dapple of potato salad flew off the plate and landed in Sam's hair.

"Yum, potato salad mixed with grunge," Sam said with a laugh, and pulled the gunk out of her hair. "I am major-league filthy. I gotta catch a shower, dark or no dark."

"I don't suppose you're going to invite me to join you?" Danny asked.

"A guy who just bopped me with potato salad?"

"I could wash your hair for you," Danny offered.

"In your dreams," Sam replied, and stood up. She stretched out. "Whew, I am totally beat." She looked over at Emma, who sat with her head against Adam's shoulder. "I just want you to know, I am not at all jealous of your modeling job tomorrow, Miss Thing."

"Miss Thing?" Emma repeated with amusement.

"Everyone at the theater calls everyone else Miss Thing," Sam explained.

"And just why is it that you aren't jealous?" Danny asked.

"Because I know who the photographer is," Sam confided.

"Who's that?" Danny asked her.

"Flash Hathaway."

Emma blanched. Flash Hathaway was a photographer who kept showing up in their lives. First, on Sunset Island, he'd lured Sam into having some revealing lingerie shots taken of herself, and then Flash had exhibited the photos without Sam's permission. Then, Flash was a press photographer on Johnny Angel's tour with Flirting With Danger, and Johnny Angel ended up wrecking Flash's cameras because of some pictures Flash had taken of Johnny and Sam.

"Can you imagine?" Emma shuddered. "That guy keeps coming back into our lives, sort of like the flu." She looked at Sam. "You are kidding, Sam . . . aren't you . . . ?"

"You never know," Sam said philosophically. "If I were you, I'd take some bug spray, just in case."

"Now what would Emma do with bug spray?" Adam asked.

"Well, if it turns out Flash really is at the photo shoot," Sam said, "I suggest you spray the little cockroach first and ask questions later!"

TEN

"You really don't mind going with me?" Emma asked Carrie as they got ready to leave for her modeling job the next afternoon. The power had come back on at about three o'clock in the morning, and Carrie's parents had dropped her back in the city at about 10:00 A.M.

"How could I mind?" Carrie asked as she tied the laces on the new black hiking boots she'd bought in a little shoe store in the East Village. "I can't decide if these shoes look good or stupid," she added, examining her leg.

"Good," Emma decreed, slipping into a pair of white jeans. "They look very cute with that short dress."

Carrie stared at her reflection in the floor-length mirror on the wall of Liz's loft. "And what am I doing wearing a mini-dress, will you answer me that? What possessed me to buy this?"

Emma looked over at Carrie. She had on a black high-waisted mini-dress covered in pink exclamation points and question marks. "It's very retro," Emma observed.

"Please tell me I don't look ridiculous," Carrie pleaded. "This dress looks more like something Sam would wear."

"I'm telling you the truth, you look absolutely darling," Emma promised.

"I went crazy at that used clothing store," Carrie said with a sigh. "I just couldn't believe I could get so much stuff so cheap."

Emma pulled a white cotton T-shirt over her head. "Should I take makeup, do you think?"

Carrie shrugged. "You're the one that knows about this stuff, not me."

"I'm just nervous," Emma said absently. She turned around and looked at Carrie. "I can't believe I'm going to model."

"Why not?" Carrie asked. "You're gorgeous."

"I'm not gorgeous and I am short," Emma responded.

Just at that moment the intercom buzzed, meaning that someone was downstairs.

The girls looked at each other.

"You expecting anyone?" Emma asked Carrie.

"Not a soul," Carrie said.

Emma went to the intercom. "Yes?"

"Hi, it's Matt Carlton," came a tinny voice through the intercom. "I'm on my lunch break!"

"Come on up," Emma said, and she buzzed Matt in. She turned to Carrie. "Why do I have this feeling he's not here to see me?"

"He could have called," Carrie said defensively.

"He could have, but he didn't," Emma said, just as Matt knocked on their front door. She opened the door. "Hi, there!"

Matt gave Emma a quick hug. "Hi. I hope you don't mind my just stopping over—I was in an impetuous mood." He walked over to Carrie. "Hey, you look great."

Carrie blushed. "Thanks. We were just leaving."

Matt looked crushed.

"We've got a few minutes," Emma said. "Anybody want a Coke or anything?"

"No, thanks," Matt said. "Carrie, could I talk with you a minute?"

"Talk," Carrie said tersely. She felt off-kilter, seeing Matt. *Be honest. You're just afraid you could really have feelings for him,* she realized. *It's making you be nasty to protect yourself.*

Matt sighed. "That was my polite way of saying I want to talk with you alone."

"I'll go take a quick walk around the block," Emma offered.

"You don't have to do that," Carrie said quickly.

"Yes, I do," Emma replied. "I have an errand to run, anyway," she improvised. She grabbed her purse and headed out the door.

"So . . ." Carrie said, sitting on the couch.

"So . . ." Matt said, sitting next to her.

"You're the one who wanted to talk," Carrie pointed out.

"I know," Matt agreed. "But you're not making this easy."

"Look, I told you at lunch the other day, there just isn't any future for us," Carrie said earnestly. "It's nothing against you, Matt. I just have other things going on in my life."

"Yeah, that's what you told me," Matt agreed. "But, you know, I'm a hardheaded kind of guy." He moved closer to her on the couch. "I kept remembering how things were with us at Paradise Island—"

"That was a tropical vacation. I lost my head—"

"You're not really the head-losing type, are you?" Matt asked her.

"Maybe not," Carrie conceded. "But even a levelheaded girl like me can lose it sometimes." She fiddled nervously with a loose thread on her dress.

"I just had such a great time with you at lunch," Matt continued. "And here you are, and here I am . . ."

"So that means we should be together?" Carrie asked.

Matt's huge brown eyes looked at her. She studied his mouth and remembered what it felt like when he'd kissed her on the beach, how she'd kissed him back so passionately and . . .

No, Carrie told herself firmly. *I am not some stupid, fickle kid. I really love Billy. I will not get sucked into this, no matter how much I like Matt.*

Carrie reached over and took Matt's hand. "Listen, Matt," she began. "I really like you. A lot. But I really am in love with my boyfriend. If it was you, you wouldn't want me messing around behind your back."

"I wish it *was* me," Matt said with a smile. He kissed Carrie's hand. Then they both stood up.

"Well, you can't blame me for trying," Matt replied.

"I'm very, very flattered," Carrie admitted.

"Will you be at the opening of the show?" he asked her.

"I wouldn't miss it." Carrie promised.

"Friends?" Matt asked.

"Absolutely," Carrie replied.

Matt held out his arms and wrapped them around Carrie. She smelled soap and a faint hint of some masculine-smelling cologne. For just the tiniest moment she wanted badly to say yes. *I'll be with you! Billy will never know!* But she didn't. Instead, she hugged Matt hard and showed him to the door.

Emma and Carrie decided to walk from Spring Street to the fashion shoot—it was only about a twenty-minute walk. All the way from the loft to the photo shoot, the two friends swapped stories about the blackout.

"All I could do," Carrie told Emma as they walked together, "was think about the adventures you and Sam were having."

Emma laughed. "They were some adventures, all right."

"And I was stuck in New Jersey with my parents!" Carrie complained. "At least we drove to the Palisades to take a look at the city."

"What did it look like?" Emma asked, stepping back from the curb at the corner of

Houston and Broadway to avoid a truck careening past.

"Blacked out," Carrie said deadpan. "Really blacked out."

Emma laughed. "You want to talk about adventure," she said, "think about those people on the one hundred and tenth floor of the World Trade Center. They had to walk down!"

"Good thing Sam wasn't there," Carrie said. "She'd have complained her legs were already sore from play rehearsal and called for a rescue helicopter!"

"They were all busy," Emma replied.

"Then she'd still be there! Stairs and Sam do not agree," Carrie responded as they continued walking along. Carrie was lugging one of her camera bags with her. "You really think they'll let me take pictures at this thing? I feel kind of like an idiot lugging this stuff."

"Maybe, especially if Gillian is actually there," Emma mused. "And if not, afterwards we'll do our own fashion shoot."

"Cool," Carrie replied. "It'll be fun. I've never done this kind of thing before. Do you have any idea what this shoot is about?"

"Not at all," Emma said as they continued walking down Houston Street toward First Avenue. "I tried to call Gillian, earlier, but I couldn't get through."

This was a pretty mixed section of the city, with hip-looking clubs with names like Beirut mixed in with used clothing stores, cheap jewelry boutiques, and ethnic food shops.

"You think I look all right?" Emma continued. "Maybe I was supposed to do something with my hair other than wash it."

"Emma, your hair is perfect," Carrie said. "Anyway, they'll probably have stylists there."

"I don't know," Emma replied. "I'm babbling. I suppose I just want to make a good first impresion."

"I seriously doubt that you ever made anything but a good first impression in your entire life. You were born making a good impression."

The girls walked past the subway station at the corner of First Avenue and Houston Street and turned left on First Avenue.

"Seven blocks to go!" Carrie said gaily. "You still nervous?"

"A little," Emma admitted.

"Me too," Carrie said, "and I'm not even having my picture taken." They continued walking in silence, past the incredibly diverse stores and people that made up this part of the East Village section of Manhattan. They saw post-punk rockers with safety

pins in their [...]
way to noon ma[...]
7th Street, and scr[...]
have nothing better to[...]
noises at them as they wa[...]

"Well, that's lovely," Emm[...]
sarcastically.

"They're harmless," Carrie said[...]
shrug.

Outside the address Gillian had given—
where the girls found a nondescript, five-
story red brick building with a fire escape
running down to the street, and a typical
New York-style front stoop—was parked a
black limousine and a couple of panel trucks,
obviously there for the photo shoot. There
was also an earnest-looking young man wearing glasses and carrying a clipboard.

Emma approached him. "I'm Emma Cresswell," she said.

"Oh, hi!" the guy said to her. "We're expecting you!" He turned a page on his clipboard
and checked off Emma's name. "Go right on
up—they're starting soon." He pointed to the
steps, which Emma and Carrie started to
climb. There was a small first-floor landing,
and then the narrow staircase started up
again. Emma and Carrie looked at it dubiously and then began to climb.

ears, old Polish ladies
ss at St. Ignatius Church on
iffy men who seemed to
do than make kissing
lked by.

commented

with a

...hit the
...this?"
...n black
...leather
...air, came
...artments.
...na. "I was
...y a finder's
...asked her. "I
...what your rent

"Hey, I g... the girl said. "It's only nine hundred m... ucks a month."

"How many rooms?" Carrie asked.

"Three," the girl said, "but the bathtub's not in the kitchen. See you guys." She pounded down the stairs two at a time, leaving an astonished Carrie and Emma in her wake.

"I grew up around here. I knew apartments were expensive in Manhattan, but wow! That's a lot of money," Carrie marveled. "I don't see how I'll ever be able to afford to live in this city!"

Emma looked at her with surprise. "I didn't know you wanted to."

"I'd love to sometime," Carrie replied. "Maybe one day you and me and Sam will live here together."

"Whew," Emma said, when they hit the fourth-floor landing. "Who'd live like this?"

At that moment a girl dressed in black tights, a black T-shirt, and a black leather jacket—with black, short, spikey hair, came out of one of the two fourth-floor apartments.

"I heard that," she said to Emma. "I was lucky to get this place. I had to pay a finder's fee!"

"I'm really curious," Carrie asked her. "I mean, do you mind my asking what your rent is?"

"Hey, I got a great deal," the girl said. "It's only nine hundred fifty bucks a month."

"How many rooms?" Carrie asked.

"Three," the girl said, "but the bathtub's not in the kitchen. See you guys." She pounded down the stairs two at a time, leaving an astonished Carrie and Emma in her wake.

"I grew up around here. I knew apartments were expensive in Manhattan, but wow! That's a lot of money," Carrie marveled. "I don't see how I'll ever be able to afford to live in this city!"

Emma looked at her with surprise. "I didn't know you wanted to."

"I'd love to sometime," Carrie replied. "Maybe one day you and me and Sam will live here together."

pins in their ears, old Polish ladies on the way to noon mass at St. Ignatius Church on 7th Street, and scruffy men who seemed to have nothing better to do than make kissing noises at them as they walked by.

"Well, that's lovely," Emma commented sarcastically.

"They're harmless," Carrie said with a shrug.

Outside the address Gillian had given—where the girls found a nondescript, five-story red brick building with a fire escape running down to the street, and a typical New York-style front stoop—was parked a black limousine and a couple of panel trucks, obviously there for the photo shoot. There was also an earnest-looking young man wearing glasses and carrying a clipboard.

Emma approached him. "I'm Emma Cresswell," she said.

"Oh, hi!" the guy said to her. "We're expecting you!" He turned a page on his clipboard and checked off Emma's name. "Go right on up—they're starting soon." He pointed to the steps, which Emma and Carrie started to climb. There was a small first-floor landing, and then the narrow staircase started up again. Emma and Carrie looked at it dubiously and then began to climb.

"New York would never be the same!" Emma replied.

The two friends laughed together as they continued climbing. Two more flights and they were finally on the roof.

And what a roof! The top of the building showed a wonderful view of the whole New York skyline looking north to the Empire State Building and south to the World Trade Center. And at that moment, the roof was a sea of people—some in suits, some with wardrobes full of clothes, some photographers.

"Look over there!" Carrie tugged at Emma's arm as she spoke and pointed to someone sitting on one of the risers separating that building from the one next to it.

Emma looked. Sitting on the riser was none other than New York Mets baseball star Shannon Berman, looking supremely confident, dressed in a baseball uniform that looked sort of like her Mets uniform. Right near her was a black woman who looked to be in her late twenties, dressed just like the girl on the fourth floor, who was in the process of giving Shannon a manicure.

"I'm going to make myself scarce for a while," Carrie said, edging over toward a spot that seemed out of the commotion.

"Okay," Emma replied, "I'll check in . . . if I can find out where to check in."

Carrie sat down, and Emma looked for another of the ubiquitous young men with glasses and clipboards. She quickly found one, and he ushered her over to a group of seven other young women, all about Emma's height and size, who Emma quickly understood were the other models for the shoot. Emma joined the girls, who were listening to still another young man with glasses and a clipboard speak.

". . . so the thing is," the guy said, "we're doing this shoot for Ever-Nails. It's a nail care company. Here's what the ad is going to look like."

Emma peered at him as he pulled out a computer-generated photograph of nine baseball-uniformed girls, with a tall one in the middle and four smaller girls to either side, and the New York skyline as the backdrop. The tall girl in the middle was obviously going to be Shannon Berman. The other girls all had their hands in the pockets with baseball gloves under their arms, and Shannon Berman would be the only one with her hands out—her perfectly manicured right hand holding a baseball in a knuckleball grip, the other one facing the camera.

I have to admit it, it's really clever, Emma

thought, reading the caption at the bottom of the mock-advertisement. EVER-NAILS: WHAT TO TURN TO WHEN THE BIG CITY TOSSES YOUR NAILS A KNUCKLER. *Someone got paid a lot of money to think that up!*

"Okay, let's get dressed and then we'll do hair and makeup," the spectacled-guy said, and steered the models over to a makeshift changing room set up on the roof.

Okay, world of modeling, Emma thought, *here I come, ready or not!*

Leave it to Carrie, Emma marveled, *the nothing-ventured, nothing-gained kid. She's talking the head photographer into something, I just know she is!* As the shoot had been winding up, and an assistant photographer had taken over for the main photographer—not Flash Hathaway, Emma was happy to see—Emma had watched with interest as Carrie had approached the chief and began explaining something to him in her usual earnest fashion.

The chief photographer now was walking back toward them.

"Excuse me, ladies," he said to all the models, "but this girl went to the same high school I did—I don't want to say how long ago *I* was there! She's photographed for *Rock*

On magazine and I'm going to give her five minutes with you."

Carrie introduced herself to the other models and congratulated Shannon Berman on her first Mets game.

"Glad you guys enjoyed yourselves," said Shannon with a grin.

Then Carrie leaped into action, taking picture after picture, trying to make the most of her five minutes with these top models. The head photographer stood over by the side, his eye on his watch, a bemused expression on his face.

"Time's up!" he called, after Carrie had been at it for exactly five minutes. "It's a wrap! Thank you very much."

Emma strode over and joined Carrie.

"How'd you do it?" she asked her friend in total amazement.

Carrie shrugged. "Nothing ventured, nothing gained," she said philosophically. "The worst he could have said was no."

"Wouldn't you have been embarrassed if he did?" Emma asked her as all the people started filing down off the roof of the building.

"A little," Carrie admitted. "But he would have forgotten me in two minutes. So it's no big thing."

"You're amazing," Emma exclaimed. "The

only way I'd ever have the nerve to do something like that would be to pretend to be my supercilious mother, and then I'd get turned down for sure!"

"Anyway," Carrie said, "I can't wait to see what they look like. I've never taken these kind of pictures before. Hey Emma, do you realize you're going to be in an advertisement with Shannon Berman?"

The two friends then looked at each other, and they both cracked up. "And you don't even like baseball!" they said at the same time.

"You sure this is where Emma and Carrie said they'd meet us after the shoot?" Sam asked Danny dubiously as they were led by a black-clad waitress to an outdoor table at a restaurant on St. Marks Place called Mapa. "This doesn't really look like Emma Cresswell territory." Sam glanced over at the next table, where two young women with matching long, sheer flower print dresses and matching blond Mohawk-style haircuts were talking in low voices.

Danny laughed. "It's the right place, all right."

"I'm gonna ask those girls who did their hair," Sam cracked.

"Wait!" Danny instructed. "First tell me how rehearsals are going."

"It ain't awful pretty so it must be pretty awful," Sam summed up. "Nancy Pumpkin is always fighting with Laszlo over something or other. Then she gets pissed off and goes to her dressing room and we hear loud crashing noises, and then if we're lucky she'll come back and we can keep rehearsing. Once the stage manager went back there and told her to get her butt back on the stage. She threw a lamp at him."

"Drag," Danny commented. "So the show's not really getting any better."

"You got it," Sam replied. "Hey, can we get a menu here?" A tiny Asian waitress overheard them.

"Yeah?" the waitress said in a slight Brooklyn accent.

"Menus?" Sam asked.

The waitress pushed two menus at Danny and Sam, and then strode away.

"Service with a smile," Danny commented, "that's what New York is famous for. So anyway, you don't have much hope for the show. You open in what, like four days?"

"Mmm-hmmm," Sam mumbled, looking at the menu. "Is there any *meat* on this menu?"

"You still haven't invited your parents, huh?" Danny asked.

"Nope," Sam replied. "I mean, who are my parents, anyway? Susan out in California? Mom and Dad in Kansas? Wouldn't it just be peachy to have all of them here at once?"

Danny didn't crack a smile. "I think you know who you consider Mom and Dad, don't you?"

Sam nodded. "The Junction, Kansas duo," she said.

"That's right," Danny agreed. "And don't you think that they'd be disappointed if you opened on Broadway and you didn't tell them?"

Sam shot Danny a cold smile. "As I recall, there was something important in my own life that they neglected to tell me."

"I thought you guys had worked all that out. If you don't tell them," Danny insisted, "you're as wrong as they were."

"I'm so sure!" Sam snorted. "I don't think forgetting to tell someone that you adopted them is the same as not sending out an invite for a bomb show, do you?"

"You are being deliberately obtuse," Danny replied evenly.

"I don't even know what 'obtuse' means," Sam said irritably.

Danny just looked at her.

"Okay, okay," she finally said. "You think I need to call them?"

"Sam I know you know the answer to that," Danny responded.

"Danny Franklin," Sam said, "if you weren't here, I'd never do this."

Danny grinned.

"And because the waitress still hasn't come to take my order for bean sprout surprise," Sam continued, "I'm gonna do it now. Where's a pay phone?"

Sam got up from her chair and wandered into the interior of the restaurant. Carla and Vernon Bridges were about to find out that their daughter was opening on Broadway.

ELEVEN

"Okay, I did it," Sam announced when she returned to the table. "Now they know." The waitress was just delivering the food Danny had ordered, and Sam wrinkled her nose with distaste. "What is that?"

"Soy-tofu burger for you, veggies, rice, and beans for me," Danny replied, reaching for the soy sauce.

Sam stared skeptically at the patty on her plate. "I don't suppose there's any actual meat in this thing, huh?"

"It's made from soy and tofu," Danny explained. "What did your parents say?"

"Hi, Sam, honey, great to hear from you," Sam reported as she gingerly poked her soy burger with a fork.

"What else?" Danny asked her.

"They're coming, you jerk. I can't believe you talked me into this."

"Hey, you can't honestly tell me you're not glad," Danny stated, taking a sip of his herbal iced tea.

"I don't know what I am, besides grossed out at this *thing* you ordered for me to eat," Sam said with a sigh. She put down her fork. "Can you imagine my parents in New York City? It's like a bad movie, and I'm the star!"

Danny laughed and took another bite of his veggies. "I doubt your parents can imagine their daughter in New York City."

"Actually, I always threatened them that this was where I was going to end up," Sam replied. "But New York City is like another planet to my parents. My dad asked me if he should bring his gun."

"Oh, that's great," Danny snorted, shaking his head ruefully.

"I told him not to bother, that most people get shot here by snipers from skyscrapers, so a gun wouldn't help," Sam said. "He wasn't completely sure I was kidding!"

Danny looked down at Sam's uneaten soy burger. "This is the first time I ever saw food in front of you that you didn't devour."

"It's soy," Sam said with disgust. "We grow soy in Kansas. It's cattle feed!"

A number of diners turned to look at her, with amused expressions on their faces.

"What's *your* problem?" Sam asked the

people at the next table. "Last time I looked, Kansas was still part of the United States."

"Kansas is for Dorothy and Toto," one of the mohawk girls said drolly. "No one actually *lives* there."

"Well, I'm from there, and I did live there, and it's pretty terrific," Sam heard herself say. She turned quickly to Danny. "I didn't just defend Kansas, did I?"

"You did," Danny confirmed.

"If it's so terrific there, what are you doing here?" one of the mohawk girls asked snottily.

"Observing the local animals in their natural habitat," Sam rejoined.

The lighter-haired mohawk groaned. "I think that was supposed to be a clever comeback," she informed her friend.

"Hey, Betsy, Debby—I got us a ride home back from the city!" a girl at the door to the restaurant called to the two mohawk girls. "He's a friend of my brother's and he said he's only gonna wait two minutes, so hustle!"

Sam started to laugh with a mouthful of herbal iced tea and it came out of her nose. "I see I'm not the only out-of-towner here," she announced.

Both mohawk girls shot Sam a look that could kill, threw some money on the table and hurried out of the restaurant.

"Too funny!" Sam snorted with laughter.

"You know, one of these days you're gonna get smart with the wrong person and end up with their fist in your face," Danny said mildly.

"Puh-leeze," Sam replied airily. She pushed the offending soy-tofu burger out of her face. "We are definitely going to have to go for ice cream after this."

"So when are your parents arriving?" Danny asked.

"The day we open," Sam said. "It's the earliest they could come. That is, if they can get plane tickets."

"What about tickets to the play?"

"Emma's already bought fifteen. You never know when we might need an extra."

"Good thinking," Danny said with a nod.

"Credit cards are wonderful," Sam agreed. "Good thing she bought opening night."

"Why's that?"

"Because there probably won't be a second night," Sam laughed. "Gallows humor, y'know."

"So is that why you don't seem more nervous about your big Broadway debut, because you think it'll only run one night?" Danny asked Sam.

She stirred her iced tea absently with the

straw. "Oh, I'm plenty nervous," she admitted.

"But you just don't let it show," Danny concluded.

"Something like that."

"Why is that?" Danny asked softly.

Sam shrugged uncomfortably. "Oh, well, you know me, put on a happy face and all that."

"But you don't have to do that with me, Sam," Danny said.

"Habit," Sam mumbled, staring into her tea. She looked up at Danny. "Hey, let's not get all serious, okay? Let's talk about ice cream. I'm up for a triple scoop with nuts and sprinkles—"

Then Sam saw Danny's face change. It got really serious all of a sudden.

"You okay?" she asked him quickly.

"Yeah," he said, smiling a little. "Mostly."

"What's up, pardner?" she asked him. "Tell the amazing Samantha, psychic of Kansas!"

Danny nodded. "I mean to."

What's this all about? Sam thought. *I hope he's all right.*

"Soooooo?" Sam prompted, imitating a German inquisitor about to torture an American spy in a grade B movie. "You vill talk! Now!"

Danny pushed a spinach leaf around with his fork before he spoke. "I don't know why

I'm really making such a big deal out of this."

"Out of what?"

"Because when I last saw you," he continued, "on Sunset Island, you told me that all you really wanted to be with me was friends."

"Yeah," Sam agreed, though she felt uncomfortable.

Because lately I've been thinking that maybe Danny really could be more than that, and maybe I was just blinded by my lust for Pres.

"Good," Danny replied fervently. "Because that's how I feel too, now."

"Great!" Sam said, even though she wasn't totally sure she meant it.

"Cool," Danny responded, "I'm glad you feel the same way. Because the thing is, I'm getting kind of serious with somebody back home. I wanted to tell you—I don't know why I feel so weird about it."

What! Sam shouted to herself. *You can't do that!* Sam forced herself to smile.

"Oh, really," she said, trying to look nonchalant but actually very shaken by her own reaction. "Who is she?"

Danny's warm grin got warmer and wider. "Her name is Megan Carmony. She's an artist and a singer—I met her at a club back home."

"Gee, that's nice," Sam replied.

"Aren't you happy for me?" Danny asked.

"Sure, I'm happy for you!" Sam answered, though there wasn't much happiness in her voice. "So, listen, if you're so crazy about this girl, why were you asking me just yesterday if you could take a shower with me?"

"Force of habit?" Danny asked.

"You tell me," Sam replied.

"I guess some part of me wanted one more try with you," Danny said honestly. "But you've made it pretty clear that it's never going to happen for us."

"Well, you know me—honest Sam!" Sam quipped lightly. She bit her lip and looked at Danny. "So what's this Megan look like?"

"It's the strangest thing—she looks kind of like you," Danny replied. "She's tall and has red hair, too—maybe it's my type!—but not as thin as you."

Great, just great, Sam thought. *Someone who looks a lot like me, but also has hooters. That's fabulous news.*

"I hope the two of you are very happy," Sam said, knowing that she couldn't have possibly said anything any dweebier, but having no idea what else to say.

"I'm glad you're not upset—" Danny began.

"Me?" Sam said lightly. "Upset? Why should I be upset? I'm happy for you."

Yeah right, Sam thought. *As happy as if a*

ton of bricks had just now landed on my lap. Megan Carmony, I don't know who you are, but whoever you are, Danny Franklin's too good for you.

But he's not too good for me.

"So, how do you like the view?" Adam covered Emma's hand lightly with his own as they stared out at the nighttime Hudson River from the fifty-fifth floor of the Gulf + Western building at the intersection of Broadway and 60th Street.

"What's not to like?" Emma replied, squeezing Adam's hand in her own.

What's not to like, indeed? she asked herself. *Most people would kill for a date like this one. Chinese food at a very untouristy place in Chinatown, then a cab ride uptown to a destination that Adam insisted on keeping secret, and now this! I had no idea this place even existed!*

"Glad you feel that way," Adam replied. "This is a secret spot. Don't tell anyone."

"Trust me," Emma said, "I won't." Adam had told her earlier that not a lot of people knew about the cocktail lounge on top of the building that housed the offices of Paramount Communications, Inc. And it was obvious from the uncrowded lounge that he was right.

"Did I mention how beautiful you look tonight?" Adam asked softly.

Emma looked down at the all-white chiffon dress that billowed in the breeze, skimming her body and ending just above her knees.

"Thanks," Emma said. "You're kind of beautiful, too."

"So, Emma Cresswell," Adam asked her, in his light, slightly flirtatious tone, "what am I going to do about you?"

Introduce me to Kurt Ackerman? Emma said silently to herself. The instant the thought formed, she realized how horrible it was. *Do I secretly wish I was still in his arms?* Emma thought sadly.

Adam tactfully ignored her silence and took a sip of the Campari and soda he'd ordered. Emma didn't know anyone besides her Aunt Liz who actually drank Campari— she'd tasted it once and it reminded her very much of cough syrup.

"I really have been asking myself what I'm going to do about you," Adam mused. "The more I'm with you, the more I like you."

"I feel that same way about you," Emma replied softly.

Adam took another sip of his Campari and looked pensively out at the city. It was a sea of lights, in stark contrast to the recent blackout. Glancing to his left, he could see the dark expanse of Central Park, with the brilliant island of the Tavern on the Green restaurant aglow on one of its flanks.

"That's good," he said, a broad grin spreading over his face. "Actually, that's great."

"I'm glad," Emma answered truthfully.

"But you're scared," Adam said, looking at her closely.

"In a way," Emma responded.

"In a big way," Adam said, setting his lips at that cute angle Emma found totally irresistible. He turned back to Emma and gently touched her face. "But you need to know I'm nothing like him."

"Kurt has a lot of wonderful qualities—" Emma began.

"Hey! You don't need to defend him to me," Adam said.

"I know," Emma replied, brushing a windblown lock of hair from her cheek. "But I feel like I do. I know it's crazy!"

"It's not crazy," Adam replied. "I know how much you cared for him."

"I still care for him," Emma admitted in a low voice.

Adam looked shocked. "You still—?"

"I can't help it," Emma said, tears coming to her eyes. "Believe me, I know it's over. And I know we weren't right for each other, but . . ." She put her hand over her heart.

"It hasn't been very long. I still have a terrible ache, right here."

Adam put his hand over Emma's hand. Then he lifted it and kissed it. "It's okay, Em," he said gently.

For a few minutes they were quiet, gazing out at a huge ocean liner that was making its way up the Hudson River toward one of the steamship docks on the west side of Manhattan island.

"I just got so scared," Emma finally whispered.

"Of what?" Adam asked. "Tell me."

Emma bit her lower lip. "The feeling of being tied down, of being controlled," she admitted.

"I don't want to do that to you—" Adam began.

"Neither did Kurt, at first," Emma interrupted. "But the more involved we got, the more things changed. Until finally I felt like I couldn't breathe."

Adam nodded and stared out into the night.

"And the money thing," Emma continued earnestly. "I can't make myself not be rich. I am rich. There's nothing wrong with being rich!"

Adam laughed. "You won't get any argument from me."

"But Kurt hated it," Emma continued. "It was as if I was somehow . . . somehow tainted for having money!"

"Hey, I have no problem with your family's money," Adam said. "I'm counting on it to finance my first feature—"

Emma's face blanched.

"Only kidding!" Adam said quickly. "Geez, you really were burned."

Emma nodded.

Adam leaned over and kissed her softly and sweetly. "Emma, Emma, Emma," he murmured. "There's only one thing to do, then," he said gently. "And that's to go slower than slow."

Emma nodded gratefully. Then, a niggling thought cropped up in her mind, a thought she tried to knock down, but which grew like a bubble until it burst, and she had to put it into words.

"Adam, can I ask you something?" she said, a little trepidation in her voice.

"Anything," Adam replied, guilelessly.

"How can you be so willing to wait?" Emma asked. "You don't already have a girlfriend, do you?"

Adam smiled slightly, and then grinned broadly.

"Emma Cresswell," he said, "you realize

you are not the only person who's been burned in the past, don't you?"

"You mean—"

"Remind me to tell you about Paige sometime."

"Tell me now," Emma prompted.

"Forget it," Adam replied. "I'm in too good a mood."

He reached over and brushed his lips against Emma's cheek in the exact place his hand had been stroking.

"Oh, Adam," she sighed, and wrapped her arms around him.

"Yes," he murmured huskily, and held her against him, until it was Emma who reached up for a kiss.

TWELVE

"Three more days until we open," Sam mused. "I can't believe it. Help!" She reached over and took another bite of Greek moussaka that had been delivered by the 24-hour restaurant just around the corner from the loft.

"It doesn't seem to have affected your appetite," Emma noticed.

"I need sustenance to get me through this," Sam said, gobbling down another huge bite. "Mmmm, this Greek food is great."

"You think all food is great," Danny said.

"Not that veggie crap you tried to make me eat in the village," Sam reminded him with a shudder. "No one actually *likes* that stuff, do they?"

It was dinnertime, and Emma, Carrie, Sam, Matt, Adam and Danny's schedules had all meshed. There was yet another major set construction problem at the theater which caused Laszlo Comfort to dismiss the entire cast of *Helen!* for an extended dinner break. Sam and Matt had taken a cab together downtown, and Emma had ordered in a feast from the Acropolis diner—delivered in only twenty minutes—which all of them were now consuming with gusto.

"Did you see the article in today's *New York Times* about *Helen!*?" Adam asked Sam and Matt.

The two of them shook their heads, as their mouths were too full with Greek salad and moussaka to say no.

"It wasn't very complimentary," Adam reported. "Basically, this reporter sort of trashed Nancy Pumpkin."

"Easy to do," Sam said.

"I think the reporter said something about how she was refusing to wear the costumes that were made for her."

Matt, who had swallowed first, laughed. "It's true," he replied. "She wants to wear one of her all-leather rock and roll outfits. She says it makes a better statement."

"About what?" Emma asked, puzzled.

"Beats me!" Matt answered. "Ask Nancy. Not that she'll actually answer."

"And not only that," Sam put in, "but I

heard she's gained like fifteen pounds since she was fitted for those costumes."

"Is she talented, at least?" Carrie asked.

Matt shrugged. "She can sing rock, that's for sure."

"Hey!" Carrie spoke up. "When do we get to hear one of the songs from the show?"

"Sam hasn't sung any of them for you yet?" Matt asked her.

"No," Carrie replied. "We asked. She refused."

"Well, these songs don't have an actual melody," Sam reported. "They're just too awful, I can't subject them to it."

"Come on," Matt chided her, "give them a tune!"

"Sorry," Sam insisted. "They're just going to have to wait to hear 'See No Evil Hear No Evil Say No Evil'."

Emma nearly choked on her Greek salad. "You're kidding," she sputtered. "You're making that up."

"I wish I was," Sam said, rolling her eyes skyward. "But I'm not."

"I can see why *The Times* reporter is so optimistic," Danny said, deadpan.

"I can't wait for my parents to see it," Sam responded. "They'll never look at theater the same way again."

"Neither will the world," Carrie joked.

Just then the phone rang. Emma wiped her fingers off on her napkin and reached for it.

"Hello?"

"Emma? It's Billy!" a voice said through the phone.

"Oh, hi," Emma said, sneaking a quick look over at Carrie and Matt, who were laughing together at some joke of Danny's.

"Hey, you don't sound very happy to hear from me," Billy said jovially.

"Oh, I am," Emma assured him.

"So, is my girl there?"

"She sure is," Emma said. "Just a sec." Emma put her hand over the phone and looked over at Carrie. "It's for you."

"Me?" Carrie asked with surprise.

Emma nodded. "Why don't you get it on the cordless in the bedroom?" Emma suggested.

Carrie looked puzzled. "Here's okay," she said, reaching out for the phone.

"No, the bedroom is better," Emma said pointedly.

A light dawned on Carrie's face. "Oh! Sure!" She got up and scurried to the back of the loft, picked up the cordless phone and switched it on. "Hello?"

"Yeah! I love the sound of that voice."

"Billy!" Carrie cried happily. "Oh, Billy!"

"So, here I am in Nova Scotia visiting

friends, and I got this real urge to talk to you," Billy said.

"I'm so glad you called," Carrie breathed, sitting on Emma's Aunt Liz's bed.

"Hey, I really miss you," Billy said huskily.

"How much?" Carrie asked in a low voice.

"Lots," Billy reported. "I keep having these sexy dreams about you."

A shudder of happiness ran down Carrie's spine. "You might want to try a cold shower," Carrie said with a giggle.

Billy laughed. "You're tough, aren't you."

"You know I'm not," Carrie replied softly.

"That's true," Billy agreed. "Smart, and gorgeous and sexy and terrific, but not so tough. So, what are you doing?"

"Just hanging out," Carrie said. *With a really cute guy who wants to go out with me*, she added guiltily in her mind.

"I know you better than that," Billy replied. "You never just 'hang out.' You've probably photographed half of Manhattan by now and set up appointments with every gallery to show your pictures."

"I'm trying to just have fun," Carrie said.

"Not with anyone in particular, I hope," Billy said pointedly.

Carrie blushed. *It's as if he can read my mind*, she thought. *But I have nothing to feel guilty about. Matt is just my friend. So what if I'm attracted to him? I haven't acted on it!*

"Carrie?" Billy asked. "You didn't answer me."

"No, of course not with anyone in particular," Carrie replied a bit tensely.

"You okay?" Billy asked.

"I'm fine," Carrie replied. "Really."

"You miss me?"

"Tons," Carrie promised.

"Hey, Billy, I need to call and find out what time the movie starts!" a female voice called to Billy at his end.

"Who's that?" Carrie asked.

"My friend Allen's sister," Billy replied.

"Billy?" the girl's voice said again, sounding closer this time. "Come on, sweetie, you know how I hate to miss the beginning of movies!"

"Sure, Sherry, just a sec," Billy told her. "Carrie? You still there?"

"How would you know how much she hates to miss the beginning of movies?" Carrie asked Billy, feeling a hot flush of anger come to her face.

"Because I've known her since she was ten years old," Billy said easily.

"And just how old is good ol' Sherry now?" Carrie asked.

"Twenty," Billy replied, amusement in his voice. "Hey, are you jealous?"

"No," Carrie said coolly.

"You are!" Billy cried, laughter in his voice.

"I'm not," Carrie replied hotly. There was a beat of silence. "What does she look like?"

"Oh, she's about five foot eight, with long blond hair, a perfect body, and the face of an angel," Billy replied seriously. "And she's an astrophysicist, did I mention that? And, oh yeah, she does volunteer work for Mother Teresa and—"

"Billy Sampson, quit teasing me," Carrie interrupted.

Billy couldn't stop laughing. "Okay, I'm sorry. Listen, I'm flattered that you care."

"You know I care," Carrie said in a low voice.

"Prove it," Billy said huskily.

"It's a little difficult over the phone."

"Okay, prove it when we get back to the island."

"I will," Carrie breathed.

"You have nothing to worry about, babe," Billy promised sincerely. "I love you."

"I love you, too," Carrie said, wishing that Billy was with her right that very moment.

"So, I'll see you soon. Take care," Billy said, signing off.

Carrie clicked off the phone and sat there, staring into space.

I do love him so much, she thought to herself. *And the only reason I got so jealous was because I'm here with Matt having fun. Even if I haven't done anything with Matt, I've sure thought about it.*

She remembered something her history teacher had told her about President Jimmy Carter, when he was asked whether he had ever cheated on his wife. He had said no, but he had definitely lusted in his heart. "I guess I'm kind of like Jimmy Carter," Carrie whispered out loud, a rueful smile on her lips. "I am lusting in my heart!"

"It never changes," Emma said, bemused, as she surveyed the constant wild scene in Washington Square Park. She, Carrie, Adam, and Danny has decided to go for a walk to try to digest their enormous dinner—Matt and Sam had to get back to the theater for evening rehearsal. Now, the four friends were walking north through Washington Square, and the scene was exactly as crazy and chaotic as it was the first time Emma and her friends had visited it.

"Want to sit a while?" Adam asked as they approached a small crowd gathering around a guy who was giving an impromptu performance on a unicycle in the middle of the square.

"Good idea," Carrie responded, rubbing her stomach. "That food was good, but kind of like eating lead."

"No kidding," Danny added. "I feel like someone dropped a few weightlifting plates in my stomach."

Emma led the way over to an empty bench, and the four of them plopped down on it to watch the show. The guy riding the unicycle was really talented—not only could he go in seemingly any direction that he wanted, but he also could juggle four apples at the same time.

At that moment, a tall, skinny guy wearing an old U.S. Army fatigue jacket and a baseball cap approached the four of them.

"Smoke, sinse," he said quickly under his breath. "Good smoke."

"Uh-uh," Adam replied.

"Hey, it's great stuff," the guy insisted.

"Not into it," Danny told him.

The guy took out a cigarette. "You got a light?" he asked Danny.

Danny fumbled in his pocket and pulled out a pack of matches from a downtown restaurant, and he handed them to the guy.

"Thanks, man," the guy said. He lit his cigarette, then slipped his hand into Danny's pocket, returning the matches. "You sure you don't want some of this primo stuff?"

"I'm sure," Danny replied.

The guy wandered off, and as if by magic, an entire squadron of uniformed and plainclothes cops swooped down from nowhere.

"Look!" Carrie cried. "They're going to bust him right in front of us!" About four of the officers converged on the dealer who had just approached them. Emma looked to the left and to the right. All up and down the paved pathway where they were sitting, drug arrests were being made.

And then, the seemingly impossible happened. The four friends saw one of the plainclothes cops point directly at them, and then a whole group of police came at them at a dead run.

"No!" Emma yelled.

"You're making a mistake!" Adam cried.

"Turn out your pockets!" the oldest of the policemen yelled, pointing at Danny.

Danny turned his jacket pockets inside out, and a small plastic bag fell to the ground. "That's not mine," he cried. "That guy must've put it in there!"

"Yeah, sure. You're under arrest!" the policeman said to all of them, picking up the plastic bag. "You have the right to remain silent. Anything you say can and will be used against you in a court of law. You have the right to an attorney. If you cannot provide one for yourself the court will appoint one to represent you. Do you understand these rights?"

"You're arresting us?" Danny asked incredulously. "But we didn't do anything!"

"I saw the perp with his hand in your pocket, kid," one cop said.

"He was returning some matches!" Danny yelled.

"Tell it to the judge," the arresting cop said.

This is my worst nightmare come true! Emma thought frantically. *They're arresting us, and we haven't done anything at all! We told the guy to go away!*

"What's the charge?" Adam demanded to know.

"Heroin possession," the cop said gruffly. "Good luck at your arraignment!"

"But the guy was selling pot, not heroin!" Adam protested.

"Hey, do I look stupid enough to buy that line?" the cop said with disgust.

"But . . . this can't be happening!" Emma cried.

"It's happening," Danny said in a steely voice.

"But it's illegal to be arrested falsely!" Carrie cried.

"Well, I guess they don't know it's false," Danny said. "I can't believe this."

"This is ridiculous!" Emma sputtered. "I've never done a drug in my life!" She marched over to two of the cops. "Excuse me, officers, but clearly there's been some mistake."

The cop just gave her jaded looks.

"We don't do drugs," Emma said simply.

"Yeah, right," one young cop said, pretty much ignoring Emma as he filled out some papers.

"But—"

"Look, I haven't got time to carry on a conversation with you now," the cop said gruffly. "You'll have your chance at the station. Just stand over there with the others."

Emma looked around. All over the place, police paddywagons were arriving. This obviously was a planned operation, and they'd had the bad luck to be in the wrong place at the wrong time.

"My father is Brent Cresswell," Emma announced in desperation. Although she hated to use her family name, she couldn't stand to see them all arrested for something they didn't do.

"Well, goody," the older cop jeered. "My father is Bruno Patarucci. Now go stand with the others."

Carrie glanced over at Emma. "If only Kat and your dad could see you now," she said, attempting a small smile.

Emma winced. *My mother would be mortified. Correction, if my mother saw me like this, she would have a fainting spell*, she thought.

"Okay, guys," the head cop said, "to the north end of the park. Move!"

Adam, Danny, Carrie, and Emma stood up and were herded by the cops into a group of about fifteen other people who had also been arrested in the big bust. Many of the other people were also complaining about having been arrested for doing nothing, but their pleas were all falling on deaf ears.

"Damn," Adam said, as he stood with his friends, waiting to get loaded into one of the big paddywagons for the trip down to the courthouse. "Wrong place, wrong time. I should have known."

"Should have known what?" Emma asked.

"Operation Frustration," Adam mumbled.

"What?" Carrie asked, puzzled.

"I read something about it," Adam explained, trying to make some room for himself in the gaggle of waiting bodies. "They're busting small-time dealers and buyers."

"The question is," Carrie said, "what do we do now?"

The four of them looked at one another. No one had a quick answer.

"Don't we get a phone call when we get booked?" Emma asked.

Adam nodded. "I think so," he said.

"I guess . . . I can call my parents," Carrie said grimly. "They're going to be overjoyed."

"Just tell them the truth," Emma advised her.

"Well, of course I'm going to tell them the truth," Carrie replied testily. "But there's that moment when they hear I was arrested and before I explain that I didn't do anything when they're both going to want to disown me!"

"They'll probably end up releasing us anyway," Danny said hopefully. "I mean, come on, there's no evidence!"

"I hope you're right," Emma responded, but she really didn't want to find out.

"Okay, let's move 'em out!" yelled one of the blue-clad cops to the group the friends were in, his voice amplified by the white bullhorn he was holding. Emma and her friends filed forward, all the way to the north end of the park, where they were herded into the last paddywagon that was lined up on the street.

"Man, it's dark in here," someone said.

"Lemme out, I'm claustrophobic!" cried another voice.

In the corner, a girl with stringy blond hair was crying. "I am dead meat," she sobbed. "I already have one conviction. I am so screwed!"

"Shut up, Wendy," her friend snapped. "Just shut the hell up!"

The metal doors to the paddywagon slammed shut, and as the vehicle began to pull away, a single electric lightbulb turned on to illuminate the interior. Emma could see two rows of benches down both sides of the windowless vehicle on which were seated about twenty of the people who'd been arrested.

"Gee, this is fun," Adam cracked to no one in particular.

"Yeah," Carrie said, "great. I'm still thinking about how my parents are going to kill me."

"They won't kill you," Danny replied.

"And I'm sure yours are going to be overcome with joy, too, Carrie said." She slid into a deep funk, and Emma really couldn't blame her very much. In fact, most of the noise in the paddywagon died down as the vehicle rumbled downtown through the streets of Manhattan.

What am I going to do? Emma asked herself. *What are we going to do? What if I actually get convicted? My future is ruined! The Peace Corps will never take me with a drug conviction on my record.*

From time to time Emma and her friends were jolted off their seats as the truck rumbled over a pothole.

BOOM! The paddywagon was jolted still again by another pothole. And then the most amazing thing happened. The doors of the back of the paddywagon swung wide open, and the light of the evening poured through. The impact of the last pothole had been enough to somehow shake the door open, though Emma had heard the sharp clang when the policemen locked it.

Immediately, everyone stood up and started jumping out of the wagon. The driver of the paddywagon had no idea that the doors had sprung open, because he continued to drive onward. Fortunately for the people jumping, they were on a congested street, so he wasn't going very fast.

"Is this some kind of trick?" Carrie yelled.

"Don't know!" Adam yelled back.

"Guilty people are getting away!" Emma cried.

"Let's go!" Adam screamed.

"No!" Danny yelped.

"We didn't do anything!" Adam insisted. "Let's go!"

Adam jumped up and grabbed Emma's hand. Then Danny and Carrie jumped up, too. Then they all jumped together, along with four or five other people in the paddy-wagon.

"Run!" Danny yelled, when they'd hit the pavement.

Within seconds, the police vehicle was out of sight, and the four friends were standing in the middle of the street in a circle.

"Where are we?" Carrie asked breathlessly, her heart still pounding in her chest.

Emma looked around. The closest street sign was the corner of Broadway and Prince Street.

"Right around the corner from the loft!" she realized.

"Then what are we waiting for?" Adam asked. "Let's go!"

The four of them ran down Broadway toward Spring Street. Emma expected to be stopped at any minute by someone in authority, asking why they were running down Broadway looking guilty and frightened.

But this is New York City, she told herself. *You could walk along naked and no one would bother you.*

She was right. No one so much as batted an eye at them all the way home.

THIRTEEN

"We've been reading *The New York Post*," Carrie reported to Sam the following morning. Carrie turned up the sleeves of her flannel nightshirt and reached for her coffee.

"Yeah?" Sam asked sleepily. She had just stumbled out of bed, and she padded across the loft in her bare feet. The long T-shirt she wore read ALMOST FAMOUS.

"We're not in it," Emma said with relief. She retied the sash of her lavender silk robe and reached for a muffin.

"What a shame," Sam replied, stretching. "I was hoping for the big headline YALE GIRL AND BOSTON HEIRESS IN JAILBREAK! I can't believe that happened to you guys last night."

"I had nightmares that I was in prison," Emma reported with a shudder.

"Well, I'm bummed that you didn't make *The Post*, that's all I have to say," Sam stated, opening the refrigerator and searching for some orange juice. "It would have been almost as good as getting into *The National Enquirer*."

"Oh, God, my mother would die," Emma said. "Believe me, in my family you are only allowed to appear in the paper on the society pages—or when you marry and when you die. And you had better do both tastefully."

"What time is it, anyway?"

"Eight-thirty," Emma told her, taking a bite of a muffin.

"And I start rehearsal at two today and go until ten at night—tell me that's humane," Sam groused.

Carrie pushed an already-filled coffee cup toward their friend. "I got this ready for you," she said with a smile.

"You're a great humanitarian," Sam said, taking the coffee, putting it to her lips, and taking a huge gulp all in one motion. "You're nominated for Pope."

"Not me. I look fat in white," Carrie said with a laugh.

"Oh, you don't look fat in anything," Sam corrected her.

"You're curvy," Emma said. "Curvy is good."

"Curvy is great!" Sam agreed, sipping her coffee.

"Oh, I guess everyone wants what they don't have," Carrie said philosophically.

"Waste of time," Sam opined loftily. She thought a moment. "Well, I wouldn't mind having your headlights and Emma's wallet, but other than that—"

"Did anyone ever tell you how crude you are?" Carrie asked Sam with a grin.

"It's one of my most endearing qualities," Sam replied, sipping her coffee. She reached for a muffin. "At least there's food. This looks good." She took a bite of the carrot muffin. "I'm an idiot," she said blithely, as she chewed.

"Why do you say that?" Emma asked.

"Because I told Danny I'd go with him to the Statue of Liberty and Ellis Island this morning," Sam replied. "I should be sleeping."

"What's wrong with that?" Carrie asked directly. "It sounds like fun."

"Yeah," Sam answered. "We can spend the morning talking about Megan Carmony. What a blast." Sam had already filled in Emma and Carrie on her conversation with Danny about his new girlfriend down in Florida.

"You don't have to talk about her," Carrie suggested.

"I hate her," Sam seethed.

"You don't even know her," Emma reminded her.

"So what?" Sam asked. "Why should that matter? Since when do you have to know someone to hate them?"

"Well, silly me," Emma replied, rolling her eyes.

"There's only one reason for you to hate her," Carrie said, draining her coffee and getting up to pour herself another cup.

"Why do I have a feeling that you're going to tell me what that reason is?" Sam said lightly.

"Because you want Danny," Carrie said.

"I don't," Sam insisted.

"Then why do you hate Megan Carmony?" Carrie asked.

Sam stared at Carrie with narrowed eyes. "Would you please stop being so logical and mature? It bugs the hell out of me." She reached for a second muffin and buttered it angrily.

"Why don't you just admit that you like him?" Emma asked her softly.

"I do like him," Sam stated. "After you guys he's my best friend. But the operative word is friend."

"Okay, then, what you're saying is that you're so small-minded that you don't want your 'friend' to be happy," Emma concluded.

"You two are ganging up on me!" Sam said. She swallowed a mouthful of muffin and took a sip of her coffee, then she looked at her two friends. "All right," she sighed. "I'm confused. I admit it."

"That's a start," Emma approved.

"So why don't you just level with him?" Carrie asked reasonably. "Just tell him how you feel!"

"I wish I knew how I felt," Sam lamented. "Back on the island, I just wanted to be friends, but now that he's with this girl Megan, I think maybe . . . I want more. But I mean, it's not just her. I've been thinking about Danny a lot anyway," Sam confessed.

"Beware of what you want," Carrie quoted, as if she was reading a Chinese fortune cookie, "you may get it."

"Yeah, but what if you don't know what you want?" Sam asked plaintively.

"I think you and Danny make a great couple," Emma said firmly

"What about me and Pres?" Sam asked.

"You broke up," Emma reminded her. "Besides, I think you're better suited to Danny, actually."

"Ha, you probably just want Pres for yourself!" Sam shot back playfully.

Emma couldn't meet Sam's eyes. The truth

of the matter was when they had all been on tour together, she and Pres had been attracted to each and she had kissed him once. And she had loved it. And she'd felt guilty about it ever since.

"Well, I've got a game plan for today," Sam decided. "Ellis Island will be really romantic. And I'll wear my black tank top—that ought to do to turn him around. I won't even mention what's-her-name."

"Just don't do that unless you're sure you really want him," Carrie said seriously. "Danny is too great of a guy for you to play games with."

"I hear you loud and clear, O Mature One," Sam replied. "So, what are you guys up to today?"

"Good question," Emma mused. "We were thinking about going to the Museum of Modern Art—Carrie wants to see the photography exhibition, and I want to show her Monet's 'Water Lillies.'"

"Yawn," Sam said.

"Or we might just go back to sleep," Carrie added playfully.

"Count me in on that," Sam replied, looking wistfully at the clock.

"Forget it," Emma cautioned, "Danny will be here in forty-five minutes."

"The whole world's against me," Sam whined jokingly.

"Too bad it's not Danny Franklin who's against you," Carrie joked back, wiggling her eyebrows.

"I'll drink to that," Sam declared, lifting her coffee cup to the sky. "On the other hand, we open the show the day after tomorrow. Maybe I'll save the drink until then!"

Emma and Carrie did go back to sleep after Sam and Danny had left for the Statue of Liberty and Ellis Island, but the phone rang just an hour later and woke them up again. Emma went to answer it.

"Hello?" Emma asked sleepily, picking up the phone.

"Hey, cutie," Adam replied, "you're famous."

"What are you talking about?" Emma asked him, totally puzzled.

"Haven't you seen it?" Adam asked. Emma could hear the rustling sound of newspaper in the background.

"Seen what?" Emma queried. "Oh, my God, there's a story about us running away from the paddywagon!" Her heart sunk until it couldn't get any lower. *My mother is going to find out now, and I'm going to be in major trouble*, she thought frantically.

Adam laughed. "We're safe on that account. No story about our getaway. Must be an everyday thing. But you got *The Post*?" Adam quizzed.

"Sure," Emma answered. "We were looking at it this morning, for, you know—"

"Well, you were looking in the wrong section," Adam said. "Go get it." Emma got out of bed, went to the kitchen, got *The Post*, and returned back to the phone.

"Okay," she said. "I've got it."

"Page twenty-five," Adam commanded.

Emma turned to the page twenty-five. And there, staring at her, was a photo of herself. Along with seven other girls in baseball uniforms, and Shannon Berman, looking supremely confident. It was the advertisement for Ever-Nails, and Emma had to admit that she looked great in it.

"You've got a future in the business," Adam said.

"But I don't want a future in the business," Emma said. "It's totally superficial! It has nothing to do with who I am!"

"You can make lots of money," Adam reminded her softly. Then they both laughed. They knew that Emma didn't need to worry about earning money.

"And you might even get famous," he continued.

"I don't want to get famous!" Emma maintained. "I just want—"

"I know what you want," Adam interrupted her, "and I'm sure you will get it."

Just then the call-waiting on Emma's line clicked.

"Hold on a sec, Adam," Emma said, "I've got to check this call." She clicked over.

"Emma Cresswell speaking," she said.

"Emma, darling," an Australian-tinged voice cooed at her. "It's Gillian. Have you seen the advertisement? It's brilliant! Listen darling, I want you today to go to—"

"Gillian?"

"Yes?"

"Hold on a moment," Emma said. "Let me get off my other call."

"Certainly."

Emma clicked back to Adam.

"Adam?" she asked, "are you still there?"

"At your service," he replied.

"Listen," Emma said, "It's Gillian Garrett. And I think she's calling me about another job. I don't want to get trapped into doing more and more of this!"

"Do what you gotta do," Adam said.

Emma sighed. "Okay, I'll call you later. Bye!"

She clicked back over to Gillian.

"Gillian?"

"Yes, darling?" Gillian asked.

"If you're calling me about another modeling job," Emma said, taking a deep breath, "I have to tell you I don't think it's a good idea for me to get any more involved right now. I really appreciate what you've done for me and all, but I'm going back to Sunset Island soon—really I never expected to get work in the first place—"

"Emma," Gillian interrupted. "It's all right. I'm not going to pressure you into anything. But, if you're interested, I'd love to call you on your island if anything should come up there."

Emma breathed a relieved sigh, then smiled. "I'd like that," she said.

"So this is Ellis Island," Sam said, stepping off the ferryboat that had brought Danny and herself to a small, rocky island in New York harbor. As they filed off the boat along with a big crowd of tourists, Sam could see that the island had several low-slung buildings on it, as well as a commanding view of lower Manhattan.

"Let's tear all this down and build our dream mansion here," she joked.

"It's a national landmark," Danny reminded her.

"Our dreamhouse could be a national landmark," Sam countered, as they followed the crowd of tourists along a pathway that led to the museum of immigration that Danny insisted that Sam had to see. "Sort of like Graceland, only cooler," she said.

"I bet even Elvis Presley had relatives that came through here," Danny said.

"I know, I know," Sam answered. "Twelve million immigrants got processed here. You told me."

"Including my grandparents," Danny reminded her.

"From Poland to New York to Miami Beach," Sam exclaimed. "That's some strange trip!"

"No stranger than from England and Ireland to Chicago to Kansas," Danny countered.

On the ferry over to Ellis Island, Danny and Sam had compared notes for the first time about their family histories. Sam had felt pretty weird about it, because though she had a pretty good sense of her mother and father in Kansas' family tree, she basically knew nothing about her birth mother, Susan Briarly's ancestors. Her birth father, Michael Blady, she knew came from a Norweigan Jewish family that lost nearly all its members in the Holocaust.

I feel really weird about that, Sam thought

to herself. *Like I don't really know who I am. And if you don't know who you are, how can you really know about anything or anybody else?*

"I guess not," Sam mused. "But how could anyone voluntarily move to Kansas?"

"You were defending Kansas in that restaurant a couple of days ago," Danny said as they joined the line waiting to get into the museum of immigration.

"That was different," Sam cracked. "People were dissing my state. Only residents are allowed to dis their state."

"Oh," Danny said, "I see." They both cracked up.

Danny and Sam paid their admission price, and started wending their way through the museum. The museum was actually a set of restored buildings on the grounds of Ellis Island, they read off the large posters adorning the walls—buildings through which millions of immigrants to the United States passed and were processed before being permitted to become residents, especially during the end of 1800s and the early part of the 1900s. Ellis Island had been closed as a processing station many years before, but as she and Danny walked over the old flagstones and corridors and into the huge, cavernous, medical examination room where each and every immigrant had to pass a medical checkup before being allowed to continue the process, Sam got the eeriest feeling.

It's as if I can actually hear the sound of a hundred foreign languages being babbled at once, like I can smell the fear and excitement of the people who spent weeks in crummy steerage on crummy boats from Europe, she thought, a shiver running through her. *Was this how Susan's mother and father came here? Why did they come?*

Finally, they came to an immense wall that had been erected on one side of the island. As they got closer, Sam saw something remarkable about it.

"It's covered with names!" she exclaimed.

"You're right," Danny replied. "Names of immigrants who came through here. It's a wall of honor."

"How do you get your name up there?" Sam asked.

"You had come through here on your way into America," Danny explained, "and then you had descendants who want to remember. They register you. Come here, I want to show you something."

Danny took Sam by the hand—she had to admit that it thrilled her, even though she couldn't put Megan Carmony out of her mind—and pulled her down toward one end of the wall.

"It's around here someplace," he was mumbling to himself.

"What?" Sam asked.

"There!" Danny cried, triumphant. "Look!" He pointed at a section of the wall, outlining four names with the forefinger of his right hand.

MIRIAM GRUENWALD
EMMANUEL GRUENWALD
MOSHE FRANKREICH
LEAH FRANKREICH

"Who are they?" Sam queried, puzzled.

"My grandparents," Danny said proudly. "Mimi and Manny are my mother's parents, Moshe and Leah are my father's."

"But your last name is Franklin, not Frankreich!" Sam exclaimed.

Danny laughed. "Oh, some overworked immigration officer probably got tired of trying to spell all these weird names," he chuckled. "So he turned Frankreich into Franklin. Anyway, everyone can spell it."

"I'm glad my last name's Bridges," Sam said emphatically. And then another voice spoke inside her head.

It is and it isn't, the voice said. *Actually, it's*

Blady, and there were a lot of Bladys who didn't make it out of Nazi-occupied Norway alive. You don't see their names on this wall, do you?

"Can you imagine what it must have been like, coming to a new country, not speaking the language, not having any money?" Danny asked her.

"Sure," Sam replied. "I never have any money." She looked at Danny's serious face. "I was only joking."

Danny smiled sadly at Sam. "You don't have to keep up that laugh-a-minute bull with me, Sam," he said softly

"I don't, huh?" Sam replied in a low voice.

"Yeah. Being deep is not a negative quality, you know."

"No one ever called me deep in my whole life," Sam replied.

"Look at the wall," Danny told her. "So many of your biological family didn't make it out of Nazi-occupied Europe to have a chance to have their names there. How does that make you feel?"

I was just thinking the same thing myself! "Sad," Sam replied honestly, tears coming to her eyes. "And . . . and like I'm a part of something . . . bigger. Something I want to know more about."

Danny grinned at Sam and squeezed her hand. "That's my girl," he said.

I want to be your girl! I do! Sam thought. *You're the only one who always challenges me to look deeper into myself. You're the only one who thinks I'm smart, and sensitive, not just some cut-up who—*

"Sam?" Danny asked, jarring her out of her reverie.

"Huh?"

Danny handed Sam a small camera. "Take my picture in front of the wall, will you? I want to give it to Megan."

FOURTEEN

"You sure you guys don't want to come to dress rehearsal?" Sam asked Carrie and Emma as the three of them lay around on the big rug in the loft, eating yet another Chinese takeout early dinner right out of the cartons. "The Wolf Man said that it's okay if we invite some friends."

"Hey, speaking of the Wolf Man, how come you haven't been talking about him lately?" Emma asked. "Did he decide to hit on someone else?"

Sam shrugged and finished an egg roll. "He keeps making these comments about how he can't wait until the second day of our run—which is when we're supposed to have our big date. But other than that, he's left me alone."

"Maybe he's too busy getting *Helen!* opened to be thinking about women," Emma suggested.

"Not from what I hear," Carrie said. "I hear he's been pretty cozy with some actress named Chili."

Sam's jaw dropped open. "Chili Dumont? How do you know about her?"

"Matt told me," Carrie reported. She opened a carton of rice and ate a mouthful.

Sam leaned close to Carrie. "Tell the truth. What you really want to do is to jump his bones, am I right? You want to feel those hunky, muscular arms wrapped around you, you want to feel his steamy mouth on yours and—"

"Shut up!" Carrie said with a laugh. She picked up a pillow and heaved it at Sam. Sam ducked and stuck her tongue out at Carrie. "Oh, very mature," Carrie added, still sputtering with laughter.

"I've decided, I'm definitely never growing up," Sam said. She took a slug of Pepsi. "Seriously, how do you do it?"

"Do what?" Carrie asked.

"Stay true to Billy."

"I love Billy," Carrie replied easily.

Sam pushed some chicken with cashews around with her fork. "So . . . what's that like?"

"I don't know how to explain it," Carrie said slowly.

"I do," Emma said softly. "It's like . . . all

you do is think about that person. You can't think about anything else—"

"That's not love," Carrie said firmly. "That's infatuation."

"Okay, then, what's love?" Emma asked.

"Well, it's when you care about someone as much as you care about yourself, I guess," Carrie said.

Sam snorted. "Gimme a break, Alden. You read that in one of those stupid books in the self-help section of the library, right?"

"I cared about Kurt that much," Emma said in a low voice. "So, was that love?"

"Who knows?" Carrie said with a sigh. "I don't have any answers." She put down her carton of Chinese food and pulled her knees up to her chin. "What really gets me is how you can really and truly love one guy and still be attracted to another."

"Ha!" Sam cried. "So you really *do* want to jump Matt's bones!"

"Well, what if I do?" Carrie asked. "That doesn't mean I have to act on it."

"You know what I think about sometimes?" Emma asked them. "I think about how I've waited this long to make love for the first time, which I'm glad about, really, but . . ."

"But?" Sam prompted.

"But when I finally do it, what if it's not as

good as all the stuff that led up to it, you know what I mean?"

"Yeah, like can it really be as good as just kissing and all that?" Sam filled in.

"Right," Emma agreed. "Sometimes I just feel like if I don't do it with Adam, I'll die right on the spot," she admitted. "And then I tell myself that it's way too soon, and I should wait."

"Maybe you need to give yourself some time to get over Kurt," Carrie suggested gently. "Before you rush into anything heavy with Adam, I mean."

"I know, that makes sense," Emma agreed with a sigh. "But when I'm with Adam I can't think clearly! It's like . . ."

"Like your IQ takes a nose dive?" Sam put in.

"Yeah," Emma said. An ironic smile came to her lips. "It's funny. I've traveled all over the world, I've done so many things, but when it comes to guys I feel totally stupid!"

"Just ask me, the Guy Guru," Sam suggested, finishing off one carton of the Chinese food. "I don't know what I just ate, but it was de-lish," Sam added, reaching for another carton.

"Tell me, O Wise One," Carrie teased, "how is it that you are the Guy Guru when you can't even handle the guys in your own life?"

"Well I'm only the Guy Guru for my friends," Sam replied breezily. "For myself, I'm totally lost."

"Who isn't?" Emma agreed.

"Carrie isn't," Sam replied. She finished chewing and took a long slug of her Pepsi. "Isn't it funny, how Matt and Adam and Danny all ended up here at the same time that we're here?"

"Danny came to see you," Carrie reminded Sam.

"Well, can you blame him?" Sam replied blithely.

"And Matt lives here," Carrie continued, ignoring Sam. "So any time I came to New York, he'd be here."

"Carrie Alden, you are too logical," Sam huffed. "What about your passionate, romantic soul?"

"I'm saving it for Billy," Carrie said, wriggling her eyebrows suggestively.

"Oo, big talker," Sam scoffed. "You haven't even done it with him yet!"

"'Yet' is the operative word there," Carrie teased.

"Just be sure to share every detail with your two terminally-virginal best friends," Sam declared.

"Sex is private," Emma said firmly.

"You know what my mom used to say to me about sex?" Sam asked her friends. "She used to say: 'Why should the guy buy the milk if the cow is giving it away for free?'"

"Yuck!" Carrie cried.

"Tell me about it," Sam agreed. "I go: 'Mom, excuse me, but women are not cows.' She just said, 'You get my point, honey.'"

"She meant well," Emma pointed out.

"I guess." Sam sighed. "Anyway, I'm one of the oldest living virgins in America, so she's getting her wish so far."

"Hey, speaking of parents," Carrie said, "yours are going to be here soon, aren't they?"

"Yeah. They called to say they got an earlier flight after all and were coming in tonight. I told them to just come straight from La Guardia airport to the loft—I gave them directions over the phone."

"But you'll be at the theater," Emma reminded Sam.

"Oh," Sam answered, swallowing another mouthful. "Well, we can just leave them a note."

"Sam!" Carrie scolded her. "This isn't Sunset Island. You don't leave people notes." She turned her attention back to the carton of Hunan chicken she was eating.

"I knew that," Sam replied, mock-defensively.

"Youch!" Carrie cried, "I just bit into a hot pepper!"

Sam reached over and tossed a fresh can of Diet Pepsi, which Carrie immediately cracked open and drank down.

"Better?" Emma asked.

"Yup," Carrie replied. "Watch out for the little red things if you try this. Now, what was I saying?"

"You were on my case about leaving my parents a note, I think." Sam grinned.

"That's right. You trust us with your parents?" Carrie teased her.

"They're from Kansas," Sam responded with a shrug, as if that explained everything about them.

"Anything we need to know about them?" Emma asked Sam, her well-bred Boston hostess instincts taking over, as she crunched thoughtfully on a fortune cookie.

"My father likes Velveeta cheese on his mashed potatoes," Sam intoned, "my mother puts Miracle Whip on Ritz crackers, and if either of you turn out like either of them, our friendship will officially be over!"

The girls laughed, but then Carrie turned serious. "I mean, we don't really know very much about them," she said reasonably.

"There's not much to know. Earthlings of Kansas, that's them," Sam joked as she poked her fork one last time into the container of cold noodles with sesame sauce—a dish she had come to adore once Emma explained that the noodles were served cold on purpose.

"Carrie's right," Emma said. "I don't even know what their names are, or what they do for a living."

"You don't talk very much about them," Carrie noted.

Sam sighed. "Okay, okay, ladies and gentlemen of the jury. Exhibit A: my parental units. Mother's name is Carla, father's name is Vernon. Mom works in a pharmacy, Dad teaches high school. Case closed."

"What subject?" Carrie asked.

"Driver's Ed," Sam explained. "And he coaches football. I still can't figure out why they decided to adopt a girl."

I'm being hard on them, Sam thought guiltily. *They really are so much more than that.* "Actually, they're pretty decent," Sam told her friends. "I mean, they're good people."

"What time are they getting here again?" Carrie asked.

"Same time as my dress rehearsal," Sam answered. "Their plane gets in at eight; they should be here by nine-thirty."

"Assuming they can get a cab right away," Carrie replied.

"I'll be amazed if they get here at all," Sam snorted. "My parents in New York City. Who'd have thought those words would ever be used in the same sentence?"

Emma and Carrie laughed, and Sam got up to get ready for rehearsal.

"Hey, Sam?" Carrie asked.

"What's up?" Sam said.

"I just wanted to know if you're nervous," Carrie asked.

"About what?" Sam queried. "Dress rehearsal?"

"That," Carrie agreed, "or maybe about your parents coming here."

Sam forced a laugh. "Never let 'em see you sweat," she replied.

Never let 'em see you sweat, Sam thought to herself, as she waited backstage at the Fanny Bryce Theatre along with the rest of the cast of *Helen! Well, if they could see me now, they'd see me sweating. From frustration! I've been cooling my heels here for three and a half hours, and we haven't even started yet! She glanced at her watch—it was eleven-thirty, and the dress rehearsal was supposed to have begun at eight.*

The stupid show's supposed to be over by

ten-thirty, Sam reminded herself. *I should be home with Emma and Carrie by now, correcting all the things my parents told them about me!*

So far, dress rehearsal had been an unmitigated disaster. First, while Sam had been warming up with the other dancers before the show, a piece of scenery that was supposed to "fly in" from above the actors' heads during a crucial moment accidentally broke loose from its mooring lines and came crashing down on the stage. Nancy Pumpkin starting screaming that a stagehand had done it on purpose because he hated her. Then she'd stomped into her dressing room and it had taken Laszlo Comfort thirty minutes to coax her back out.

The accident had happened very close to Sam, and she got a sickening feeling in her stomach when it happened. It reminded her of when she was out on tour with Flirting With Danger, and a lighting instrument over the stage at Madison Square Garden had broken loose and conked her on the head.

That put me in the hospital, she remembered as she heard the scenery crash down. *And they say lightning doesn't strike twice in the same place. That's a little too close for comfort for me!*

It had taken quite some time for an emergency piece of scenery to be fashioned, and then another crisis erupted. While the tech people were handling the emergency, Nancy Pumpkin left the theater. She didn't show up again for an hour and a half.

And her head was shaved.

Nancy said that it came to her in a dream the night before that if she shaved her head the play would open to rave reviews. It would be an entirely new symbolic interpretation of Helen Keller, she explained. Of course, there was no time to clear it with Laszlo, so she just went ahead and did it anyway. She was sure it would be okay.

Naturally, a huge fight ensued, in which Laszlo and the playwright accused Nancy of deliberately sabotaging their play, and in which Nancy screamed at the two of them that you can't sabotage something that's already so embarrassingly awful you were sorry you were even associated with it, and in any case you don't even want your family to see you in it.

Gee, great, Sam had thought. *Mine is coming. This whole thing is mondo-depressing.*

"Bad dress rehearsal, great opening," Matt Carlton quipped to Sam, pulling her back to reality as she played the last couple of hours over in her mind.

"Says who?" Sam replied glumly.

"Old Broadway saying," Matt explained.

"Created by Matt Carlton," Sam suggested, "to cheer up depressed dancers from Kansas?"

"I wish I could take credit for it," Matt said, smiling, "but I can't. Not that I don't deserve it!"

"Tell me that this isn't the worst dress rehearsal you've been in, and I'd feel a lot better." Sam sighed.

"I can't—" Matt replied.

"I knew it!" Sam retorted.

"—because this one hasn't even started yet," Matt continued, looking at his watch. "But if we don't get going soon, I'm gonna grow roots."

Just then the familiar voice of Neil Glascow, the intrepid assistant stage manager, rang out backstage.

"Places everyone!" Neil called. "Five minutes!"

And at that moment, the pit orchestra launched into the overture to *Helen!*, beginning with a piece of music that the cast had nicknamed the DDB theme . . . short for deaf, dumb, and blind.

"Places! Places!" Neil called.

"Here we go," Sam said to Matt.

"Hold on tight," Matt suggested, "and fasten your seatbelts!"

* * *

"Sam actually knows how to milk a cow?" Carrie chortled, hitting herself on the knees with glee.

"Yes indeed," Vernon Bridges said, reaching over and taking another couple of grapes from the bowl of fruit that Emma had thoughtfully put out for Sam's parents after they arrived at the loft. They'd gotten in at 10:45 P.M.—their plane had been delayed, and then it had taken forever for them to get a cab at the airport. But they were too excited to sleep, and insisted on waiting until Sam got back from dress rehearsal before taking another cab to the Gramercy Park Hotel, where their travel agent had made them reservations. They had rambled on and on about how Ruth Ann, Sam's little sister, couldn't come because she was working as a counselor at Girl Scout camp, and how the entire town of Junction, Kansas, had made a card and signed it, sending Sam good wishes on her Broadway debut. Then they had launched into stories about Sam's childhood, which was a total hoot.

"She never told us she had a more than a passing acquaintance with farm animals," Carrie said, still laughing.

"Oh, my, yes," Mrs. Bridges agreed. "When

she was five, she had a pet pig that she entered into the Kansas State Fair—"

"Sam had a pet pig?" Emma shrieked.

Mrs. Bridges nodded. "She called him Cookie, after the Cookie Monster from Sesame Street. She just dearly loved that pig."

Carrie had to wipe tears of laughter from her eyes. "A pig named Cookie. . . ."

"Sam claimed Cookie was smarter than most people," Mrs. Bridges went on fondly. "She wanted Cookie to sleep with her and Ruth Ann in their bedroom, but we had to draw the line somewhere."

"So one night we found Sam out back asleep in the hay with the pig!" Mr. Bridges finished.

Carrie and Emma both laughed so hard their stomachs hurt. "We're never going to let her hear the end of this," Emma promised.

Mrs. Bridges looked contrite. "I hope she won't mind us telling you—"

"Oh, no," Carrie assured Sam's mother. "I'm sure it's fine."

"Because she's been kind of . . . funny lately. . . ." Sam's mother left the rest of her thought dangle. She stared down nervously at her hands.

"She took the news about her adoption mighty hard," Sam's dad said in a low voice.

He gave Emma and Carrie a plaintive look. "Sometimes I have a hard time talking to my own child."

"We're just so grateful she invited us here for her big night." Sam's mother rushed in to cover for her husband's embarrassment.

"She wanted you here," Emma insisted.

"Did she?" Mrs. Bridges asked, her face lighting up.

"Of course she did, that's why she invited us," Mr. Bridges told his wife. He looked at Emma and Carrie again. "If you don't mind my asking . . . is her . . . the other woman here in town, too?"

Carrie thought about this a moment. *Other woman. Oh! He must mean Susan, Sam's birth mother in California!* "No, she's not here," Carrie said.

A tremulous smile spread over Mrs. Bridges' face. "It would have been okay if she was here," she said. "I just . . . wanted to know."

"You're her mother," Emma said softly.

"Does Sam say that?" Mrs. Bridges asked.

"Of course Sam says that," Mr. Bridges said gruffly.

"I know, I'm just being silly," Sam's mother declared. She nervously pulled a loose thread from her skirt. "Well, enough of this serious stuff! I'm just as excited as I can be. I never thought my Samantha would be in a Broadway show!"

"Has she told you much about it?" Mr. Bridges asked eagerly. "Sam's mother and I really enjoy the theater. We go to a Broadway series that tours through Topeka whenever we can. We just loved *Cats*! Is Sam's show anything like that?"

"Uh, not exactly," Carrie said, biting her lower lip. "It's . . . different."

"More serious?" Mrs. Bridges asked.

"Uh . . . kind of," Carrie agreed.

"It's a musical about Helen Keller," Emma explained.

Mr. Bridges looked confused. "But Helen Keller was deaf, mute, and blind. So how could she sing and dance?"

Carrie and Emma looked at each other, both at a total loss for words.

"Gosh, I guess that's just the miracle of show biz for you!" Carrie finally said heartily. "I'm sure it's going to be . . . memorable!"

FIFTEEN

"I'd like to place an order for a dozen yellow roses," Carrie said into the phone as quietly as she could, not wanting to wake either Emma or Sam, who were sleeping late.

"Sure, miss," the guy at the florist's shop Carrie had called replied. "Delivered?"

"Please," Carrie answered.

"Where, when, and to whom?" the guy asked her.

I can't believe I'm doing this, Carrie thought to herself. *I shouldn't be doing this. But I am doing this. Hey, I have nothing to feel guilty about! Matt is my friend! And yellow roses are supposed to be for friendship, so it's okay to—*

"Yo, lady, you still there?" the guy at the florist's called into the phone. "Where you want these sweet things delivered?"

"Sorry," Carrie said, brought back to her

phone call. "Deliver them to the Fanny Bryce Theatre, tonight around six o'clock. Bring them backstage, please. It's for the opening of *Helen!*"

"Miss, I know all about the opening of *Helen!* My cousin Freddie is in the stage-hands' union. The show's supposed to be a major dog, by the way," the guy at the flower shop said, sounding bored. "You didn't say who to give 'em to. You want the whole cast of this show to share 'em, or are they for one particular person?"

"Maybe the show will be a big hit," Carrie insisted, crossing her fingers superstitiously.

"Yeah, and maybe I'm gonna marry Madonna, babe," the guy on the phone said. "Now who are the flowers for?"

"Matt Carlton," Carrie said, forgetting momentarily that she was trying to keep her voice low. The guy at the florist's was really starting to irritate her.

"Oooooo," a voice cooed knowingly from across the loft. Carrie looked to see who was cooing. It was Sam.

"It's not what you think—" Carrie began.

"Oh, sure," Sam said breezily. "You know I say go for it, girlfriend. Two guys for every girl, that's my motto. Glad to see you're catching on!"

"Yo, miss, try to stay with me here!" the

guy from the florist's called into the phone. "Whaddaya want the cute little card to say?"

"Just say 'Break a leg,'" Carrie instructed.

"Breaking new ground in theater flower cards," the guy observed dryly. "How do you want it signed?"

Carrie thought for a moment. *Not "love," that would be all wrong. But not "sincerely," either, because that sounds too formal. . . . What about "fondly"? Yes, that'll do.*

"Make it, 'Fondly, Carrie,'" Carrie instructed.

"Ooooooo," Sam cooed again.

"Fondly?" the guy repeated derisively. "This a cousin you really hate, or what?"

"Look, do you have some kind of a problem?" Carrie asked him irritably. "I mean, you're not funny."

"I am, too, funny," the guy said. "I do stand up at The Improv on open mike night. I slay 'em. Let's have the credit card info."

Carrie gave the guy her mother's Visa Card number—her parents let her charge some things so long as she paid them back immediately—and the order was completed.

"So, have fun at the bowser show tonight," the florist guy said before hanging up.

Well, I won't be relating that conversation to Sam, Carrie thought to herself as she got herself a diet Coke from the refrigerator. She plopped down on the couch and put her legs up.

"Carrie, I am so disappointed in you," Sam said, affecting a somber tone.

Damn. I know I screwed up by doing that, Carrie thought to herself.

"You're right," Carrie replied guiltily. "It's so disloyal to Billy." She thought for a second. "No, it isn't disloyal. I'm allowed to have a guy as a friend. And a friend sends a friend flowers on opening night! Right?"

"You are such a good girl," Sam chuckled.

"I'm just trying to do the right thing," Carrie replied.

"And that's why I'm disappointed in you." Sam grinned.

"Would you please quit saying that?" Carrie asked. "I didn't do anything wrong!"

"Wrong-amundo," Sam replied. "In this case, the right thing is order flowers for *moi* before you order them for a measly guy. Even if the guy is Matt Carlton."

Carrie laughed. "I should have known. Anyhow, give us a chance. You haven't been forgotten."

"Cool," Sam replied. "Carrie Alden, there is hope for you yet!"

Emma, Carrie, Adam, and Danny all met up with Sam's parents at the Gramercy Park

Hotel at six o'clock for drinks in the lobby, and then shared two taxicabs for the run up to Broadway and the theater. All of them were decked out—Danny had on a navy-blue blazer, khaki pants, and a denim shirt with a Mickey Mouse tie, and Adam had on a great-looking Italian suit with shoulder pads and baggy pants. Emma wore a simple black dress, short and straight with a matching jacket and her grandmother's pearls, and Carrie had on an oversized black-and-white houndstooth jacket which Sam had insisted she stud with rhinestones, over a black mini-skirt and a black scoop-necked leotard. Sam's mother had on a kelly-green dress with a pink sash, and a striped pink and kelly-green jacket, while Sam's dad had on a charcoal gray suit with a ghastly tie covered with cherries.

Where did Sam get her great fashion sense? Emma wondered.

"You two look gorgeous," Adam had commented when Carrie and Emma walked into the lobby of the hotel. "I'll take you both."

The opening of *Helen!* was the talk of the town—it was a slow news day in Manhattan, and it was pretty common knowledge that the show had, as they say on Broadway, "problems." Emma and Carrie had even seen one TV theater critic give a report in which she predicted the play would not even open that night.

"But she hasn't even seen it!" Carrie had protested.

"So what?" Emma had observed wryly. "Since when do you have to actually see a play in order to trash it?"

They put Sam's parents into a taxi with Danny, then Carrie, Adam, and Emma got the next one.

"Where to?" the cabbie asked, sucking the last drag off his cigarette before flipping it out the window. Emma directed the driver to the Fanny Bryce Theater.

The street in front of the theater was packed, and it took a really long time for the taxis to make their way through. Up and down the street were all kinds of media equipment trucks and limousines. Finally, the taxis let them out about a half block from the theater—it was just too big a crush. The six of them piled out of the cabs and started to walk.

"Isn't that Burt Reynolds?" Carla Bridges asked, pointing to a man entering the theater.

"And isn't that Sharon Stone?" Danny pointed out another famous actor.

"And isn't that the heiress Emma Cresswell?" Carrie joked, pointing directly at Emma. Even Emma had to laugh.

Finally, they made their way into the theater, had their tickets torn by an usher, were handed Playbills—the program for the performance—and were led to their seats. Emma had purchased tickets for seats that were in what she said was the perfect location—the orchestra section at about the twentieth row.

In their seats, they opened their Playbills.

"Vernon!" Carla Bridges cried almost immediately. "Turn to page twenty-six!"

Sam's father quickly opened to the page his wife had specified. And by that time, Emma, Carrie, Danny, and Adam had all found it, too. There, in black and white print, along with the biographies of Nancy Pumpkin, Matt Carlton, and all the other actors and creative personnel working on *Helen!* was Sam's biography.

Samantha Bridges (chorus dancer): A proud native of Junction, Kansas, Sam is making her Broadway debut in *Helen!* Sam has performed at Disney World in Florida, on Paradise Island in the Bahamas, at Madison Square Garden with rock star Johnny Angel, and currently is a featured backup singer with the New England-based rock band Flirting With Danger. Sam dedicates her performance to her mother and father, and to her best friends, Emma and Carrie, "the wind beneath my wings."

"I can't believe she put us in her bio!" Carrie cried, tears coming to her eyes. She looked over at Emma, who was also tearing up.

Sam's mother reached over for Carrie's hand. "She said her mother and her father here. Do you think she means us?"

Carrie squeezed the older woman's hand. "I'm absolutely certain," she said fervently.

"Well, bless her heart," Mrs. Bridges murmured. She took out a tissue and dabbed at her eyes. Sam's dad was trying hard to choke back his own tears.

This is probably the biggest thing that's ever happened to them, Emma thought. *Getting to watch their daughter perform on a Broadway stage, in a Broadway show—even if it might not be the greatest show on earth. When they adopted Sam, did they have any idea that this was going to happen? Does any parent have any idea of what's going to happen to their kid?*

At that moment, the house lights dimmed and music began to well up from the orchestra pit. Carrie reached over and squeezed Emma's right arm, and Adam reached over and squeezed her left arm. The musical theme that Sam had described to them began to soar toward the ceiling.

Helen! was about to begin.

"I'm so nervous for her!" Carrie whispered to Emma.

"Let's just pray it's not as bad as Sam thinks it is," Emma whispered back.

The overture finished and the curtain rose, revealing a set that looked like a house and a garden. The audience applauded politely.

"They like the set," Danny whispered hopefully.

"Sort of," Adam amended.

Music swelled up again. Eight girls and guys danced out on to the stage. They were all wearing paper bags over their heads. You could only tell male from female by looking at them below the neck.

"Sam said she was in the opening number," Sam's mom hissed to Carrie. "Which one is she?"

Carrie had no idea. "Uh, the tall one on the end," she guessed.

The cast started signing.

"This is the world for Helen.
No light, no sunlight on her face.
Does she even know she's a member of
the human race?"

Now the dancers groped around the stage blindly, bumping into each other and falling over, rolling across the stage while a singer in the pit took over the refrain of the song.

"She's deaf! She's blind! She's really, really dumb!
Can Helen ever overcome?"

A pitiful scream rang out from inside the house on stage, and then just as the dancers had rolled into the wings, Nancy Pumpkin ran out of the house, shrieking at the top of her lungs.

She shrieked again to the music, and tore at her hair. But evidently she forgot she was wearing a wig, so her hair came off in her hands.

She stared at it, shrieked again on pitch, then plopped it back on her head at a cock-eyed angle.

Carrie and Emma stared at the stage with their jaws hanging open.

"I'm Helen! They think I'm dumb
Yes, they think I'm on the run
From life! But they're all wrong.
I'm Helen! I must be strong!
I want to taste the world
This is where I belong!"

Now Nancy ran over to a picnic table that had been set up near the front porch of the set, and she began to gobble all the food that had been pre-set there. She smeared her face with chicken, then stuffed in chocolate cake, then washed it all down with a pitcher of some liquid, which dribbled into her cleavage. Then she ran to center stage, threw her arms wide, and began singing again.

"I'm Helen!
I'm not a fool!
So why should I live by their rules?
I'm special but I don't know why
I'm Helen, watch me fly!"

Then, to the astonishment of the thousand people watching the opening night of *Helen!*, the star of the show was lifted off the stage by a hidden pulley system. She flew over the heads of the first rows of the audience, shrieking "I'm Helen! I'm Helen!" Just as she got to the third "I'm Helen!" the cable holding her bobbled, and she screamed and grabbed for her wig, which flew off of her head and landed on a man sitting in the fifth row center.

As the cable carried Nancy off the stage, the orchestra music came to a flourishing finish.

The audience was completely silent.

And that was the high point of the show.

"Okay, we're going to be very upbeat when Sam comes in," Carrie instructed everyone.

They were in a private room at Sardi's restaurant, where the opening night party was being held. Since there hadn't been any previews, the producer had managed to get someone at *The New York Times* to promise to send a copy of the next day's review.

Emma, Carrie, Danny, Adam, and Sam's parents had prearranged to meet Sam at the party.

"How can we be upbeat?" Danny asked glumly. "That was the wackiest thing I ever saw in my life!"

"I thought Sam danced very nicely," Sam's mother said lamely.

"And what was the water dance thing in the second act?" Danny continued incredulously. "They actually made the dancers spell out the word 'water' with their bodies."

"Having that pool of water on stage was a nice touch, I thought," Sam's dad put in.

"But it did seem kind of tasteless, didn't it, having Helen throw off her clothes to splash in it practically naked?" Sam's mother commented with a furrowed brow. "It didn't leave much to the imagination."

"How about when the dancers had to pretend they were part of a water fountain, and they actually spouted?" Danny marveled. "It's amazing how much water one person can hold in her mouth."

They all fell silent, shaking their heads ruefully.

"Sam looked great, didn't she?" Sam's dad finally said.

"Yeah, in the two scenes where she wasn't wearing a paper bag over her head," Danny said with disgust. "I'm sorry, but Sam is really talented. I'm just . . . I'm ticked off on her behalf."

There was a commotion at the door to the private banquet room, and most of the cast from *Helen!* came in.

"Get me a drink!" a chorus dancer screamed. "Get me lots of drinks!"

"Sam! Over here! Danny called when he saw Sam across the room.

Sam said something to Matt, who was standing next to her, and the two of them made their way across the room.

"Okay, you hated it, you don't have to be nice," Sam said, hugging her parents.

"We though it was . . . creative," her mother managed.

"Mom, it sucked," Sam snorted.

"Watch your language, miss," her father warned her.

"Sorry Dad, but I call it like I see it. Oh, this is my friend Matt Carlton. He played Helen's dad."

"It's a pleasure to meet you," Matt told Sam's parents.

"You were very good," Sam's father told Matt. "Your solo was the best moment in the show."

"Thanks," Matt said. "Too bad I'll never get to sing it again, huh?"

"Would they really close it that fast?" Emma asked.

"You'd better believe it," Matt replied. "That's show biz." He turned to Carrie and took her hands in his, then he kissed her lightly on the lips. "That's for the flowers. No one ever sent me flowers before."

"No kidding?" Carrie marveled. "I figured you theater types get flowers all the time."

"Nope," Matt replied. "I was really touched."

"Hey, Emma bo-Bemma," Sam cried, "I have a feeling those four dozen long-stemmed red roses were your idea, am I right?"

"Guilty," Emma said with a grin.

"You are too much, girlfriend!" Sam said, throwing her arms around Emma. Then she hugged Carrie. "I love you guys!"

"You're not upset that the show wasn't a success?" Emma asked Sam.

"What have I been telling you guys all this time?" Sam asked them. "I said it was going to be a major oink." Sam shrugged philosophically. "What the hell, I had fun."

"Sam, your language—" her father warned her again.

"Oh, Dad, I'm not in Kansas anymore!" Sam laughed. Her father's face looked stern. "Okay, okay, I'll watch it."

Everyone partied in the banquet room and got silly, reliving the worst moments of the show. Nancy Pumpkin guzzled a bottle of champagne all by herself and took off to hurl in the ladies' room. Some tables had been cleared to make room for a small dance floor. Adam danced with Emma, Carrie danced with Matt, Danny danced with Sam, and Sam even danced a fox trot with her dad. Everyone seemed to be having a good time—it was as if they all already knew they were about to be unemployed, so there was no anxiety about the reviews.

"I predict the worst reviews for any show ever to open on the Great White Way," Sam said.

"Samantha, darling, having fun?" Laszlo Comfort asked, coming up to Sam and putting his arm around her.

"A blast," Sam answered honestly. She introduced him to her parents.

"You have a charming and talented daughter," he told Sam's parents.

"Thank you, we think so," Sam's mother said, beaming with pride.

Laszlo pulled Sam away from the others. "Our date is on for tomorrow, right sweet one?"

Sam laughed. "Oh, Laszlo, that was only if we ran two nights, and you know no one expects to go on again!"

"Well, I admit, I wasn't crazy about the show myself when I took the job," Laszlo said. "But if the backers want to throw their money away, there's not much I can do about it, is there?"

"It could have been worse, but I don't know how," Sam said.

"This means if the show closes our date is off?" Laszlo asked.

"Yep," Sam said cheerfully. *What the hell—he can't fire me*, Sam said to herself. *There's not going to be a show to fire me from!*

"Hey, everyone!" one of the associate producers yelled, running into the room. "I just got a preview copy of *The Times*!"

"Someone get Nancy!" a chorus girl yelled.

"She's passed out in the john," someone reported.

"Okay, listen up, everyone!" the associate producer called out.

"We were having a good time. Why ruin it?" Chili Dumont shouted.

The associate producer ignored her and quickly opened to the review.

> **_HELEN!_ SPEAKS TO ME**
> BY CHILTON PENNYSWORTH
>
> Last night Broadway history was made at the Fanny Bryce Theatre with artistic daring, audacious nerve and a hint of kitsch. That's _Helen!_—one of the funniest, most thought-provoking, most original pieces of theater this reviewer has seen in a decade. Taken at face value, the unenlightened might not appreciate _Helen!_ for the miracle it is. Yes, this show was a major risk. But the stylized humor juxtaposed against the screaming, ranting rock brilliance of Nancy Pumpkin proves that the risk was well worth taking. . . .

The room was silent.

"You're making that up," someone finally said.

Even the associate producer who had read the review looked stunned. "I swear to God, it says all that right here."

The executive producer ran over to Laszlo Comfort and smacked a loud kiss on his cheek. "I knew you could do it, babe! I always believed in you! We're a hit!"

SIXTEEN

Everyone was screaming, crying, and yelling for joy.

Except Sam. Sam just looked confused. She grabbed Matt Carlton. "Wait a sec, I don't get it," she said. "How can we be a hit just because one guy says he actually liked *Helen!*?"

"It's not just one guy, it's Chilton Pennysworth of *The New York Times!*" Matt exclaimed with excitement. The joy in the room was infectious and a huge grin spread across Matt's face. "He's the only reviewer that really matters. If Chilton says we're a hit, we're a hit!"

"But . . . but . . . the guy must be delusional!" Sam sputtered.

"He makes or breaks every show on Broadway," Matt explained.

Danny shook his head in consternation.

"You mean it's an Emperor's New Clothes kind of thing? In other words, if he says something is good, and all the people who think it's trash are just too plebian to appreciate real art, then he's right and they're wrong? And thousands of people are just too insecure about their own taste in art to call him crazy?"

"Something like that," Adam confirmed.

Carrie grabbed Sam's hands. "Do you know what this means? You're in a Broadway hit! Your career just got launched!"

"I just can't believe it!" Sam said. "I mean, I am not stupid. *Helen!* seriously sucks, doesn't it?"

"It sucks," Adam, Danny, Carrie, and even Emma said all at once. Even Sam's father didn't bother to say anything about anyone's language.

"What can I tell you?" Matt Carlton said, throwing up his hands. "Show biz is bizarre! But this means I'm employed for a while, and I'm going to celebrate! Come on, Carrie. Let's dance!" He pulled Carrie away to the dance floor, where dozens of people were pouring champagne over themselves and dancing up a storm.

"I'm really happy for you, honey," Sam's mom told her daughter, kissing her on the cheek. "I don't pretend to understand it, but I'm happy for you."

"Thanks," Sam said, still in too much of a daze to feel anything except shock.

"Uh-oh," Emma murmured, her neck craned toward the other side of the room.

"Uh-oh what?" Sam asked Emma.

"Uh-oh, Laszlo Comfort is headed this way."

"I guess he wants to congratulate me," Sam said.

"And I guess he wants to set up the time for your big date tomorrow," Emma whispered to Sam.

Sam's mouth fell open.

Oh, no, Sam thought with panic.

A date with Laszlo.

Who is now directing me in a Broadway hit.

"Quick! Run to the ladies' room!" Emma improvised, pushing Sam in the opposite direction from Laszlo.

"What's that all about?" Danny asked as Sam took off toward the ladies' room.

"Oh, you know, nerves and all," Emma called sweetly.

"Hello, dear heart, where is your luscious friend?" Laszlo asked Emma after kissing her hand.

"She's . . . otherwise engaged at the moment," Emma replied.

"I wanted to give her her first kiss of

congratulations," Laszlo said. "I always believed *Helen!* would be a big hit. Never listen to the nay-sayers, I always say!"

"That's the spirit!" Adam said cheerfully.

"Only someone of Chilton Pennysworth's obvious brilliance could appreciate the true artistic nuance of my show," Laszlo said earnestly.

"Oh, we couldn't agree more," Adam replied, egging Laszlo on. Emma had to bite her lower lip to keep from laughing at his ridiculous turnaround.

"Well, when my young redheaded lovely comes back from wherever it is she went, please tell her to find me and let me know what time our date is tomorrow after the show," Laszlo requested.

"Wait a minute, what date?" Danny asked.

Laszlo looked at Danny for the first time. "Who are you?"

"Sam's boyfriend," he said in a steely voice.

Emma and Adam looked at Danny with surprise. He didn't flinch.

"Oh, really," Laszlo said mildly, pulling on his beard. "Well, not to worry. I don't have permanent designs on her."

"Yeah, well how about if you don't have any designs on her at all?" Danny asked. "How about if you drop dead?"

"I can't right now," Laszlo replied seriously.

"I have a Broadway hit." He turned to smile at Emma, and he kissed her hand again. "Do tell Sam to find me across the room." Then he strolled away.

Emma looked at Danny, who was still seething. "I thought you had another girlfriend."

Danny threw up his hands in exasperation. "Only because Sam doesn't want me. I thought I made that really clear!"

Sam crept back out to her friends. "Is the coast clear?"

"You're going out with that idiot?" Danny demanded.

Sam's eyes got wide. "What's it to you, Mr. I-have-a-girlfriend-named-Megan-Carmony?" Sam asked belligerently.

"At least Megan isn't old enough to be my parent!" Danny fumed. "Wait, make that grandparent!"

"Look, you are totally out of line," Sam snapped. Her parents were looking at her askance.

"Mom, Dad, I'm not really going out with him," Sam hastened to explain.

"It sure sounded like he thought you were," Sam's dad said. "The dirty old man. I should have belted him one."

"Gee, Dad, that wouldn't have been a very good idea," Sam said.

"Yes, it would," Danny put in. "I agree with your father!"

"Well, goody for you two!" Sam yelled.

Carrie and Matt came back from the dance floor, both sweating from their wild gyrations. "Whew! It's hot out there," Carrie said, fanning the back of her neck. "Oh, I just saw Laszlo Comfort on the way over here, and he wants you to come talk to him about tomorrow night," Carrie reported to Sam.

"He said, 'Tell her not to be a sore loser,'" Matt reported. "What is he talking about?"

Everyone stared at Sam.

"Excuse me, Samantha?" a short guy in cowboy boots said, coming over to Sam. "You don't know me, I'm Arthur Leonard, the executive producer of *Helen!*"

"Oh, I do know you," Sam said, smiling prettily. "Thanks for believing in the show."

"Hey, I'm a risk-taker. I believe in art—that's why I'm in this biz, you know? People think it's for the money, but they just don't understand. Anyway, could I speak with you a minute?"

"Sure," Sam said.

God, I hope he doesn't expect me to go out with him, too, Sam thought to herself.

"Excuse us," Mr. Leonard said, directing Sam to a quiet corner of the room.

"Samantha, you're a very good dancer—" the producer began.

"Thank you," Sam replied.

"But, you know, you were a last minute replacement," he continued. "Frankly, when you came into the show we didn't think we had much of a chance of success—it's tough when you're an artistic original like Nancy Pumpkin to get people to take you seriously."

"Uh huh," Sam said, keeping her mouth shut for once.

"Anyway, this is very hard for me to tell you," the producer said, looking serious, "but . . . you're out of the show."

Sam's jaw fell open. "I'm WHAT?"

"Out of the show," the producer repeated easily. "No hard feelings, okay?"

"But . . . why?"

"Well, Nancy has her own ideas about who should be in the chorus," the producer explained. "Like, for example, her little sister Celeste."

"Her little sister Celeste," Sam repeated dully.

"Right," Mr. Leonard confirmed. "Celeste is a dynamite dancer. She's tall and thin and has red hair. But she's been in rehab and she just got out. So now Nancy wants her in the show."

"And she's replacing me?" Sam asked incredulously.

"Well, you were the last one hired, so you're the first one fired," he explained. "Besides, Celeste is the same type as you. We can't have two of the same type in the show."

"But . . . but . . . I'm in the Actor's Equity Union now! I have a contract!" Sam exclaimed. "Aren't there rules about things like this? I mean, are you allowed to do this to me?"

"You'll get severance pay and all that," the producer said. "And if your union wants to take us up on charges, so be it. Meanwhile, you're out and Celeste is in. She's been studying all the choreography, so she can go into the show tomorrow. Sorry, kid. But you're beautiful and a real trooper. I'll use you again in something else, and that's a promise from Artie Leonard." He smiled at Sam and walked away.

Sam couldn't believe it.

She wandered back to her friends and her parents.

"What did he want?" Carrie asked Sam. "Did he give you a raise or something?"

"Not exactly," Sam said. "He fired me."

Silence.

"He WHAT?" Carrie screeched.

"He fired me," Sam repeated. "Nancy

Pumpkin's sister is coming in to do my part."

"But he can't do that!" Adam protested. "You're in the union!"

"He said let the union take him up on charges," Sam said. "He didn't seem very worried abut it."

Sam's mother hugged her shell-shocked daughter. "Oh, honey, I'm so sorry!"

"Now I'd like to go punch out that director *and* that producer!" Sam's father threatened.

"Just forget it, Dad," Sam said wearily. "That won't help."

"Maybe not," Vernon Bridges said. "But I'd feel better."

Somehow word spread quickly that Sam had been fired, and people began to look over at her and point to her, whispering to each other. Nancy Pumpkin finally made her way out of the john and gave Sam a really bitchy smile.

"I'm going to go kill her," Sam threatened.

"Ignore her," Emma advised. "She's drunk anyway."

Two more girls pointed over at Sam.

"Everyone knows," Sam said miserably. Tears began to roll down her cheeks. "I don't want them to see me cry!"

Emma and Carrie both put their arms around Sam. Sam let the tears fall down her cheeks. "I . . . I just can't believe this happened!" She roughly brushed away her tears with the back of her hand.

"Come on," Emma coaxed. "Let's go outside for a minute."

Emma led Carrie and Sam through the wild party and found a back door that led into a tiny side street. The three girls stood outside in the night air.

"God, why does this stuff happen to me?" Sam wailed. "I got fired from Disney World and now I got fired from Broadway after one night. It isn't fair!"

"No, it isn't," Carrie agreed. She rummaged in her purse and found a tissue, and she handed it to Sam.

"I'm afraid this is just one of those awful things that you don't have any control over," Emma said softly.

"I'd like to go kill Nancy Pumpkin!" Sam seethed between sobs.

"If it makes you feel any better," Carrie said, "the show really is awful."

Sam thought a moment, then she managed a tiny laugh. "It is, isn't it?"

"The worst thing I've ever seen," Emma said earnestly.

Sam had to laugh at that, which made Emma and Carrie laugh, too.

"Look at it this way," Emma said. "Now you get to come back to Sunset Island with us."

"To babysit for the monsters," Sam groaned.

"To hang out with us," Carrie corrected Sam. "The island just wouldn't be the same without you."

Sam blew her nose. "Do you think I'll ever really be a success at anything?" she asked them in a small voice.

"Hey, as far as we're concerned, you are a mega-success," Carrie said fervently.

"Oh, I am not," Sam replied. "I screw everything up. I screwed up my relationship with Pres, then I screwed up my relationship with Danny. I made my parents feel awful for not telling me I was adopted. I got fired from two dancing jobs . . ."

"Uh-oh, it's a pity party for Sam!" Carrie teased.

"Shut up," Sam said mildly. "I deserve it. I just feel like . . . like you two really have everything together, and I never do."

"I don't know how you can say that," Emma said softly. "I hurt Kurt, the first guy I ever loved. Now I'm afraid to get involved with Adam, because I don't think I even know what love is anymore. I want to go into the Peace Corps, but they turned me down until I'm older. I did one modeling job and then decided I wasn't interested. I mean, what is so together about my life?"

"You're rich—you don't have to have your life together," Sam said glumly.

"Now, you don't really believe that, do you?" Emma asked.

"Only sort of," Sam replied honestly. She took a deep breath and looked over at Carrie. "No peppy speech from you?"

"I'm pepped out," Carrie replied. She sat down on a block of cement someone had left near the door. Sam and Emma sat down with her.

"I hate what just happened to you," Carrie continued earnestly. "It makes me sick."

"Yeah," Sam agreed. "Tell me about it."

"But, look, at least you tried. You auditioned for a Broadway show, and you got in! You got to actually dance on Broadway! That's more than most people ever get!"

"Most people don't get fired from Broadway, either," Sam added. "I'm so humiliated in front of my parents!"

"Sam, they love you. It doesn't matter to them," Emma said firmly. "And it doesn't to us, either." She stared up at the sliver of sky she could see and thought a moment. "It's like . . . it's like Carrie having the nerve to ask to take those photos when I did that modeling job with Shannon Berman," Emma explained slowly. "She didn't let her fears stop her, and she got what she wanted."

"So, I didn't let my fears stop me, and I got fired!" Sam exclaimed.

"Yeah, but look at all the good things that happened before that," Emma pointed out. "And you never know. Maybe someone you were in this show with will get you an even better dancing job one day. Maybe it will be Matt Carlton!"

Carrie sighed. "He's a great guy, isn't he?"

"He is," Emma agreed.

"So is Billy," Carrie added. "And I love Billy."

Sam and Emma looked at her.

"But I keep wanting Matt to kiss me!" she blurted out. "Oh, I hate myself!"

All three girls broke out laughing.

"Look, all we can do is the best we can do," Carrie finally said.

"Whatever that means," Sam added.

"It means . . . it means we're best friends and we're having a blast," Carrie said firmly. "For right now, that will have to do."

Sam laughed out loud. "Hey, I just thought of something!"

"What's that?" Emma asked.

"Now I don't have to go out with Laszlo! I'm not in the show!"

"That's good news," Carrie said with a grin. "And speaking of Laszlo, guess what Danny told him while you were hiding out."

"What?" Sam asked.

"Danny told Laszlo that you were his girl-friend!" Carrie said.

"He did?" Sam asked.

"Absolutely," Carrie said. "He still wants you."

"He doesn't," Sam said. There was a hopeful look in her eyes. "He does? He really does?"

Emma and Carrie nodded. Sam stood up. "I have to go throw my arms around him! No, that's too obvious. I'll play it cool, I'll—"

"Sam! Don't play anything!" Carrie cried. "Just go be honest with him!"

"Okay," Sam said seriously. "I will. Well, I'll try, anyway." She looked at Carrie and then at Emma. "Did I ever mention that you two are the best friends anybody ever had in the history of the planet?"

"You may have mentioned it," Emma said with a grin.

"Well, it's true, but don't let it go to your heads," Sam said. She hooked one arm through Carrie's arm and the other through Emma's. "Shall we?"

The three of them marched back into Sardi's, ready to take on the world.

SUNSET ISLAND MAILBOX

Dear Readers,

So, how goes it out there? I am back home in Nashville after spending the summer in Indianapolis directing my play Candy Store Window. It was a great experience and I'm happy to say we got rave reviews. I invited Chali Thakrar, a smart, funny, terrific fan who lives nearby and who wrote me terrific letters, to be my guest at the play. We had a wonderful time meeting each other in person.

The letters and pictures I've been getting lately have been just incredible. Thanks, Tracy Barnes of Albuquerque, New Mexico, for being so honest. To Nicole Miller of Sterling, Virginia—a person who laughs at your dreams is a person afraid to follow his or her own dreams. And to Erika Perry of Springdale, Arizona—your ideas were just brilliant!

How do you like the two guys on the cover? Mondo-cute, huh? Can you imagine how much fun my editor, Lisa Meltzer, and her assistant, Susanna Frohman, have when all these guys come to their office to audition for the covers? And I never seem to be in New York when they're doing the photo shoots!

HOT NEWS FLASH! Coming next summer, the younger teens from Sunset Island get their own series! Yes, it's Club Sunset Island, starring Becky and Allie Jacobs, and two new girls who I think you'll love. And of course, I'll keep writing the regular <u>Sunset Island</u> books, too.

I can't thank you all enough for your loyalty to me, Sam, Emma, and Carrie! Keep those great cards and letters coming, and don't forget to let me know if you want your letter considered for publication.

See you on the island!
Best—
Cherie Bennett

Cherie Bennett
c/o General Licensing Company
24 West 25th Street
New York, New York 10010.

All letters printed become property of the publisher.

Dear Cherie,

I love all your books. My favorite character is Sam, because I am also a dancer, and she's wild, just like me. My mom also reads your books after I am done with them. She also says I remind her of Sam.

I have a problem. I really like this gorgeous guy, but he only likes me as a friend. I don't have what it takes to ask him on a date. The last guy I asked on a date never gave me an answer. Can you please publish this? I'd like to hear what other people would say to do.

Love, your longlasting fan,
Nadine Louise Soderberg
Shelton, Connecticut

Dear Nadine,

Before I wrote to you, I went to my husband for some guy advice on this question. He told me that most guys are very flattered to be asked out. Do it casually, and invite him to something you know he likes to do. I know it's scary but nothing ventured, nothing gained, right? Do the rest of you have any good advice for Nadine? Let me know, I'll pass it on!

Best,
Cherie

Dear Cherie,

Last year I used to write all the time. I even began a "book" but toward the end of the story I couldn't finish it. It seemed stupid. I seem to have writer's block. Is there anything you can do to help yourself get unblocked? Can you suggest anything to help me stick with it?

Sincerely,
Christina Silves
Albuquerque, New Mexico

Dear Christina,

It seems to me that there are two voices inside everyone's head. One voice says, "Go for it! You can do it!" and the other voice says, "What you're doing is stupid, so just give up." It's always a war to listen to the positive messages and not the negative ones. This is true whether you are trying to write, sing, dance, do sports, or anything that has meaning to you. Believe me, I've been through this myself. If you try forcing yourself to write a little every day, and you let go of caring whether what you're writing is any good, you free your creative self and stop beating yourself up. I know this sounds trite, but it's true—the only failure is not to try. Good luck!

Best,
Cherie

Dear Cherie,
I have just recently started to read your Sunset Island *books. The trouble is, I can't find any of the first books in the series. I want to collect all of them, but I don't know where to find them. Any suggestions?*

Sincerely,
Emily Wilk
St. Clair Shores, Michigan

Dear Emily,

I get asked this question a lot! You can find a complete list of the <u>Sunset Island</u> books published to date in the front of this book. Just circle whichever books you're missing, and take the list to your local bookstore. If they don't have those books in stock, ask them to special order them for you, or look for the order form in the back of most of the <u>Sunset</u> books. Then they will call you when the books arrive at their store.

Best,
Cherie